Praise for Victoria Wilcox

"Through her intimate, firsthand knowledge of Doc Holliday, his youthful environs and his living relatives, author Victoria Wilcox has discovered and distilled much of Doc's actual history, weaving it in with passed-down family folklore. This firsthand account of Doc's travels and acquaintances rivals other historical novels like *Gettysburg* and *Killing Lincoln*. Although much of Doc's life is shrouded in mystery, this is the best book yet that traces his life, entertainingly mixing known historical facts with educated guesses. It is a must read for anyone searching for a seamless Doc Holliday biography."

Don Weber, *NY Times bestselling author of "Silent Witness"*

"This wonderfully written novel brings together one of the great stories of the American Frontier. Author Wilcox has done a superb job through fiction of creating a sense of time and place and giving us an intriguing look at one of the most controversial figures in the West — Dr. John Henry Holliday."

Casey Tefertiller, *Author of "Wyatt Earp: The Life Behind the Legend"*

"As a biographer of John Henry 'Doc' Holliday, I can only be envious of Victoria Wilcox's telling of his story. The facts of a life so intriguing — and the gaps in the facts — are cruel dampers to the historian, limited as he is by the record. Wilcox pursues the truth in a powerful and moving novel that is not tainted by the legend of its central character, trapped by the documentary evidence of his life, or tempted to ignore history. She tells his story with an intimate voice that is surprisingly fresh and compelling. Here, Doc is alive and his world real — wonderfully so."

Dr. Gary Roberts, *Author of "Doc Holliday: The Life and Legend"*

SOUTHERN SON

THE SAGA OF DOC HOLLIDAY

Books in the Southern Son Saga

Inheritance

Gone West

The Last Decision

SOUTHERN SON
THE SAGA OF DOC HOLLIDAY

INHERITANCE
Book One

Victoria Wilcox

KNOX ROBINSON
PUBLISHING
London • New York

KNOX ROBINSON
PUBLISHING

3rd Floor, 36 Langham Street
Westminster, London W1W 7AP
&
244 5th Avenue, Suite 1861
New York, New York 10001

Knox Robinson Publishing is a specialist, international publisher of historical fiction, historical romance and medieval fantasy.

First published in Great Britain in 2013 by Knox Robinson Publishing

First published in the United States in 2013 by Knox Robinson Publishing

A CIP catalogue record for this book is available from the British Library.

ISBN HC 978-1-908483-55-3

ISBN PB 978-1-908483-56-0

Map illustration by Paul Hughes

Typeset in Bembo by Susan Veach
info@susanveach.com

Printed in the United States of America and the United Kingdom.

Download the KRP App in iTunes and Google Play to receive free historical fiction, historical romance and fantasy eBooks delivered directly to your mobile or tablet.

Watch our historical documentaries and book trailers on our channel on YouTube and subscribe to our podcasts in iTunes.

www.knoxrobinsonpublishing.com

For my mother

Beth Wanlass Peirson

From whom I inherited a love of reading, research,

and traveling into the past.

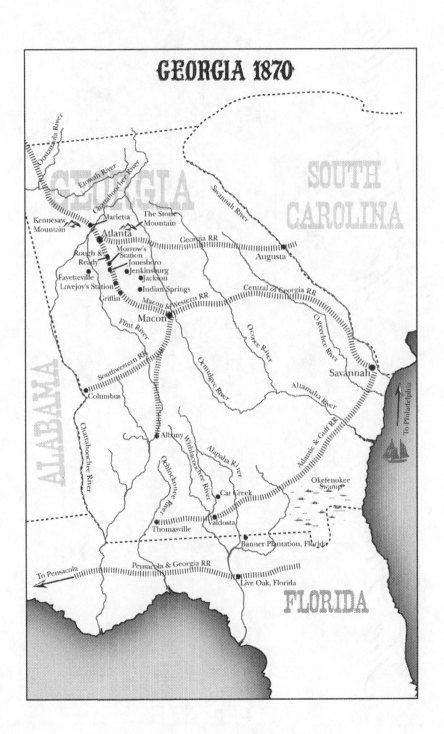

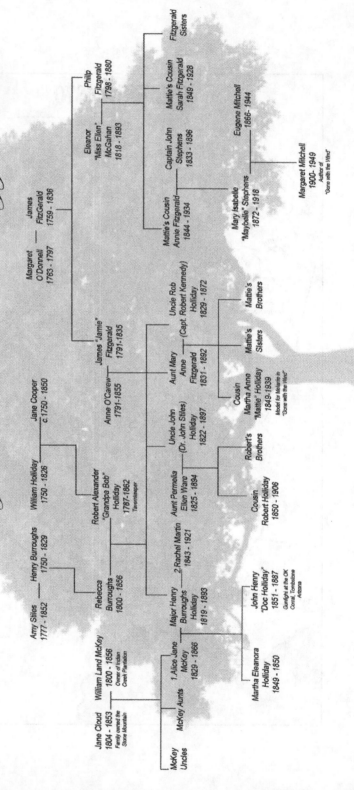

The Hollidays & The Fitzgeralds

Jane Cloud
1804 - 1853
Family owned the
Stone Mountain

William Land McKey
1800 - 1856
Owner of Indian
Creek Plantation

McKey Aunts

McKey Uncles

Amy Stiles
1777 - 1852

Henry Burroughs
1750 - 1829

William Holliday
1750 - 1826

Jane Cooper
c.1750 - 1850

Margaret
O'Donnell
1763 - 1797

James
FitzGerald
1759 - 1836

Rebecca
Burroughs
1800 - 1856

Robert Alexander
"Grandpa Bob"
Holliday
1787 - 1862
Tavernkeeper

James "Jamie"
Fitzgerald
1791 - 1835

Anne O'Carew
1791 - 1855

Eleanor
"Miss Ellen"
McGahan
1818 - 1893

Philip
Fitzgerald
1798 - 1880

Fitzgerald
Sisters

Mattie's Cousin
Sarah Fitzgerald
1849 - 1928

1. Alice Jane
McKey
1829 - 1866

Major Henry
Burroughs
Holliday
1819 - 1893

2. Rachel Martin
1843 - 1921

Aunt Permelia
Ellen Ware
1825 - 1894

Uncle John
(Dr. John Stiles)
Holliday
1822 - 1897

Aunt Mary
Anne
Fitzgerald
1831 - 1892

Uncle Rob
(Capt. Robert Kennedy)
Holliday
1829 - 1872

Mattie's Cousin
Annie Fitzgerald
1844 - 1934

Captain John
Stephens
1833 - 1896

Mary Isabelle
"Maybelle" Stephens
1872 - 1918

Eugene Mitchell
1866 - 1944

Martha Eleanora
Holliday
1849 - 1850

John Henry
"Doc Holliday"
1851 - 1887
Gunfight at the OK
Corral, Tombstone
Arizona

Cousin
Robert Holliday
1850 - 1906

Robert's
Brothers

Cousin
Martha Anne
"Mattie" Holliday
1849-1939
Model for Melanie in
"Gone with the Wind"

Mattie's
Sisters

Mattie's
Brothers

Margaret Mitchell
1900- 1949
Author of
"Gone with the Wind"

The water is wide, I cannot get o'er –
Give me a boat to take me home.
My true love waits on yonder shore,
So far away, so long alone.

But love is gentle and love is kind,
And love can soothe a lonely heart.
The more we seek, the more we find,
Love keeps us strong though we're apart.

Irish Folk Song

Chapter One

John Henry Holliday believed in heroes – he came from a long line of them, after all. From his distant Irish ancestors who had fought English invaders down to his father and uncles who fought Yankee oppressors, the Hollidays were famous for being fighting men. And so it was with some disappointment that John Henry listened to the eulogy being read over his grandfather Robert Alexander Holliday's grave that gray November day when Grandpa Bob was buried in the family plot in the Fayetteville Cemetery. For though Bob Holliday had been a loyal Southerner all his life and had passed a fighting spirit on down to his descendants, he had never himself raised arms in any kind of fight, and to young John Henry's way of thinking that was a real shame.

Not that Grandpa Bob had lived a shameful life, as a whole. He was well-loved by his family and well-respected by the little Georgia town he had helped to settle, and as the owner of the most popular tavern on the Jonesboro Road, he was a man of many friends as well. In fact, it was "Uncle Bob's Tavern" that had helped to put Fayetteville on the map in the first place, giving thirsty travelers a pleasant place to stop on the long ride from Newnan to Decatur. In those early pioneer days, when most of Georgia was still fresh out of the Indian Nation, hotels were few and far between, and a country tavern seemed like the very center of civilization. With his genial personality, and the help of his wife and six living children, Bob Holliday had prospered in the inn-keeping business and in the farming business, as well, with an eight-hundred acre place south of town and even a few hard-earned slaves to help till the soil.

No, there was nothing all that shameful about Grandpa Bob's life except for the peace of it, and that wasn't really his fault. He couldn't help having been born too late to fight against the British and too early to fight against the Yanks. Still, John Henry felt disappointed as the preacher pronounced the eulogy. Not a single battle

1

to his grandfather's credit! Not even a sword, like the one Great-Grandfather Henry Burroughs had used in the Revolutionary War, to pass down to a hero-worshipping grandson. Just a lot of talk about hard work and responsibility, and Bob Holliday's word being as good as his bond, and where was the heroism in that?

John Henry sighed as he shivered in the damp November chill, wishing that the funeral would hurry and get over. The sermon had been going on for what seemed like hours already, and there were still the benediction and the burial to go, the clumps of red clay falling with a hard finality on the pinewood box in which his grandfather was laid out. Grandpa Bob's remains had been in that box for two days now, resting for viewing in the best parlor of Uncle John's big white-columned house just off the Fayetteville town square, and John Henry had been obliged to stand as honor guard while the whole village came through to pay their respects, a grandson's duty to his grandfather's memory. For a restless eleven-year-old boy, standing still for any time at all was difficult; standing with his head bowed and a properly mournful countenance on his face was torture.

But no one could have guessed by looking at him how hard John Henry had to work at being reverent. With his blue eyes downcast under sandy lashes and his lips moving silently in response to the prayers, he was the very model of good behavior. He was a handsome boy, dressed for the funeral in his Sunday-go-to-meetin' suit, his fair hair pomaded neatly into place. He had his father's high cheekbones, his mother's fine narrow nose and expressive mouth, an easy grace about him that matched the rhythm of his slow southern drawl. And if it hadn't been for the way he kept fiddling with his hands and fussing with the wool cap he held in front of him, one would have thought him a properly placid child. But there was nothing placid about John Henry. He only stood so politely still because he had been trained by his mother to be polite. Left to his own whims, he would have bolted from the cemetery long ago, grabbed the first horse he found tied to a rail, and headed off into the open countryside for a fast ride.

It wasn't that he didn't truly mourn his grandfather's passing, of course. John Henry had loved Grandpa Bob as much as the rest of the grandchildren, though since he lived away off in Griffin, thirty miles to the east, he didn't get to visit as often as the rest of the Fayette County clan. But his father had brought him to Fayetteville with enough regularity that he knew his grandparents and aunts and uncles well, and considered his first cousins to be his closest friends, and he had actually cried himself to sleep the night he heard that Grandpa Bob had died, though his father would have called that an unmanly show of emotion had he known.

His mother knew, though she never said a word about it. Alice Jane McKey Holliday was a well-bred woman and a dutiful wife, and she would never dream of discussing something of which her husband disapproved. If Henry Holliday had ordered their son to keep his emotions in check, then she would never reveal that she had heard the boy's weeping as he buried his face in his feather bed pillow in the room next to her own. But the next morning, she had laid her hand on John Henry's shoulder, and said in her sweet and sensitive voice: "It breaks all our hearts to lose your Grandfather. Why, heaven itself must have been cryin' some last night." And John Henry knew that she had heard him, and would keep his confidence.

He stole a glance at his mother, noting how she stood near the grave with her eyes prayerfully closed, her face in pale repose under the dark veil of her silk mourning bonnet. On the bodice of her black mourning dress, she wore the symbol of another death, an ebony broach set with a lock of hair taken from her dead baby daughter. The somberness of Alice Jane's attire contrasted sharply with the alabaster whiteness of her skin, and emphasized the dark shadows that showed beneath her eyes. The shadows were caused, she said, by too many sleepless nights worrying over the health of her husband, who had recently returned from the War on a medical discharge. But it wasn't just worry over her husband's illness that caused her tired and drawn appearance. Alice Jane had been sick for some time herself, suffering from an undulant fever and a nagging cough, and the added strain of caring for her husband in his recuperation was wearing her to the point of exhaustion.

Her husband's early return from Virginia, occasioned by a long bout of camp sickness, had been the sad ending to a proud military career. After enlisting as Captain Quartermaster of the 27th Georgia Infantry, Henry Burroughs Holliday had been promoted to Major on Christmas Day of 1861, and seen action from Williamsburg to Seven Pines, Mechanicsville to Malvern Hill. But in the the defense of Richmond, the spring rains had turned the green countryside of Virginia into a muddy bog that spread disease through the camps of tents and shacks, and Major Holliday had taken sick along with his men, suffering from a bout of watery dysentery that had threatened to waste him away. The camp doctor tried every remedy he had, but Henry finally had to surrender to the sickness and resign his commission with the Army, returning home to Georgia in the early fall of 1862. For the proud Major, it was a galling defeat. But though his Confederate gray uniform hung loosely on his illness-ravaged figure, Henry Holliday still looked like a hero to his son, with his black Irish hair streaked with silver and his eyes a cool uncompromising blue – eyes that could chastise with only a glance, as John Henry knew only too well. But John Henry didn't mind his father's militarily disciplined demeanor. A hero was supposed to be strong, after all, and John Henry was proud to be a hero's son.

Henry Holliday was the bravest man his son had ever known, beholden to no one, afraid of nothing – a legend and a legacy impossible to follow. Henry had been a fighter since he was old enough to load a gun and had already fought in two wars before the struggle for Southern independence began, winning his first commission at only nineteen-years-old as a Second Lieutenant in the Creek Indian War. When the War with Mexico broke out, Lieutenant Holliday had signed up again and served with valor from Vera Cruz to Monterrey, coming home in glory and full of stories to tell of the great adventure – of rough and wild Texas where longhorn cattle grazed on endless acres of grassland, of strange Spanish Mexico and the fierce Indian warriors of the western deserts. John Henry had been raised on his father's war stories and thought them even more exciting than the penny-novel tales of Daniel Boone and Davy Crockett that were so popular with other boys. When John Henry's father talked of Texas, there was a gleam in his eyes that made the adventure seem so real that John Henry could almost picture himself there, too.

But for now, Henry Holliday's eyes were staring dispassionately ahead of him, as he stood beside the open grave, a shovel in his leather-gloved hands. As the oldest of Grandpa Bob Holliday's four living sons, it was Henry's right to place the first spadeful of dirt on his father's coffin as they lowered the box into the ground – a privilege he would have missed if he hadn't returned from the War just a few weeks before. Now, instead of commanding men, he was at the forefront of a cemetery full of mourners, spreading out around the graveside in a dark and somber circle of family and friends. Grandpa Bob's sons and daughters stood closest to the coffin, the men wearing black armbands in honor of their deceased, the women with their grieving faces hidden behind the heavy veils of black mourning bonnets. Behind them stood the daughters-in-law, sniffling daintily into their black-trimmed handkerchiefs and trying to keep all the cousins quiet while the preacher rambled on. Past the family were the neighbors and business associates, hats in hands and heads bowed. And past them, at a properly respectful distance stood the Negro slaves, swaying and murmuring in musical lamentation.

If only the preacher would say a final "Amen" and get on with it! John Henry's

4

already thin patience was wearing even thinner, and he let out a loud sigh and shifted his weight from one foot to the other, trying to keep himself warm in the wintry chill of the air.

"Stop fiddlin', Cousin John Henry!" The whispered words came as both a scold and a tease, and he turned to look into the watchful eyes of his cousin Mattie, who was standing just behind him in the circle of grandchildren. As the oldest of the girl cousins, Mattie Holliday had always made it her business to keep an eye on the others, and especially on John Henry who had no sister of his own to look after him, and he usually didn't mind too much.

Mattie was all right, for a girl, with a bright sense of humor and an adventurous streak to match his own, though she was getting too grown up and ladylike to show it very often. Young ladies of almost thirteen-years-old couldn't keep throwing their skirts up to ride horses the way Mattie used to like to do when she and John Henry had been children together. For all her growing up, though, Mattie still looked childlike. She was just a little thing, barely as tall as John Henry though she was eighteen-months his elder, with eyes too large for her little heart-shaped face, too wise for a girl her age. And though she wasn't really what one could call a beauty, those eyes of hers were beautiful: dark brown flecked with streaks of gray, changing in the changing light, calm and deep as evening shadows in the woods along the river.

"I'm not fiddlin', Mattie," he whispered back. "I'm just bored, that's all."

"How could you be bored at Grandpa's funeral? I should think you'd be cryin' harder than the rest of us, seein' as how you were his favorite."

"Says who?"

"Says everybody. You're the only son of his oldest son, aren't you? That's bound to make you the favorite."

John Henry shrugged, feeling the uncomfortable weight of his special place in the Holliday family: only son of the oldest son, primary heir of the Holliday clan, and future guardian of the family's good name, as well. For as long as he could remember, he had been taught that it would one day be his responsibility to represent the Holliday family to the world. The family, he knew, would always be watching.

But for now, the only one watching was Cousin Mattie, and sparring with her was more entertaining than listening to the preacher, anyhow.

"And I guess you don't call that fiddlin'," he said, "playin' with those rosary beads of yours."

"I'm not playin'," she retorted. "I'm prayin' to the Blessed Mother for Grandpa's soul."

Mattie always took offense whenever anyone derided her Catholic traditions. Though the rest of the Holliday family was Irish Protestant, John Henry's uncle Rob had converted to Catholicism when he married Aunt Mary Anne Fitzgerald, and their five daughters all worshipped the Virgin Mary and the Roman Pope. *Popish*, John Henry's mother called them, though the Hollidays generally tolerated the Fitzgerald's religion.

"...and it wouldn't hurt you to do some prayin', too, you know," Mattie added.

"Oh, I'm prayin', all right," John Henry replied with a grin, "I'm prayin' this preacher gets done with his preachin' so I can get to supper soon! I'm starvin', aren't you?"

"No," Mattie answered piously, her brown eyes averted from his mischievous gaze.

"We're havin' smoked ham and sweet potatoes," John Henry tempted, "hot buttered biscuits, pecan pie...can't you just taste it, Mattie? Bet you can! Bet you're as hungry as me, under all that proper religion of yours..."

And just as he had expected her to, Mattie rose to the challenge.

"John Henry!" she said loudly, forgetting herself for a moment too long, "you are just shameful! I don't know why I even bother to help you behave!"

And as she spoke, her voice rising above the solemn sound of the sermon, the crowd of mourners turned to stare at the auburn-headed girl whose cheeks were blushing crimson with embarrassment. Only the preacher seemed unaware of the disturbance, and kept right on with his sermonizing, quoting endlessly from the Holy Book: "...that it is written, Death is swallowed up in victory. O death, where is thy sting? O grave, where is thy victory? The sting of death is sin; and the strength of sin is the law..."

John Henry quickly bowed his head to hide a laugh, though Mattie heard the sound of it.

"Very funny, John Henry! I hope you're satisfied now that you've made a mockery of me in front of the whole family. Have you no decency at all?"

"Aw, Mattie," he drawled, "I was just foolin' around, you know that! I wasn't tryin' to get you in trouble. Besides, everybody knows you're too good to make a fuss in public. I'll own up, if anybody asks."

"I still say you're shameful, not carin' anything about Grandpa bein' dead."

"I never said I didn't care. But my Pa says a man's got to quarter his feelings and not cry over somebody dyin'. So I'm not cryin', that's all."

Henry Holliday's word was law to his son, and he was careful to obey – though it wasn't really his father's strict discipline that kept John Henry on the straight and narrow path, but his mother's gentle persuasions. Like cousin Mattie, his mother was always watching him, making sure that he was behaving himself as a gentleman, and John Henry didn't like to disappoint her. He loved his mother as much as he idolized his father, and her good opinion of him mattered more than any tempting misbehavior – most of the time. There were days when his adventurous streak got the better of him and made him throw caution to the wind and commit some ungentlemanly act or other. Then Alice Jane would reprimand him and call him to repentance, her sweet voice tinged with the suffering of a loving parent: "John Henry, dearest, I am so very disappointed…" and John Henry would be truly ashamed of his sin and beg for her forgiveness, which of course she always gave.

But Cousin Mattie wasn't nearly as forgiving as his mother, and she was still fuming over the embarrassment of having all the family turn those chastising eyes upon her.

"I don't know why I even talk to you," she whispered, "you're such a child, John Henry, and a spoiled one, too! It's a shame you don't have any brothers or sisters. I bet that would teach you to be a little less selfish."

"I am not selfish!" he protested – though in truth he'd been accused of it before, mostly by the cousins who all came from large families and had to share everything, including their beds. As an only child, John Henry seldom had to share his room or his things with anyone else, though he didn't see as how that made him selfish. It wasn't his fault that his mother had never had another baby after he came along, or that his only sister, Martha Eleanora, had died as an infant before he was even born.

Mattie, on the other hand, was the oldest of five children, and proud to be from a large and growing household. It seemed like her mother, Aunt Mary Anne, was always either caring for a new baby or expecting another. In fact, it was only since Uncle Rob had gone off to the war that Aunt Mary Anne had not been in the family way – though John Henry wasn't supposed to notice such things. Still, as a curious youth, he couldn't help but wonder where all those babies came from, and why Uncle Rob and Aunt Mary Anne should have so many and his own parents had only him. There was some mystery to it, he knew, and he intended to unravel it one day…

"Curiosity killed the cat, John Henry," Mattie whispered, as if reading his thoughts. "What are you ponderin' on, anyhow? You've got that wonderin' look on your face again."

"I'm wonderin' how much longer this service is gonna last," he snipped, uncomfortable at the way Mattie always seemed to see right through him. There were some thoughts a boy didn't want to share with a girl. And to his relief, before Mattie could question him anymore the preacher gave a final and dramatic, "Amen!" and the men began their burden of covering over Grandpa Bob's grave.

It was the sound of the dirt going down, heavy spadefuls of damp red clay, that caught John Henry's attention. His father's was the first shovel to swing and drop, committing Grandpa Bob to the ground, then Uncle John and the rest of the pallbearers followed after and the ladies began to sing a hymn to cover the morbid sound.

Amazing Grace! How sweet the sound,
That saved a wretch like me!
I once was lost, but now am found,
Was blind, but now I see...

Above the sound of the rest, John Henry could hear his mother's voice, so sweet and musical that it seemed to float out over the cemetery, and he felt the poignant beauty of the moment rise up inside him.

"John Henry!" Mattie exclaimed, "Take that hat back off your head! You know you can't cover yourself 'til after the service is through. It isn't proper!"

But John Henry didn't answer, as he pulled his wool cap onto his sandy hair and down low.

"John Henry!" she started again, but stopped when he turned and gave her one quick look from under the brim of the cap.

"Well, it's a funeral, isn't it?" he said, sniffing back unmanly tears. "I reckon I've got a right to mourn a little."

"Oh, honey," Mattie said, her scolding voice going soft, "so you really do care about Grandpa's dyin', after all!"

"I told you I did," John Henry said, defending himself as he struggled with the sudden emotion. Then he added, "Hey, Mattie? You won't tell anybody, will you? I mean – you won't tell my Pa that I was cryin'?"

"I won't tell a soul," she replied. Then she leaned over and kissed him once on the cheek, a sisterly sign of affection. "It'll be just our secret always, I promise. No one but me will ever know what a soft heart you really have. Now let's go on and get to supper. You're right, I am just starvin'!"

"No, you go on ahead and get started without me. I think I'll stay around here a little longer."

"Whatever for? I thought you couldn't wait for this funeral to get over."

"I'm just not ready to go yet, that's all. Save me a plate, all right?"

And as Mattie picked up her skirts and went off with the rest of the mourners, their mood lightened now that the last benediction was spoken, John Henry stepped closer to the graveside. The fresh red earth was mounded over Grandpa Bob, a spray of red fall leaves taking the place of flowers on the grave. Then, with no one but the angels in heaven looking on, John Henry let the tears come. His grandfather may not have been a hero, but John Henry was going to miss him all the same.

~~~~~~~~~~

Dr. John Stiles Holliday, John Henry's namesake uncle, was the only doctor in Fayetteville and, as such, had one of the nicest homes in town: two-stories tall with a row of white columns across the front and eight fireplaces inside, one in every room. To John Henry, the house seemed like a mansion with its glistening floors of Georgia heart pine and lofty ten-foot ceilings, its two front parlors and string of servants quarters out back. And though Uncle John's home was really just a townhouse that doubled as a medical office, compared to John Henry's family's neat little cottage in Griffin, it was elegant.

Now, with the eight fireplaces blazing and the funeral supper laid out on tables in the dining room, the parlor, and the front hall, the house looked fit for a party. Only the black draping that covered the mirrors over the fireplaces and the pictures on the walls showed that the family that lived there was in mourning. While neither Uncle John nor Aunt Permelia were superstitious folk, they still held with the old traditions and had ordered that all the reflective glass in the house be covered to keep the dearly departed's soul from looking back into the mortal world – though John Henry wouldn't have minded seeing his Grandfather's ghost smiling back at him from the other side.

While the adults took their funeral supper in the dining room and the parlor, the children were served from tables in the entry hall and had to seat themselves on the stairs, two cousins to every step. But though the stairway was crowded with Holliday children, they all knew that somebody was missing, and the talk soon turned to Cousin George, Uncle John's oldest son, away at military school in Marietta.

"...best school in the whole state!" George's younger brother Robert said proudly. "My father says it's a real honor to the whole family for George to be goin' there. 'Course George always was a smart one – like me!" he added with a laugh and a wink. "In fact, I bet ol' George makes Captain of the Cadets real soon. He's sixteen-years old now, you know, plenty old enough to see some service."

"Oh, Robert!" cousin Mattie exclaimed, "you don't think the cadets will have to go off to the War, do you? They're just students still..."

"That's true, but I wouldn't be surprised if General Lee called them all up to fight one of these days. You heard about the Battle of Sharpsburg back in September? They say Bobby Lee lost ten-thousand men on Antietam Creek up there in Maryland, almost a quarter of his whole army. He may need all us boys to go fight the Yanks, soon enough."

"Well, I'd go, if they'd let me!" John Henry said fiercely, the War talk bringing out the Irish in him. "I'd whip those Yanks good!"

"Don't be silly, John Henry!" Mattie's younger sister Lucy said with a laugh and a toss of her long dark braids. "You're only eleven-years old, and mighty scrawny. You couldn't even whip Cousin Robert, let alone a Yankee!"

Twelve-year-old Robert Holliday grinned at that. "Don't taunt him, Cousin Lucy. You know John Henry's always ready to make a fight, even if he is little!"

As the two boy cousins closest in age, John Henry and Robert always had a sort of sibling rivalry going on, though they were good friends most of the time. They even favored each other in looks, with the same Irish blue eyes and high Holliday cheekbones, and strangers sometimes mistook them for brothers. Still it irked John Henry that Robert was older by a year and always would be, giving him a superior edge in the circle of cousins.

"I'm ready to take you on, anyhow," John Henry boasted. "I may be younger'n you, Robert, but I bet I could take you in a pistol fight. My Pa says a pistol makes all men look about the same size."

"Now stop it, both of you!" Mattie scolded. "Such talk! I thought you two were best of friends, not enemies."

"We're friends, all right," Robert replied. "It's just a little friendly competition between cousins, that's all. So what do you say, John Henry? Shall we make it a real competition?"

"I'm game," John Henry answered. "What'd you have in mind?"

"Just a little tree jumpin', that's all."

10

"Tree jumpin'?" ten-year old Theresa asked. "What's that?"

Robert lowered his voice conspiratorially before answering, evidence that tree jumping was not approved of by the adults. "Tree jumpin's a game George and I invented before he went off to school. There's this oak tree outside my bedroom window, and if you stand in the windowsill and jump out far enough, you land right in the tops of the branches. Like landin' on a feather bed, if you do it right."

"And if you do it wrong?" Lucy asked.

"Then you break your neck, no doubt," Mattie observed, "and land in a heap on the ground. Sounds like a stupid game to me, and I forbid John Henry to participate in it."

"And who made you my Mammy?" John Henry snapped back. "I swear Mattie Holliday, sometimes you act like an old maid! But I don't guess I have to be scared of tree jumpin' just 'cause you are..." he let his words hang in the air, like a challenge, knowing that the one thing Mattie hated was to be called a coward. For all she was a girl, she had the same unthinking courage as the Holliday men, afraid of nothing.

"I am not scared!"

"Then prove it," John Henry replied. "I dare you!"

Mattie sat still for a moment, the color rising prettily in her pale cheeks. Then she gave a quick nod of her auburn head. "All right, I will! I'll beat you both at your stupid tree jumpin', and I'll go first, as well!"

"Oh no, Mattie!" Lucy gasped, "you'll kill yourself for sure!"

But Mattie had already pushed her plate off her lap and was climbing over the other cousins to the top of the stairs, where Robert's room was the first on the second-floor hall.

Robert's jumping tree was a good six feet away from the window, though the spreading branches did reach close to the white painted clapboard siding of the house — almost close enough to make a jump from the open window possible. But if the jumper didn't leap quite far enough...

"It's a long way down, isn't it?" five-year old Roberta asked as Mattie pulled her skirts up past the hem of her pantalettes and climbed onto the window sill. It was a twenty-foot fall at least onto the hard-packed earth of the side yard where Uncle John kept his wagon and carriage. Mattie hesitated just a moment, then took a deep breath and bravely jumped out into the cold night air.

Lucy and Theresa both screamed at once, then Roberta and baby Catherine started crying, and all John Henry could think was that he was going to hell for sure with his own cousin's blood on his hands. He'd killed Mattie by daring her to jump out the window, just as much as if he'd pushed her.

"Did she fall?" he asked, his heart racing.

"I can't tell," Robert said, "but I didn't hear her hit the ground."

Then, as if sharing the same thought, they both bolted from the room and went racing down the stairs and out of the house, heading for the side yard.

"Mattie!" John Henry cried, and Robert echoed him, "Mattie, are you all right?"

And to their relief and amazement, they heard an answering sound of laughter coming from under the jumping tree where Mattie was lying in a heap of leaves and broken branches, her skirts up over her head and her drawers shining white in the moonlight.

"I did it!" she said, laughing and crying all at once. "Did you see me do it? I jumped out the window, just like you dared me to!"

But before they could join in her excitement, there were scolding words behind them as Aunt Permelia's little mulatto housemaid, Sophie, came running out onto the porch.

"Mercy, Miss Mattie! I see you all right, and I'm ashamed to say your cousins seein' you, too, with your underpinnin's all open to the night air like that. Where'd your decency go, Missy? And what's all this screamin' and hollerin' goin' on, anyhow? Shame on y'all! Makin' a circus out here and your grampa jest buried this day and not even cold in his grave…"

Sophie had uppity ways for a serving girl, John Henry thought, even if she was descended from the Governor of South Carolina, being the illegitimate daughter of the Governor by one of his favorite slave women. But good blood lines or not, Sophie should have kept her nosey self out of the cousins' business, and he was about to tell her so when another voice spoke from out of the darkness – one that made John Henry stop cold in his tracks.

"Leave them be, Sophie," Henry Holliday said, as he stepped down into the side yard. "I'll handle this," and Sophie replied with a hasty "Yessir, Mr. Henry, Sir."

Henry Holliday was a commanding presence, standing militarily straight in the moonlight. Even in undress, without his officer's frock coat and with his uniform vest unbuttoned and hanging loose on his illness-gaunt figure, Henry looked every inch the officer he was trained to be, accustomed to giving orders and being obeyed.

"Well, Mattie, are you hurt?"

"No Sir, Uncle Henry," Mattie answered, quickly pulling her skirts down to cover her underthings. "I'm just tousled a little. My petticoats flew up and broke my fall, I guess. We were just playin'. Robert told us about his jumpin' tree, and then John Henry dared me..."

"Did he?" Henry asked. "Well, boys, it seems like we have some talkin' to do. Sophie, you go on and take Miss Mattie back inside and let Dr. Holliday have a look at her, make sure there's nothin' broken. John Henry, you and Robert make yourselves comfortable."

Comfort, however, had little to do with a lecture by Major Holliday. Henry had never been much for conversation, and when it came to chastising his wayward son, he tended to be brief, to the point, and painfully blunt.

"What the hell did you boys think you were doin', anyhow?" he asked as soon as Mattie and the maid were safely out of earshot. "You could have got your cousin killed."

"We didn't make her do it, Uncle Henry," Robert said with an apologetic smile. "It was her idea. We were only bein' gentlemanly, lettin' her go first..."

Henry's sudden anger cut into Robert's excuses. "Damndest pair of gentlemen I ever saw! Lettin' a lady put her life on the line like that! John Henry, tell me a man's duty toward his womenfolk."

John Henry's answer came easily, having been memorized as part of his family training from toddlerhood. "A man's duty is to protect his womenfolk, Sir."

"Yet you dared your cousin Mattie to jump from a window?"

"Yessir."

"You're pretty brash and bold with your dares, aren't you, son? Have you ever jumped from that window yourself?"

"No, Sir."

"Then how did you know it could even be done?"

"'Cause Robert said so, Sir," John Henry explained in his own defense.

"We never really did it, though," Robert mumbled. "George and I just talked about how fun it would be to try it..."

"Damn if I haven't raised a fool for a son!" Henry exclaimed. "John Henry, next time you want to make a dare, you better make sure you can beat it yourself first!"

"Yessir," John Henry nodded.

"Yessir, what?"

"Yessir, I'll make sure I can beat it myself."

"All right, then," his father said, "let's see you do it."

"Do what?" John Henry asked, bewildered.

"Let's see you beat the dare," Henry said coolly. "I want to see you jump from that window yourself and make it down as good as little Mattie did. " 'Course without all those skirts and petticoats of hers, you're likely as not to break your neck. Now get up those stairs and get to it. Robert, you go on inside and start makin' your apologies to your cousin."

Robert nodded obediently, then darted into the house as though afraid his uncle would decide to include him in the punishment as well, for punishment it certainly was. Without the thrill of the game, without the excitement of all the cousins watching, jumping from the window seemed like a stupid and dangerous thing to do, indeed.

But Henry had given his command, and John Henry resolutely climbed the stairs and made his way to Robert's bedroom window. The room was empty now, the rest of the children all gathered around Mattie downstairs, and the only sound John Henry could hear was the loud thumping of his own heart as he climbed up into the open window, balancing his smooth-soled leather boots on the wide window sill, and looked out into the night.

The limbs of the jumping tree were a black silhouette against the moonlit sky, and down below in the darkness his father was waiting for him to prove himself against a dare. He put one foot out the window and took a quick breath the way he had seen Mattie do, steeling himself to step into thin air. But just before he jumped, a strong hand grabbed hold of him and pulled him back into the room.

"That'll do, son," said Henry Holliday.

"Pa, I thought you were still down there..."

"I followed you up. I don't want you to get hurt, son. I just want you to learn to think before you speak, and not let the Irish in you get the better of your judgment. You've got a tendency to be impetuous, I fear. But God knows, your mother would never forgive me if I ever let anything happen to her boy." And for a moment, John Henry thought he saw something soft go across his father's stern face, something warm like the flicker of the oil lamp lighting Robert's room.

"But I would have jumped, Pa," he said eagerly, basking in the unexpected warmth in his father's cool blue eyes, and in his heart he added: *I'd do anything for you, Pa...*

"I know, son. But I hope this particular lesson's already been learned. Now get on down there and say you're sorry to your cousin Mattie. And let's not hear any more about this jumpin' business, all right?"

"All right," he said, but hesitated a moment before obeying. "Pa?"

"Yes, son."

"I just wanted to say...I..." he stammered, unsure of how to put the feeling into words.

"I'm listenin', John Henry."

"I'm glad you're home, Pa."

And Henry nodded, accepting the welcome.

~~~~~~~~~

The easiest part of his punishment was asking for Mattie's forgiveness, since he didn't really care whether she forgave him or not. As long as she wasn't hurt, he didn't see that any harm had been done. She could rant and rave at him all night if she wanted.

But Mattie wasn't angry a bit, only flushed with the excitement of her brave feat.

"My mother says I should be ashamed, jumpin' out a window like a boy! But I think she's most upset about my skirts comin' up. Sophie told her you boys saw my underthings – did you?"

"I don't know," John Henry lied, "maybe. I wasn't thinkin' about underthings just then."

The truth was that he had indeed noticed Mattie's drawers as she lay in the pile of leaves with her skirts all around her neck. Robert had noticed, too. How could they not? Neither of them had sisters, so girl's underclothes were something novel to them both. He'd seen the hem of Mattie's pantalettes before, of course, as she pulled her skirts up to ride horseback and as she stood in the window before jumping. But never before this night had he seen all the way up.

"Well, I don't care if you did see," she said with a toss of her auburn hair. "You're just a child, anyhow."

"I don't guess you're so grown up yourself," he shot back, "or you wouldn't have been jumpin' from the window, and all."

Mattie clenched her fists and pursed her lips, and John Henry wasn't sure whether she was going to hit him or cry. Then she squared her small shoulders and put her chin up in the air.

"I am still waitin' for your apology, Cousin John Henry. And I'll tell your father if you don't make it good."

She had him there. So he launched into the prettiest words he could find to beg her forgiveness. Better to humiliate himself in front of a girl than to earn his father's displeasure again, and he got down on one knee and bent his head like a true penitent.

"Mattie Holliday, I am sorry for darin' you to jump out of Robert's window – even if you did take me up on it of your own free will – and I hope you will forgive me for bein' so ungentlemanly." Then he looked up at her from under his sandy lashes, his blue eyes as full of repentance as he could make them appear to be.

"Get up off the floor, John Henry! You're makin' a fool of yourself! Of course I'll forgive you, don't I always?" and when he grinned up at her, she smiled reluctantly. "I never saw a boy who could get into so much trouble, or get out of it so easily!"

"That's 'cause I'm so charmin'," he said without a trace of sarcasm. "My mother taught me to be a gentleman. Besides," he added with another grin, "you always did like me special."

And Mattie had to smile herself at that. "I always did," she said fondly, "ever since you were a baby. I guess if I'd had a brother, I'd want him to be just like you. Even if you are trouble most of the time."

"Aw, Mattie! I thought I was your best sweetheart! That's what you always used to call me when we were little, remember?"

"*You* still are little," she teased, reaching up to pat him on the head and tousling his sandy hair. "But I guess you'll always be my best sweetheart, trouble or not."

~~~~~~~~~~

They all stayed over at Uncle John's house that night, the adults filling the beds and the children sleeping together on pallets on the floor. But in spite of the cramped accommodations, John Henry slept well. He liked being surrounded by his family. He felt safe inside that close circle of cousins and aunts and uncles, and only wished that his three Holliday uncles still off at the war could be with them, too. Uncle Rob, Mattie's father, was still off fighting, as were Aunt Martha's husband, Colonel James Johnson, and Aunt Rebecca's husband, John Jones. In fact, of all the men in the family, only Uncle John Holliday had not gone off to war, choosing instead to serve in the Georgia Home Guard Cavalry. As a doctor and a surgeon, his medical skills would be needed at home should Georgia ever be threatened with direct attack by the Federals.

For as long as he could remember, John Henry had been fascinated by his uncle's medical practice. He loved to spend time in the everyday parlor Uncle John used as a medical office, looking through the medicine bottles in the tall apothecary cabinet and admiring the collection of surgical tools stored neatly near the examining table: saws and lancets, bone forceps, bullet extractors, and long-handled surgical probes. His uncle even had a real human skeleton hanging on a metal frame, left over from his school days at the Medical College of Augusta - a gruesome and wonderful sight for a wide-eyed eleven-year-old boy.

The medical office was just off the entry hall, with one door leading to the side yard so that patients could come and go without disturbing the rest of the family, and another door leading to the guest room where surgical patients could stay over a night for observation, and it was there that John Henry would sometimes hide, leaving the door to the office open just a crack so that he could hear Uncle John's conversations with his patients. A boy could learn a lot about life that way, he'd discovered through the years, overhearing everything from headache remedies to tooth pullings — and sometimes far more private matters. He was eavesdropping, he knew, but he excused himself with the notion that he might someday follow his uncle into the professional field and would need all the knowledge he could glean.

And so it was that on the morning following the funeral, as his father saw to packing up the spring wagon for their trip back home to Griffin and John Henry stole a few free moments listening near the medical office door, he overheard his uncle in intimate conversation with his mother – and wished that he hadn't heard at all.

"Alice Jane, my dear," his Uncle John said in a voice surprisingly tender for a doctor's office. "My dear, sweet sister-in-law..."

"Please, John, don't," John Henry's mother said, her own lovely voice full of emotion. "Don't say anything just now. Henry mustn't see I've been cryin', or he's sure to suspect somethin'. You must promise me."

"But he's my own brother! I don't know how long I can go on bein' disloyal to him like this."

"He'll find out soon enough, and we'll deal with it then," Alice Jane said. "And when the time comes, I'll tell him myself, in my own way. You must promise me!"

"If only he hadn't come home just now, and sick as he's been," Uncle John said. "I do hate to burden him with the news of this..."

"Then it must remain our secret, dear John. Now kiss me and wish me well, for I've a hard road ahead, it seems."

"You have such strength, my dear! All right, then. I'll keep my silence awhile longer."

Then came a brief silence when his uncle must have given his mother the asked for kiss. And sitting on the floor of the room next door, his head leaning against the doorframe, John Henry felt his heart slowly turn over inside of him. How could Uncle John be so despicable? And how could his perfect mother welcome his uncle's advances? Oh, if only he hadn't been listening at all...

Then he heard his own name, and he had to keep on listening.

"And what of the boy?" his uncle said. "What about John Henry?"

"My darlin' boy..." Alice Jane said on a sigh. "I suppose my little sisters will have to look after him. Margaret and Ella and Helena are livin' with us now, you know, since our own father passed away. Until they're married themselves, they can tend to him."

"He could come here. He'd have a good home here. My boys are like brothers to him already."

"No, dear John. His father would never let him go, you know that. But perhaps Henry will remarry, give my son a new mother..." Then she began to weep. "Oh, John! It's leavin' my little boy that makes this so hard! I don't think I can bear it!"

"Then we won't talk of it anymore. God willin', he'll be grown before the time comes."

Then there was another long pause that might have been another embrace, and John Henry thought that he would never again hear anything as awful as that intimate silence. But there was more, and worse. For when his uncle spoke again, his voice cooler now, professional again, his words had nothing at all to do with any supposed faithlessness, and John Henry knew he had been rash in judging him.

"You may have years yet, Alice Jane. Consumption is a long illness. And there are spontaneous remissions..."

"Miracles, you mean? Then I'll pray for a miracle. But you must remember that Henry's not to know until I'm ready to tell him. It won't help him recover from his battle sickness to be worryin' about me. And he'll need all his own strength, soon enough. So, brother to my husband or not, you must be my own doctor first and promise to keep my confidence. And if you do love me as a sister, as you say, you'll honor my request, and not tell Henry that I have the consumption."

Consumption – John Henry mouthed the word in disbelief. He knew from other overheard diagnoses that consumption was always fatal. But worse than knowing that his mother was dying, was knowing and not being able to tell.

The homeward road from Fayetteville to Griffin led through dense woods and across winding streams that often washed out the low wooden bridges, and there was always the possibility of some adventure along the way. Now and then a deer would leap out of the green darkness and cross the path before them, and Henry would grab at a loaded rifle and try for a quick shot, startling the stillness and leaving a smell of gunpowder in the air. And sometimes, John Henry would imagine that the deer was followed by the quick silent footfalls of Indians, their dark skins hiding them in the darker shadows of the trees. But that was just imagination, he knew, for the Indians who had walked the paths and followed the deer were gone now, driven out by the white men, though their names remained on the countryside: Chattahoochee, Etowa, Kennesaw, Oconee. He liked to let the words linger in his mind like an incantation, bringing the past back to life. And sometimes, he imagined it was Yankees in those shadowy woods, and his father's shot had been lucky and found its mark in a blue-coat's heart. The Yanks weren't nearly as romantic as the Indians, but with the War still dragging on, they were a more likely foe.

But on this long trip, he hadn't the heart to watch for deer or worry about the Yanks. He was weighed down with the awful secret he had just discovered, and all he could think about was the fact that his mother was dying.

"You're quiet today, John Henry," Alice Jane said, looking back to where he sat on a pallet of blankets in the wagon bed. "Aren't you feelin' well?"

And it was all he could do to keep his emotions in check, looking back at her sitting beside his father on the board wagon bed. But he mustn't let on what he had learned, so he shrugged his shoulders under the wool blanket that covered him, keeping him warm in the chilly November air, and said: "I'm fine, Ma."

"Probably just worn out from the visit," his father said, and glanced at his wife. "You're quiet today, too, Alice Jane. Somethin' on your mind?"

"Nothin', dear," she said, and John Henry believed it was the first time he had ever heard his mother tell a lie.

"Then why aren't you singin'?" Henry asked. "You're usually like a lark on these trips. John Henry, has your mother ever told you she could have been an opera singer, if she hadn't got married to me?"

"Yes, Pa," John Henry said, "she told me."

Alice Jane McKey's lovely soprano voice was famous around Griffin, and folks said she could have been an opera diva, if she hadn't married so young. But when handsome Lieutenant Henry Holliday had come calling, fresh from his service in the Mexican War, Alice Jane had fallen head-over-heels and forgotten about everything else. Within just a few months they were married, and by the end of their first year together Alice Jane was a mother. And though her little Martha Eleanora had lived only a few months, John Henry came along soon after, and Alice Jane had been a devoted mother ever since. She still sang some, though, for weddings and funerals and such, and gave piano lessons to neighbor children. All the McKeys were musical, from Aunt Ella and Aunt Margaret who played piano for Sunday services, to Uncle Tom McKey who had gone off to War as a musician in the Griffin Light Guards Band.

"Well," Henry said, "let's hear a song. No point in havin' a wife with a pretty voice if I can't have some entertainment to help me drive."

And as Alice Jane obediently started into the strains of a hymn, John Henry thought he knew why she had chosen this particular one:

> *"Abide with me, fast falls the eventide!*
> *The darkness deepens, lord with me abide!*
> *When other helpers fail and comforts flee,*
> *Help of the helpless, O abide with me!*
>
> *Swift to its close ebbs out life's little day.*
> *Earth's joys grow dim, its glories pass away.*
> *Change and decay in all around I see,*
> *O Thou, who changest not, abide with me..."*

Her voice broke on the words and she started to weep, and John Henry reached out to touch her shoulder as if he could comfort her pain.

"I'm sorry," she said, reaching a gloved hand to his. "I guess I'm still feelin' poorly about Grandpa Bob's passing."

"I know, Ma," he said, and meant *I know*. "Pa? Is Uncle John really a good doctor? I mean, does he really know all that much about things?"

"He knows more than most of these country doctors do, since he went to the medical college for his degree. Why do you ask?"

And when he hesitated a moment too long in answering, his mother gave him a questioning look, and he had to turn his eyes away from hers.

"Aw, you know I always liked to watch Uncle John work," he said, which was true at least, though not really an answer to his father's question. "In fact, I've been thinkin' about bein' a doctor myself one day. You know Uncle John let me help when he pulled Littleton Clark's tooth last time we came to visit?"

"Your mother mentioned somethin' about that."

And with the subject safely changed away from his mother's illness and his own ill-mannered eavesdropping, he went on more easily.

"I was thinkin' that maybe I could go over to Fayetteville next summer when school is out, spend some time in Uncle John's office. I could assist him again and learn a whole lot..."

"Not next summer, son," Henry said. "Next summer we'll be busy movin'."

"Movin'?" Alice Jane said in surprise. "Movin' where? What are you talkin' about, Henry?"

"I'm talkin' about gettin' out of Griffin before the Yankees get here. You know Lincoln's issued an Emancipation Proclamation, freein' all the slaves in the rebel states? I fear that once the emancipation takes effect come January, things are gonna get hot down here in Georgia, and I don't want my family anywhere near it."

"But where will we go?" she asked, bewildered. "Everything we have is here; your family in Fayetteville, my family in Griffin. We have my sisters livin' with us. What will they do? And our baby girl is buried in Griffin! We can't leave her all alone..."

"We're goin' down to south Georgia," Henry stated, ignoring her protestations, "a little place called Valdosta, and your sisters will just have to come along. I hear the land down there is good for cotton."

"What land?" Alice Jane said, her voice growing desperate. "We don't own any land down there! Please, Henry, surely you're not serious about this..."

But he was serious, and seemingly set upon his new plan.

"We'll have some land soon enough," he replied, "once my father's estate is settled. You know that place of his out by the Harp's farm? Well, John's neighbor, Colonel Dorsey, has made an offer on it, and a good one for these hard times. Once the sale's done, my brothers and I will split the profit as our inheritance. There ought to be plenty to buy a place down in Valdosta, and some field darkies as well. You'll see, Alice, it'll be like a new life for us, and in a few years..."

"In a few years..." she echoed, and John Henry expected to hear her start weeping again, thinking of how few years she might have to share her husband's dream. But instead she smiled bravely and put her hand on Henry's arm. "It sounds wonderful, my dear. You'll have so much to do, so much to think about. Why, I believe we'll love livin' out in the country, won't we John Henry? You've always wanted a horse of your own. Now maybe you can have one."

"Yes, Ma," he said, and thought that, in her own genteel and ladylike way, his mother was as much of a hero as his father was.

Chapter Two

Griffin, 1863

John Henry's hometown was one of the prettiest little cities in Georgia, dotted with red brick shops and white frame houses on the tree-lined streets that rose up from the railroad tracks. Griffin had been born in the prosperous 1840's as a cotton shipping center on the Macon and Western Railroad, and by the start of the War it boasted a population of three-thousand, making it the busiest town between Atlanta, forty miles to the north, and Macon, sixty miles to the south.

Henry Holliday had come to Griffin soon after its founding, looking for the opportunities a railroad town could offer a young war veteran, and Griffin had rewarded him well. From his first job in town as a clerk for the local druggist, he quickly rose to become a landholder, joining in the buying frenzy whenever a new section of town lots was opened up. But the biggest opportunity that Griffin had offered Henry Holliday was the chance to meet and marry Miss Alice Jane McKey, the eldest daughter of one of the wealthiest plantation owners in that part of Georgia. Alice Jane's father, William Land McKey, owned hundreds of acres of prime cotton land on Indian Creek in nearby Henry County, and dozens of slaves to make the land produce; her mother, Jane Cloud McKey, was kin to the Elijah Cloud family who had first settled the area and had thousands of acres of cotton and hundreds of slaves of their own. So when Henry Holliday, who had plans to become a wealthy planter himself, married into that Southern aristocracy, his future was pretty much assured.

John Henry took his aristocratic heritage for granted, since many of the children he knew in Griffin had wealthy planter relatives, too. It was the bounty of his grandfather's Indian Creek Plantation that he had enjoyed, caring little about the cotton that had made the McKeys rich. It was the peach and plum orchards he loved, the Muscadine arbor heavy with ripening grapes, the beehives humming with honey bees, the clean-swept dirt yard where he could sit under the shade of a dogwood tree and eat bowls of bread and fresh sweet milk. On his grandfather's plantation, there had always been good things to tempt a visiting grandchild's appetite: beaten biscuits, red-eye gravy, farm-raised chicken with doughy dumplings, peach pot pie smothered with cream and cane sugar, and sometimes, on special occasions, a glass of Syllabub made of sweetened milk curdled with homemade wine. To John Henry, the plantation was the Promised Land and he was one of the chosen people, fed on the manna made by the Negro slaves who worked his grandfather's land.

Slavery may have been a "peculiar institution" as Northern abolitionists liked to call it, but for the wealthy planter class of Georgia and the rest of the Southern states, it was an institution that worked well. The whites ruled, the blacks obeyed, the cotton economy prospered, and the rising generation was taught to expect that things would always go along as they had for two-hundred years of Southern slavery. John Henry had been raised that way, knowing that when he turned twenty-one he would inherit some of the McKey land and the slaves that came with it, and he had fond memories of going with his grandfather to the auction block down by the railroad tracks where Mr. Daniel Earp, Griffin slave trader, sold males and females right out in the open.

The Earps and their kind held a unique place in Southern society. Though the service they provided of procuring human chattel for the slave trade was an essential part of the plantation economy, the slave traders themselves were despised. Slave dealers were commonly known to be liars and cheats, using unscrupulous means to obtain slaves for sale, since the legal importation of Africans had been ended by federal law in the early part of the century. Wise plantation owners were cautious when dealing with slave traders; nice folks avoided them completely.

While John Henry's parents didn't own dozens of field slaves, they did have enough House Negroes to keep their home running smoothly. The Holliday's pretty cottage on Tinsley Street in downtown Griffin was kept clean by the colored housemaid, the meals prepared by the colored cook, the clothes cared for by the colored washerwoman, the buggy driven by the colored driver. The slaves were such an integral part of the family's life that when nightfall came and they went to their own cabins behind the main house, the big house felt quiet and empty without them. For John Henry, it was hard to imagine a world without slavery, a world where black and white weren't so completely dependent upon one another. But that was the world the Yankees were fighting for. For nearly two years, the War of Secession had ravaged the land as the North fought to abolish slavery and save the Union, and the South fought to preserve the Constitution and its guarantee of States' Rights. And though both sides claimed to be guided by divine providence, neither side had made much progress. The North was out-generaled, the South was out-numbered, and the war thus far had been one long, bloody stalemate.

Griffin felt the continuing weight of the war more than most Georgia towns, as it served as one of the main training centers for Georgia troops. Every week, the trains went out carrying men armed with devotion to the Cause and shouting the Rebel Yell, high and wild as a band of banshees. The sound of that yell would always remind John Henry of the war: of streets filled with soldiers dressed in Confederate gray, of shops emptied of goods as the Union blockade closed all the ports from Charleston to New Orleans.

Times had gotten hard in the promised land in the two years since the war began, and the once-rich cotton economy was nearly at its breaking point. By that spring of 1863, flour was selling for $65 a barrel, bread was going for $25 a loaf, and the Confederate dollar was as good as worthless. In April there were bread riots in Charleston. In May the Confederate States' government asked planters to give up their cash crop cotton land for planting corn and potatoes to feed the starving people of the South. In June General Lee's army, having already foraged away all the food in Virginia, moved north through the Shenandoah Valley and into the farm land of Pennsylvania looking for rations and a chance to wage one final battle that might end the war while the South still had the strength to win. In July, in the shadow of the Blue Ridge Mountains, in the quiet Cumberland Valley town of Gettysburg, the army found its fight.

All four Griffin newspapers carried the story of the Battle of Gettysburg as front-page news, but it wasn't until a letter from cousin Mattie's father arrived that the family realized how close the battle had come to home. Uncle Rob Holliday had been there at Gettysburg during the fighting, serving as a Captain Quartermaster under General Longstreet, though his own regiment had been kept back to cover the retreat. It was a heavy blow, he wrote, a hard defeat to accept, with twenty-five thousand Southern casualties in two days of desperate fighting and entire divisions decimated.

Then, before the news of Gettysburg had even grown cold, came reports of the fall of Vicksburg on the Mississippi River as the Yankee General Ulysses S. Grant completed the encirclement of the Confederacy. There would be no more easy victories for the South, with the shipping lanes of the Mississippi River cut in two and General Lee's army limping back from its defeat in Pennsylvania. But the war wasn't over yet, and Henry Holliday was more determined than ever to move his family far from the battlefront.

~~~~~~~~

Though John Henry's mother never complained about moving away from Griffin, there were tears in her eyes as she packed their things, and her younger sisters complained enough for everyone, anyhow. How would they get along in such an uncivilized place as south Georgia? Where would they live? Where would they go to church in that God-forsaken wilderness? Nineteen-year-old Ella and seventeen-year-old Helena worried that their brothers, Will and James and Tom, all of them off fighting, might not be able to find them once the war was over. And Margaret, twenty-four years old and promised to a soldier named Billie Wylie, worried that he might not find her, either, and she'd end up an old maid. But Henry Holliday gave little heed to his sisters-in-law. He was their guardian; they would be obliged to go wherever he wanted to go, and he wanted to go south.

John Henry was the only member of the family who joined Henry in looking forward to the move, though he felt like a traitor to his mother for doing so. But for a restless twelve-year-old boy, going south seemed like the adventure of a lifetime. Two-hundred miles to Valdosta! It would be the longest trip he had ever taken and the longest time he'd ever spent on a railcar, and that was fine by him. He had always loved the railroad, ever since he first knew the sound of the steam engines coming into town. The trains roared in on iron rails, bringing people from places he had never seen, taking them away again to places he had only heard about. To him, the railroad was a romance and an adventure, and now it would be his turn to travel off into the unknown. If only his mother weren't so sad about leaving...

But how could she not be sad, leaving her baby behind, buried on a hill outside of town? Nearly every Sunday that John Henry could remember, his mother had made a pilgrimage to the city burial ground to lay flowers on his sister Martha Eleanora's grave, and many a time he had happily accompanied her. He liked sitting beside her as she drove the buggy out of town and across the low wooden bridge that led to Rest Haven Cemetery. He liked kneeling beside her on the grassy ground as she wove fresh cut flowers into pillows or wreaths to adorn the grave. He liked being alone with her and the sister he had never known, feeling close to them both and special as the only living child of his beautiful mother. So when Alice Jane asked him to go with her to the cemetery one last time to say a final farewell to little Eleanora before they left Griffin for their new home, he was glad to go along.

It was sultry hot that August afternoon and John Henry was sweating in his wool jacket by the time they reached the Holliday plot at the top of the graveyard hill. He would like to have been coatless in his cotton shirtsleeves on such an uncomfortable day, but visiting the cemetery was almost a religious event for his mother, and religious events demanded a certain amount of decorum, so he wore his suit coat and tried not to complain of the heat. His mother was nearly as warmly dressed as he was, in her high-necked blouse and wide-sleeved jacket, her full cotton skirt and layers of petticoats, though she seemed not to be feeling the heat as badly as he was. His young aunts said it was the hoop skirts the ladies wore that helped to keep them cool, holding up the weight of all those petticoats and allowing a little breeze to blow past the legs. Of course, he would never dare to discuss such delicate things as skirts and petticoats with his ladylike mother.

"John Henry, you clear away the weeds from Ellie's grave while I sort these flowers," his mother said as she gracefully gathered her skirts and climbed down from the buggy, and he obediently set to work pulling at the long grass that threatened to cover over the granite headstone.

In Memory of Martha Eleanora
Daughter of H.B. and A.J. Holliday
Who died June 12th 1850
Aged 6 Months 9 days.

John Henry did the ciphering in his head, adding up that his sister Ellie would have been thirteen-years old now, had she lived, and wondered as he always did what it would have been like to have had a living sister instead of this small grave for a sibling. Her simple stone stood upright on a marble base at the head of the tiny plot, the footstone only two feet away. And underneath, six feet down in the red Georgia clay, lay the baby girl who had died before he was even born — died of the same malady that would likely have killed him, had his Uncle John not intervened.

"Ma, tell me again how Uncle John saved my life when I was a baby."

His mother sighed as she set to arranging the flowers she would lay on the grave: yellow jonquils and purple petunias intertwined with glossy green magnolia leaves. "You know how your sister was born with a cleft in her mouth," she said softly,

27

though there was no one around to overhear the sad tale. "Ellie's beautiful little face was disfigured by a gash in her lip. But worse than the appearance of it was how it made her unable to nurse properly. The poor little thing couldn't suckle, and when we gave her cow's milk in a pap, the milk ran back out of her mouth before she could take much of it in."

"So she starved to death," John Henry said with childlike bluntness, and his mother nodded.

"When you were born with the same condition, we knew we had to do somethin' – anything – or we would lose you the same way. That's when your Uncle John brought Dr. Long down here from Jefferson County to assist him in an operation."

"Dr. Crawford Long," John Henry added, proud that his life was connected to the famous surgeon who had pioneered the use of ether in surgery. He'd heard that story a hundred times as well.

"That's right. Dr. Long was your Aunt Permelia's cousin on her Ware side, so he came as a favor to the family. Permelia came too, as a nurse to your Uncle John. You were only two months old at the time. So tiny, so helpless! But tiny as you were, they didn't dare wait any longer to do the surgery."

"So Dr. Long gave me the ether in a cloth over my nose, and Uncle John mended me up."

Alice Jane nodded. "Your Uncle John did a wonderful job. He sewed the cleft in your lip together, and did the same with the opening in your mouth. And then there was nothin' to do but pray that you would survive the surgery, and recover."

"But I did. You can hardly even see the scar on my lip anymore, and I don't lisp at all…" though he still remembered the pain of being laughed at by taunting schoolmates.

"No, sweetheart, you are just perfect now. You've done well with your voice lessons, learnin' to speak properly, and when you're grown to be a man, you can wear a nice mustache to cover that little scar line that remains. No one will ever know how close you came to joinin' your sister here in the cemetery. I will always know, though, and be forever indebted to your sweet Uncle John for savin' my precious baby. He's a brilliant man, a talented physician."

John Henry sat quietly for a moment, though his thoughts were racing. If his uncle were indeed as brilliant as all that…

"Ma? Do you reckon Uncle John might find a cure for other kinds of sicknesses someday? I mean, he cured me, didn't he?"

"He did indeed."

"Maybe someday he'll find a cure for typhus," he suggested, "or cholera," and when his mother nodded, John Henry gathered his courage and went on. "Maybe he'll even find a cure for – for consumption," he said quickly, his words rushing out with childish hopefulness. "Do you reckon he could, Ma? I reckon he could. I reckon he could cure anything. I'll bet, if he worked on it hard enough, he could figure out what causes the consumption, and make it go away. Oh, Ma!" he said, his heart coming up in his throat, "he has to find a cure for it. He just has to!"

"John Henry, sweetheart," his mother said in surprise, "what is all this? Whatever is wrong?" Then she laid down the wreath of flowers she had been fashioning and looked into his distraught face, her voice a worried whisper. "You haven't been talkin' with your uncle, have you? Surely, your Uncle John has told you nothin'..."

"I heard, Ma! I heard it all! I was right next door, listenin' from the other room when Uncle John told you about havin' the consumption! I didn't mean to hear about it, honest I didn't. I was just tryin' to learn somethin'..."

Alice Jane let out a sound like a painful sigh, then touched a hand to his hair and said sadly: "Well, I suppose you learned somethin' all right. I'm sorry that you had to hear. I didn't mean for you to know so soon. I'd hoped to keep it private for a while longer, at least until we'd got moved and settled in. Your father doesn't need to be dealin' with this just now..."

"But maybe Uncle John can cure you, Ma, before Pa has to know. Maybe he can save you like he saved me."

"Oh, my sweet boy!" his mother said as she pulled him close to her. "I do hope you are right. I pray to God for such a miracle! But I also trust in God's divine providence. If Jesus means for me to be cured, I will be. Of that I have no doubt. But if this illness should take me..."

"No, Ma!"

"...if this illness should take me, then that is God's will. You must believe that. But John Henry, your mother is not dead, so there's no need to mourn just yet. And God willin', I'll live long enough to see you grown and with a family of your own before I die, as a proper mother should. That's what I want, more than anything, for you to grow to healthy manhood and find a life that'll make you happy. I want you to know the joy that I've known in raisin' you, for you've been the light and the love of my life. But for now, we must decide how to keep your father from findin' out."

"You're still not gonna tell him?" he asked in surprise.

"No, I am not. It'll do him no good to know, and may harm his own recovery. So, my dear boy, you'll have to share my secret a little longer. Now it must be our secret, together."

"Our secret," he repeated, and somehow having a confidence with her made him feel better, though it was a heavy secret to share.

"Now promise me one thing, dear. Promise me that you will never forget your sister here, for I fear that when I'm gone no one will remember to care for her grave. Promise me that you'll come back here in days to come, and tend to Martha Eleanora's grave for me."

"But all I can do is weed. I can't make those fancy flower things like you do."

"Why, of course you can. You have good talented hands – you're learnin' how to play the piano, aren't you? It won't take you long to catch on to flower weavin'. Just take a stem like so..." and she nodded for John Henry to follow as she pulled a jonquil from her basket.

"But flowers are women's work!" he protested. "That's what Pa says, flowers and sewin' and tendin' to babies..."

"Is that so? Well, if your Uncle John hadn't done such a fine job sewin' up your lip when you were a baby, you wouldn't be nearly so handsome now. He's handier with a needle and thread than any woman I know, and he's a fine man all the same."

She had him there. "I guess I could try and make one of those wreath things like you do. Just as long as you don't tell Pa, all right? I'll catch hell for sure, if he sees me makin' pretty things."

"Mind your tongue, John Henry. Gentlemen don't need to curse to make their point. But I promise I will keep your secret, as you must promise to keep mine, and not tell a soul until I give you leave. Now take those flowers left in the basket there, and do as I do, but make haste, for this heat will make them wilt before we're half done."

~~~~~~~~~~

The Hollidays weren't the only refugees that hot summer of 1863. It seemed that everyone in Georgia was going somewhere on the trains, trying to get out of the way of the Yankees. And swelling the crowds of civilians were thousands of Confederate troops, packing the rail cars as they followed their orders east to the sea and along the Georgia coast.

John Henry had never seen so many soldiers at one time or heard so much commotion, with the shouts of military commands, the frantic cries of lost children and frightened women, the roar and hiss of the steam engines and the grinding clang of the wheels on the rails. Everyone was hurrying, panic driven to get from where they were to somewhere else, and at every stop there was a fight for tickets, hoping that the cars weren't already full of troops, vying with the other refugees for space on a box car, some place to put the household belongings that had been dumped on the side track at the end of the last leg of the journey. And when his family finally did get settled, crowding into the dark and airless back of a boxcar with the crates and Alice Jane's piano, the train slowed to a stop at every little village so the conductor could pass along the news of the War to the anxious crowds gathered by the tracks.

"What do y'all hear from Gen'ral Lee's army?"

"My boy's in Virginia, have y'all heard anything from up there?"

"Is the fightin' still goin' on in Tennessee? We haven't heard from Uncle in more'n two months now."

"Where's that damned Yankee Sherman? Give us one good fight and we'll whip 'em yet!"

Then finally Valdosta, near end of the line for the Atlantic and Gulf Rail, sixty miles from Thomasville, hundreds of miles from anyplace else one could call civilized. South Georgia was barely out of the woods and Valdosta was still just a frontier outpost in a humid, insect-infested wilderness. But rough as it was, just a scattering of business houses around a wooden courthouse, Valdosta was full of the bustle and building that filled all refugee towns.

Henry Holliday listened to the commotion, breathed in the thick piney air, and smiled. For $35,000 Confederate, his entire inheritance from his father's estate, he bought three-thousand acres north of town, past Cat Creek. It was beautiful land, high fertile ground that ran across a ridge between the road and the woods. An old house faced onto the road, and behind the house the land spread out, sandy and level, covered in tall grass and dog fennel that waved in the slow summer breeze. Past the house, the road wound on around a bend and disappeared into the woods again. It was new land, wild country that still had a soul to it, ready for a man and his family to settle and tame.

They were far from the battlefront now, but in that primitive environment life itself was often a battle. Henry took his son out and taught him how to use a rifle – how to tear the paper cartridge open with his teeth and pour the black gunpowder down the barrel, slide in the ball and ram it home with the ramrod, set the percussion cap against the hammer and pull the trigger back to half-cock, then aim and wait. The waiting was the hardest part for John Henry, the huge gun pulled up to his shoulder, near as long as he was tall and near as heavy as he was, too. Even his father's Colt's Walker pistol was heavy in his hands, but John Henry seemed to have a natural feel for it, learning how to shoot the eyes out of a rabbit when it stopped to look at him before it started running.

There were other lessons Henry had for his son, things every Southern gentleman should know, like honor and responsibility and the importance of hard work. And with his father's guiding hand, John Henry learned to care for a horse of his own, and spent long hours racing across the grassy fields and dirt roads that led from the farm toward Valdosta. He learned to hunt from horseback, one hand on the reins, one hand on his gun, firing low from the hip without slowing to aim. And in the cool evenings after his mother had gone to bed, he learned to play a friendly game of cards, bluffing without blinking, and besting his father so many times that Henry said he was glad he hadn't taught the boy to wager as well. Those were happy days for John Henry, with his father's time and attention, the sun on his skin, the wind in his face, and a wild new world to explore.

But his mother made sure it wasn't all too wild. She continued his music lessons on the spinet piano in the parlor, saying that his agile fingers seemed to have a natural affinity for the instrument. And though his father thought piano-playing sissified, his mother insisted that it was manners, not muscles, that were the real proof of a man. But a gentleman must be educated as well as mannered, so he was enrolled in the day school over in Valdosta, where the local children were taught grammar and history, mathematics and penmanship, and recited together the opening lines of their reading primer. His mother nodded in approval as he practiced for her:

"Do not lie, my son; a good boy will not lie. It is a sin to lie; and a good boy will not sin."

The day school wasn't the caliber of the fine institutions in Griffin, of course, but at least it was an education, and John Henry was sent packing every morning for the seven-mile ride into town, leaving the farm before daybreak so he wouldn't be tardy. The first class sessions were held in the rough wooden courthouse until a real school building could be readied, though even that was a slap-dash affair with no sash or shutters and only boards nailed across the windows to keep out the weather, and the students had to do their work by the weak light of a lamp of plaited rags dipped in melted tallow. By the time class was over for the day, twilight was coming on and John Henry rode home watching out for "haints" and "boogeymen" as the darkness closed in. The woods were full of such things, he knew. He'd been raised on the stories told by the Negro slaves who worked the land and knew what kind of spooks hid out in the shadows. And just to be safe, he kept his right hand on the butt of his gun, ready to draw and fire at the first frightening sound.

But the most frightening sound of all in that wilderness was his mother's coughing in the night. Her miracle hadn't come yet, and she often took to her bed with fever and exhaustion. And though Henry was concerned and wanted to send for the doctor, she insisted that there was no need.

"I'm fine, Henry," she would say with eyes closed as she drifted off to sleep soon after supper. "I just need a little rest, that's all. I'm sure I'll be feelin' better soon enough. Now tell John Henry to play something for me on the piano while I rest. I do so love to hear him play."

~~~~~~~~~~

In the north the War dragged on as the Union General Sherman kept pushing his forces deeper into the Confederacy, and every week more refugees arrived in Valdosta fleeing ahead of the Yankee destruction. One Southern village after another was becoming a ghost town as the families refugeed and neat town squares and comfortable old homes were left empty, waiting for the destroyer. Sherman had promised to enter the South with the sword in one hand and the torch in the other and carve a forty-mile wide road to the sea where a crow could not find its supper. He meant to punish the rebels, and if the helpless wives and children of the South suffered, so much the better; their husbands and fathers, hearing of the carnage, would give up their Cause and surrender to save their families. But the Yankees had never understood the heart of the Southern people.

On through the summer of 1864 the Federal troops kept moving south, driving the Army of Tennessee and destroying the rail lines that kept the Confederacy alive. If the rail hub of Atlanta could be taken and her railroads crippled, the Confederacy would suffocate. The Yankees pushed on toward that goal, moving south into Georgia from Dalton to Resaca, past Kennesaw and on toward Decatur, where they made their headquarters while the siege of Atlanta began. The Confederates fought valiantly to defend their ground, but they couldn't counter the flanking movements of a hundred-thousand Yankee soldiers. Soon Atlanta was surrounded on three sides with only the southern roads toward Macon and Savannah still open. But as long as the Confederates could hold the southern railroad, Atlanta could survive.

John Henry listened with the excitement of a thirteen-year-old boy to the stories of the battles, imagining the gunfire and the cannon blasts echoing against the brass hot summer sky, the smoke hanging thick as thunderclouds before the sun. Then late in August, the fighting suddenly stopped as the Yankees disappeared into the wooded Atlanta countryside. At first there was the desperate hope that Sherman had given up and moved his troops back north to Tennessee, but it was only a hope. The Yankees were moving south in force, heading on toward the Macon and Western rail line, the final iron road that connected Atlanta to the coast. The Confederates tried to hold them at Rough and Ready, ten miles south of Atlanta, but the Yankees pushed on and headed for Jonesboro and the final bloody battle of the War in Georgia.

When John Henry heard about Jonesboro, the War suddenly ceased to be just an exciting story for him. His cousin Mattie's family lived in Jonesboro, in a pretty house on a shady lane near the railroad. He remembered it with fondness and disbelief. Jonesboro wasn't a place where battles were waged. Jonesboro was sunlit summer afternoons and backyard barbecues, birthday parties and Christmas gatherings. Jonesboro was old trees big enough to climb and grassy hills just right for rolling down. Jonesboro was little girl cousins who played dolls on the front porch and dress-up in the attic, and let him be the hero of all their make-believe stories. Jonesboro was warmth and home and family, but not war; never war. But the Yankees were moving south, and Jonesboro would be caught in the firestorm that Sherman was lighting from Atlanta to the sea.

Surely the family would leave before the fighting started, surely Aunt Mary Anne would take the children and refugee south to safety as Uncle Rob had instructed her to do if the Yankees ever came near. Soon now they would hear from her, have a message that she was safe and coming to Valdosta with the children to wait there until Uncle Rob returned from the War. But no message came, not in the first days following the battle, not in the days and weeks that came after that. All through the warm days of Indian Summer and into the first cool days of fall they waited, and still no word came, and John Henry pondered on what the Yankees could do to the families of Confederate soldiers.

It was a crisp day in mid-October when Henry Holliday made the seven-mile trip to Valdosta to take care of some business and left his horse saddled at the rack across from the depot, and was done and about to go on home when the train pulled in. So he took his time packing his saddlebag, always waiting for what news the trains might bring. Maybe there would be some mail with a message of hope from Jonesboro, or word from his brother Rob, and he waited and watched as the passengers left the train. Then, in the steam that rose up from the engine, he saw a small woman climb down from a boxcar and help three little girls down after her. She turned to find her bearings, and for a moment she disappeared into the steam as if she'd only been a phantom and not there at all. But as the air cleared, Henry saw her again and recognized her at last. It was his own brother's wife, Mary Anne Fitzgerald Holliday, and she was crying thankful tears at the sight of him.

~~~~~~~~~~

That night after her little girls had been settled down to sleep, Aunt Mary Anne tried to tell her brother-in-law what had happened to the family. Alice Jane had already gone on to bed, worn out from the excitement of the day, she said, but John Henry stayed up, lingering in the shadows, hoping to hear about the War and the battle that had finally taken Atlanta. And he wanted to hear about Mattie and Lucy as well, away in Savannah for the time being, safe behind convent walls. But it would be ill-bred of him to interrupt the conversation and ask questions, so he watched and waited and listened.

Aunt Mary Anne looked weary as she sat in the old rocking chair in front of the parlor fire, her face drawn and dark-shadowed around deep blue eyes. She'd been beautiful once, he'd heard tell, in those long-ago days when she was the sixteen-year-old bride of his father's younger brother. But five baby daughters and four years of wartime had aged her, like all the women he knew. Her voice was still beautiful though, a lovely lilting combination of Irish brogue and Southern drawl.

"I never believed the Yankees would get past Atlanta," she said, speaking softly so as not to wake her sleeping children. "Who could? With General Hood in command I thought surely we were safe. Rob served with him and said he was a fighter if ever there was one."

John Henry's thoughts ran ahead of the story. He knew his Uncle Robert Kennedy Holliday's line of command and recited it to himself: Seventh Georgia Regiment, Anderson's Brigade, Hood's Division, Longstreet's Corps. Hood's men served with General Lee at Gettysburg, some of the hottest fighting of the War. But General Hood had been injured there, and in Georgia he'd proven that the fight had gone out of him.

"Hood's a fool," Henry said, "sendin' half his cavalry off to Tennessee. An army's blind without the cavalry as scouts. He didn't even know Sherman was movin' on Jonesboro."

"We had no word the Yankees were comin'," Aunt Mary Anne went on, "not until Kilpatrick's raiders came through town. They burned all the business houses and tore up the railroad tracks. We hid in the attic and watched them do their work – a whole regiment on horseback with their guns at the ready."

"And why didn't you leave?" Henry said, his voice was softly critical, but Mary Anne took no offense.

"I couldn't. My old Uncle Roddy was desperately ill, and couldn't be moved. He lived with us, you know. All I could do was pray that the Yankees wouldn't come back, or that Uncle Roddy would be taken soon..." She stopped talking for a moment and lowered her eyes in shame. "It's a hard thing, Henry, prayin' for someone's death. But that is what I did, prayed for his release so the children and I could leave Jonesboro."

"There was nothin' wrong in it, Mary Anne. We do what we have to do in wartime."

She nodded, understanding more of war than she ever should have known. "I sent for a priest, but no one could come. There were so many soldiers dyin' in Atlanta – they said the streets were full of the wounded. I feared that Uncle Roddy would die without final confession, as if God wanted him to prove his perfect abandonment to the Holy Will, but Father O'Reilly blessedly came down from Atlanta in time for the last rights. Uncle Roddy passed away the end of August, peacefully, in his sleep."

"Well, God rest him," Henry said. "Roderick O'Carew was a fine old man."

Mary Anne crossed herself, honoring her dead. "I had to take his body to Fayetteville for a Catholic burial in the family plot, but there were rumors the Yankees were comin' back. A regiment of our boys, down from the fightin' at Rough and Ready, warned us that Sherman himself was on the way."

"And were the Yankees comin'?" John Henry spoke up from the shadows, so intent on the story that he forgot himself.

"Hush, son! Remember your manners," his father scolded.

"It's all right," Mary Anne said as she turned to look at her nephew. "Yes, John Henry, the Yankees were comin'. The day after we buried Uncle Roddy the Fayetteville Road was filled with bluecoats. We heard them comin' before we saw them, like a low rumblin' of thunder movin' in from the west – thousands of men and hundreds of wagons, comin' right toward us. The clouds of dust they kicked up turned the whole sky red as blood. I watched that red cloud movin' in and knew that it was too late for us to get out of Jonesboro."

John Henry's eyes opened wide, picturing the whole Yankee army invading the town and the brave Confederate soldiers frantically digging in for the defense.

"By the time our boys got there the Yankees had the high ground outside of town, waitin' for them, and we were trapped between the Confederate lines and the railroad. I had to get the children away from there before the firin' started, so I loaded the wagon with everything I could carry out of the house and set out toward my Uncle Phillip Fitzgerald's plantation."

"But Rural Home is south of Jonesboro," Henry said, "right along the line toward Lovejoy's Station. There must have been Yankee cavalry all through that countryside!"

"I kept to the old trails we used to use before the railroad came through, and took to the trees every time I heard a sound." She paused before going on, sighing. "The Yankees had gotten there before we did and set up headquarters in Uncle Phillip's house, but we were not harmed. Some of the Yankee soldiers were Catholic raised and remembered their duty as Christians, though they were not so honorable about Uncle Phillip's property. They ruined his farmland, drivin' their wagons and runnin' their horses through the cotton and the corn. Then they set fire to everything else that remained, and when they left they took all the animals along with them, leavin' Uncle Phillip destitute. I couldn't ask him to care for my family when he had nothin' for his own. At the end of two weeks when the soldiers moved on, I took my girls and went back home."

She stared into the fire and John Henry watched the light flicker across her face, thinking of the fires the Yankees had set when they took over Jonesboro. They'd torn up the railroad tracks and heated the rails over bonfires until the metal was soft enough to twist around the trunks of pine trees, leaving "Sherman's Bow Ties" that couldn't be straightened and re-laid by the Confederates.

"All along the road there were mounds of dirt where the dead had been buried – there must have been thousands of them. At the edge of town were trenches where the troops had dug in and breastworks beyond. Church Street was just behind the lines and had taken heavy fire from the Yankee artillery, and our house had been right in the middle of it. It was all but torn apart by the shelling, the windows shattered, the walls filled with spent bullets, everything inside broken or stolen."

John Henry's heart was fairly bursting out of his chest. Now the story was getting really good – breastworks and trenches, artillery and gunfire! He held his breath and waited for more.

"Behind the house, in the garden, were two more graves: Confederate dead, Colonel Grace of the 10th Tennessee and his chaplain. They say that Colonel Grace was wounded during the first day of the battle so his troops moved him behind the lines to the garden of our house. His chaplain went there to minister to him and was givin' him the last rights of Holy Church when he was struck and killed by a shell. There'd been no time to move them before the Yankees came over the lines, so Colonel Grace's men buried them there where they died, under the trees in our backyard. I like to think that at least they were near a Catholic home when they passed. Maybe one day they can be moved to a proper site, in consecrated ground."

John Henry had to bite his tongue to keep from asking Aunt Mary Anne to tell the story again. To have a garden that was a cemetery was gruesome enough, but to have two war heroes buried there – now that was really something! His father shot him a look of warning, and he quickly wiped the hopeful smile from his face. He'd be sent on to bed for sure if he acted childish at a time like this. Still, dead heroes buried in the garden was mighty exciting!

Mary Anne didn't see the look that passed between father and son. She had closed her eyes for a moment, exhausted by the memory and the retelling of it. "There was nothin' left to stay for, so we set out to make our way here. I had no way to contact you, Henry – I didn't even know for certain where your farm was. But I prayed for guidance, and look at the miracle of it: when we finally arrived in Valdosta there you were at the depot, as if God himself had led us every step of the way."

John Henry was moved by her faith, and in her telling of the story, it did seem that some providence had saved the little family.

"But what about Mattie and Lucy?" He was startled to hear his own voice speaking his thoughts out loud. He looked quickly at his father, but Henry said nothing this time, and Mary Anne turned to answer him directly.

"They are still safe, praise God. I was able to see them when we passed through Savannah. The convent will keep them until the end of the term. Their father thought it the best place for them during wartime. The Confederate soldiers were always gentlemen of course, but I wouldn't trust the Yanks, not even the officers."

Henry nodded his approval. "Did Rob take the girls there himself?"

"Yes, in spring, when he was home on furlough."

She rested her hand absently against her full gathered skirt, and Henry asked softly,

"And when is the baby due?"

John Henry started with surprise. He hadn't even noticed his aunt's swollen figure hidden under the long shawl that stayed draped around her. But Mary Anne didn't blush at Henry's question, though men weren't supposed to comment on such things.

"Christmastime, or sooner. It's been hard on the baby, I fear, all this refugeeing. But I think it'll be a boy this time, Henry. I've prayed for Rob that it be a son." Then she looked up and her eyes were filled with tears. "I want a son to carry on his name, if he doesn't come home again."

She said it with such courage, acknowledging the danger of her husband's long years in the War, and Henry reached out and took her hand in his, speaking gently.

"He'll be home, Mary Anne, and he'll be proud of that son. A man always is."

John Henry was surprised to hear the compassion in his father's voice. Henry had never spoken so gently to Alice Jane, even while he tended her on her sick days. He was always polite, of course, cool and efficient in seeing to her needs, but never did he treat her with such heartfelt kindness. And suddenly, John Henry understood something elemental about his father, something his mother surely already knew. Henry hated weakness, and illness was weakness, and poor Alice Jane, through no fault of her own, was both ill and weak. But Aunt Mary Anne, in spite of all she'd been through, was still strong, and in the quiet shadows, John Henry could see the admiration in his father's eyes.

~~~~~~~~~~

Aunt Mary Anne's baby came early as she had thought it would, but the tiny boy was all Holliday and a fighter from the start. Mary Anne named him James Robert after his grandfather and father, but the family soon shortened that to Jim Bob, a good Southern nickname that John Henry had suggested. The baby was the center of attention from then on, and even Alice Jane found the energy to join in the adulation.

Infants were a mystery to only-child John Henry. He watched with bewilderment as the women and girls all fussed endlessly over the new baby, envying his father's freedom to leave the house every time the baby wailed, as Henry was suddenly finding town business more demanding than usual. Still, having Aunt Mary Anne's brood wasn't such a hardship, as long as cousin Mattie was on her way — she and

Lucy would be leaving Saint Vincent's Academy at the end of the term in mid-December, and with the Yankees moving ever closer to Savannah, the girls wouldn't be going back to school.

John Henry went along with his father to the depot to meet their train, eager to see Mattie's familiar face and have her company once again. He was already full of plans for how they would spend the time together, riding and exploring the wilds around his father's farm. But as the train pulled in and the passengers stepped down from the cars, his plans vanished into the thin winter air.

The little girl he loved was gone and in her place stood a stranger with Mattie's eyes and a woman's body, her long auburn hair pulled up from her neck, her small shoulders squared against the world. John Henry's heart fell – did everything always have to change? He'd already lost the rest of his childhood, and now Mattie was gone too.

But then she saw him standing on the platform and her face broke into the wide smile he remembered, and she ran down the steps to embrace him.

"John Henry, it's so good to see you again! I hoped you'd be here! How's my mother? Is the baby well? Oh, I just know we're gonna have the most wonderful Christmas!" And she kissed him on the cheek and hugged him again.

Her words tumbled out so fast that he hardly had time to answer, but it was just as well. For having her arms around him gave him a strange new sensation, pleasant and unfamiliar. She was still Mattie, but someone new as well, and he hardly knew what to make of it. And it was hard to keep his eyes on her face as she spoke, and not let them stray down to the curving figure in her small-waisted traveling dress. She looked like the girls who had grown too old for school, and left to stay with relatives and look for husbands in other towns. She looked like the girls he silently stared at as they walked home from Church, hips swaying in wide hoop skirts.

She was still talking, asking his father a hundred questions, telling Lucy to help with their bags, and still hanging onto him with one hand that sent shivers up his arm and made him dizzy. She didn't see the blush rise up in his face when she spoke his name. She didn't hear his young voice crack when he stammered an answer to her questions. And she didn't know that, for the first time in his life, John Henry Holliday was falling in love.

Chapter Three

Valdosta, 1864

None of them would ever forget that Christmas, the last one of the War. It came at the end of a cold, gray December when the air hung heavy with an icy fog over the red fields, and even the sun seemed to have been captured by the Yankees and carried away. Yet in the midst of the suffering, life went on. Babies were born and christened, sweethearts met and made promises to one another. That was the year when John Henry's Aunt Margaret McKey was married on Christmas Day when her soldier-beau from Griffin, Billy Wylie, came home from the army on furlough – thirty days for a wedding and a honeymoon, then back again to join his regiment in Virginia.

They were married in the parlor of Henry Holliday's farmhouse, standing in front of the fireplace and attended by Margaret's two younger sisters, Ella and Helena, as bridesmaids. Margaret wore the same wedding dress her sister Alice Jane had worn at her own wedding sixteen-years before, while Billy Wylie wore his Confederate gray uniform, threadbare but freshly pressed. Henry Holliday gave the bride away, handing her over to Billy while all the ladies cried, then the party moved to the dining room for the finest Christmas dinner that could be had in those hard times: roast turkey and salt ham, sweet potatoes and stewed pears, corn muffins and French honey bread, and a white pepper lemon cake with cane sugar icing on top. After dinner there were toasts to the happy couple, with brandy for the grownups and cider for the children.

Then came the dancing, the parlor furniture pushed out of the way and Alice Jane playing waltzes on the piano. Henry gallantly asked all the ladies to dance, laughing as he turned one sister-in-law after another across the wide plank pine floor, then he bowed to young Mattie and offered her a dance, too, while John Henry sat by his mother's side at the piano and watched with pride. His father was as handsome as ever in his gold-braided Major's uniform, his hair thick and shiny with pomade, his face sporting a stylish mustache and goatee. The move to Valdosta had been good

41

for him, helping him recover the strength he had lost during his hard year of service to the Confederacy.

Billy Wylie, dancing with his new bride close in his arms, leaned toward Mattie and smiled. "You're sure growin' up, little Miss Mattie. Pretty soon it'll be your turn for a weddin'!"

Margaret laughed with him, "And who will you pick, Mattie? Who are you fond of?"

"Why, I'm gonna marry little John Henry, of course," she said with a smile. "We've always been sweethearts, haven't we honey?"

She looked at him with bright eyes, and he flushed with embarrassment.

"I'm not aimin' to marry just yet!" he answered, too seriously. "I'm just waitin' 'til I'm sixteen, so I can join the army and go fight in the War."

A sudden chill ran through the room, as if the door had been opened a crack to let in the cold world outside, and Margaret gasped.

"Oh no, you mustn't say such things! Why, the War will be over long before you can go. Won't it Billy?" she asked, looking up anxiously at her new husband.

"Sure honey, we'll have those Yanks licked real soon. Why, I hear General Longstreet is givin' 'em a good whippin' right now. I bet we're done with 'em by summertime."

Aunt Mary Anne sat in the warm corner by the fire, listening while she rocked baby Jim Bob. "Rob is serving with General Longstreet," she said quietly, half to herself and half to the baby, and Henry stopped dancing and looked down at her with concern.

"Now, Mary Anne, you mustn't worry yourself about Rob. Quartermaster's just about the safest job there is in the army. The officers have to protect the supplies, no matter what. And Billy's right; Longstreet will have the Yankees beaten back in no time."

Mary Anne smiled at him bravely. "You're right, of course, Henry." Then she looked back down at the baby, but as she bent her head John Henry saw a tear fall and drop onto the sleeping baby's cheek.

The conversation needed to change direction, and Henry gave it a gentle push.

"Well, Mattie, you are a mighty fine dancer," he said, "and much too good for an old man like me. Why don't you see if my son will dance with you? I expect he's tall enough to partner you now."

John Henry started and tried to protest but Mattie was already at his side, maneuvered there by Henry on his way to the punch bowl.

"Well, Cousin," she said, "it seems I have an empty space on my dance card. Would you care to step in for my last partner?"

She was just teasing him, smiling the way she always had when they'd played together as children, but John Henry wasn't sure just how this game was played. But she didn't wait for his answer, taking his hand in hers.

"Aunt Alice Jane," she called to his mother, "play that waltz again, won't you? That lovely one by Franz Liszt."

"Oh do," Margaret agreed. "That's one of our favorites, isn't it Billy? 'Dream of Love' I think they call it."

Alice Jane was too intent on her music to notice that her son was squirming and wishing that she would plead sudden sickness and stop playing altogether. He didn't know how to dance and didn't want to learn now, just when everyone was treating him like a grown-up and listening to his talk of joining the army.

Mattie laughed at his furtive look toward the door. "Don't be shy, honey, it's only a little waltz. Just hold me like this," she said, lifting his left arm with her hand as his right arm slid behind her back. "That's right. It's easy. Now watch my feet," and she did a little side step in the square of space between them, her feet moving one-two-three with the music. He didn't have much choice but to follow along, without making a scene that would appear rude. "That's it. Just keep movin' like that. Why, you're a real natural dancer, John Henry. I think you must have been practicin' with some other girl behind my back."

"Why are you talkin' to me like that, Mattie?" he said, scowling. "You don't even sound like yourself anymore. They've ruined you up at that convent school, with all that lah-de-dah talk."

"Why, I'm just tryin' to talk sweet to you, the way a young lady should at a dance."

"I liked you better the way you used to be. I miss the old Mattie."

"Silly thing," she said, looking into his face, "I'm still here."

And in her round brown eyes he did see the same girl he had always known. One thing about Mattie's eyes — they could never be dishonest.

"And I wasn't teasin' you about the dancin' either," Mattie added. "You are good."

"Did you mean that other thing you said, about us gettin' married?"

Mattie responded with a laugh. "Of course not, silly! I was just talkin'. Everybody knows I'm gonna marry a Catholic boy. Though I suppose you could convert. My father converted when he married my mother."

"I couldn't do that!" John Henry whispered in shock, casting a furtive glance toward Alice Jane. "My Ma would tan my hide if I ever joined that papist religion!" It was just an echo of his mother's words and he hardly knew what it meant, but Mattie was offended nonetheless.

"Well, that's just fine, John Henry! I had no idea that you disapproved so of my faith," and she pulled herself away from him and put her nose up in the air.

"I'm sorry, Mattie. It's just that," his voice dropped to a whisper again, "you know how my Ma is about religion. It's real important to her that I believe what she does." He glanced back at Alice Jane again, just to make sure she wasn't listening. "But I think religion's pretty awful boring, mostly. Maybe it'd be more fun to be Catholic."

"Religion is not supposed to be fun, John Henry! Besides, nobody's gettin' married for a while, anyhow. You've still got to go fight for the Cause and all."

Now they were talking about something interesting again, and his face lit up. "I wish I was sixteen already! I'd be a hell of a fighter, Mattie!"

He felt very grown up, swearing in front of her like that, and she blushed just the way a lady should and said, "Oh, I know you would!"

She sure looked pretty when her cheeks went pink like that and her eyes were dancing, and her words made a wave of boldness sweep over him.

"Would you wait for me, Mattie?" he said, knowing that a soldier should have a special girl waiting for his return. "Would you be my sweetheart while I was gone?"

"Of course I will, honey," she said, and took his hand in hers, squeezing it gently. "Best sweethearts always, I promise."

"Always," he repeated after her, and thought that he would never in all his life see anything lovelier than Mattie's eyes in the firelight.

~~~~~~~~~~

Aunt Mary Anne's family stayed on at the farm through the rest of the winter and on into the spring, waiting for some word from Uncle Rob. They'd had no letter from him since Christmastime when he was sent on detachment to North Carolina with a wagon train of supplies, and the talk was that he'd been taken prisoner by the Yankees. But Aunt Mary Anne refused to believe that awful possibility and spent her days quietly tending to her baby and writing and sending off letters that were never answered.

To Mattie fell the task of watching over her little sisters, and she amused them by taking them on long walks into the countryside, making trails through the tall grass, following the rabbit and deer into the dark woods along the ridge. On Saturdays when his school was out John Henry joined them, hitching two horses to the spring wagon and driving them all down the old Troupville Road to where the Little River and the Withlacoochee River ran together.

There where the two green rivers met the water slowed and wound past sandy shoals, sheltered by overhanging trees that filtered long shadows across the stream – a perfect, natural swimming hole. At the water's edge, with the air full of the sounds of insects in the trees, John Henry sat on the soft grass and took off his shoes, rolled up the legs of his homespun trousers, and waded out into the water. If the girls hadn't been along he'd have taken off the rest of his hot, heavy clothing as well and gone skinny dipping, feeling the grass and the fish skimming past his skin. But with the girls there he had to keep his clothes on and act like a gentleman.

Mattie helped the little girls tie up their skirts into their waistbands and left Lucy to watch them play at the river's edge – the fear of water snakes was enough to keep them from wandering too far into the river. Then Mattie tied up her skirts too, and followed her cousin out into the cool, dark water.

John Henry watched her as she walked toward him in the golden light, the sun glancing off her auburn hair and making her eyes close in a squint against the glare, wrinkling her nose. She laughed as her skirts billowed up above the water and dipped her hand to chase a passing fish. The water on her clothing made it hang tight against her body, and John Henry stared through the shadows at the curve of her waist, the rise of her breast. He was mesmerized by the closeness of her and felt a sudden surge of something he didn't understand, a need to touch her and feel that curve against his wet skin. Mattie turned to look at him as if hearing his thoughts, and he felt himself flush with embarrassment.

"John Henry, what are you starin' at? You look like a big catfish, with your mouth hangin' open like that."

He choked on her teasing words and turned aside, mortified that she had seen him looking at her that way. *Stupid, stupid girl!* he thought with anger and embarrassment. And feeling a need to prove something, he dove into the water and swam out toward the deeper, faster flowing stream. He was a good swimmer, but his heavy clothes slowed his movements and the branches of the underwater bushes caught and pulled at him, starting to drag him down.

Mattie saw and screamed at him, "John Henry! Hang on honey, I'm comin'!" and she gathered up her dress and tried to follow him into the deeper water. But the weight of her long skirt held her back and she watched helplessly as he slipped farther and farther away from her.

But the undergrowth that entangled John Henry also kept him from being swept out into the middle of the river, and he hung onto the branches and dragged himself slowly back toward the riverbank. Finally, soaking wet and mad at himself for looking so damned foolish, he stumbled up the bank and threw himself down on the ground. Mattie struggled up through the mud and the sand and fell down on her knees beside him.

"Whatever were you doin', John Henry? I thought you were gonna drown! Are you all right, honey?"

"I just wanted to go for a swim," he muttered, not looking at her, watching as a green snake slid down from a tree at the river's edge and slipped out into the dark water.

"Well, you scared me to death. I was about to go out and save you, for heaven's sake, and you know I can't swim!"

He looked up into her serious, solemn face for a moment, then he started to laugh. "Well, Mattie, that was mighty brave of you, but who'd have saved you after you'd saved me?"

She stared at him a moment, then started to laugh. "I didn't think about that! I just knew you needed me, that's all." Then she lay back on the grass, her hand over her face to shield her eyes from the sunlight.

John Henry rolled over and looked at her lying there beside him, wet and dirty and laughing in the sun, her hair coming all undone around her face, and the feeling came again – the need to reach out and touch her face, run his fingers through her hair. It was an awkward feeling and he looked for something to say to break the silence.

"What's the little ring you're wearin'?" he asked, as the sunlight glinted off her hand.

"It's a Claddagh ring, from Ireland," she replied, holding up her hand to admire it. "It was my Grandmother Fitzgerald's. My mother gave it to me when I went off to the convent school in Savannah. She says it's an heirloom, and I am to pass it on to my own daughter someday. She says it was owned by an Irish princess, a long ways back. Imagine that."

John Henry looked closer at the ring, noting the intricate carving of two hands holding a heart with a king's crown above.

"The two hands are for friendship," Mattie explained. "The crown is for loyalty. The heart is for love. I think it's a good luck token and I wear it always." Then she smiled up at him. "Maybe I should give it to you, so you don't drown yourself!"

"Maybe you should learn to swim," he shot back, making them both laugh.

Then she sighed and said softly, "Oh, John Henry, it's so good to laugh again, like we used to in the old days. Seems like we used to laugh all the time, you and me and the whole rest of the world. Before the War. I miss those days. Seems like the best part of my life is already over."

"I don't know where my life is," he replied. "Seems like every time I get things figured out, somethin' changes. And then I'm supposed to just take it like a man, that's what my Pa says." He looked down at the ground, his fingers pulling at the wet grass, thinking that he might never be man enough for his father.

"He expects a lot from you now, I'm sure," Mattie said, "with your mother so sick and all..."

"She's dyin'," he said suddenly, surprised himself to hear the words. He hadn't planned to tell her. But being with Mattie always made him feel so safe that it just seemed to spill out of him all on its own. "Uncle John said it's the consumption, but she made him promise not to tell my Pa."

"What are you talkin' about?"

"She hasn't told anyone but me, but you see how she is. She just gets weaker all the time and coughs all night long. And last week, I saw her rinsin' out her pillowcase early before my Pa got up. There was blood on it, Mattie. She's coughin' up blood."

"Oh, honey..."

Then with the rush of words came the tears he'd held back for so long, and Mattie put her arms around him.

"My poor John Henry! How awful for you! But why hasn't she told your father? Surely he needs to know."

"My father..." he sniffed and wiped his hand at his blue eyes. "My Pa hates sick folks," he explained, "and my mother doesn't want to be a burden to him..."

The reasons didn't seem to make any sense, saying them to Mattie. But having her arms around him was comforting, the closest thing to having his mother's arms around him.

"Then we must tell him ourselves," Mattie said reasonably, "so he can do what needs to be done for her."

"No! I can't! She made me promise not to tell anyone until she gives me leave.

I shouldn't even be tellin' you. She made me promise, Mattie. I can't betray her wishes like that."

"But maybe if I tell my mother and make her promise to keep the secret, too, then we can do more to help. If I tell her it's our sacred oath, make her swear on the rosary, then she'll have to keep it secret, at least as long as we're still here in Valdosta..."

And for the first time, John Henry realized that Mattie wasn't going to stay on the farm forever, and a sudden loneliness ran through him.

"Do you have to go, Mattie? Can't you stay on here after your family leaves? My mother could use the help, and I..."

"You know I can't. We'll be leavin' as soon as my father comes home again. But it's sweet of you to want me to stay." She brushed her hand through his damp hair while she spoke, as if calming a small child. "You know we'll always be together in our hearts, John Henry, no matter where we are. You'll always be my favorite, dearest cousin."

"I love you, Mattie." He said it easily, as he'd said it all his life, like little brother to his doting sister. But now in the golden light at the water's edge, it suddenly seemed to mean so much more.

"I love you too, John Henry. I always have and I always will." And for one sweet moment in time, his mother's illness and the war were both forgotten and the world was perfect again.

~~~~~~~~

In April of 1865, the war finally ended when General Lee signed the surrender at Appomattox Courthouse, Virginia. But beyond that there was nothing dramatic to signal the end of the Cause and the fall of the Southern Confederacy – just the ghostly, desolate landscape of the conquered nation that was its own memorial. Even the assassination of Abraham Lincoln seemed little cause for celebration.

Though south Georgia had been spared any fighting during the war, a month after Appomattox one final fight came near to Valdosta. Jefferson Davis, the hunted, haunted president of the fallen Confederacy, was making a run for freedom from the Federals. His route led south from Richmond through the Carolinas and down into Georgia as he tried to reach the safety of Texas and the western territories. His plan was to cross over the Mississippi and rejoin Confederate sympathizers there where he might be able to start up the secession fight again. But he only got as far as Irwinville, Georgia, halfway between Macon and Valdosta, when the Yankees caught up with him, camped out with his family in a piney wood. The Yanks took him away in chains as a traitor to the United States of America. He said the chains made him feel like a slave.

Slowly the soldiers came home, from disbanded regiments in Virginia and Tennessee, from prison camps in the North, from lonely outposts in the far West. Most of them came on foot, walking hundreds of miles to find their homes in ruins, their families scattered. And one by one, John Henry's uncles returned from the war: William Harrison McKey, with a battle wound that refused to heal; Dr. James Taylor McKey, who had served as a field surgeon and did his best to tend to his brother's wound; and the youngest McKey brother, Thomas Sylvester, who had finished the war as a nurse in the Confederate hospital in Macon.

Tom was John Henry's favorite McKey uncle, only nine years his elder and close enough in age to be almost like a big brother. So when word came that Tom was on his way home from Macon, John Henry saddled up his own horse and tied another of his father's stock behind, and rode out to meet his uncle. It was a brave thing for a thirteen-year-old boy to do, with the roads filled with starving, desperate men who would think nothing of stealing a horse or two and leaving a young rider in a ditch. But John Henry went armed with a shotgun in his saddlebag and his father's long pistol laid across his lap, and knew that he could outshoot any man he could see. And with the headstrong determination of youth, he found Tom walking along the road from Macon and brought him back home to Valdosta. If his mother had known his plan, she never would have allowed such a thing, but his father seemed to understand his need to try himself on this adventure, and let him go.

It hadn't been hard to recognize Tom, even amidst the straggling crowds of dirty soldiers who filled the roads. Tom's red hair shone like something on fire, his usually fair complexion turned to the color of a ripe apple from weeks of walking in the summer heat. He looked more like a mischievous little boy who'd stayed out too long in the sun than a weary soldier coming home from War, but the huge knife at his side proved that Tom was man enough for the fight.

"I call her the Hell-Bitch," Tom confided as he unsheathed the knife in the barn one afternoon after his return. "She started out as a plowshare back at Indian Creek, but your Grandpa McKey had it forged into a meat cleaver for slaughterin' the hogs. When the War came, I had her forged again into this..."

He held the knife out toward John Henry and his nephew instinctively flinched away from the blade, fifteen inches long from swamp oak handle to point, two inches wide across the blade, and more than a quarter of an inch thick. Both edges of the blade were sharpened to a shine, and either side could have sliced a man clean through as easily as slaughtering a hog.

"Go ahead," Tom said, "give her a try. She's a beauty," and he dropped the Hell-Bitch into John Henry's hands.

The knife was so heavy that John Henry's arms fell from the weight of it. But once in hand, he found the knife to be remarkably well-balanced.

"You can feel the meat cleaver in her still," Tom said, "the way the blade runs up from the hilt. That angle at the point is where the corner of the cleaver-blade used to be. Give her a swing and you'll see how well she handles."

But when John Henry raised the Hell-Bitch over his head, Tom laughed. "Who taught you to knife fight, anyhow? You can't throw a knife that big! You just cut with it."

Tom took the knife back and slid it into the holster, then swung the rawhide bandoleer over his shoulder, pistol-style. "She's a cross-draw weapon," he explained, "like this." Then in one quick move, he pulled knife from sheath and pointed it at John Henry, upside down in his hand so that the monstrous cutting edge was clean against his nephew's throat. "That's how you knife fight with the Hell-Bitch. One fast slice, and your enemy don't have a jug'lar anymore."

John Henry swallowed hard, though he knew his uncle would never do him any harm. "Did you ever...kill anybody with it?" he asked, half hopefully.

"Never had reason to," Tom replied. "Once I showed her, the discussion was generally over. Besides, I didn't get into much fightin', bein' in the regimental band and all. Mostly, I just carried her like a saber, for show, though she hides neat when she needs to. But no, she's got nothin' but pig blood on her. I've seen enough man's blood to fill me up for life, anyhow."

"But you said you never killed anybody..."

"Didn't have to," Tom said, his bright smile fading and his eyes taking on a distant look. "You heard how I finished the war by servin' in the military hospital up in Macon?"

"I heard."

Tom shook his head. "You never heard nothin', boy. Nothin' about what that hospital was like."

"Tell me?"

"I'll tell you, though tellin' don't do it justice, and I hope you never have to learn what it's like for yourself. War's a terrible thing, John Henry, and the hospital ward's as bad as the battlefield. Men come in, all shot up, bleedin' still or so far gone they don't have nothin' left to bleed, gangrene in their wounds, smellin' worse than anything I ever smelled. Plenty of them died before the doctors could do anything to help them. Plenty more died after the doctors worked on them, hackin' off their arms or legs. Out back of the hospital was a dead house to store the bodies until we had time to bury them. Sometimes that dead house was so full we couldn't put any more in, and we had to stack up the corpses outside. The stench of it was somethin' you wouldn't ever forget. Some of them we never even knew their names, never could write home to their families or sweethearts to say how they died – not that the homefolks would have wanted to hear how it happened. Though knowin's better than not, I reckon."

"We haven't heard anything about my Uncle Rob, not since the war ended," John Henry said. "He was in a prison camp, last time there was any news."

"Well, there's hope in that, anyhow," Tom said, as he slid the knife back into its sheath and pulled the bandoleer from his shoulder. "And your Aunt Mary Anne's a pray-er, with that rosary of hers. Prayin's better than just waitin'."

"She says he's comin' home for sure, but I don't know how she knows. What do you think, Tom? Do you think Uncle Rob is comin' back again?"

Tom was quiet a moment before answering. "That's hard to say, John Henry, that's hard to say. War's a funny thing. Some men go off and come home again just fine. But there's some that come home and never do come back."

~~~~~~~~~

While the family waited and Aunt Mary Anne prayed for Uncle Rob's safe return, John Henry had to keep going to school – his mother insisted on it. A gentleman's son still needed an education, even in a world rent apart, and John Henry didn't mind too much. The seven-mile journey to school and back was a good excuse to take his horse for a fast ride, especially since the Cat Creek Road was pretty much deserted, the only traffic being an occasional gray-coated drifter heading home. And so it was that on one late May afternoon as he was on his way home from school, he nearly ran down one of those drifters.

The man was walking right down the middle of the dusty road, his head bent and his feet dragging, and he hardly moved at all when John Henry hollered at him to get out of the way. If the horse hadn't been so well trained to John Henry's hands, wheeling around and rearing its front legs clear off the ground, the man would have been trampled for sure. But even with the whinnying of the startled animal and John Henry's shouts, the soldier barely moved at all. And the way the man just stood there, staring out of deep-set eyes and skinny as a rail, gave John Henry a spooky feeling, like seeing a skeleton come to life. He was glad to get his horse turned back toward home and take off again in a cloud of dust.

"It was the strangest thing, the way he just stared," he told Mattie awhile later, as he brushed down the horse. "It was like he was seein' a ghost, though he looked more like the ghost than me."

"You should have stopped to ask if he needed help," she chided as she held out a handful of feed to the horse. "He might have been lost, or hurt. He might have needed a place to stay."

"He might have been armed and crazy, too, and ready to kill me for all I know. I should think you'd be more concerned for my safety than for the welfare of some stranger. I could have been hurt myself, you know, the way my horse reared up. If I didn't have such a good seat..."

"If you hadn't been racin', your horse could have stopped faster. Seems like it's your own fault she reared on you. You ought to be more careful, John Henry. Next time you will run somebody over." Mattie had a way of sounding sweet even when she was scolding him, but he still didn't like the lecture.

"It's our road!" he retorted. "If folks walk down the middle of it, they're gonna get run over!"

"John Henry," she said, shaking her auburn head in that slightly superior way of hers, instructing a wayward child. But the instruction didn't come, as she looked up from the horse and across the yard, her little mouth slowly dropping open in astonished silence.

John Henry, turning to follow her gaze, saw the same scarecrow-man he'd nearly run down on the road, dragging slowly up to the front gate.

"Aw, hell!" he complained, "that's him. Now I suppose you're gonna ask me to apologize to him and fetch him a plate of supper."

But Mattie had no reply as she dropped the rest of the feed from her hand, picked up her calico skirts, and ran across the yard toward the gate. And to John Henry's amazement, she threw herself into the drifter's arms.

"Mattie!" he called. "What do you think you're doin'? Mattie!"

But she didn't answer him, as she buried her face in the drifter's chest and started to cry. Then, for the first time, John Henry really looked at the man, his gaunt face half-covered in an unkempt black beard, his dirty uniform coat still carrying the gold collar badges of a Captain in the Confederate States Army. It was no drifter that he had almost run over, but his own uncle, Captain Robert Kennedy Holliday, Mattie's beloved father come home at last.

Uncle Rob looked so different from the hale and healthy man who'd left Georgia four years before that John Henry hardly recognized him. But Mattie knew him, even with his haggard appearance. Her heart told her it was him the minute she looked up toward the road.

"You never forget someone you love," she explained breathlessly, hanging onto her father as though she'd never let him go again and smiling through her tears, "and you never stop believin'! We knew you'd come home again Pa, Mama and I. Even when they said you were in a Yankee prison camp, we knew you were comin' home!"

"A Yankee prison camp?" he said, as though he'd hardly understood her words, looking dazed and confused at having his daughter back in his arms again. Then he nodded slowly. "That's right, that's right. But the damn Yanks couldn't keep me away from my girls. I've walked all the way home. Signed their Oath of Allegiance at Raleigh, and walked all the way home. Where's your mother, Mattie?"

"In the house, nursin' the baby. We've got a brother now, Pa. Did you get our letters? You never answered."

"A brother?" he asked, his heavy brows lifting in surprise. "You mean the baby was a boy this time?"

"Yes, Pa. A beautiful little boy. Mama named him James Robert, after you and Grandpa Fitzgerald. But we call him Jim Bob. John Henry here thought of it."

"John Henry?" Uncle Rob said, turning his dazed eyes toward his sandy-haired nephew. "I thought you looked familiar, back there on the road. But you've gotten so tall..."

"It's been four years, Sir. I'm all grown up, now."

"That's what he always says. He's still just thirteen, though. Now come on in the house and see the baby. Oh, Pa! We've missed you so much!"

But Uncle Rob hesitated, looking down at his worn and dirty clothes.

"Maybe I should get cleaned up a little first. Where's the well, John Henry? I should wash some of this road dust off before going in. I know how Alice Jane is about her clean floors."

"My mother won't worry about the floor," John Henry said, shooting Mattie a look that meant she wasn't to say what she knew about his mother's condition. "She doesn't care so much about the house anymore, anyhow. You come on in right now, Uncle Rob. And Sir?"

"Yes, John Henry," his uncle said, as Mattie pushed open the gate and led him up the walkway.

"I'm sorry about almost runnin' you down, back there. If I'd known it was you..."

"It's all right, John Henry," his uncle said somberly. "I've had worse things done to me, these past months, than bein' kicked up by a horse."

And as Uncle Rob followed Mattie into the house, welcomed by a cry of joy from the ladies inside, John Henry wondered just what the Yankees had done to his uncle in that Northern prison camp. Robert Kennedy Holliday had been a bright and jovial man before the War, always ready with a smile and a taunting joke. Now he didn't smile at all, not even when he heard that his wife had finally given him his longed-for son.

Damn Yankees, John Henry thought. Damn Yankees.

~~~~~~~~~

Uncle Rob had reached the end of his long walk, but his journey wasn't over. He was restless to get back to his own home in Jonesboro and see what was left of his house and business buildings there. He was near penniless, worn out and disheartened, but he had a large and helpless family to provide for and he needed to get his affairs back in order again. So as soon as he'd had time to rest up a little and arrange for the journey, he took his wife and children back home to Jonesboro and John Henry had to say goodbye to Mattie. She'd been his only friend on the farm for the better part of a year, and having her gone was going to leave him lonely. But though he hoped for a last private moment with her to bid her a proper farewell, she was too busy doting on her father to pay him any attention. And as John Henry watched her ride away in the heavy-loaded wagon, seated between her father and little sisters, he wondered if he would ever see her again.

With Mattie and her family gone, the farm seemed suddenly quiet again, even though his McKey uncles were staying on awhile longer. It was Uncle James McKey, with his surgical training, who finally told Henry Holliday the truth of his wife's illness. He'd seen enough men die after battle, he said, to know when death was coming on. Since he had last seen her four years before, his sister Alice Jane had become just a shadow of her former self. Her porcelain fair complexion was now utterly transparent, the veins showing blue through the skin; her graceful figure was wasted away to emaciation; her lovely singing voice was hoarse and breathy from ceaseless coughing spells.

"She never would let me send for the doctor," Henry Holliday said in his own defense.

"You surprise me, Henry," Uncle James said, as they took their home-rolled cigars outside after supper. John Henry couldn't help listening, as he was outside, too, the June night so thick and heavy that he couldn't abide being indoors. While his father and uncle talked, he pretended to be absorbed in the lanky movements of a daddy-long-legs crawling across the porch rail.

"I've never known you to bow to a woman before," Uncle James commented. "You should have sent for medical help long ago, when somethin' might have been done. Maybe with enough food, proper air and exercise..."

"I won't be chastised by you, James," Henry said. "If you don't like the way I run my home, you can leave now. You might find some place to stay over in Valdosta."

John Henry wasn't surprised by his father's stern words to his Uncle James. Henry was often stern these days, more so than usual since the bottom had dropped out of the cotton market and their whole cash crop wouldn't bring enough to pay for next year's seed. Henry had been too troubled by the farm and his finances to pay much attention to what was happening at home.

But Uncle James was as hard-headed as his brother-in-law.

"Surely you had to notice how thin she's gotten, Henry. Unless, of course, your attentions have been turned elsewhere." Then he said in subdued tones: "I hear your neighbor Mr. Martin has a comely daughter, and available, since her fiancé was killed in the war."

"How dare you, James McKey! Have you no decency? How dare you make such accusations right here in my own home!"

"Calm down, Henry," Uncle James said smoothly. "I'm not makin' accusations. Just take it as a warnin', for if there is anything untoward going on between you and Martin's daughter, word will surely get out about it. This is a small community, and talk travels fast. And it won't be just the community, but our family that you will have to answer to, if you ever do anything to dishonor Alice Jane."

"I'll admit that I go over to the Martin place some," Henry said, "but it's strictly business when I do. Mr. Martin and I are working on a plan to plant some new trees in that back orchard, as his land adjoins mine there. And God knows I could use a new cash crop just now."

"Then I wish you success in your business venture, Henry. But you've drawn me off the subject. Alice Jane needs medical attention, and soon. I'll do what I can, but I fear her disease has gone on far too long now to have any hope of remission." Then he sighed heavily. "Poor, dear sister..."

But Henry didn't answer, and John Henry knew the conversation was over. It would have been better, he thought, if his mother could have told Henry in her own gentle way. Without her tempering influence, his father was a man of hot passions.

He didn't dare ponder long on the thought that those passions might include the neighbor's twenty-two year old daughter Rachel, who was indeed comely as his Uncle James had said. John Henry had seen her in the orchard himself on occasion, a plump young woman with a ready smile and a mane of yellow hair. But surely his Uncle James was as wrong in his assumptions as John Henry had been years ago when he'd overheard what he thought was love talk between his mother and his Uncle John Holliday. His father was too honorable a man to do anything so dishonorable as what Uncle James suggested. His father was a hero, after all.

~~~~~~~~~

Though the War had ended, the Yankee occupation went on. Georgia had been made a Department of the Military Division of Tennessee, stripped of its status as a sovereign state, and the Federals made regular forays to the farms around Valdosta. They were searching for Confederate contraband, horses mostly, and took every animal with a CS brand, leaving many of the families in the county with no means of transportation – not that there was much of anyplace to go. Most of the stores in town were closed, and even the day school was on permanent summer vacation and wouldn't reopen again, leaving John Henry with nothing much to do but farm chores and target shooting, and no one to talk to, now that Mattie was gone.

His McKey uncles had moved on too, taking up some land together just over the Georgia-Florida line, a place they called "Banner Plantation." They had hopes of putting in a cotton crop and making back some money for the family once the market rebounded. But for the present, they were busy clearing land and planting food crops, not cash crops. Their sisters Ella and Helena went to join them, though they came back to Cat Creek to visit with Alice Jane as often as they could.

At his mother's bidding, Aunt Ella and Aunt Helena took John Henry to Sunday Services at the Methodist church whenever they came to visit, as Alice Jane had become too weak to leave home and take him herself. Though she'd been raised as a Baptist and married as a Presbyterian, Alice Jane had recently taken fellowship with the Methodist-Episcopal sect, and her sisters had joined with her. It didn't matter to John Henry which service his aunts took him to, as all the churches met in the same building, anyhow, where Union Church was held and the congregations took turns having their own pastors speak. Methodist was first and third Sundays, Baptist was second and fourth. As long as there was covered dish supper after the sermon, John Henry didn't much care who was doing the preaching.

His mother cared, though. She wanted him to understand the gospel as she believed it, and she even had the Methodist minister, the Reverend Newt Ousley, come out to the house to write her testimony for her so that John Henry would have it to remember her by. Her biggest quarrel with the Presbyterians was over the doctrine of election, as she explained to her son while he sat by her bed for his evening devotional and prayers.

"The Presbyterians believe that some men are chosen, elected to salvation from before the foundation of the world. I think such a doctrine denies the power of our Savior to redeem the wicked from their sins. I believe that as long as a man is willin' to repent and turn to Jesus, he can always be forgiven and begin again on the saintly road. Do you understand what I'm talkin' about, John Henry?"

"Yes, Ma, I reckon so."

"Then you must always remember that Jesus loves you and died for your sins. *Though your sins be as scarlet, they shall be white as snow; though they be red like crimson, they shall be as wool.*"

"Isaiah Chapter One, Verse Eighteen," he said, trained to quote back chapter and verse whenever his mother recited the scriptures, as she believed that Bible study was as important a part of his education as reading and writing and arithmetic. "Ma? Do you reckon that Jesus thinks I'm a sinner?"

He didn't like to think he was, but he wasn't always righteous, either. He still liked to play childish pranks, like hiding frogs in the laundry for the housemaid to find, or taking fruit from the neighbors' trees. And sometimes, when his mother was resting and his father was away, he even stole a sip or two from Henry's whiskey bottle which was kept hidden away under the sideboard in the dining room. But those were small enough sins, he hoped, to go unnoticed by God's all-watching eye.

"He thinks you're a boy, I'm sure," his mother replied. "And like most boys, you're still learnin' how to behave, and sometimes digress from the paths of rectitude. There are some boys, for instance, who would seek out the opportunity to drink liquor, even if they had to steal it from someone else. I would be terribly disappointed, John Henry, if I ever heard that you had done such a thing."

Though she was gazing placidly at the Holy Bible she held in front of her, her pale face as serene as ever, she had clearly just uncovered his crime and chastised him for it, and John Henry felt like a sinner, indeed. All his father's rantings couldn't put the fear of the Lord into him like a few gentle words from his mother.

"I'm sorry, Ma," he said, his eyes lowered with shame under his sandy lashes. "How did you know?"

"Whiskey has its own aroma, John Henry. A lovin' mother can smell it on her wayward son. I fear you have too much of your father's hot Irish blood in you and a tendency to be rebellious at times. Like the wheat and the tares, there is both good and bad in you. But you must crush the tares, lest you be plucked out at the harvest."

Sometimes the meanings of his mother's religious symbols eluded him, though he was sure she'd read him something somewhere about wheat and tares. But he was spared having to give the reference, chapter and verse, when his mother closed her eyes and sighed.

"I am very tired, John Henry. Do you mind if we finish our devotional early? You go ahead and kneel by my bed and say your prayers. Then maybe you can go into the parlor and play me somethin' soothing on the piano while I sleep. You know how Mother loves to hear you play."

~~~~~~~~

The only school in session that fall was run by an ex-Confederate officer for the boys who had served under him, most of whom had gone to fight for the South before finishing their studies and had returned after the War as unlettered adolescents unfit for anything but fighting. So to help them catch up with their book learning and to keep them out of trouble, their former commander started up a little school on his own farm and taught them everything he could remember from his own school days.

The most popular of those young veterans was a lad named Dick Force, who'd

58

gone off to the War at only fourteen-years old and come home again at nineteen with a knowledge of the world well beyond his years and an outspoken hatred of the Yanks. The younger boys called him "Captain" even though he had never risen past private, and idolized him because he'd been wounded slightly in the fighting at Gettysburg, though he was well enough recovered to get into fist fights with his friends. John Henry knew him by sight, as the Force family also attended Methodist services at the Union Church, and he thought the Captain seemed like a worthy idol. He was a head taller than the rest of the older boys, broad-shouldered and already wearing a small mustache, and the girls all giggled around him whenever he came through the door.

The only folks who didn't show Dick Force his accustomed deference were the newly freed slaves, and their bold insolence was more than an irritation to him and his friends. And most irritating of all was the federal Bureau of Refugees, Freedmen, and Abandoned Lands — the "Freedmen's Bureau" that had been created to negotiate labor contracts between the former slaves and their former owners. To the white folks of Valdosta, the Freedmen's Bureau was just another Yankee effrontery, made all the worse when Washington sent in black soldiers to oversee the operation.

"But a nigra's still a nigra," Dick Force proclaimed to his friends, "freed or not. And I ain't about to bow to a nigra, even if he is dressed up in Yankee blue."

Dick threw those words around a lot, but when he threw them at a black soldier in front of the Freedmen's Bureau offices, he ended up in jail. Under martial law, he didn't even have the right to speak his mind. If it hadn't been for his friends sawing away the window sash of his cell to help him escape, Dick might have languished in that jail cell forever.

John Henry heard of the escape from his church friends in town, and thought it a wonderful adventure, though the story would have been better if the Captain had done some fine shooting along with his fast run from the authorities. Word went out that Dick had taken his favorite horse and gone west to Texas, though most everyone knew he was really just hiding out in the swampy countryside until things cooled down a bit in Valdosta. To keep him comfortable in his hideaway on the banks of the Withlacoochee River, the town boys formed a sort of underground railroad running him meals and fresh bedding taken from their own homes.

John Henry had little problem adding his own portion to the contraband, as his father was busy all day and his mother was sick in bed. No one paid any attention when he packed meals from the dinner leftovers and stole a little of his father's whiskey from under the sideboard in the dining room. For Dick's horse, he brought feed and fresh apples from the orchard his father shared with Mr. Martin. He sometimes saw Martin's daughter Rachel there picking apples too, and she always smiled and waved at him. She must like apples a whole lot, he thought more than once, to spend so much time in the orchard.

It was on one of those bright fall days, just past noon, as he was getting ready to go pay a visit to the Captain, that all hell broke loose – at least that was the way it looked to John Henry. He'd just saddled his horse and slid his double-barreled shotgun into the saddle scabbard when a strange darkness began to creep over the sky. At first he thought it was some straying raincloud drifting across the sun and dimming the afternoon light, but the sky was cloudless blue as it had been all week. It wasn't a fog coming in, either. Fogs came in early in the morning or late at night, starting down by the river and rising up over the fields of cotton and corn and sugar cane. This sudden darkness seemed to be coming from nowhere and everywhere all at once. The horse noticed the strangely waning light, too, and started whinnying and shying from his touch. Then the dogs on the porch started howling, and the cows in the pasture started lowing like it was coming on dusk, and from the distance came a moaning sound from the hired negroes in the fields.

"Damn if it isn't Judgment Day!" he whispered to the horse and himself both. "Do you reckon those darkies know somethin' we don't? Sounds like they're callin' to the Lord for mercy." He had a passing thought that he ought to be calling to the Lord for mercy, himself, but he had his hands full with the horse and couldn't fall to his knees just then. And thinking of praying, he thought of his mother and let the horse go, still saddled and ready for a ride.

"Ma?" he called, as the chill of the gathering darkness seemed to spread right through him. He had the awful feeling that the darkness was the angel of death passing over the farm, and his mother was about to die.

"Ma!" he cried, as he ran across the horse lot and the back yard, bounding up the back steps of the house and bursting into her room. His mother lay still as a corpse, her eyes peacefully closed.

"Oh, Ma!" he whispered, and dropped to his knees beside her bed. "Oh, Ma!" and the words choked out of him as he buried his head in her coverlet. "I love you, Ma! Please come back to me. Please come back..."

"I love you, too, son," Alice Jane said, her sleep disturbed by her son's pleading. "Come back from where?"

"I thought..." he was almost afraid to look up at her for fear that she was a specter already. "I thought you were dead, Ma. I thought the dark was the angel of death."

"The dark?" she asked, then she smiled weakly and reached out her hand to touch his sandy hair. "Why, that's just the eclipse comin' on, John Henry. Didn't your father tell you?"

"Pa's gone, out at the orchard or somewhere. I was goin' out too when the sun started to go away."

"The sun's not goin' away, though it looks like it is. It's just an eclipse, when the moon passes between the earth and the sun, and blocks the light. It's a miracle in the sky..." She stopped talking a moment, and took a ragged, weary breath. "I saw a miracle myself, once..." Her eyes closed again, and for a moment John Henry thought she had gone back to sleep.

"What was that, Ma?" he asked, fearful of her sleep almost as much as he was of her death. One day she might drift off and never come back again.

"They called it the Fallin' of the Stars," she said, her eyes still closed. "It happened away back in 1833 when I was just a little girl. My father woke us all with his shoutin', tellin' us to come look quick."

"And what did you see?"

"The stars fallin' down from the sky. My father called it a star-shower. It looked like the whole sky was comin' down in a fiery blaze, so bright and hot that I thought the stars would set the ground on fire. But they never really touched the earth. My father said they all burned up before they reached the ground. It was on that night that I first understood the glory of God, when the heavens came right down into our barnyard." Then she started coughing, so hard that her whole body heaved with the sound of it, and John Henry had to look away. He couldn't stand to see her sick like this, and couldn't stand the helpless way he felt in the face of it.

"I'll go now, Ma," he said, standing up and taking a step away from her. "You need to rest..."

"No!" she said quickly, her eyes wide open again. "I want to tell you somethin', John Henry. I felt the heavens close to me the night of that star-shower, but I feel them closer now. You know your mother is gonna be passin' on..."

He nodded an answer, his heart too full for words. *I know*, he thought. *I have known too long...*

"I am not afraid to go, John Henry. The Lord has been good to me, and I expect he'll be merciful to me when I cross. But I do worry over you, my sweet boy. I do worry about your welfare. You have so much that is good within you, if you will only hold fast to the things I've tried to teach you and stay close to the Lord and keep his word..."

"I will, Ma! I will be good, I promise!"

"Remember how I loved you, and how God loves you." Then she added softly: "Your father loves you, too. I know he may not show it very often, but in his heart, he cares for you more than he even knows. Be patient with him, please. As our Lord is patient with us in our weakness, learn to be patient, too."

He nodded again, trying hard to hold back tears, but his mother closed her eyes again, worn out from the words. "Now go on outside and see the eclipse, John Henry. It won't last too long. It's a miracle in the sky, and you may never see another one. Go see it for me, too, all right?"

"All right, Ma," he said, leaning down to give her a kiss before he left, thankful beyond words that she was still alive. "I love you, Ma," he said again, knowing he could never say it enough.

Outside, the sun had all but disappeared, only a circle of light hiding behind the darkness of the moon. But at least it wasn't Judgment Day yet, he thought with relief, or the Angel of Death passing over either – not yet.

~~~~~~~~~

But the Angel of Death was hovering nearby and it came on dark wings at Christmastime and wearing Yankee blue. For the Yankees had not forgotten the embarrassment of young Dick Force's escape from his military jail cell, any more than they had forgotten that the Southerners had been their sworn enemy, and they were only waiting until the Captain came out of hiding to make him an example to the people of Lowndes County. And unwittingly, Dick Force obliged them by answering an invitation from his sister to leave his river hideaway and come join the family for Christmas Dinner. If his sister hadn't invited the whole church congregation to come along too, he might have had a peaceful meal.

John Henry was part of the crowd of well-wishers standing in the Force's front yard on the cold December afternoon when Dick rode up the long dirt drive to his home. His sister was waiting for him on the porch, laughing about the surprise he would have when he saw the whole Methodist congregation there to welcome him home. But just as the Captain turned his horse into the yard and raised a hand to wave at his sister, shots rang out from the trees along the drive. The Captain cried out and slumped forward over his horse as his sister screamed, but no one dared run to his aid as the Yankee Lieutenant rode out from a hiding place in the trees. It seemed that word of Dick Force's visit home had reached the garrison, as unguarded words always reach someone's waiting ears.

"You Rebs can run all day if you want," the arrogant Yank said as he rode onto the drive, his revolver still smoking in his hand, "but this is our country now, and we'll find you eventually. Let young Force here tell you how much good your swaggering and swearing will do. You're beat, Rebs!" Then he wheeled his horse and rode right down the driveway, safe from retribution in that goodly group of church members, while Dick Force lay panting for breath and bleeding on his saddle. To John Henry, still angry over what the Yanks had done to Mattie's father, it was too much to be born. He was about to run for his own horse, where he kept his shotgun hanging from his saddle scabbard, when one of the church founders stepped out onto the porch.

"Leave him be," Major William Bessant said, raising his hands as though preaching a sermon, though his real career was the law. Bessant was the leading attorney in Valdosta, and folks listened when he spoke. "Boys, pull the door off that outhouse and carry Dick inside on it. And the rest of y'all listen to me. Evil work was done here today, we all know that. Dick's crime didn't deserve jailin', let alone shootin'. He's just a hotheaded boy, still angry over the War and the way the darkies are turnin' against us, sidin' with the Yanks. It's an insult to all of us that Washington sent colored troops here to keep their peace, and no wonder Dick felt like insultin' one of them. I feel like throwin' some insults their way, myself. But my friends, look where Dick's insults have led. He's shot down right in his own yard, and we have no authority to do anything about it. As long as that Federal garrison is camped out in our streets, they are the law. But there is a higher authority than the United States government. The wicked may be in power, but God is in his heaven." Then his voice rose, and he stood, white-haired and glorious as an Old Testament prophet full of righteous indignation. "Vengeance is mine, saith the Lord, and I will repay!"

Major Bessant's words were meant to calm the angry crowd, but they only made John Henry's blood boil all the hotter. Vengeance might indeed be the Lord's, but sometimes the Lord's work needed human hands.

Chapter Four

Valdosta, 1866

But vengeance waited while Dick Force languished of his gangrenous wounds and the winter came on even harder than the one before, the weather so cold that cowsmilk turned solid in the milk buckets and crops froze right in the ground. Deer made bold by a lack of forage came out of the woods and down into the farmyard to share the horses' feed, and yellow-eyed possums slunk under the porch, looking for remains of the cats' dinners. Even the people seemed like feral creatures, lean and hungry and desperate. The only good news was the end of the Yankee occupation and the slow awakening of the businesses in town, though times remained almost as hard as they had been during the war.

"Might as well live away up in the mountains, for this cold," Henry Holliday said as he came in from the orchard one evening, chilled and rosy-cheeked from the frigid wind. "Get me a drink from under the sideboard there, John Henry. I may lose this crop, too, if the weather doesn't break soon, damn the weather and the Yankees both. I've got enough trouble already, what with the cut worm and the boll weevil and the rust."

John Henry opened the sideboard door slowly, hoping that his father wouldn't notice how much of the liquor had disappeared. Though he'd stopped stealing his father's whiskey for himself following his mother's chastisement, he'd borrowed enough for the Captain to nearly empty the bottle.

"Where's my drink, son?" Henry said, and John Henry poured all that was left into a tumbler. Enough, he hoped, to satisfy his father.

"Looks like it's almost gone, Pa," he said with studied blue-eyed innocence as he handed his father the glass. "Guess you'll be needin' to get some more."

But Henry seemed, thankfully, not to be paying attention to him as he pulled off his heavy great coat and thick woolen gloves. "Damn that fool Congress up in Washington with their Constitutional Amendments! First the Thirteenth to free the

65

slaves, now this Fourteenth they want ratified givin' all coloreds the rights of white men. Freein' the slaves was one thing, but making them equal to whites! 'Civil Rights' they call it. What about my civil rights? My people helped to build this country. My grandfathers fought in the Revolutionary War. Hell, I fought for the United States, myself, back in the Mexican War!"

John Henry was used to his father's tirades and usually didn't pay much attention, but his ears perked up when Henry mentioned Mexico. Those stories were still his favorites, far more adventurous and romantic than the cold reality of the War of Secession. In exotic places like Vera Cruz and Monterrey, in the wilds of Texas and the paradise of California, the Americans had fought against foreign imperialists and added a million square miles to the American territories. The Mexican War had been a hero-maker, giving glorious careers to future Rebels and Yankees, both: Winfield Scott, George McClellan, Ulysses S. Grant, even General Robert E. Lee, himself. Henry Holliday had fought beside all those men, and come home a hero, too.

And Henry had brought more than just his brave stories home with him. He'd brought an unusual souvenir as well: a Mexican orphan boy named Francisco Hidalgo, whose parents had been killed in the fighting. Henry, who was still a bachelor at the time, had given the boy a home and sent him to school, and Francisco had repaid him by serving as his valet and teaching him the tricks of the Mexican card game called Spanish Monte. It was a complicated game that matched suits to a dealer's hand, and the American soldiers had picked it up and tried to cheat using marked cards. But the Mexicans knew how to win with straight cards, and Francisco had passed the skill along to Henry, and it had paid off well in the saloons of Georgia.

Francisco was grown and married now, living on a farm in Jenkinsburg, near to Griffin, and until John Henry's family had moved away to Valdosta, they had paid him regular visits. Henry treated him like one of the family, kin almost, and Francisco returned the sentiment, naming one of his own sons John in honor of John Henry. And when Francisco went off to defend the Confederacy as a private in the Georgia Volunteer Infantry, he took one of Henry Holliday's pistols with him. But John Henry's fondest memory of Francisco Hidalgo was the Spanish he had learned from him as a child. Being able to understand and speak a little of a foreign language gave him a certain status among his schoolmates who were still struggling with English rhetoric and basic Latin grammar.

And thinking of English and Latin, he remembered something the town boys had told him. "Pa? Did you know there's a new school opening up over in Valdosta? The *Valdosta Institute* they're callin' it. I hear the teacher's as good as anybody up in Griffin or even Atlanta."

"I heard about it."

"Well, Sir, I'd like to go, if you could spare the money to send me."

"You know there's nothin' to spare, boy!" Henry thundered. "Everything I had was Confederate, and Confederate's gone bust now. Be lucky to find enough to pay the taxes on the place this year. Where do you suppose I'll get money for a luxury like school?"

"But school's not a luxury, Pa! I need my schoolin', if I aim to be a doctor like Uncle John one day. I need to get my education..."

"You need to learn to work harder, and earn what you get in life. I haven't noticed you puttin' out much effort to help around here. Looks to me like you spend most of your time ridin' off to go shootin'."

"I do my chores, Pa. I help take care of Ma, too. And you've got the darkies to do the field work..."

"Don't you listen to anything I say, boy? We haven't got any darkies anymore! Half the hands have run off to join the Yanks, the rest want me to pay them royal wages for their work. Pay them! Hell, I've paid for them over and over again already, buyin' them off the auction block, givin' them homes and clothes, feedin' them. And where am I supposed to get the money to pay them with? Between the cost of seed and this damn winter that won't break..."

"I'm sorry, Pa," John Henry said quietly, trying to assuage his father's growing anger. "I didn't know..."

"What you don't know could fill a book, boy! Now pour me another drink. This one's not makin' a dent."

But there was no more whiskey to be poured. His father had already drunk the last of what was left in the bottle, and John Henry felt a wave of dread come over him. Henry was angry enough already without learning that his own son had been stealing from him.

"There...isn't anymore, Pa," he muttered, not daring to look his father in the face. "I reckon you've already drunk it all."

"Hell if I did," Henry said, his steely eyes narrowing. "I know how much I drink, and how long the liquor will last. I had enough 'til next month, unless someone's been sharin' it with me..."

But before his father could make the accusation that would lead to a beating, a gentle voice spoke from the bedroom doorway.

"Someone has been sharin' it with you, Henry," Alice Jane whispered hoarsely as she steadied herself with one hand on the doorframe, her white nightdress draping around her like a shroud. "I've been drinkin' a little, now and then, to help with the pain. You needn't take on after John Henry about it."

"You?" Henry asked, his dark brows lifting in surprise. "I've never known you to touch a drop of liquor in your life."

"My brother James suggested it," she said. "Shall I write to him that you disapprove?"

"James told you to drink?"

"Yes," she said, and John Henry was surprised by how coolly she could lie. He was sure she had never touched a drop of the whiskey herself, and was only saying so to protect him from his father's wrath. "Now what's all this fussin' that woke me? Surely a little missin' liquor can't have made you so angry, Henry."

"It's my fault, Ma," John Henry said quickly. "I just asked if I could go study at the new school in town. I didn't know that things were so hard around here."

"Spoiled, that's what he is," Henry said. "Thinks the world comes on a golden platter. That's your doin', Alice Jane, yours and your sisters' for dotin' on him all the time. Thinks the world owes him everything."

"You're right, of course, dear," she agreed. "We do dote on him over much. But that's because he's the only child. You know I would have been thankful for more children, if the Lord had seen fit to bless us. Is this new school so very expensive?"

"Everything's expensive these days," Henry replied, but his hot temper seemed to be cooling some in his wife's gentle presence.

"But surely we can find the money somewhere," Alice Jane said. "You know how well he always did in school." Then she added in measured tones: "You know how I feel about his education, Henry. If I leave him nothin' else, I want to leave him educated, as a gentleman's son should be. I want to know I did the best by him, when I am gone..."

When I am gone, John Henry's thoughts echoed silently, surprised to hear his mother allude to her own mortality. For though the family all knew now that she was indeed dying of the consumption, the sad truth of it was never mentioned aloud. But now she was using her own illness to fight for his happiness.

Henry sighed as though unaccustomed to acquiescing. "All right, Alice Jane, if that's what you want. I'll scrape the tuition together somehow, if I have to sell off some of the farm to do it. The land's not worth much to me these days, anyhow, without enough hands to work it. Hell, maybe I'll even hire myself out to the Freedmen's Bureau. I hear the government is lookin' for local agents, now the occupation is over." Then he turned his gaze, cool as blue steel, on John Henry. "But I'll expect you to prove yourself deservin' of the honor, boy. I want to see top marks in every subject, and perfect attendance as well. No use joinin' the battle unless you plan to fight to the end." Then his gaze shifted to the old sword that hung over the fireplace, the sword great-grandfather Burroughs had used in the Revolutionary War, and he sighed again.

"I had hoped you might follow me into the military one day," he said, "fight for your country like your forebears did. But I don't reckon there'll be much call for Southern soldiers anymore." And as he spoke, there was such sadness in his voice, such wistfulness for those glory days gone by, that John Henry felt a pang of remorse.

"I'll do my best in school, Pa," he vowed. "I promise I'll make you proud of me."

"You do that, son," Henry said heavily. "Our pride's about all we've got left, these days."

~~~~~~~~~

The Valdosta Institute was located in the remodeled old day school building and run by the erudite Professor S.M. Varnedoe and his sisters, Miss Sallie and Miss Lila Varnedoe, newly arrived from Savannah, and dedicated to bringing modern education to the backwoods boys and girls of Lowndes County. The coursework they offered was challenging, combining the basics with a heavy dose of classical language and literature. While penmanship still counted, composition and recitation became the true test of knowledge, and the students spent every Friday in written and oral examinations. But despite the rigors of the routine, the students quickly came to love and admire their new instructor. Professor Varnedoe's techniques stirred his pupils' sense of pride and ambition, and their reward was his benevolent smile and happy laughter. Learning with Professor Varnedoe was a joy.

The highlight of the school week was the Friday afternoon recitation contest, when the students entertained each other by reading their compositions aloud and reciting the long poems Professor Varnedoe assigned to them: *William Tell*, *The Midnight Ride of Paul Revere*, *The Death of Napoleon*. The best orators in school were

Willie Pendleton and Constantia Bessant, Major Bessant's pretty young daughter, but Sam Griffin was John Henry's favorite, hands down.

Young Sam had a fervent love of the South, a fervent hate of the Yankees, and a way with a patriotic theme that could make an audience burst into applause. And as the son of the owner of the town's general store, he often came prepared with cinnamon bark candy in his pockets to share, as he did one school day in spring.

"For the ladies," he said with a brown-eyed grin, sneaking some out at recess time as he and John Henry loafed in the schoolyard. "Give a bite to Thea Morgan over there, I'll bet she gives you a kiss for it."

"Thea?" John Henry asked in surprise, stealing a glance at the skinny, pale-eyed girl who stood staring back at him from the shadows near the outhouse. "Why'd she do such a thing?"

"She's sweet on you, don't you know?" Sam replied with a laugh. "Constantia Bessant told me so, and if Constantia said it, you can bet it's true. Any girl with the grit to stand up to that Yankee soldier the way she did is bound to be tellin' the truth."

John Henry's head shot up, the cinnamon bark and Thea Morgan forgotten all at once. "What Yankee soldier?"

"Why, the one that arrested Dick Force, back last fall, didn't you hear? It was Constantia Bessant first found out about the Captain bein' in jail. She was passin' by the jailhouse that day, goin' home from my Pa's store, when one of those uppity darky soldiers pushed his bayonet at her and told her to go on and git. Well, you know Constantia. She wasn't about to git just 'cause some Yankee darky told her to, so she turned around and told him he could go on and git himself right back up to Washington. And that was when she saw who it was that darky was guarding."

"You mean the Captain?"

"Sure enough!" Then Sam Griffin started into an oratory to rival anything he'd ever presented in school. Sam was an actor at heart, and he could copy almost anyone's voice, as he did now, letting his voice go high and flirtatious like Constantia Bessant's.

" 'Why if it ain't the Captain! Whatever are you doin' in that jail cell, Dick?' "

When John Henry laughed at the mimicry, Sam changed characters, his voice growing low and angry like Dick Force's. " 'They say I choked a darky, and I am under arrest.' "

Then, quick as a wink, he became Constantia again.

" 'Well, I am goin' home and choke two or three of them myself, and then they will arrest me, too. And as this building belongs to my father, we will just turn them all out and take possession.' "

John Henry, playing along with the performance, looked concerned as he asked: "And did you get arrested, too, Miss Bessant, Ma'am?"

"Hell no!" Sam laughed in his own boyish voice. "But Constantia did go right on home and tell everybody that Dick was in jail. It was just awhile later that Alex Darnell and Jack Calhoun came and helped him to escape. So I reckon you could say that Constantia showed those Yankees what's what, helpin' get Dick out of jail."

John Henry nodded, a hot light in his clear blue eyes. "I sure would like to show those Yanks a thing or two, myself! The way those darky soldiers parade up and down this town is more than a man ought to have to bear, and pushin' a gun at a lady like that...Why, if my Pa wasn't agent for the Bureau, workin' with the Federals and all, I might just teach them a lesson in manners!"

"I'm with you, there, John Henry," Sam agreed. "Too bad we're not old enough to join up with Alex and Jack. I'll bet we'd see some fightin' then."

"What are you talkin' about, Sam?"

Sam looked around quickly, then spoke in hushed tones. "I'm talkin' about vigilantes! That's what Alex and Jack are puttin' together. I heard 'em plannin' in the back room of my Pa's store when they came in for a drink the other night. Alex and Jack and the Captain all fought in the War together, so they know somethin' about fightin'. They say that if the Captain dies, there's gonna be trouble, one way or another. I tell you, John Henry, I sure would like to join up with them and make some trouble myself!"

"Vigilantes," John Henry said, the word rolling off his tongue with a satisfying sound. "Vigilantes! For the honor of the South!"

"For the honor of the South!" Sam Griffin repeated. Then he shrugged. "But us being only fourteen and all, they ain't gonna take us in. Hell, John Henry! Sometimes I think I'm gonna bust before I get a chance to do a man's work!" But Sam's mood could change like quicksilver, and he let out a sudden laugh. "But I know one thing we can try that's man's business..."

"And what's that?"

"Kissin' women! Tell you what, you give that piece of cinnamon bark to Thea Morgan, and I'll bet you two bits she lets you kiss her at the next barn dance."

"You're on," John Henry readily agreed. Since his childhood days with cousin

Robert, he couldn't resist the thrill of a contest – especially one where a wager was involved. "And how about you, Sam? You gonna try for a kiss, too?"

"Sure am," Sam said with a grin. "I aim to kiss Constantia Bessant!"

John Henry let out a whistle. "You do dream big, Sam! Constantia's the most popular girl in school. What makes you think she'll kiss you?"

Sam grinned again as he pulled a paper-wrapped wad of sticky candy from the pocket of his homespun trousers. "Cinnamon bark, John Henry! She's got a real sweet tooth, that's what I hear. And I've got the best supply of sugar in town. Why, by the time I'm done passin' around candy to all the pretty girls, Valdosta's gonna be needin' a dentist."

~~~~~~~~~~

"...*more than kisses, letters mingle souls*," John Henry recited, and though he should have known what to say next, his mind kept drawing a blank. "*Sir, more than kisses, letters mingle souls...*"

"Yes, yes, Mr. Holliday," Professor Varnedoe said, "you have already said that. The next line, please." The professor looked at him patiently as did a classroom of young faces, all waiting while John Henry struggled with his final Friday recitation. Professor Varnedoe had assigned him selections from the English writer John Donne, and until this last poem, John Henry had been making a competent presentation. But though he'd read the words of the poem dozens of times and recited them to himself nearly that many times more, until this very moment, the meaning of the lines had alluded him. Now he stood suddenly understanding what the poet had meant, and feeling so overwhelmed by the truth of it that he could think of nothing else.

"...*more than kisses*," Professor Varnedoe prompted, and John Henry took a breath and tried again.

"*Sir, more than kisses, letters mingle souls,*
For, thus friends absent speak."

"Very good, Mr. Holliday. Now, that wasn't so very difficult, was it? Class, you may offer Mr. Holliday a round of applause. Next, I believe we will hear from Mr. Albert Pendleton, Jr."

And as the class clapped heartily at his dubious achievement and the next reciter came forward, John Henry quickly took his seat on the bench behind his wood plank desk. Sam Griffin, sitting on his right side, leaned over and winked, and pointed to where Thea Morgan sat across the aisle on the girl's side of the classroom. Thea was looking back, her cheeks in a flush that made her skinny, pale face seem almost pretty. Why did she have to blush like that? John Henry thought, and right here in class, too. Surely, everyone would guess what she was blushing about and would think that she and John Henry were sweethearts.

His first kiss had been nothing, really, and he almost felt bad about taking Sam's wagered two bits for accomplishing it. Thea Morgan was as meek and mild-mannered as she looked, and she didn't put up any fuss at all when he held her by the hand and led her behind a bale of hay in the barn near the Darnell's Livery Stable the night of the spring dance. Getting her there, out of sight of the chaperones, was easy enough, and getting the kiss wasn't much harder. After stalling a bit out of his own nervousness, wondering just how he ought to go about it, he figured he might as well get on with it and he just up and kissed her. It was over almost before he realized that he'd done it, and there was Thea, looking at him with her pale eyes shining and a funny-kind of smile on her thin lips. But there was so little of anything remarkable about the feeling of kissing those lips that he reckoned he might as well have kissed the family cow or his favorite riding horse. So though it was the first kiss of his young life, it was nothing much to remember.

What he did remember from that warm evening in mid-May was Colonel William Bessant interrupting the barn dance to announce that Dick Force had died. It had taken five long months for the Yankee bullets to do their work, but the slow poison of the gangrenous wounds had finally killed the Captain, as sure a murder as if he'd died the same day he was shot. And without Colonel Bessant there at the dance to soften the news and try to calm the angry young crowd, there would have been trouble in Valdosta that night for sure, for murder demanded justice, or vengeance at least. But Colonel Bessant reminded them all again that the Lord would surely repay what they could not, and it was best for the townspeople to keep their tempers and their tongues. In the heated atmosphere of the times, even a rumor of revenge could bring down a flood of Federal soldiers on them all.

The dance was quickly dismissed, as was school for a few days, and the students sent home to cool their heels and their hot heads. But for John Henry, living away out in the country, seven miles from school and Sam Griffin and the rest of the boys, the time away only made his anger grow. Dick Force was only nineteen-years-old when he died, just five years older than John Henry himself, and too young to suffer such a lingering and loathsome end. Why, if he'd had any say in the matter...

But he had no say, nor even a chance to talk out his frustration. His mother was sick in bed most of the time, too ill to be disturbed. His father was busy with business and the job he had taken as local agent for the Freedmen's Bureau – and even that rankled John Henry. Working for the Bureau was nearly as bad as being a Yankee, in his mind, and he tried not to remember that his father had only taken the Bureau job to make the money to send him to school.

He was still in that solitary and sorrowful mood when a letter came for him from Jonesboro. Cousin Mattie had finally written to tell him how things were going back in her hometown – a hometown that she hardly recognized anymore since Sherman and his soldiers had swept through.

Nearly the whole town is burnt up, she wrote, her neat handwriting filling the front, back, and margins of the one small sheet of stationery, an economy necessitated by the high price of writing paper since the War. *Broad Street is changed so, you'd hardly recognize it. Where the rails used to run down the middle of the road, there's two roads now, one on each side of the rails. The Yanks lowered the town side of the street and dumped the dirt on the McDonough side to raise it, which they supposed would make it harder for us to get around. They burnt the old train depot, up on the north side of town past Aunt Martha Holliday Johnson's house, and tore up all the tracks along through there, but there's talk of building a new depot when there's any money for it. My father's warehouse where he had his mercantile is just a pile of bricks and charred boards, like most of the rest of downtown. The Courthouse is gone, and the Academy, and lots of folks lost their homes. Our home is still standing, though in disreputable shape, the wall plaster is broken and full of holes from gunshots and the clapboards were stolen by the Yanks for firewood, so we hear. Mama said she told you about the graves in our vegetable garden, Captain Grace and Father Bleimal. How sad it all is! When I went to the convent school in Savannah, I left a pretty white house with flowers in the yard. Now I've come home again, but it hardly seems like home anymore. I miss the way things used to be. Do you feel the same? How I wish we could talk to one another again...*

He knew just how she felt, and wished so much, as she did, that they could talk again. But Jonesboro was so far away, farther even than Griffin, and he was buried out in the quiet of the countryside. If only he were older, he thought for the thousandth time, and had some say in his own life....

But at least he had Mattie's letter, and reading it over again and again until he almost had it memorized made him feel closer to her. Dear cousin Mattie, who understood him and cared about him as no one else seemed to. So on this final day of Friday recitations, the last week of the school year, the poet's words were alive in his heart:

"*Sir, more than kisses, letters mingle souls,*
For, thus friends absent speak."

Thea Morgan could smile at him all day if she wanted to, and dream a hopeless dream that he would ever kiss her again. It was cousin Mattie who had his heart and always would.

~~~~~~~~~

Summer came too soon that year, and with the end of the school session, John Henry found himself alone again on his father's farm with only the field hands and his horse for company. Most days, as soon as his chores were done and his piano practice was over, he'd be off riding somewhere, shooting at rabbits or fishing in the green waters of the Withlacoochee. But wherever he'd gone to spend the days, he was always home again for his evening devotional at his mother's bedside.

It was there by his mother's side that he celebrated his fifteenth birthday, while Alice Jane lay coughing with the consumption that racked her ravaged body. And though the August day was sweltering, even the heat of the south Georgia summer didn't seem to warm her anymore, and she shivered as she lay under a heavy quilt.

"I am so sorry, my dear," she said breathlessly, "I should have planned a party for you..."

"Don't be silly, Ma. What do I need a party for? I'm nearly a man now. Besides, who'd come all this way just to celebrate with me?" And though he tried to make his voice sound light and uncaring, there was something wistful in it. Who would come out so far just to see him, anyhow? Only Sam Griffin maybe, and Sam was busy helping out in his father's general store that summer, where he was no doubt filling his mind with thoughts of vigilantes and other town-boy excitements.

"Nearly a man..." Alice Jane echoed. "Look at you! My sweet boy, so grown up. I am glad there is so much McKey in you..." She reached her hand to his face, fair and freckled from the summer sun, then touched his sandy hair, threaded with traces of reddish-gold.

He did look some like his mother's side of the family, that was true, with the McKey's Scots-Irish coloring and clear china-blue eyes, the graceful gait and aristocratic bearing. But the rest of him was all Holliday, with his father's high cheekbones and squared jaw, his peaked hairline and hair-trigger temper.

"I do have something for you, though," she whispered, "a birthday gift."

"What gift, Ma?" he asked, as his gaze went quickly around the little room, falling on washstand and chair, wardrobe and trunk before settling back on the quilt-covered bedstead. "I don't see any presents."

"Your gift isn't here. It's back in Griffin. I wanted you to have it as part of your inheritance from my father's estate. The money may do you good one day. You remember Indian Creek, your Grandfather McKey's plantation?"

"Sure, Ma, I remember." How could he ever forget? Indian Creek had been like paradise to his childish mind, and at the mention of it, he could almost taste the Muscadine grapes that grew on the arbor, almost feel the breeze blowing over the endless acres of cotton and corn and sugar cane. Paradise lost, he thought, like everything else he loved. Like his mother, who was dying.

"I tried to keep some of the plantation for you," she went on, struggling for breath, "but all that's left now are the house lots in town and the Iron Front..."

"The Iron Front?"

"It is...a business building...my father invested in it..." her voice broke then, torn by a coughing fit, and John Henry pulled the covers closer around her.

"Don't talk now, Ma," he said gently. "You can tell me later." Or never, he thought with a shudder. What did he care about a building, anyhow? Even Indian Creek Plantation wouldn't make up for his mother's fading life, or his own frustrated one.

"Yes," she whispered, "later..." and she closed her eyes. "Happy Birthday, my dearest..."

"Thank you, Ma," John Henry said. And as he bent to kiss her cool damp brow, his heart repeated her words, *Happy Birthday...*

~~~~~~~~~

The one pleasure that he could offer her in her failing days was the piano music she so loved, though she was too weak to play for herself anymore.

"You play for me, John Henry," she would whisper in her breathless voice. "I do love to hear you play." So he would open the sheet music that she had taught him and stumble through Schubert and Liszt. But as the days passed and September and Indian Summer came on, Alice Jane no longer had the strength to ask him to play, or even to listen, and the music ended altogether.

It was an awful death that came to take Alice Jane Holliday that warm evening in September, slipping from consciousness as her lungs filled with water and she lay drowning in her bed. Her sisters and brothers, come up from Florida to be with her at the end, tried to comfort one another by speaking of that peaceful land beyond the grave where Alice Jane would live forever in eternal light. But all John Henry could see was the darkness of the world that only his mother's company could chase away, and in the darkness, the end finally came.

He waited in the shadows outside her room, listening to the hushed voices beyond the door. He recognized his father's voice, and Uncle James McKey who was her attending physician, and heard the muffled sound of his aunts' weeping. And he wanted to go in and wanted to run away at the same time, so he sat transfixed, listening but not wanting to hear. In his hands he held a small, leather-backed photograph of a beautiful young woman in a ruffle-lined bonnet. She held a baby boy in her arms, fair haired and wide eyed, cuddling against her for comfort. He could hardly remember his mother looking like that, young and serene, but he could still feel the warmth and safety of her arms around him, and knowing that he was losing her was more than he could bear.

Then the bedroom door swung open and his aunts shuffled past him, clinging onto each other and not noticing him through their weeping. His father noticed him though, as he sat on the floor with his back against the wall, his shoulders shaking with the emotion that he could not control.

"No cryin', boy. I will not have you cryin' like some girl. Do you understand me?"

"Yessir," John Henry said, his words trembling out.

"Your mother has gone on to a better life, God rest her soul. A better life than I ever gave her. Maybe she will finally find some happiness now." And for a moment, his father seemed to be looking right through him and into some other place. Then his eyes focused again on the frightened boy before him, and he said sternly: "Get up from there and do somethin' to help your aunts. I don't want to see you cryin' anymore."

John Henry pushed himself up from the floor and tried to wipe the tears from his eyes without his father seeing, but Henry wasn't looking at him, done giving what little consolation he would, and John Henry hurried past him down the hall to find his aunts. But what he wanted was to go back into that sick room, kneel down by his mother's bed, and cry himself to sleep at her side.

His mother would have understood, and let him cry.

~~~~~~~~~

She was buried in a plot in Sunset Hill Cemetery in Valdosta, where magnolia trees shaded the sparse grass and squirrels chased across the graves. And standing by his father, hat in hand and eyes swollen from two nights of silent weeping into his pillow, John Henry felt that his own life was over as well. He'd known his mother was dying; for years he'd lived with the pain of the knowledge of it. For years he'd listened to her struggle for breath until she'd suddenly stopped breathing. No breath, no life, only an empty silence, a void in his life where she had always been, a chasm in his heart that nothing would ever fill.

But the hardest part of his mourning was having to go back to school, knowing his mother would want him to do well in spite of his loss, knowing his father expected it. Perfect attendance and top marks were still Henry's requirements for continued education, and John Henry had no choice but to comply, though he often found his eyes so clouded with emotion that he could hardly read the books before him. If only he could talk to someone, share the anguish of his loss, he might be able to handle it all better. But his father had ordered him not to cry, so he kept the pain inside and kept the tears to himself. And when the well-meaning Misses Sallie and Lila Varnedoe expressed their condolences and concern, he couldn't even bring himself to thank them.

He was still mourning his mother's death, feeling lost and alone without her and doing poorly at school because of it, when his father stunned the family by announcing that he would be marrying again. It had been only three short months since Alice Jane had died, and though the usual mourning period of three years might be shortened if the widower had small children at home who needed tending, John Henry was fifteen-years-old and hardly a child anymore.

"Your mother would have wanted it," was all the explanation Henry offered his son on that cold December afternoon as he saddled a horse and rode off to marry young Rachel Martin, his neighbor's daughter. The Reverend Newt Ousley, his mother's minister, was to perform the ceremony – a deed that seemed nearly as disloyal as his father's taking Rachel to wife.

Suddenly, all those visits his father had made to the Martin's orchard seemed sinister in retrospect, and John Henry remembered the words his Uncle James McKey had thrown at his father one hot summer night: *"I hear Mr. Martin's daughter is comely, and available. If there is anything untoward goin' on between you and Martin's daughter..."* But surely, Uncle James had been wrong. Surely there had been nothing between Henry and Rachel while Alice Jane was still alive. But the hasty marriage brought rumors that rippled all across Lowndes County. Three months was hardly any time at all to mourn a beloved wife. Three months looked more like a hurried engagement before a shotgun wedding, making an honest woman out of a married man's mistress.

Though John Henry tried not to hear the talk in town, in the quiet of the country nights he couldn't help but hear Rachel's soft laughter from the room next to his own. He was old enough now to know what went on between man and wife, and the thought of Rachel in his father's arms both fascinated and repulsed him. She was so different from his refined and cultured mother, a raw and earthy farm girl with little education and a fine lust for her new husband. But if the nights were hard for John Henry, the mornings were worse, listening to Rachel's humming as she cooked breakfast over the big iron stove. And Henry, smug and smiling, would come out of their bedroom and look at her with satisfaction.

It wasn't surprising, the way they were carrying on, when Rachel became pregnant. And though she miscarried that baby and then another one, she vowed that she would keep trying until she gave her husband a new son – a pleasure that John Henry secretly prayed she would never have. Henry Holliday already had a son to whom he paid little enough attention as it was.

But John Henry didn't have long to suffer feeling like an intruder in his father's honeymoon cottage, for Henry took a sudden desire to rid himself of the farm and move into town. The cotton crop was failing again, he complained, and business in Valdosta was starting to pick up at last. So the Hollidays sold off some of the plantation land and bought a town house across from the railroad tracks on Savannah Avenue, and just down the road from the store where Henry set out to sell buggies for a living. When the buggies sold well, he signed on as a dealer of tickets in the Georgia State Lottery, and soon he was able to buy his new wife a whole new set of furniture and some pretty new clothes to go with it. Life was good again for Henry Holliday, and John Henry wondered if his father ever even thought about Alice Jane anymore, or remembered that he still had a son who needed him.

Chapter Five

The Holliday house on Savannah Avenue was typical of its time and place: a single-storied wooden structure, clapboard-sided and shuttered at long windows, with two bedrooms, a parlor, and a dining room that doubled as a winter kitchen. The floors throughout were wide-planked Georgia heart pine, the plaster walls white-washed, the mantels and moldings Tung-oiled until they shined. The front door, with its six-paned glass transom and double panels, opened onto a wide front porch that looked over the fenced-yard toward the railroad tracks and the town beyond. Flowers bloomed along the dirt walk that led from the house to the road, and the well in the front yard was shaded by a neatly painted well-house. Altogether it was a pleasant home, as pretty as its mistress, and a place that John Henry stayed away from as much as possible.

Not that anyone noticed his absence. It seemed that nobody noticed John Henry Holliday these days, or cared that he started staying out later than he should, coming home with a trace of whiskey on his breath. His mother would have noticed and scolded him into repentance, warning him against friends who drank liquor and bet money on cards and made trouble for the town, even if they were all sons of fine Confederate families. But John Henry found them to be good company, still loyal to the Cause, still spoiling for a chance to beat the Billy Yanks who were running their town.

The Federals were back in force after Georgia had refused to ratify the Fourteenth Amendment aimed at granting the former slaves full rights as citizens of the United States. Coloreds were, after all, naturally inferior to Whites, and lacking the mental and spiritual judgment that citizenship required. So although the Fourteenth Amendment had already been passed by a majority vote in the North, the Southern Democrats were morally opposed to it.

With the renewed flood of Federal soldiers came a greedy band of northern politicians, ready to reap a profit off the Yankee occupation. They offered to pay forty acres and a mule to any black man who voted Republican – the forty acres stolen, of course, from the broken-up plantations of the former slave owners. "Carpetbaggers," folks called those thieving Yankee politicians, saying it like a cussword, and considered them to be only slightly above the turncoat Southern scum called "Scalawags" who sold out their own people to curry the favor of the Yanks. In those turbulent times the Ku Klux Klan arose to protect the rights of white southerners, and Negro Loyal Leagues were formed to defend the newly given rights of former slaves. On both sides of that Fourteenth Amendment battlefield tempers were running so hot it seemed the War might just catch fire all over again.

Some of those fiery tempers belonged to the hot-headed young men who called themselves "Vigilantes," sworn to uphold the honor of the South. Though their actions put them somewhere outside the law, their names ran like a roster of some of the finest families in Valdosta: Jack Calhoun, Alex Darnell, Ben Smith, J.J. Rambo – good boys all of them, as long as they weren't pushed too far and they weren't drinking too much. But the Yankees were pushing hard, and there was always plenty of whiskey flowing when the Vigilantes got together amid the shipping crates and flour barrels in the back room of Griffin's general store. Mr. Griffin himself was too busy to pay much attention to what went on back there, as long as the place was left clean and no dry goods disappeared. Only his seventeen-year-old son Sam, who fancied himself a Vigilante too, knew what plans those boys were making. Only Sam, and his pal John Henry Holliday, who spent every afternoon playing cards with the Vigilantes and besting them over and over again at Spanish Monte.

"Damn you, Holliday!" Alex Darnell cursed, "I'd shoot you for a card cheat if I could figure out how you're cheatin'!"

"He ain't cheatin'!" Sam Griffin said, springing to his friend's defense. "He's just better than you, that's all. Learned it from his Pa's Mexican servant-boy before the War, ain't that right, John Henry?"

"Francisco taught me some things," John Henry agreed. "But even if I was cheatin', Alex would never know it. He's too busy swiggin' that bottle to pay attention to the hands like he ought."

"You talk mighty bold for a youngster," Alex said darkly, though he was only a few years past being a youngster himself. "You might just stay a youngster forever, if I get anymore sick of listenin' to your chatter."

"Cool down, Alex," Jack Calhoun cautioned. "You get to fightin' here, and Mr.

Griffin will ask us to find somewhere else to do our drinkin', and I for one would miss this fine view."

The fine view to which Jack referred was a clear sight through the open freight doors of the storeroom and into the alleyway behind. For though the alley was just a muddy track overgrown with weeds and overhung with shaggy pines, it offered privacy from prying Yankee eyes – and privacy was what plans like theirs demanded.

"Now y'all listen up," Jack Calhoun went on, "the time's comin', soon enough, and we've got to be prepared. There's a big political rally comin' at the Courthouse for a carpetbagger runnin' for United States Congress. Seems to me like we ought to give him a warm welcome, show him what we think of his tellin' Yankee lies around Valdosta."

"Welcome him?" Alex Darnell asked. "Seems more like we ought to chase him out of town."

Jack Calhoun shook his head, a weary young War veteran burdened with leading a pack of ignorant, hotheaded boys. But those boys were old enough to load a gun and fire it, and plenty willing to fight with him against the Yankees who had beaten him and murdered his best friend, Dick Force.

"Chasin's too good for Mr. J.W. Clift," Jack replied, "stirrin' up these nigras to vote for him, tellin' 'em how the Yankees saved 'em, how they owe their salvation to the Republican government. Forty acres and a mule! Might as well promise 'em the moon!"

"So what are we gonna do?" Ben Smith asked, "if chasin' him out of town's too good?"

Jack Calhoun took a slow look around the storeroom, his eyes resting for a moment on each of his listeners, before going on in hushed, unhurried tones.

"I've been thinkin'," he said, 'bout how easy it would be to set a charge of gunpowder under those Courthouse steps, light it up just when Mr. Carpetbagger Clift starts makin' his speech. There's enough space under the steps to set a keg, I reckon."

"A keg!" Sam Griffin gasped. "But that much powder could kill somebody! We don't want to make a murder, do we?"

"We may have to make a murder," Jack answered, "to make the point. They won't be sendin' no more Yanks to Valdosta after we send this one home in bits and pieces. " 'Course, the Courthouse will take it pretty hard in the blast. But hell, what's one building compared to what the Yanks have done to us?"

They all knew full well that sending one Yankee home all rearranged would only bring more fighting to their town – but fighting was what they wanted.

"So who's in?" Jack asked. "I want to know right now. Anybody who's out, get out now before I say anymore."

Alex Darnell was the first to break the answering silence. "My father's got a fresh stock of horses, if murder's what it comes to. We can all ride out of town as soon as the place goes up. With the commotion it'll be awhile before anyone comes lookin' for us."

"And where'll we go, if we do have to run?" J.J. Rambo asked. "They'd look down by the river, where Dick hid out. I don't mind killin' a few Yanks, but I don't relish gettin' killed myself."

"We could go to Texas," John Henry suggested, as he sat on a crate of dry goods and counted up his penny-ante Monte winnings. "My father was there in the Mexican War. He's told me about it a hundred times at least. I could get us there without any trouble at all." At sixteen-years-old he was the youngest of the Vigilantes, but he reckoned that he ought to be able to add his say.

"The hell you could!" Alex Darnell said. "I wouldn't follow a youngster like you to Sunday School, let alone all the way to Texas!"

"Why don't we just shoot Mr. Congressman when he gets off the train?" Ben Smith asked, raising an imaginary pistol. "I could hide out in the trees on the other side of Ashley Street just like a sharpshooter."

"And get yourself caught before he'd even hit the ground," Jack Calhoun pointed out. "No, it's got to be the explosion that does it. That way we've got the smoke and noise to cover our work. Besides, blowin' up the Courthouse makes a statement to the Yanks, like I said."

"We still haven't settled on where we'll ride off to," said Sam Griffin. "Alex's horses won't do us much good if we ain't got no place to go."

"How about my father's farm?" John Henry said. Though he was disappointed that the boys hadn't gone for the idea of Texas, a romantic and adventurous destination, the remaining portion of his father's plantation property was far enough out to make a good stopping place. "It's past Cat Creek. There's nothin' around for miles, and I know all the trails through the woods."

"Sounds good," Jack Calhoun said with a nod. "If it comes to runnin', we'll take Alex's horses and make a run for Major Holliday's farm. You sure your father won't mind us using his place for a hide out?"

"My father doesn't give a damn what I do," John Henry said sullenly. "Does anybody have any more whiskey? I need another lick."

"You better stop that drinkin' for a while," Jack advised. "You'll need your wits about you, if you're playin' mole."

"Playin' what?" he asked, bewildered.

"Mole," Alex Darnell said under his breath, "underground varmint. Just a low-down card cheat..."

"I said that's enough, Alex," Jack Calhoun warned again. "Mole's the one who goes underground, finding out what we're not supposed to know. I figure your bein' Major Holliday's son, you know your away around that Courthouse. Be easy enough for you to wander around without gettin' noticed."

"Not as easy as it used to be," John Henry said, "since my father's not Agent for the Freedmen's Bureau any more. You know they let all the local men go, once Martial Law come back around."

"Even so, folks are used to seein' your face around there. Won't seem too strange to have you back around again, snoopin' a little."

"All right," John Henry nodded. "So what do you want me to find out?"

"Particulars about Mr. Carpetbagger Clift. When he's comin' to town, when he's gonna make his speech. We'll wait to move on your information."

"Sounds to me like everything hangs on Holliday," Alex Darnell complained. "What if he gets it wrong, and it's one of our boys who's on the speaker's platform? I don't like trustin' so much to a youngster, let alone a card cheatin' one."

There was only so much that John Henry's pride could take. He hadn't had to cheat even once against Alex, the boy was such a bad player.

"I may be young," John Henry said, "but I can do the job. And I reckon I'll be a good mole, too. No one would ever suspect me of lowerin' myself to your level, Alex Darnell, and joinin' in on somethin' like this."

"If you think you're too good for this," Jack Calhoun said, "then maybe you'd best get out now, before somebody does get hurt. If there's local men around when the Courthouse goes up, your father's likely to be one of them."

John Henry shrugged an answer. "My father always wanted me to be a soldier like him. I reckon he'd understand about the risks of war. But don't you worry about Major Holliday. He's a hero, you know. He can walk on water."

Then he took a long drink from the new bottle J.J. Rambo offered him, and felt the liquor burn its way past his aching heart.

~~~~~~~~~~~~

Getting into the Courthouse to listen for information wasn't too hard, as his father had done business for the Freedmen's Bureau and his own face was familiar to the military guards there. And even if he hadn't looked so familiar, who would think to question such a well-mannered and gentlemanly young man as John Henry Holliday? Although he was nearly as tall as his father, he was still a narrow-shouldered lad, beardless and blue-eyed, innocent-looking if not innocent in his heart.

"Excuse me, Sir," he addressed the military commander, "but I hear there's gonna be a political rally comin' up soon..."

And the commander nodded and told him everything he wanted to know, the boy so obviously awed at the privilege of speaking to a real Federal Officer that he almost blustered with excitement.

"Why yes, son, a big rally for Mr. J.W. Clift. He's running for United States Congress. He's a powerful man, Mr. Clift, voting registrar for the whole state of Georgia. Appointed by General Pope himself."

John Henry's eyes widened in studied surprise. "Is that a fact?" he asked, letting out a whistle to complete the purposed effect. "Sir, you don't suppose – I mean, if I was to stay out of the way and all..."

"Go on," the commander said with a smile, enjoying the boy's stammering subservience, so unexpected in a Rebel's son. "Spit it out. I haven't got all day."

"Well, Sir, I sure would like to stay around here and help out some. Sure would be an honor to help get things ready for a United States Congressman comin' to town."

"I suppose that could be arranged," the commander answered with a generous smile. "You go on over to my aide and get yourself a pass written up. A boy ought to know what's going on in the world, and make himself some use in it."

"Oh, thank you, Sir!" John Henry gushed, "I surely do thank you!"

The commander was easy, a fool like most Yanks, full of pride and blind to what was going on around them. It was amazing that such fools had won the war, John Henry mused, considering the cunning of their opponents.

But not all the Yanks were so blind. There were some who'd had their eyes opened, since their days of slave-laboring, and were still watching – like the guard who stood at the entrance to the commander's office. He was a big black man, a former slave from one of the plantations near to the Holliday place, who'd run off to join the Union Army as it marched through Georgia. Now he was back in Lowndes County again, dressed smart in a new uniform of Federal blue, and feeling his position of importance as guard for the commander's office. And maybe it was the Yankee blue the man wore with such seeming ease, or maybe it was seeing a familiar face himself, but the sight of the darky drove John Henry to forget his carefully crafted subservience.

"Out of my way, boy!" John Henry ordered as he tried to push past the guard. "I need to see about a pass."

"I ain't no boy to you, no how," the guard said, pulling up his rifle so fast it nearly knocked John Henry down. "And I ain't movin' out of the way jest 'cause some Reb' chile say so."

"You will move, or answer for it!" John Henry said angrily. "I've got business here, and no darky's gonna get in the way of it, least of all some run-away field hand puttin' on airs."

If he'd had a pistol on him, he would have pulled it just to make the point. As it was, all he had was words and the arrogance of being born to the ruling class. But he also had enough of his father's steely-eyed nerve to make the soldier back down a bit.

"And what business is it you got?" the guard asked.

"No business of yours," came the cool reply. "Business for the commander himself – he's sent me to get a pass. Now let me through, or I'll report you for insubordination."

The guard hesitated a moment before pulling the rifle away from John Henry's ribs. "All right, you go on. But I'll be keepin' both my eyes on you. Like I kept both my eyes on that Dick Force 'fore he run from jail. We got him after. We'll get you, too, if you're up to no good."

John Henry knew full well that the man meant what he said, like he knew that he had only himself to blame for bringing the scrutiny. He should have put away his pride and been ready to bow and scrape before the guard the way he'd bowed before the commander, playing the game of guileless country boy that worked so well to win Yankee confidence. He could still do it now, if he wanted, and probably should...

Instead, he put his narrow shoulders back, turned his clear blue eyes on the guard, and drawled with all the arrogance of his fallen class:

"You do that, boy. You just keep right on watchin'. And maybe someday you'll even learn somethin'. But I doubt it."

Then he pushed on past and into the aide's office, hearing the click of the hammer on the rifle behind him and hardly caring at all. As his father had said: pride was about all they had left, these days. Pride and a plan, and that seemed like more than enough.

~~~~~~~~~~

The fourth of April dawned damp and warm, a mist rising up from the Withlacoochee River bottoms, the air all lazy and sweet with the smell of honeysuckle starting to bloom. Above the fields of fresh-plowed Lowndes County, whippoorwills sang and Jayhawks coasted against the sunrise, singing of growing things and life renewed, while in the dank alley behind Ashley Street, dark with overhanging pines and the shadows of secret plans, the Vigilantes readied for the death of a man they had never met and hated all the same. And as they finished their preparations, checking one last time on the position of the powder keg hidden under the Courthouse steps and stashing pistols in saddlebags for their horsed getaway, the Atlantic and Gulf Line Railroad hissed into town spreading a pall of black smoke across the white-cloud sky.

The crowd at the depot was mostly Yankee soldiers, making a big show for one of their own, but there were plenty of curious townsfolk as well, and the atmosphere was more like a holiday celebration than a coming election. Even the train came dressed for the party, decked out in drapes of red, white, and blue, its platforms hung with bunting and its engine and caboose flying flags of stars and stripes. Foreign flags, John Henry thought, as he stood close by the regimental commander and waited for Mr. J.W. Clift to appear - foreign flags that would drape the coffin of a dead carpetbagger on his way home.

It was amazing how calmly John Henry could think of such things, murder and mayhem and all. But he'd lived so close to them for so long, most of his growing-up life, that death and destruction seemed of little consequence anymore. Everyone lived and everyone died. At least this man's death would count for something, and that was more than most people got. It was more than his mother had gotten, anyhow. Alice Jane Holliday had died for nothing, her passing hardly even remembered by most folks.

Seeing his father striding toward the train platform, smartly dressed in a gray frock coat and tall top hat, didn't calm him any. Though Henry Holliday no longer had his position with the Freedmen's Bureau, he was still a plantation owner and a powerful man among the citizens of Valdosta, and had been personally invited by the Regimental Commander to come welcome the train. A dubious honor,

John Henry thought. His father should have proudly turned down the invitation and watched the train arrive from the comfort of his own front porch, since the Holliday's new home was just across the railroad tracks on Savannah Avenue. But Henry obviously enjoyed being courted for his vote, as he readily accepted the Commander's invitation. At least his father had left Rachel at home, John Henry thought with grudging gratitude, though home was so close that everyone could see her standing out in the fenced front yard, giggling like a girl and waving a white handkerchief at the arriving train. Did she realize that the handkerchief looked like a sign of surrender? John Henry had little enough respect for Rachel as it was, and she was doing precious little to earn any more.

The brassy noise of the regimental band pulled his thoughts away from Rachel and brought him to quick attention. The band was playing *Dixie* in honor of the vanquished foes, then broke into a rousing rendition of *The Battle Hymn of the Republic* – half the crowd cheering one tune, half the crowd cheering the other. But as they started into *The Star Spangled Banner*, the music was blessedly drowned out by the squeal and moan of the braking train, iron on iron, a truer anthem of America. Then J.W. Clift himself finally appeared, smaller than John Henry had thought he would be, balder and rounder, and looking hardly worth all the effort that had gone into his imminent demise. But when he took a place on the back platform of the train and raised his arms to quiet the noisy crowd, his words had a fierceness that belied his small stature and meek appearance.

"My friends! My dear, Southern friends!" His voice had a nasal tone that spoke of his Northern birth. "What an honor it is to come among you! What a beautiful country you have here, so full of opportunity for those who seek and strive! Why, just this day I was crossing through the great swamp the Indians called the Okefenokee, a land of alligators and venomous snakes. A dangerous land, certainly. But it occurs to me that with some effort that land might be rid of its alligators, and those waters made safe for navigation, those swamps made healthy for cultivation. So it is all over the beautiful Southland in these days following our recent conflict. The land is ripe and ready for the taking, once the alligators are rid from our midst. My friends, there are alligators among us! But cast your vote for J.W. Clift, and I will vow to rid these swamps of danger. Cast your vote, men of Lowndes County, for J.W. Clift, and let us strive together to make our country safe!" Then, as if on cue, the brass band started up again, this time offering a discordant version of Stephen Foster's *Suwannee River*, an ironic choice, considering the alligator talk.

The Courthouse had no real porch around it, so a raised platform had been constructed for the rally, leading off the wooden staircase and placing the speakers high above the crowd where their voices could carry out over the townspeople who had come to enjoy the spectacle. John Henry was enjoying it himself from his chosen vantage point in the doorway of Griffin's General Store. Behind the store, Alex Darnell's horses were saddled and ready to ride as soon as Jack Calhoun lit the fuse that would blow the Courthouse high into the blue spring sky. Jack had insisted on being the lighter; he was the oldest of the Vigilantes, he said, and more experienced at such things from his time in the artillery during the War. But John Henry figured there was more to Jack's insistence than strategy. Killing J.W. Clift was Jack Calhoun's way of taking personal revenge on the Yanks for the death of his friend Dick Force.

"Everything's ready, just about," Sam Griffin said as he stepped out from the store behind John Henry, sharing his space in the doorway.

"Just about?"

"Jack's nervous we didn't put enough charge in the keg, after all. I told him it was plenty, that my Pa would notice if I took any more. He's fidgety, though. Says if it doesn't blow clean, they'll be more trouble. So I just snuck him a little more. He's puttin' it out there now."

"In front of everyone?" John Henry asked, impressed by Jack's bravery.

"It'll be all right. Nobody's watchin', anyhow. They're all caught up in Mr. Carpetbagger."

"My dear Southern friends!" Clift was saying, "my dear *colored* Southern friends..." and he waited for effect while the colored men in the crowd, along with a few colored women, cheered him. "My dear *colored* friends," he said again, his voice rising like a preacher's putting down Satan and raising up righteousness, "shall you forever be in bondage to your old owners? Did our beloved, martyred President Lincoln not set you free?"

There were murmurs of assent, "yes, yessir," the voices droned, "Massa Lincoln set me free. He died to set me free..."

"Did not the God of Heaven make you equal? Then be a man!" he thundered. "Let the slave-holding aristocracy no longer rule you! Vote for a constitution that will educate your children free of charge! Vote for a constitution that relieves the poor debtor from his rich creditor! Vote for a constitution that allows you a liberal homestead for your families! And more than all, vote for a constitution that places you on a level with those who used to boast that for every slave they were entitled to a three-fifth's vote in congressional representation!" Then his voice dropped to a dramatic whisper. "My dear colored friends. Is this not freedom? Education without charge, relief from your debts, a home for your family, a place in society beside the men who were your oppressors? Does not this country owe you as much?"

"Amen, amen, this country do," came the reply.

"Then, friends, there is only one thing for you to do. Vote Republican in the coming election, elect me and the men like me, who will see to it that all these things are given to you. Turn away from the Democratic-Conservatives who have held you in bondage these many years. The Republican Party offers you ease and equality, and asks nothing but your vote. I ask again, dear friends, is this not freedom?"

"What's takin' Jack so long?" Sam asked, growing restless as the speech ran on. "He should have had that powder placed by now, with no train and all..."

"What did you say?"

"I said he decided to light the fuse with no train. Said it would blow better that way."

John Henry stared at him in disbelief. "It won't blow better. It'll blow him up! You can't light that much powder at the keg. Surely Jack knows that, his bein' in the Army with Dick Force and all..."

And as Sam looked back at him in horror, they both realized at the same moment what Jack Calhoun's real plan was. He aimed to blow up the Courthouse all right – and himself along with it, going to meet his lost friend in some better world.

"We've got to stop him before he kills himself!" Sam cried.

"No we don't," John Henry said with a sudden comprehension of the situation.

"What do you mean? Of course we do!"

"Not we," John Henry said steadily, "me. I'm the only one can get close enough to the Courthouse right now without drawin' suspicion. Jack's already crawlin' around under the stairs. If you start crawlin' around down there, too, the Yanks will figure somethin's goin' on. The guards are used to seein' me there. Likely they'll let me pass without lookin' twice."

Sam considered only a moment before nodding. "All right then, John Henry, you go. I reckon I better stay behind, keep an eye on things here at the store."

He couldn't blame Sam for looking relieved. Neither one of them wanted to take a chance at being blown up.

Getting close to the Courthouse was the easy part, pushing his way through the crowd of onlookers listening to the speeches. But getting close to Jack was another story. There was a ring of Yankee soldiers on the ground around the speaker's platform, rifles raised and aimed into the crowd. They meant business and they weren't letting anyone through – not even a polite Rebel boy.

"But Sir," he said with wide-eyed pleading, "my Pa's up on that speaker's stand, and I got to get a message to him!"

"Give me the message, and I'll pass it on," the guard said, standing his ground.

"I can't, Sir. It's..." he cast around in his mind, looking for some likely-sounding excuse why he should be let through. "It's personal," he said at last. "It's my Ma, you see. She's in a way of needin' him bad."

And something in his words struck the guard as very funny, and he let out a laugh.

"Well, Son, if your Mama's in a way of needing a man all that bad, you just run and tell her the Regiment will be right down to take care of her!"

It took John Henry a moment to understand the Yankee's lewd joke, and by then he was too scared to be angry. With every passing minute, Jack Calhoun was getting closer to lighting that keg and blowing them all up. Somehow he had to get through that military guard.

But the soldier kept laughing, and his laughter caught the attention of one of the other guards, a big black man in Yankee blue.

"What's so funny?" he asked.

"This Reb boy wants to get through the guard," the first soldier replied. "Says his Mama's needing his Papa home right away – says she needs a man. I say we go take care of her ourselves, so his Papa don't have to be disturbed. What do you think about that?"

But the black man didn't laugh. He just looked at John Henry with a gleam of recognition in his eyes, then he smiled with teeth as white as a panther's.

"I know this boy," he said smugly. "I know his Pa, too, and he ain't even on the stand. Seems to me this boy's been lyin' to you, and I'm wonderin' why. What's he want to do that he shouldn't ought to be doin'?" Then he pushed the barrel of his rifle against John Henry's ribs. "What you lyin' about now, Reb boy?"

He almost cursed himself for not having pandered to the soldier's arrogance the last time they had met. But it was too late for bowing and scraping now. He looked from the black soldier to the white soldier, and knew there was no way he could get through them both. There was nothing left to do but yell.

"Gunpowder!" he hollered at the top of his lungs. "Under the stand! There's a keg of gunpowder about to blow down there!"

The sudden panic surprised him, as his warning was answered by screams from the onlookers and a near riot on the speaker's stand. The guards around the steps were pushed aside as a flood of politicians shoved each other down from the stand, stepping on anything and anyone in their way. John Henry only hoped the screaming and the running had made Jack Calhoun reconsider his suicidal plans.

But as he tried to push his way through the confused guards to find Jack, the black soldier grabbed ahold of him and held him back. "Not so fast. The commander will be wantin' to speak to you, Reb boy who knows so much. I reckon I was right in keepin' my eyes on you."

John Henry's own eyes were fixed on the crawlspace under the steps, where two more guards were pulling another young man out from the shadows.

"Jack!" he called out, unable to free himself from the soldier's grasp enough to manage a wave. "Jack Calhoun! You're still alive!"

But there was no answering greeting, only the dull stare of a young man whose death wish had been dashed like the rest of his hopes. Jack was alive, all right, and it was John Henry's fault that he was.

"Friends, huh?" the black soldier said, smiling. "Well, I guess you can have some company when you hang. You know they hang traitors, don't you? String 'em up like this..." and to demonstrate, he yanked on John Henry so hard his feet came right up off the ground and he yelped out in pain.

Then a voice spoke from behind them, cool and commanding.

"That'll do. You can put him down now."

And to his relief, John Henry looked up into the steely eyes of his father, come to rescue him.

"And why should I do that?" the soldier asked, putting John Henry down but keeping a strong hand on him. "Don't look to me like you got any say around here anymore, Major Holliday. You been put out as Freedmen's Agent. And this boy's goin' up to talk to the Commander, tell him what he knows."

For all his commanding presence, Henry Holliday was still no physical match for the soldier, big and heavy-muscled as a plowhand. But what Henry lacked in stature he more than made up for in boldness.

"Well then, we'll just go together to see the Commander," he said with a nod. "And I'm sure he'll be interested in hearin' how you've been mistreatin' the boy who just saved his life. Probably give you jail time yourself for your rough handlin' of him, or run you out of the service altogether. 'Course there's always plenty of work to be done back in the fields where you come from. I'm sure I can manage to find you a good position around the County somewhere."

For a moment the soldier's big black hand tightened on John Henry's shoulder, and he winced in pain again. Then the man loosened his grasp a little.

"What do you mean, the boy who saved his life? This boy's been in on somethin' for a while. I know it."

Then to John Henry's astonishment, he heard his father let out a laugh.

"What you know ain't worth listenin' to!" Henry said, laughing again, loud and robust like John Henry had never in life heard him do. Henry rarely even smiled; he never laughed.

But he was laughing now, so hard that there were tears coming down his face.

"Big Nigger like you gets a nice uniform, thinks that makes him smart! Of course my boy's been up to somethin'! He's been workin' for the Commander for months now, doin' errands and such. You think just because the Yanks freed the slaves, they know how to get along without someone doin' their business for them? Why, without John Henry and boys like you, your commander couldn't take himself a decent piss. In fact, the commander was just tellin' me as much the other day, glad he's got a big buck like you waitin' on him hand and foot..."

It was all a lie, of course, and John Henry knew it. But the soldier didn't know as much as he thought he did, least of all the cunning of a Confederate officer who was trying to save his son.

"You been talkin' with the Commander?" the soldier asked, wavering a little.

"Just 'cause Washington put me out as Agent don't mean the Commander's done with me," Henry replied, lying again. "So let's go, boy. Let's see what your Commander has to say about all this."

If the soldier had been a Northern colored, or even a Southern city colored, he might have held his position. But he was a plantation colored, born and bred, and used to being ordered around by arrogant Southern planters.

"I say let's go, boy," Henry said again, his voice hanging on the word *boy*. "Or let my son go and get along about your business."

There was nothing the soldier could do under the circumstances but release John

Henry and walk away, broad shoulders hunched like he'd been horse whipped.

"Oh, Pa!" John Henry said, turning back toward his father with a heart torn between relief and amazement. "You saved me..."

But he'd barely gotten the words out when Henry's hand came down across his face, slapping him so hard it nearly knocked him over.

"Don't you ever shame me again, d'hear me? Don't you ever make me grovel for you again! Bad enough you waste all your time down at Sam Griffin's place, drinkin' and such, but goin' in on this fool business..."

"It wasn't fool business, Pa. We were Vigilantes..." The word had seemed so adventurous, until now.

"Gunpowder in the hands of children looks like fool business to me. And it don't make no difference to me who got it, or why, so save the excuses. You're just damn lucky I happened to be nearby or you'd be headed off to jail by now like your fool friends. I expect Sam Griffin was in on this too, and Darnell's boy Alex..."

"Jail?" John Henry said, rubbing his aching jaw as he stared wide-eyed at his father. "They're goin' to jail?"

"That's what we do with law-breakers in this country. Just pray the commander turns them over to the civil authorities instead of lettin' the military deal with them. It's Martial Law, John Henry, and we're still the enemy. Now get on home and make yourself useful. You're done with those boys."

~~~~~~~~~

Henry was right about the boys being thrown into jail, and it didn't take the Federals long to get them there. Once the unexploded powder keg was hauled out from under the Courthouse steps, bearing the mark of Griffin's General Store, the soldiers knew right where to look for the rest of the conspirators. They made quick work of it and found Sam Griffin still at the store, waiting for his friends to return, along with Alex Darnell still holding his father's horses out back for their getaway. By nightfall, all the boys had been rounded up and hustled off to the same dank jail cell from which they had once helped Dick Force to escape. All the boys except John Henry, whose father had gotten him off in the nick of time.

So while his friends spent the night on the hard plank floor of the County jail, John Henry tossed and turned on his feather mattress. He deserved to be in jail with them; he almost wished he were. For though his father would surely mete out punishment for his misdeed, knowing his friends were suffering without him made him feel all the more guilty. Nothing Henry could do to him would be punishment enough to make up for his undeserved freedom. Even Henry's open hand across his face hadn't hurt all that much. Angry as his father had been, it was the most attention he had paid his son in longer than John Henry could remember.

But the boys didn't have to languish in jail for long. As soon as the commander turned them over to the civil authorities, the Sheriff took bond and set them free again, pending civil action. The Superior Court could deal with them when the calendar opened up some. Until then, the judge was busy with more important matters, like a neighborly disputation over a fence line and the theft of some prized chickens. The opinion of most of the good people of Valdosta was that the boys had meant no real harm since the keg had been found to have no fuse or train attached. Surely, they couldn't have meant to light it, only scare folks a little. And as it was, it was the coloreds in the community who were scared the most, fearing that the unlit gunpowder was a warning to them of what would happen if they dared to vote Republican in the upcoming election. Thanks to the gunpowder plot, there'd likely be a landslide victory for the Democratic-Conservative ticket, come Election Day. So all in all, things had come out fine, and the town turned its attention to other matters.

But the Federals weren't so easily distracted. Gunpowder under a speaker's platform, exploded or not, was clearly an act of aggression. And since the speaker on the platform had been a United States official, a Registrar of Voting assigned by General Pope himself, the gunpowder plot was an act of treason as well. So once word got to General Meade in Atlanta that traitors to the United States of America had been set free by the local authorities, the boys were in worse trouble than before.

The first John Henry heard of it was a banging on his bedroom door late one moonless night.

"Get up and get dressed!" his father's voice commanded.

Even half-asleep, John Henry knew better than to disobey his father, and he rolled out of his rope-slung bed and reached for his clothes.

"What's goin' on, Pa?' he said, opening his bedroom door and blinking in the light of the oil lamp his father held to light the dark hallway.

"You're goin' to Jonesboro. Pack your things, and be quick about it."

"Jonesboro? But it's the middle of the night! Why am I goin' there?"

"To save you from your own fool self," Henry said. "Colonel Bessant's in the

96

parlor. He's just got word that the Yankees are comin', General Meade's men. They're plannin' on takin' your friends off to prison in Savannah to stand a military trial. So I'm gettin' you out of town before they get here."

John Henry was wide-awake by now, but his father's words still made no sense to him.

"But why should I leave town?" he asked. "You got me off already. I didn't even get arrested. What can the Yankees do to me?"

"Plenty, if your friends decide to talk. 'Cause arrested or not, you're still as guilty as the rest of them. Now pack up. We haven't got much time."

But John Henry had no desire to be leaving town just when things were getting hot again.

"But Pa, what if Jack and the boys need my help? They'll think I'm a coward, or worse, for runnin' away..."

"Runnin' is what you should have done the first time you heard of this business. A boy's got no place playin' in a man's work."

"I'm not a boy!" he said stubbornly. "I'm near seventeen-years old now, nigh unto bein' a man myself..."

Henry cut him off with a cold glare.

"Are you man enough to hang? For that's what General Meade plans to do with those boys, once he's finished tryin' them. Treason's a hangin' crime, John Henry. You think you're man enough for that?"

The thought of his friends with their necks in a hanging noose made him feel so strangled himself that he couldn't even speak an answer. But his heart was racing like a horse whipped to a lather. How could he leave when his friends might need him? What would they think of him when they found out he'd gone off and left them? And how could his father not understand that his place was with the Vigilantes, not away off in Jonesboro hiding out like some sissy boy?

But he couldn't disobey his father, so he did as he was told and packed his things, ready for the long ride to Jonesboro. And the only consolation he could find was that Mattie would be there, and she, at least, would understand.

Chapter Six

Mattie Holliday had other things on her mind that summer, however, for Mattie had a beau, a young Confederate veteran from South Carolina whose wife had died during the bombing of Charleston and left him with a baby daughter to raise. Mattie hadn't actually met him yet, but they had exchanged letters and he was hoping to come to Jonesboro to court her. Her father had known him during the War and said he was a fine man, and her mother was delighted that he too was Catholic – there were so few Catholic boys in Georgia. It seemed a match made in heaven to everyone except John Henry, who couldn't believe that Mattie could be so disloyal.

"You can't be serious about this, Mattie!" he said, as they walked home from town together one warm evening soon after his arrival. "You don't even know him!"

"My father knows him and, of course, I trust his judgment for me. And besides, I think it's terribly romantic, the tragic young war hero and his motherless babe, saved from a life of desolation by true love come again. It fairly sweeps me off my feet!"

"Well, it sounds like dime novel nonsense to me!" John Henry said as he kicked at the dusty road in disgust. "Suppose he's crippled from the War, with one arm and a big glass eye? He wouldn't seem so romantic then, I bet!"

Mattie looked up at his flushed face and laughed. "Why, John Henry Holliday, I do believe you're jealous!"

He knew he was, but he couldn't let her know that. "Don't be stupid, Mattie. I just think you're too young for this kind of talk. Next you'll be thinkin' of marryin' this soldier."

"Well, of course, silly, that's why he wants to court me," she said condescendingly. "I'm eighteen now, plenty old enough to marry. Why, my mother had a husband and two babies by the time she was my age!"

How was it possible that Mattie had suddenly grown so much older? The year-and-a-half between their ages stretched out like an eternity in his mind. "I just think that you ought to wait for awhile..." He shrugged, not knowing what else to say, but his heart went on, *wait until I'm older and can ask for your hand...*

Mattie smiled at him with sympathy, the way she looked at her little sisters when they fell and bruised a knee. "Oh honey, I know we've always been best sweethearts, but that was just child's play. I'm a woman now, with a woman's heart, and I need a family of my own to love and care for. I wish you'd be happy for me."

And reflected in her shining eyes he saw himself the way Mattie saw him: just a tall, awkward boy who followed after her with loving eyes and silent longings. But his arms ached to hold her close and make her forget that soldier, make her forget anyone but him. There was a long silence between them, then Mattie slipped her hand into his and stood on tiptoe to kiss his cheek.

"Why, John Henry, I think it's sweet that you care for me so. I'm sure I'd be hurt if you weren't a little jealous. Please don't let this spoil our summer together. I'm so happy to have you here."

They walked on home, hand in hand as always, but he could still feel the touch of her lips on his face, and in his heart he heard the words that she had said when they were children together: *"I love you, I always have, and I always will."*

~~~~~~~~~~

Mattie's gentle rejection didn't help his mood any that summer. He was still angry at his father for sending him away from home and confused by a world that made even less sense now than it had during the War. If the Cause were just, why weren't they still fighting for it? And if it were unjust, why had they ever fought at all? He was at that idealistic age when everything needed an answer and all he seemed to have were questions – and his exile in Jonesboro wasn't helping any. His father had told Uncle Rob to put him to work, so John Henry was given a job at the newly completed granite train depot doing menial tasks no one else wanted to do: raking the gravel rail bed, scrubbing the wood plank walks, hauling coal and water – hard physical labor that was surely beneath his station, but left him with little time or energy to misbehave. After a long day in the scorching summer sun he was ready for a good meal and a soft bed, but there was still more work to be done. The horse in the barn behind the house needed tending, the kitchen garden was growing tall and thick with weeds, and Aunt Mary Anne always had extra chores to be done as well. The work went on right past sundown, six days a week.

On Sundays, there were family visits with relatives living out in the county – Aunt Martha Holliday who was married to wealthy Colonel Johnson and lived in a big house north of the depot, and Aunt Mary Anne's uncle Phillip Fitzgerald who still lived on the old plantation south toward Lovejoy's Station. John Henry sat quietly during those visits, dressed in his best wool suit, hot and uncomfortable in stuffy dark parlors, knowing he was the object of family talk –

"You remember Cousin Henry Holliday's boy, John Henry? He's here visitin' with Rob and Mary Anne for a while. His father had to send him here after that unfortunate trouble down in Valdosta…"

"Well, we've sure never had any trouble like that in this family before. Must be somethin' from that McKey side of his. You know how quiet his mother always was, and they do say still waters run deep..."

Then the voices would drop to a whisper and he would feel himself turning red with embarrassment and anger. If he hadn't been raised to be so polite he sure would set them all straight. Wasn't anything wrong in what he'd done, nothing at all. Why, there were vigilantes in every Southern town, Jonesboro even, horseback riders coming through just before sunset, guns showing, warning those free Negroes to mind themselves. Just a little show of strength to keep things orderly. Well, wasn't that what he'd done too? But they talked about it like he was some kind of outlaw.

But worse than the way the family talked about him was the way Mattie talked incessantly about her soldier-beau. Was he really handsome or just good-looking? Was he as tall as Father? Were his eyes blue as Mother's, or lighter, like John Henry's? It was hardest of all to hear himself compared to the hated stranger. It didn't matter one whit to him what the fellow was like, he was the enemy pure and simple, and Mattie was a traitor for caring about him. Hadn't she promised to always be his sweetheart? Funny how fast always could end.

~~~~~~~~~~

It was hard to get away from Mattie's soldier talk in a house that was filled with Hollidays clear up to the attic, the room he shared with little Jim Bob, the baby born to Aunt Mary Anne that Christmas in Valdosta. So sometimes at night when he thought everyone else had gone to sleep, he'd quietly climb around Jim Bob's little bed and steal down the attic stair, past the room that Mattie shared with her sister Lucy, and go outside to sit alone in the darkness of the back porch. He liked the stillness of the night when all the sounds seemed close and clear – the music of the crickets, the low drone of the katydids in the trees, and far away, the lonely whistle of a train headed south from Atlanta. And out in the moonlit shadows, under the backyard trees, there rested those two heroes buried in the garden – strange companions in the silence.

What he wanted was Mattie by his side, understanding him and helping him to understand life. What he needed was a fast horse and an open stretch of country, room to run and burn off the turbulent feelings that tore at him. So one sultry summer afternoon he quit work early and went on back to his Uncle's house, saddled the family horse, and rode out onto dusty Church Street.

Just past the edge of town Church Street joined up with the Fayetteville Road, the old stagecoach route that wound from Whitesburg all the way to Decatur. West of town, the road crossed over swampy Flint River into Fayette County where the Hollidays had first settled. To the south was the track that led down to Lovejoy's Station, through rich red farmland and cotton plantations. He turned the horse loose and took off at a gallop, headed nowhere in particular. But Uncle Rob's animal knew the country well and had made that ride to the south over and over again, and by the time John Henry tightened his hold on the reins he was halfway to Lovejoy, pulling up to the drive of Phillip Fitzgerald's place.

The Fitzgerald farm had been a fine plantation once, before the Yankees had ruined the cotton fields and everything else. But old Phillip, Irish stubborn, just plowed up the fields and started again. John Henry could see the result of that hard-headedness: acres of rich red furrows curving across the rolling hillsides, surrounding the white frame house in an ocean of cotton. Phillip had put everything he had into that ground, not minding that his home was hardly suited to a wealthy plantation owner. It was a rambling, doddering old dowager of a place, facing sideways toward the road, not bothering to put its best face forward. Phillip had bought the house along with the land when he first came to the country, adding onto it every time another daughter was born. Plenty of space was all the family needed, he insisted – what really mattered was the land.

"John Henry Holliday, is that you?" From the shadows by the front door a lilting feminine voice called out to him, and he was startled into answering.

"Yes, Ma'am. Sorry to bother you, Ma'am." He couldn't see the person to whom the voice belonged, but it sounded too young to be Phillip's wife, Eleanor. Of course, with all those daughters on the place, it could be almost anyone. The horse snorted and tossed its head impatiently, ready to move up the drive.

"Well, are you comin' on up or not? We're 'bout ready to start supper if you're stayin'."

"Hadn't planned on it. I'm just out for a ride." It was disconcerting talking to the shadows like that.

"Well, suit yourself." The voice paused for a moment, as if considering. "You tell Cousin Mattie I said hello."

He jerked the reins and the horse pulled around to the side. "Who is that up there?" he called. "Come on out where I can see your face."

Musical laughter, then a dimpled smile in a halo of golden hair: "Why, it's only Sarah, John Henry. Don't you remember me?"

Even from across the yard he could see the blue of her eyes, thick lashed and shining. She was Phillip Fitzgerald's second oldest daughter, close to Mattie's age and every inch a young woman. She was tiny like all the Fitzgerald girls, with that wasp waist just about as big around as a man's two hands put together, and a softly curving figure above and below. She put her hands on that little waist and tipped her head to one side, making her curly hair bounce in the afternoon light. "Well? Are you stayin'?"

Of course he couldn't stay. No one even knew he was gone, and it would be coming on dark soon. He was just about to tell her so when his legs seemed to take a life of their own and swung him down out of the saddle and onto the drive. Sarah smiled and those dimples showed again.

"I'll go and tell cook to set another place," she said, then she turned and disappeared into the house, the porch door giving a sigh as it swung closed behind her.

So there he was joining the Fitzgeralds for supper, with a stable boy tending to his horse, and wondering all along how it had happened. He went through supper in a daze, listening to Phillip's thick brogue expounding on the price of cotton and the ravages of the boll weevil, thankful that nobody asked him how he happened to be out riding by their place just before dusk like that. And every now and then he'd look up and catch Sarah looking at him across the table with a shy flutter of lashes that set his head spinning. What was he doing here, anyhow?

Supper took forever but cleaning up took no time at all, with all the daughters rushing dishes off the table and into the kitchen. And suddenly he found himself on the moonlit front porch with pretty Sarah, a housemaid at a discreet distance, and those bright blue eyes looking up at him as if he were God Almighty. What else could he do? He slid his arms around that inviting little waist and stole a kiss from those sweet dimpled lips. And though he still had no idea how it had happened, it sure felt good to have a pretty girl in his arms. Damn Mattie for making him so miserable all summer! It gave him a sense of sweet revenge to know that it was Mattie's own cousin he kissed there in the moonlight.

Sarah laughed a little when he kissed her a second time, and it startled him. "What's so funny, Miss Sarah?"

"Nothin' at all, Cousin." He wasn't really her relation, only first-cousin to her first-cousin, but it sounded nice and friendly. "I guess I just had a mind that you and Cousin Mattie were sweethearts."

"Mattie?" He laughed too, but with a bitter edge. "Mattie's all but engaged to that soldier boy of hers."

"Well, I'm awful glad to hear it, 'cause I sure wouldn't want to steal her beau away from her." She cast her eyes demurely down, and her lashes made little crescents on her rosy cheeks. "And I had been hopin' that you might notice me."

John Henry looked down at her and began to realize just what was happening. There were seven daughters in the Fitzgerald family, and few men of any eligible age since the War. No wonder he had received such a quick invitation to supper and a gentle push toward the front porch with one of the oldest girls. Well fine, if that was the way it was. It was about time that somebody realized he wasn't a boy any longer. And Sarah was just about the prettiest thing he had ever seen. Might not be bad to be her beau, not bad at all.

"I've heard folks talkin' about what you did down in Valdosta," she said, "tryin' to chase out the Yanks and all." Her eyes were dazzling in the moonlight, staring up at him like that. "I think it was mighty brave of you."

Brave was he? "Mattie doesn't think so. She says it was just plain foolishness, and could have gotten somebody killed."

"Well, as long as you weren't killed." Her voice slowed a little as she said it, and her face dimpled again with that smile that made him feel like he'd just whipped the whole Yankee army single-handed. Why didn't Mattie ever look at him like that? She just bossed and scolded and treated him like a child the way she always had.

"I guess it was dangerous, but I'm a damned good shot. I could have handled myself, if it had come to that."

He raised his right arm over her head and aimed his hand into the starry sky, and Sarah gave a little "Oh!" when he pretended to pull the trigger.

"Wherever did you learn to shoot like that?" she asked in a flutter.

"My father taught me," he said, and knew all at once that he shouldn't have said it. He had a sudden memory of his father taking him out rabbit hunting in Valdosta. He remembered those days with a rush of emotion that stung at the back of his throat: happy days for him, before his mother had died and his father had married again.

Rachel. The memory of her laughter in the night made him sick to his stomach. He looked down at Sarah with a strange suffocating feeling and pulled his arms away from her. He didn't belong here. He shouldn't be doing this.

"Why, John Henry, is somethin' wrong? You look all pale. Why don't you sit down and let me get you somethin' to drink? Would you like a little lemonade?"

"No, I...I need to be goin'. It's gettin' mighty late, isn't it?"

"Are you sure you're all right? I can have someone drive you home in the wagon. You can tie your horse to the back if you want. Wouldn't be any trouble at all."

"No!" The last thing he wanted was to be coming home in the Fitzgerald's wagon after disappearing into the night, like some lost boy being escorted home.

"No, I'll ride. There's plenty of moonlight tonight."

"I know," she said, and turned her head up to gaze at the indigo sky, "lots of nice moonlight tonight." Then she laid her hand against his chest and asked sweetly, "You'll come again soon, won't you? Before that lovely moon is all gone?"

How had he gotten himself into this fix?

"Why, sure, I'll be back. You just keep that moon hangin' there for me." It was a boldfaced lie, and there'd be hell to pay if Mattie ever found out he'd led her very own cousin on like that. Shameful behavior. What did they do to men who seduced innocent young women? He was sure he deserved whatever it was.

He left her standing there on the porch, waving him a sweet good-bye. He would never be able to face Sarah Fitzgerald again, not as long as he lived. He was a cad and had ruined her innocence, kissing her like that right in front of the whole world. It was as good as a marriage proposal, he knew, and now here he was riding back to Jonesboro in the dark, longing to hold Mattie, wishing it had been her there in the shadows.

"Where have you been?" Mattie was waiting for him back of the house, scolding him while he unsaddled the horse. "Father is fit to be tied about the horse bein' gone, and Mother is nearly frantic." She stroked the animal's face, and in the moonlight her hair was as red-brown as its russet coat.

"I just went for a ride," he answered, trying to stay on the far side of the horse from her, avoiding her eyes.

"Fine time to go ridin', in the dark!"

"It wasn't dark when I left."

"Well, where did you go that kept you so long?"

The uncomfortable feeling he'd carried all the way home was turning to irritation. "I said I just went for a ride. What do you care?"

"I care plenty, seein' as how I had to walk all the way up to the depot today to bring you your letter. And when I got there, all hot and dusty, you weren't even around. Where did you go to, anyhow?"

"What letter?" he asked, not bothering to answer her question.

"From your father, the one you've been waitin' for. It came inside a letter for my parents."

She knew, of course, that he had been watching the mail for a letter from his father with forgiveness and a train ticket home. He was tired of railroad work and ready to get back to school. At least his summer of exile had taught him one thing: he didn't want a life of physical labor. One more year of school and he could go on to college, learn to be a doctor like Uncle John, the richest man in the family. Sure would be nice to live in a fancy house like his Uncle John's, with white columns and polished wood floors and servants bringing in dinner across the breezeway from the kitchen out back. And when he pictured himself in that kind of life, there was always Mattie by his side, dark eyes glowing, loving only him.

"Well, anyhow, here it is," she said, slipping the letter out of the hidden pocket of her skirt. "Though I don't think you deserve it after tonight."

He looked up at her with a sudden flush of color in his face, sure she was reading his thoughts. "Tonight?"

"After you stole the horse and all."

"Oh, that. I only borrowed it." Then he tore open the envelope and started to read aloud:

"Dear Son,

I hope that all is going well for you there in Jonesboro, and that you are being of

great help to your Uncle Robert and Aunt Mary Anne, and remember always your
manners and the debt of gratitude you owe them for taking you in."

He glanced at Mattie with embarrassment. His father was still lecturing him, even from two-hundred miles away –

"Our businesses here are doing well, and I hope to see a good profit at year's end. I
am thinking of adding carriages to the stock of buggies we carry in town, which should
do well here in Valdosta where there are no other carriage dealers as yet.

In light of the recent news that Martial Law has been lifted once again following the
ratification of the Fourteenth Amendment by the Constitutional Convention at Macon,
I feel that you will be safe in returning home. The military can no longer molest you for
your misdoings here, and the civil authorities are unlikely to pursue the matter further.
Your friends have all been released from their incarceration in Savannah on a $200,000
bond raised by the merchants of Valdosta. I paid a share, as well, with the stipulation
that the boys be sent away from Valdosta for a time, so there won't be any more such
trouble. Of course, I will expect you to be circumspect in your behavior when you return,
paying all due allegiance to your new government. If I, a soldier of the Confederacy, can
take the Oath of Allegiance and pledge to uphold the honor of the United States, then
you, a mere boy, can certainly bow yourself to the civil authority..."

He stopped reading and said in disgust, "How can he be so cowardly, givin' in to the Federals like that? Damn pack of lyin' Yanks!" Then he crumpled the letter and threw it to the ground.

"Hush that swearin'!" Mattie scolded him. "Mother will hear you for sure."

She handed him a curry brush, and he went to work with a vengeance on the horse's coat.

"Well it's a fact, lyin' Yanks! And after all they've done against us! After all they've done to me, gettin' me sent away from home..."

"You're talkin' nonsense. You know you got your own self sent away for tryin' to kill that congressman. If your father hadn't hustled you out of town, you might have ended up in prison like your friends, or worse. What if the soldiers had come after you, too?"

"I reckon I'm handy enough with a gun to take care of myself," he boasted. "I could have finished off a few Yanks, if it'd come to that."

Mattie stopped to look at him over the horse's back, shaking her head. "John Henry Holliday, you have entirely too much pride, and it will land you in a heap of trouble one day!"

It was bad enough to be reprimanded by his father and uncle. He didn't need to have Mattie criticize him as well.

"Don't treat me like a child!" he said, grabbing the reins away from her and leading the horse into the barn.

"Well stop actin' like one then, runnin' off without even sayin' where you're goin'!"

She stood in the doorway behind him, the moonlight making a dark halo around her. He had a sudden notion that her skin looked just like ivory silk in that silvery light, and he threw caution and good sense to the wind.

"Do you really want to know where I was?" he asked suddenly. "Well, I'll tell you. I was havin' supper with the Fitzgeralds. Miss Sarah invited me."

Mattie's eyes opened wide. "Sarah invited you? Why would she invite only you and not the rest of the family?"

"Well, I don't think she's interested in the rest of the family, Mattie," he said with a lazy drawl, taunting her. "Not like she's interested in me."

A trace of surprise and something else went across her face, then she forced a laugh. "Don't be silly, you're not near old enough for her! What do you know about courtin'?"

"Stop it, Mattie!" he said, the teasing suddenly over. "Stop treatin' me like I'm still a child!" His blood was boiling from the arguing, his mind still clouded from the confusion of the evening, and he reached for her arms and pulled her close to him.

"Let go of me, John Henry!" she said, trying to twist away from him.

"I will not."

"I want you to let me go!"

His voice was husky with emotion. "I love you, Mattie, you know I do!" he said, and bent his head close to hers, letting the sweet smell of her skin fill his mind as his arms slid around her.

She stared up at him, her eyes dark and wide as a frightened deer. "What are you doin'?"

Until that very moment he didn't know himself, but suddenly it was all so very clear. He knew just what he needed to rid himself of his frustrations, and just how to get it. "I'm gonna kiss you, Mattie, right here and now, in this lovely moonlight," he said, echoing Sarah's words without thinking.

Mattie caught her breath, "You wouldn't dare! You know I've got a beau. What would he think?"

108

"I don't give a damn what he thinks, or what your parents think either! Hell Mattie, right now I don't hardly care what you think."

He held her tighter, and she wriggled and hissed at him, "You are the most selfish, arrogant, vain..."

His kiss smothered her words into silence, and for a startled moment she stopped struggling, leaning toward him. Then she slipped one arm free from his embrace and swung back with all her might, slapping him hard against the side of his face. He let her go, stunned, and she finished the thought his kiss had interrupted:

"...despicable thing! Get your vile hands off of me!"

He laid his fingers against his burning face, speechless.

Mattie put her head up proudly. "I am goin' in the house now, and if you try to stop me, I swear I'll scream and wake my parents. And my father will not be as gentle with you as I have been. Good night, John Henry!" And she swept out of the barn with as much dignity as her wounded innocence would allow.

John Henry's mind was reeling, his ear ringing from the blow of Mattie's hand. She was right to slap him. He would have been disappointed in her if she hadn't, after he'd forced himself on her like that. But for a fleeting moment she had leaned up toward him, and almost kissed him back. He knew it and she knew it, and that was all that mattered.

Then he smiled to himself. He'd just kissed two girls in one night.

~~~~~~~~~~

He left Jonesboro two days later, taking the first train headed south, going home to face his father and the Freedmen's Bureau. He made his polite apologies to Mattie, standing under the covered platform at the depot waiting for the train, and she nodded her forgiveness. She understood, of course, that he had been distraught over his father's letter, and not at all himself. But when she raised her eyes to say goodbye, there was a spark of acknowledgment there. They were neither one of them children anymore. His kiss had changed all of that forever.

Henry met him at the depot in Valdosta with stern admonitions about staying out of political trouble, but John Henry had no intention of getting involved in that kind of business again. The Cause was truly lost when a loyal Confederate like himself could get sent away by his own folks.

" 'Course, you won't have much time to get into trouble nowadays, anyhow," Henry commented as he loaded John Henry's luggage into the wagon for the short ride home to the house on Savannah Street. "You'll be workin' after school every day now. I've got you a position in town."

"What are you talkin' about, Pa?" John Henry asked, bewildered, though he should have been accustomed to the way his father liked springing things on him suddenly. "What kind of position? Doin' what?"

"Workin' with Dr. Lucian Frink, the new dentist just moved down here from Jasper. You know how we've been tryin' to get a dentist to come to Valdosta for some time now. I guess the Institute finally attracted one, with all these new families movin' into town to enroll their children. I reckon you'd rather work for one of the medical doctors since that's the career you're aimin' at, but Dr. Frink's the one who needed help. His office is right next door to my store, so I know you'll be punctual."

"I don't know what to say, Pa. I hadn't expected..."

"You hadn't expected to work? Well, it's about time you started to pay your own way in life. I'm doin' better than I have in years, but that doesn't mean I can afford to send you to medical college. You'll have to put aside a pretty penny to pay your tuition, if you do manage to get yourself accepted."

"I meant that I hadn't expected you to find a job for me. I'm obliged, that's all."

"Damn right, you're obliged. If it hadn't been for my handlin' your trouble about the Courthouse, you'd have spent the summer in military prison like your friends. But don't think I'll come to your rescue like that again. You get yourself in another fix with the law, John Henry, you're on your own. I can't afford to risk my own good name mixin' in your misdoings. Next time..."

"There won't be a next time, Pa," John Henry assured him. "I'm through with all that, I promise. All I want to do is finish school and get on with my life."

"I'm glad to hear it. Now straighten your collar and make yourself presentable. Your mother is eager to see you, after all this time you've been gone."

"My mother?" For a fleeting moment his heart rose. Then his mind washed the pleasant impossibility away and he said heavily: "You mean Rachel."

"I mean my wife. And your stepmother, though you've never made much of an effort to make her feel like either one. She's a good woman, John Henry, and wants to be a good mother to you, if you'd let her. She's been cookin' all day, gettin' ready for your homecoming, and I expect you to behave with proper gratitude."

"Yessir," John Henry said, as the wagon turned off the dirt road and into the picket-fenced yard where Rachel had planted rows of flowers along the walk. Then, under his breath so his father wouldn't hear the sting of angry sarcasm in his voice, he added: "I'll behave just as politely as she deserves."

~~~~~~~~~~~

Things in the Holliday home were as unchanged as if John Henry had never gotten into trouble and gone away at all. Henry was still so busy with his business of carriage dealing and farming that he had little time for his son. Rachel was still intent on giving Henry a new heir, and spent her days making baby clothes that would probably never be worn, the way she kept conceiving and miscarrying one pregnancy after another. And even that was a constant reminder to John Henry of the fleeting nature of life and loyalty as his father participated lustily in Rachel's baby-making plans. Did it never occur to them that he could hear everything they were doing in their bedroom right across the hallway from his? Did they not realize that he was near eighteen-years-old now, and just hearing them made him angry and anxious all at once? To try and drown out the sound of them, he even brought the young housemaid into his own bedroom a time or two – a thing he never would have done with a white girl, of course, but Lizzie was Mulatto, and until the Emancipation had been the Holliday's bought and paid for slave, and that made any immorality more acceptable. But once he had her there he found he didn't really want her after all, and he sent her back to her loft room confused and complaining that Mr. John Henry sure did act peculiar sometimes. He knew he wasn't peculiar, though. It was just that he wanted Mattie, the way his father had Rachel, and he was sure that until he had her, nothing else would do.

It was a blessed relief to have to leave the house every morning, crossing the dirt road and the railroad tracks and walking up the hill to school for his final year of studies at the Valdosta Institute. He threw himself headlong into academics, excelling at every subject and finding that science and philosophy seemed to interest him the most. And as always, there were history and mathematics, composition and recitation, the long lines of literature to be memorized, the Latin phrases to translate and conjugate. But while others complained that Professor Varnedoe had never been as demanding as he was that final year, John Henry enjoyed the work and the security of school. The sameness of the school days, the routine of the school weeks, gave him a certain comfort in the chaos of his family life.

It was easier to attend to his studies, of course, with his friends all gone away. Willie Pendleton and Constantia Bessant had already graduated. Sam Griffin and the rest of the Vigilantes were out of prison and scattered to the homes of faraway relatives. And while John Henry still felt guilty that he had not been made to pay the price for recklessness as they had, he appreciated his freedom enough to keep quiet and behave himself. Besides, high marks would buy his ticket out of Valdosta forever, if his plans worked out. For while he had long wanted to follow in his Uncle John Holliday's footsteps and become a medical doctor, his after-school job with Dr. Lucian Frink had widened his view of the possibilities before him. Medicine was all well and good, but John Henry found that the dental work performed by Dr. Frink fascinated him even more.

Dr. Frink was the first full-time dentist John Henry had ever known, as most small-town dental work was done by physicians who pulled teeth as part of their surgical services, the way Uncle John had done back in Fayetteville. But as a graduate of the Pennsylvania College of Dental Surgery and a specialist in dentistry, Dr. Frink's work went far beyond just pulling teeth. There were decayed cavities to be cleaned out and filled with sheets of gold foil beaten paper-thin. There were crown restorations made of porcelain and gold fused together to look like real tooth enamel. There were artificial teeth carved out of ivory and set into bases of gold or vulcanized rubber. And the instruments the dentist used – forceps, turnkeys, excavators, pluggers, burnishers, burrs – were artists' tools for a profession that was as much art as science, and one that John Henry's talented hands longed to try. He had always been good at whittling, he told the dentist, and added without boasting that he was the fastest boy around when it came to draw and fire, with eyes so keen he could spot a rabbit running through the woods a hundred yards off. So when Dr. Frink smiled and said he seemed a natural for dentistry and ought to think about applying to the College of Dental Surgery himself, John Henry promised to give it some thought.

He thought about it, all right, through the long days at school and the even longer nights at home, and by the time graduation came, he had his mind all made up. With letters of recommendation from Dr. Frink and Professor Varnedoe, and with copies of his excellent grades from the Valdosta Institute, John Henry was all ready to apply to the Pennsylvania College of Dental Surgery. The only thing he needed was a promise from his father that Henry would help him pay the cost of the tuition – an exorbitant $100 per session.

It was the money that caught him up. Though Henry's business ventures were booming, he said flatly that he could not afford to send his son so far away for schooling. The Medical College at Augusta would have been one thing, but paying for the trips to Philadelphia and back and arranging for rooming in that expensive Northern city was quite another.

"Augusta was good enough for your Uncle John," Henry pronounced. "And it'll be damn good enough for you, as well."

Henry sat in the parlor, smoking his after-supper cigar and reading the paper out of Savannah, and being as dogmatic as ever. John Henry had long since stopped expecting Rachel to curb his father's swearing and smoking, the way Alice Jane had always tried to do. Rachel didn't seem to mind that the house was filled with blue smoke and blue language whenever Henry was around, though his son didn't dare emulate him. John Henry was still expected to keep a civil tongue and a cool temper, though cursing seemed more appropriate at the moment.

"The Medical College doesn't teach restorative dentistry," John Henry explained, trying for a voice balanced between instruction and supplication. "They teach extraction as part of the surgical curriculum. You can ask Uncle John about it if you don't believe me."

"Believin' you is beside the point," Henry said, taking a slow draw on his cigar. "Payin' for your expensive tastes is more like it. If you'll recall, I already sold off considerable land to pay your way through the Institute. Not to mention the money I paid into that bond to get your friends out of prison. Haven't seen much gratitude for any of that."

"I am grateful, Pa. Didn't I do well, as you told me to? I graduated top of my class, didn't I?" How Henry could always pull him away from the conversation at hand, make him feel so young and defenseless...

"Looks to me like you could learn what you need just by workin' for Dr. Frink," Henry went on, "and save me the cost of the schooling entirely. Surely he could train you good enough."

"He can train me in some things, and he'll have to, even if – even when," he corrected himself, "I go off to school. Dr. Frink will be my preceptor; the Dental College requires them. I'll work with him during the summer, learning clinical skills. But there's so much more that I need to know – chemistry, anatomy, physiology, metallurgy – it's a whole new field, Pa, a whole new world..."

"You always were a dreamer," Henry said flatly. "Just like your Ma..."

"Ma would have wanted me to go," he said quickly, taking the rare moment of reflection that Henry had offered. "You know what store she set in education. You know how much she always admired Uncle John..."

It was the wrong thing to say, John Henry realized as he watched Henry's expression change in the blink of a cold blue eye. Henry's words came out with a hiss and a cloud of smoke. "Yes, she always did admire your Uncle John, more than she should have."

John Henry felt his face flush. "You forget yourself, Pa," he said with emotion straining his voice. "My mother's memory deserves better." *And my mother deserved better than you,* he wanted to add, but kept himself from it. Angering his father would only keep him further from his goal and keep him home in Valdosta. If he wanted to leave his father's home behind, he needed to leave well enough alone. "I can come back every summer to work with Dr. Frink and earn a little money as well. The course work runs September until June, with a break until the fall..."

"Not this fall," Henry said. "This fall your cousin George Henry is gettin' married, up in Atlanta. I've been thinkin' of takin' you and Rachel along, makin' it a family reunion of sorts."

Henry hadn't said no, exactly, though he still hadn't said yes, and John Henry knew that the conversation was over for the time being. If he wanted to go in his father's good graces and with some of his father's good money, he'd have to abide by Henry's suddenly announced decision. No dental school this fall, or next spring either – then he realized what his father had said.

"A family reunion? Who all will be there?"

"Everybody, sounds like. Your Aunt Martha Holliday and Colonel Johnson and their boys, your Aunt Rebecca and that new husband of hers, Willie McCoin, and her boys. Glad Rebecca got herself married again, after your uncle John Jones got killed in the war, or we'd be supportin' her, too..."

"And Uncle Rob?" John Henry asked impatiently. "Is Uncle Rob comin'? Is his family comin', too?"

"I expect so, seein' as Jonesboro is just down the railroad from Atlanta. It's gonna be a big affair, so I hear. George is marryin' a real society girl, granddaughter of one of the biggest planters up in Tennessee. Old money. Not that old money is worth much anymore..."

Henry was about to start on another of his lectures on the economic decline of the South, so John Henry quickly excused himself from the room. If dental school had to wait, at least he had something else to look forward to. For if Uncle Rob were bringing his whole family to the wedding, then surely Cousin Mattie would be there, too. And along with his plans for dental school, John Henry had some even more personal plans, plans that he hoped Mattie would find pleasing.

He lay awake in bed half the night thinking how fine the fall was going to be after all.

Chapter Seven

Atlanta, 1869

John Stiles Holliday had been one of the wealthiest men in Fayetteville before the War came to Georgia and Fayette County became a foraging point for Yankee and Confederate troops alike. The Yanks burned most of the homes in the county, the Rebs stole most of the farm produce to feed the soldiers, and Fayette County was left nearly destitute. Then Reconstruction came, and times turned so hard that the County had to send as far off as Kentucky to buy corn and bacon for the hungry people of Fayetteville. And if the people had nothing to eat, they had less to share with the town doctor, who had taken his pay for services in cash and kind before then. Even his partnership in a general store didn't bring in enough money to support the doctor's household, so with no regular source of income and his own family of five and a houseful of servants to provide for, the good doctor had no choice but to move away, looking for better times.

Atlanta was having better times – boom times compared to Fayetteville, and soon after moving his family to the city, Dr. Holliday found himself gainfully employed again. To supplement his practice earnings he invested in another dry goods partnership, Tidwell and Holliday, and before long the dry goods store was making more money than the medical practice ever had, and Dr. John Stiles Holliday found himself in the unusual position of being a prosperous grocer with a medical degree. But that was Atlanta in the Reconstruction – fortunes were being made every day by people who didn't mind changing with the times.

After three years in their new home, the Hollidays were well on their way to becoming one of the leading families in the city. Mrs. Holliday was a pillar of the Presbyterian Church. The Holliday boys attended school at fine academies on Peachtree Street. And when the eldest son, George Henry, announced his engagement to Miss Mary Elizabeth Wright, daughter of another of Atlanta's new entrepreneurs, the event was hailed as one of the highlights of the Atlanta social season. Guests from all over Georgia were invited to attend — including the Holliday's cousins from all the way down in Valdosta.

John Henry had been to Atlanta a time or two before, traveling up from Griffin with his father on business before the war. But the town he had known then, and the city he saw now, as the train pulled in that November afternoon, had nothing in common but a name. The old Atlanta had been a busy place at the terminus of two railroads. The new Atlanta was booming, all hustle and bustle and filled with the noise of construction going up everywhere. The sound of Atlanta, as John Henry would ever after remember it, was the sound of hammer and nail, chisel and saw.

After Sherman's siege had destroyed half the city, Atlanta had lost little time in starting to rebuild. Now, a short four years since the war had ended, Atlanta was already stretching past its three-mile town limits and boasting a population of over 20,000. There were three-hundred merchants in town, fifty liquor stores, thirty butchers, ten wagon yards, and more hacks and drays than John Henry had ever seen in one place before. Atlanta, like the mythical Phoenix bird, was rising up from its own ashes to spread its wings again.

"Ain't it grand!" Rachel Martin Holliday exclaimed, putting one gloved hand to her heart as if to still its racing as they stepped down from the train at the Atlanta Depot. "I ain't never been to the city before – any city before. I figured Valdosta was a big place, 'til now. But oh! Don't Atlanta just beat it all!"

"I doubt Atlanta 'beats it all'," John Henry replied with a superior tone. "There's lots of cities bigger than this. Philadelphia for instance, that's where Dr. Frink studied dentistry. Philadelphia would make Atlanta look like a farm town, I bet," though in truth he was as awe-struck by the city as she was. But he couldn't let Rachel know that.

"I reckon you're right," Rachel said, then she grinned. "Don't your father look handsome in that new top hat of his? He didn't want to buy it, but I made him do it. I said if he was gonna make a visit to the city, he ought to look citified. Don't he look dapper?" Then she waved her hand and called out above the raucous crowd to where Henry was paying for a cab: "Hey there, Major Holliday! I sure do like that hat your wearin'!"

Henry looked almost flustered as he tipped his new hat to her, and Rachel responded by twirling around to show off her new traveling dress, gray silk and pink ruffles to match a beribboned pink bonnet. With all the ruffles and bows it looked like a little girl's dress, and nothing like the costumes John Henry's mother had favored, dark and elegant in their simplicity. Rachel was nothing like his mother, except that she shared his father's bed, and the thought of that never ceased to rankle him.

But on this trip, even Rachel's irritating presence couldn't dampen his spirits. Mattie was coming to the wedding for sure; she had written to tell him so, and he took that as a favorable sign. Favorable, because he had something important to discuss with her, something far too important to say in a letter, and he needed to know that she would be happy to see him again. Though it had been over a year since they had last been together during his summer of exile in Jonesboro, the memory of that kiss in the barn behind her father's house had stayed bright in his mind – as bright as the moonlight that had made her skin shine like ivory silk and made him lose his head for one sweet, satisfying moment. With any luck, he'd find the opportunity to kiss her again and then...

"Well, are you comin' with us or not?" Henry Holliday said, as he climbed into the hired hack and took the reins in hand. "It's a long walk out to your Uncle John's house, if you're plannin' on standin' here all day."

~~~~~~~~~~

Uncle John's home was eight blocks out Peachtree Street, past the gaudy new mansions of the Reconstruction Era and up the long hill of Forrest Avenue. The woods were still thick this far out from the city, and the road was little more than a dirt track between fields cleared for cows and chickens. But though Uncle John's house wasn't one of those elegant Peachtree Street mansions, it was substantial. Above a foundation of gray stone and red brick rose three stories of gothic elegance, with rows of balconies wearing fancy filigree woodwork and a hip-roofed verandah that curved from the front door clear around the side of the house.

Behind the house, the yard was filled with outbuildings: carriage house and summer kitchen, smoke house and dairy, horse barn and cow stall. Like all well-off city families, the Hollidays kept a cow, providing the luxury of fresh milk every day. Vegetables came from the garden behind the barn, eggs from the chickens in the chicken coop. More exotic supplies came from the family's store – cured hams from Virginia, oysters from the coast, beef all the way from Texas.

Food seemed to be the main topic of conversation that week of George's wedding, besides the decorating that needed to be done. Although the wedding was to be held at the Methodist Church and the reception at the home of the bride's parents, there were several pre-nuptial dinners being hosted at the Hollidays' home and plenty of company to entertain. The young people were recruited to help at first, until Cousin Johnny Holliday, thirteen-years old and awkward as a growing puppy, knocked over Aunt Permelia Ware Holliday's heirloom crystal punch bowl, shattering it on the shiny hardwood floor.

"Y'all get on out of here, right now!" Aunt Permelia commanded, her anger only barely restrained under her properly-mannered upbringing, and even her neatly arranged curls were starting to come undone. "Robert, take your cousins on an excursion somewhere for a while. Your aunts and I are busy enough without havin' to guard the dishware!"

John Henry was glad to be sent out of the house, for since his arrival he hadn't had a single moment alone with Mattie – though she did seem pleased enough to see him. But they were always surrounded by a crowd of cousins and aunts and uncles, and her smiles might have been meant for anyone, not just him. Nor would anyone else, without knowing what had gone on between them the last time they had been together, ever guess that her " 'Afternoon, John Henry. You're lookin' well," sounded like a love song to him, coming from her sweet lips. But did she mean it to sound so sweet, or was it just his eager heart that made it sound that way? He was in a fluster just thinking about it, and if Aunt Permelia hadn't sent them all away, he might have been the next to drop a crystal serving piece.

Cousin Robert, who at nineteen-years old had fast forgotten his country roots in Fayetteville and given his heart to Atlanta, was pleased to act as tour-guide for their excursions. With his father's two fine carriages – a phaeton with a folding leather roof and seats for six passengers, and a roofless runabout that seated four – he and John Henry could carry all the cousins who wanted to go along. Besides John Henry and Mattie and Cousin Robert, there were Robert's boisterous younger brother Johnny, Mattie's younger sisters Lucy, Theresa, Roberta, and Catherine, and Aunt Martha Holliday Johnson's boys John Allen and Daniel. But luckily, the ten cousins were a perfect fit for the two carriages – and John Henry made sure that Mattie ended up riding in the runabout next to him for their daily outings.

There was plenty for young people to see in Atlanta, and to the thrill of the boys most of the sights had something to do with the War. There was Kennesaw Mountain, where General Johnston's army had dug in to await the arrival of the

Yankees only five short years before, and where the entrenchments were still filled with the refuse of battle: bullets and buttons and sometimes even knives to take home as souvenirs. There was Stone Mountain, a mile-wide outcropping of white granite that loomed over the countryside like a sleeping dragon, and that both Rebels and Yankees had used as an observation point during the War and Indians had used as a ceremonial site before that. In between the time of the Indians and the armies, the mountain was owned by Aaron Cloud, who built an enormous observation deck at the top with a hotel at the base of the mountain. In its day, "Cloud's Tower" had attracted tourists from all over the Southern states before the Yankees came and burned it down, like they did everything else they came close to. But John Henry still enjoyed hearing the story of Aaron Cloud, as his mother's mother was a Cloud and cousin to the enterprising Aaron, which in his mind made him part owner of Stone Mountain, too.

But the sight which affected Mattie most were the countless dirt mounds that littered the city, marking where fallen soldiers had been laid to rest in mass grave trenches during the Battle of Atlanta.

"Like Colonel Grace and his chaplain," she said in a reverent voice as they drove past one after another of those trench grave mounds. "I didn't know so many folks had their gardens turned into cemeteries."

"It's a problem, all right," Robert commented, as the carriages drove side-by-side down the wide dirt expanse of Peachtree Street. "Seems like every time a builder turns over the land to lay a new foundation, there's already skeletons in the way."

They were about to turn the corner when they crossed paths with John Henry's father and Rachel riding at his side, returning from a shopping trip to John Smith's Carriage Manufactory to place an order for the store in Valdosta.

"Ordered two phaetons," Henry said, "like that one y'all are ridin' in. Might be some folks around Valdosta foolish enough to spend their money on such frivolity."

Though Henry's words sounded like an insult to anyone owning an expensive driving rig, the truth was that Valdosta's rutted dirt alleys were no place for a fancy carriage like a four-wheeled phaeton. Wagons and buggies were all that were really needed in a country town like Valdosta. Still, John Henry smarted under his father's brusque words. Without knowing about backwards Lowndes County, his cousins wouldn't understand about the phaetons, and think his father plain rude.

"I ordered some runabouts too," Henry went on, "including one for us. Figured it'll be good advertising for the business when folks see Rachel ridin' in that new carriage up the hill to town when she goes to buy dry goods, instead of walkin' a couple of blocks."

His reasoning made sense, but John Henry couldn't help thinking that his father had never bought his mother a carriage to ride in, though they'd lived seven miles out of town and she'd been sick all the time. Alice Jane had never had anything nicer than an old buggy to ride in all the years of her marriage. Now Rachel, undeserving as she was, would ride to town in style, showing off Henry's new prosperity.

But Rachel's words made John Henry forget all about his irritation at his father.

"Well, I reckon I'm gonna need a carriage to ride in," Rachel added with a grin, "now I'm in the family way again. I wasn't gonna tell anyone yet, not even your Pa, for fearin' bad luck. But when he wanted to stop off to Rich's store and buy me a new corset at that big sale, I figured I better tell him. 'Course fifty cents for a pretty French corset is a fine buy!"

There was a moment of startled silence, and John Henry felt the blood rush to his face as he blushed in embarrassment. It wasn't Rachel's pregnancy that he found so disturbing; Rachel was always either with child or trying to be. But the way she announced it so openly, along with the needless mention of his father's knowledge of ladies' underthings, was a humiliation. Both topics related to marital intimacy, and neither was appropriate in the current mixed company of young ladies and adolescent boys. What would Mattie and her sisters think? His hands tightened reflexively on the reins as though he could lead the horse to a quick run, removing his carriage and himself from the shameful situation. But before he could move or even look to see if everyone else was as offended as he was by the crass comment, Mattie smiled and reached a hand across to Rachel.

"Oh, how wonderful, Aunt Rachel!" she said, as if Henry's wife were a real relation. "I know Mother will be thrilled to hear about a new baby in the family. Congratulations to you both!"

John Henry turned and stared at her in astonishment, amazed that she could act so cordial in the face of such disgusting news, but Mattie seemed to be truly pleased, holding Rachel's hand in her own and smiling sweetly. Then she turned to her sisters, crowded together in the back seat of the runabout.

"Did you hear that, girls? We're gonna have a new cousin in the family!"

Because of Mattie's enthusiasm over the baby announcement – and her complete disregard of the corset comment – everyone else joined in the congratulations as well. Even Robert, who surely had to have known how uncouth Rachel's remarks had been, seemed unperturbed, shaking his uncle's hand heartily.

"Well done, Uncle Henry! I'll have to make sure Father makes a toast to you both at the wedding reception tomorrow evening. Just think of it, John Henry, you could have a younger brother like Johnny here to torment you!"

But it wasn't a new brother John Henry was thinking about, or even Rachel's rudeness anymore. He was thinking about what a lady Mattie was by comparison, genteel and refined and ready to diffuse a difficult situation with her sweet smile and gentle ways.

His mother, he knew, would have approved.

~~~~~~~~~~

George Henry Holliday and Mary Elizabeth Wright were married in Wesley Chapel Methodist Episcopalian Church, a most auspicious location for the Holliday family's first Atlanta wedding. The simple log meeting house was the first church established in Atlanta and one of the few wooden structures to have survived Sherman's fires, and folks said that if Wesley Chapel could withstand the burning of Atlanta, surely those married there could survive the smaller fires of family life.

The only shadow on the service came when Aunt Permelia insisted that her Mulatto serving girl, Sophie, be invited to attend the ceremony and be seated in the Holliday family pews as well. The Wrights, long-time slavers from Tennessee, objected of course. In times past, coloreds had sat apart from the white congregation in separate rows at the back of the chapel, and since the War, there'd been no coloreds in Wesley Chapel at all after the whites raised a subscription of seven-hundred dollars so the former slaves could start their own church, and the African Methodist Episcopalian Church was founded. But Aunt Permelia was adamant: Sophie Walton was like family, having come to her years ago in Fayetteville and choosing to stay on with the Hollidays even after the Emancipation. And with Georgia back under Martial Law again for ousting the newly elected black members of the State Legislature, the Wrights didn't dare make too much of a fuss. The Yankees were still in control, after all, and that meant coloreds could be seated anywhere they liked – even in Wesley Chapel Church.

The wedding reception followed at the home of the bride's parents, one of those gaudy Peachtree Street mansions that had risen up during the Reconstruction. The grand entry hall glowed in candlelight, a string ensemble played in the parlor, the dining room table groaned under the weight of a sumptuous wedding banquet, and the ballroom gleamed in polished wood floors and cut glass chandeliers with a grand piano toward one long wall and a table of refreshments against the other. In the middle of the floor a fiddle player struck up a lively tune, then the piano joined in and the guests gathered for the traditional Virginia Reel with the colored butler acting as dance caller.

"Head lady and foot man, forward and bow to your partner! Bow to your partner again! Right hands 'round, now left hands 'round, now both hands 'round and do-si-do! Foot lady and head man, forward, bow to your partner..."

It took John Henry two turns through the reel to position himself opposite Mattie, and she laughed when she saw him standing there across from her. But the reel was not a place for talking, what with the loud music and the louder laughter of the dancers, so he still couldn't do much more than grin back at her, enjoying the dance.

By the end of the reel most of the guests were too winded to go on, and the musicians struck up a gentler waltz tune instead, and though John Henry had been about to offer to get Mattie a drink of lemonade, the music made him stop in his tracks.

"Liszt," he said out loud, and felt the notes all the way down to his fingertips. For it was one of his mother's favorite pieces the musicians had chosen to play, an old love song he'd practiced as a youth...

"*Dream of Love*," Mattie said, finishing his thought. "I haven't heard that song in years, not since your Aunt Margaret's wedding down in Valdosta. Do you remember it?"

He looked into her face, flushed from the dancing, and smiling at the memory. "How could I ever forget?" he asked. "That's when I learned to dance." Mattie had been his teacher, of course, showing the steps of the waltz to an awkward boy. But he wasn't a boy anymore, and he asked with a bow: "May I have this dance, Miss Holliday?"

She was so small compared to him, her head coming no higher than his shoulder, and with her in his arms he suddenly felt taller than he ever had before. He could have kissed her on the top of her auburn head without even leaning down, or swept her up in his arms to kiss her on the face. But as the final strains of the waltz finished, Cousin George's new father-in-law, the host of the wedding, stepped forward.

"Ladies and gentlemen!" Mr. Wright announced with a broad smile, "I would like to offer a toast to the wedding couple: to my beautiful daughter Mary and her new husband, Mr. George Henry Holliday. May their married lives be as full of happiness as this night!"

"Huzzah!" the men in the room cheered, and raised their glasses to the bridal couple, while the ladies all applauded.

"And to our host and his lady," another of the men added, and the cheer went around again. It was a tradition of sorts that the first toast should be answered by a return of good wishes from the guests, then each gentleman would add his own congratulations for some other accomplishment. Everyone knew, of course, that the whole exercise was just an excuse for the men to continue refilling their liquor glasses without any dispute from the ladies. So it was good manners to continue the toasts, though continuing them often lead to some extremes:

"To Atlanta, may she continue to rise from the ashes!"

"Huzzah!"

"To the honor of the South!"

"Huzzah!"

"To Stonewall Jackson, may he rest in peace!"

"To old Abe Lincoln, may he rest in hell!"

They toasted the fallen Confederacy, the rising Klan, and their own good fortune in making money off the Yankees. They toasted each other and their families, their neighbors and their health – whatever sounded good over a raised liquor glass. Robert even added a toast to his Uncle Henry's good fortune, though he politely avoided mentioning the delicate nature of that fortune. So by the time the toasting came back around to Uncle John, there wasn't much left to say that hadn't already been said – yet his words took John Henry completely by surprise.

"To my nephew, John Henry, who'll be goin' off to dental school next year. May he find many friendly smiles – and many more rotten teeth!"

The men all laughed and shouted another "Huzzah!" but John Henry looked at his uncle in astonishment. What did Uncle John mean by announcing that he would be going to dental school, anyhow? Had his father told Uncle John about his plans? Had Uncle John prevailed upon Henry to let his son go off to school in Philadelphia? Or did Henry's sudden change of heart have something to do with that new baby on the way...

He looked across the room at his father, standing in the circle of men at the punch bowl and paying him no attention at all. Surely, that had to be the explanation for Henry's sudden change of heart. With Rachel expecting again, it would be more convenient to have the troublesome John Henry far off in Philadelphia. He didn't know whether to cheer at his good news or fling out in anger that he was being sent away again.

Mattie, who must have seen the war of emotion passing over his face, took his hand in hers.

"It's awful warm in here, isn't it, honey? Let's go find some fresh air."

But they were hardly outside on the gravel drive before her questions came flying at him like hard rain.

"What did he mean, you're goin' off to dental school? I thought you wanted to be a doctor. And where would you go? Why would you go?"

"I did want to be a doctor," he said, trying to defend himself. "But this past year, workin' with Dr. Frink, I changed my mind. I'm good at dentistry. You know how I've always been clever with my hands. Dr. Frink's written me a recommendation to the Pennsylvania College of Dental Surgery in Philadelphia..."

"Philadelphia!" she exclaimed. "But that's so far north, and in Yankee territory! Why ever would you go there?"

"There's only a few other dental schools in the country – Baltimore, New York – but Dr. Frink says Philadelphia's the best. He says, with my grades and experience workin' with him, I shouldn't have any trouble gettin' in. It'd be an honor for me to go there, Mattie, a real honor. Don't be angry, please..."

But when she turned tear-filled eyes toward him, he realized that it wasn't anger that she was feeling after all, but sadness at his leaving, and he was touched to the heart.

"Ah, Mattie," he said gently, "I won't be gone all that long. It's only a two-year course, and I won't even be leavin' until next fall. I need to work some first, to help out with the tuition and all. Fact is, I didn't know myself until just now that my father was gonna let me go. When I told him about it, he just said it was a fool idea and too expensive, like he says about everything I want to do. But somethin' changed his mind, I guess..."

He didn't tell her what he believed was true: that his going was only to get him out of the way for a new son to be born. Tender-hearted Mattie would never understand anything so cool as his father's cold affections.

"But you will be comin' back, won't you, back to Georgia?"

"Do you want me to come back?" he asked.

"Well, of course I do, you're family, after all. Family should be together."

"But do *you* want me to come back, Mattie?"

She hesitated a moment before answering, then looked up at him with a face full of affection.

"You know I do!"

He didn't bother asking for permission as he put his arms around her, bending his head to hers and feeling the chill of the November evening on her face as he kissed her quickly. And like that other night, when he'd kissed her in the barn behind her parents' house, she leaned up toward him and kissed him back, and her willingness told him what he wanted to know: that Mattie loved him as he loved her. Then, arms still around her, another question came to his mind.

"Whatever happened to that South Carolina soldier of yours, Mattie? The one your father wanted to marry you off to?"

She pursed her lips as if in disgust. "He married a rich widow lady – a Yankee widow lady! My father said it was good riddance, that he was obviously not a gentleman, after all, and no great loss to the family."

"And no great loss to you, either?" he asked.

"He was a dream, John Henry, just a girlhood fantasy. I never even knew him."

"But you know me."

"Yes, I do. I know you to the heart," she said. And when she laid a hand against his chest, he bent his head and kissed her again.

"Philadelphia!" she said when their lips parted, "It's so far away! You will write me while you're gone, won't you?"

"Of course I will. And you can write me, too. You can write me every day."

"Writing paper's too expensive for that!" she said with a laugh. "But I will think of you every day, and pray for your safe return."

"My safe return?" he asked, amused. "Whatever could happen to me in prim old Philadelphia, anyhow?"

But Mattie wasn't laughing anymore, only looking up at him with those loving eyes of hers. "You know how I've always tried to look after you, ever since we were children. Now you're goin' so far away, I won't be able to watch out for you anymore. So I suppose God will have to watch over you for me."

"Ah, Mattie!" he said, touching his hand to her face, like ivory silk in the moonlight, "I'll come back safe, I promise. And will you promise to be waitin' for me when I do?"

"Yes, John Henry," she said, the tears welling up again. "I promise!"

~~~~~~~~~

The newlyweds left that night on the late train out of Atlanta, bound for a honeymoon trip to Tennessee. As at the wedding, they both looked like fashion plates in their going-away clothes, and even the telegram delivery boy, bearing the best wishes that had come across the wire, stopped to admire them.

The Holliday cousins all escorted them to the depot, then stood together in a cloud of steam on the platform, waving them off as they left, the first of their generation to go into marriage. And watching the train as it steamed off into the night, John Henry had an idea of how he might raise some money for dental school. The Atlantic and Gulf Line Railroad in Valdosta was always looking for workers, smart young men who could learn the complexities of the railroad schedule and handle the ticket taking and selling. He'd never thought before of inquiring after the job for himself, busy as he was with school and his afternoons at Dr. Frink's office. But now that he'd finished at the Valdosta Institute, he'd have time to work two jobs and make some real money. Besides, he'd always loved the railroads, ever since he was a boy growing up near the tracks in Griffin. To him, the railroad had always seemed a romance and an adventure...

"What are you ponderin' on, John Henry?" Mattie asked, slipping her arm through his as she stood beside him on the depot platform.

"Adventure," he replied. "Life is full of adventures, and I aim to have me some." Mattie just smiled, understanding.

~~~~~~~~~

Though Henry Holliday had changed his mind about John Henry's attending dental school, that didn't mean he was willing to offer much support. He was only permitting his son's professional plans, not paying for them, and he expected John Henry to raise most of the money for his schooling himself – which turned out to be a blessing in a way. For busy as John Henry was between his days assisting Dr. Frink and his evenings and weekends as a station clerk for the Atlantic and Gulf Line, he had little time to spend at home. So when Rachel's pregnancy ended too early, like all the others had, John Henry didn't have to be around much to hear her weeping – or offer condolences he didn't feel. In truth, his only real concern was that without a baby on the way, his father might have another change of heart about his schooling and not let him go, after all. But Henry seemed resigned to sending his son off to Philadelphia, and as the time came close, he even seemed to be looking forward to taking him there.

The fancy luggage was a gift he hadn't expected. Henry presented it to him on the night before they left Valdosta, saying that a young professional man needed to have proper traveling cases. But the black leather satchel and matching train trunk, both fitted with shiny brass fastenings and bearing the gold-embossed initials *JHH*, were more than just proper. They were fine enough for a rich man's son, and had surely set his father back a bit, though Henry said nothing of the expense. He only reminded John Henry that morocco leather needed to be well-cared for, and that he would have to keep an eye on the porters and bellboys who carried his things.

If John Henry hadn't known better, he would have thought his father had finally come around to being proud of his going off to dental school. For with uncharacteristic generosity, Henry hardly complained at all about the price of their train fare from Valdosta, or their hotel accommodations in Savannah, or even their stateroom on the steamship bound for Philadelphia. And though they were five days at sea before the ship turned inland and sailed up the Delaware River, not once did Henry remind him that he could have become a doctor and done his studying closer to home at the Medical College of Georgia. And not being chastised seemed almost a sign of affection, coming from Henry.

Chapter Eight

Philadelphia, 1870

The city celebrated his arrival with fireworks and cannonades and a torchlight parade through the cobblestone streets. At least that was the way John Henry liked to think of it, not learning until later that the festivities were presented by the Philadelphia Fire Association in honor of a visiting fire brigade from New York, and he'd only happened to arrive on that same late August night. The timing still seemed a serendipity enough to make him consider the celebration partly his own, as well.

He had plenty to celebrate with the start of his professional training and his first taste of big city life both coming at once. And what a city it was! With a population of nearly three-quarters of a million, Philadelphia was the second largest city in the country. Compared to it, Atlanta with its twenty-thousand was just a town, and Valdosta, where John Henry could name almost every one of the three-hundred residents, was nothing but a bump on a backwoods road.

From Penn's Landing on the Delaware River, Philadelphia stretched for seven miles north and south, spread west for two miles to the Schuylkill River, and reached for another four miles past that into the Pennsylvania countryside. Even the city market was enormous, covering eighteen whole blocks from the Delaware to 18th Street. And with buildings as old as the Revolution and some even older than that, there was an air of steady importance about the place, as though Philadelphia had always been there and always would be. Not like Georgia, where everything was either raw and new or tumbling down from disuse. Georgia was still half frontier; Philadelphia was civilization.

His father had arranged a room for him near to the dental school in the boarding house of Mrs. Christina Schrenk on Cherry Street. The house was a typical Philadelphia dwelling place, two stories tall but only one room wide with a narrow staircase taking up most of the front hallway. The room Mrs. Schrenk gave him was smaller than his old bedroom in Valdosta, but it had a window facing out onto

Cherry Street and the use of a water closet down the hall – and the novelty of indoor plumbing made it seem like real luxury to John Henry. Back home in Georgia, most of the houses still had no plumbing at all, and bath water had to be carried in from wells out in the yard. Even his Uncle John's new house in Atlanta, elegant as it was, still had an outhouse out back. And to his mind, having the use of a flushing toilet and a bath with running water was final proof that Philadelphia was truly civilized.

His father warned him, however, about letting the luxuries of city life spoil him.

"You're here to study, not lay around in the bathtub all day," Henry said as he helped John Henry carry his heavy traveling trunk up Mrs. Schrenk's narrow stairs and into his newly rented room. "Though for the price of this place, you ought to get as much washing in as you can. Fifty dollars a month for room and board! At least the gas light should help you get through that crate of readin' material, anyhow."

The gas was another of the luxuries of life in Philadelphia as the city had been illuminated since the 1830's, with gas lamps at every street corner and gaslights in nearly every house as well. With just the turn of a key and the strike of a match, John Henry would be able to study all night long without having to worry about a candle burning down or an oil lamp running out. And he had plenty of material to study in his newly purchased library of medical books, required reading at the dental school.

"I don't reckon I'll have much time to lay around in the tub, Pa," he replied. "I'll be lucky to get through this reading at all."

"You're lucky just bein' here, John Henry, and don't you forget it. I'll be expectin' to see top marks when you come home next summer."

His father hadn't changed any since John Henry's first days at the Valdosta Institute. Henry still believed that getting an education was a privilege and good grades were proof of proper gratitude. But John Henry was prepared to be grateful, and he did indeed feel lucky to be getting away from the provincial life of south Georgia. Let his father warn and reprimand all he wanted; his own spirits were too high to take offense.

"Don't worry, Pa. I'll bring home good grades like I always did. Besides, Dr. Frink says I have a natural aptitude for dentistry. 'Good hands,' he calls it, just like you used to say about my shootin'. So I reckon I'll do all right. I won't shame you."

And though any other father might have taken the offered opportunity to say that he was not ashamed of his son, was proud even of his past accomplishments and his bright future, Henry made no reply. His only comment was that it was getting on toward suppertime, and they'd best be finding somewhere to eat unless Mrs. Schrenk had enough for an extra plate.

What Henry Holliday lacked in private emotion, however, he made up for in patriotic spirit on his tour through the old Colonial capital of Philadelphia. Though Henry's patriotism had put him on the losing side in the last War, he remained proud of his ancestors who'd fought and won the War of Revolution against the British and helped to create the United States of America. After all, it was on Revolutionary War bounty lands, won for service at the Battle of Kettle Creek, that his own grandfather, William Holliday, had made his first home in Georgia. So it was with some personal feeling that Henry took his son to Chestnut Street to see the old State House called Independence Hall and the great brass bell that had rung out the signing of the Declaration of Independence.

The bell still hung in the rotunda of the dusty hall, displayed behind a wrought iron fence that kept visitors from trying to ring it. But as John Henry and his father paid their respects to that emblem of American freedom, he couldn't help but think of the irony of its history, noted on a large bronze plaque. When it was first cast in England and shipped over the ocean to the Pennsylvania Colony, it was called the "Province Bell". During the Revolution, when it rang out meetings of the Continental Congress, it was called the "State House Bell". It was only when a group of nineteenth-century Boston abolitionists took it as the symbol of their own cause that it gained the name "Liberty Bell", for its inscription from Leviticus, Chapter 25, Verse 10: *Proclaim liberty throughout all the land unto the inhabitants thereof.* But the bell cracked soon after that, proof, as far as John Henry was concerned, that the abolition movement had cracked the country apart: North and South, Yankee and Rebel. And that was the one unfortunate thing about Philadelphia: it was still a Yankee city, through and through. Even though the War Between the States had been over for five years, the name "Rebel" still clung to anyone with a Southern accent. But the South *was* still rebellious, as far as the North was concerned, refusing to ratify one Constitutional Amendment after another until forced to do so by Martial Law. And where, John Henry wondered, was the liberty in that?

But there were other, less troubling, sights to see in Philadelphia: Betsy Ross's home where the first American flag had been sewn, Christ Church where George Washington had prayed and Benjamin Franklin was buried in the churchyard near the old city wall, the ingenious waterworks that supplied the whole city with fresh drinking water, Fairmount Park with its miles of lush green preserve along the Schuylkill River. And by the time Henry had taken him around to see it all and readied himself for his return to Georgia, John Henry was almost sad to see his father go. To his recollection, he'd never had so much of his father's attention, cool-tempered or not.

But Henry had his own business to attend to back in Georgia and could only stay long enough to see his son settled at the boarding house and registered at the dental school. For in addition to operating his Valdosta Buggy and Carriage Company, Henry was planning on running for Mayor of the town in the coming November election. It would be a tough campaign to win, as his opponent was Sam Griffin's father, owner of the only general store in town and owed money by nearly everyone in Valdosta at one time or another – and money owed meant votes in the ballot box. So it was probably the election, not John Henry, that Henry was thinking of when he shook his son's hand and wished him well, then boarded the *Steamship Wyoming*, sailing back to Savannah.

~~~~~~~~~~

The Pennsylvania College of Dental Surgery was located in a four-story brick building at the corner of 10th and Arch Streets, across from the Philadelphia College of Pharmacology, and the two schools shared more than just a street address. For with both courses of study including an anatomy laboratory, it was convenient for both to share laboratory cadavers as well. The dental students took the heads for dissection, the pharmacology students took the rest of the bodies, and where the remains went from there no one would say – though there was rumored to be a hundred-foot deep pit in the basement of the Medical College of Pennsylvania where used body parts were thrown.

Grisly as it was, cadaver study in the anatomy lab was a vital part of the dental school curriculum. A dentist couldn't very well treat a patient if he didn't know the physical structures underlying the teeth and gums: how the muscles of the mandible connected to the skull, where the nerves ran under the skin, how the arteries and veins carried blood to the tissues and bones. Once John Henry got over the initial shock of slicing into dead flesh and handling torpid bones and tissues, he found the work fascinating. The only really disturbing aspect of Anatomy Lab was that it was held during the noon hour, between Clinic and Lecture, and the students often brought their dinner to the cadaver table with them. Seeing a dental student reaching into an open cranium with one hand while holding a bite of bread and cheese in the other was far more unsettling than the lab work itself.

The students couldn't be blamed for trying to get two things done at once. With the demands of the dental school schedule, there was little time for anything but study. Mornings from eight until noon were spent in the dental clinic treating patients under the watchful guidance of the clinical professors. Afternoons from one until four were spent in lecture classes learning the medical sciences of anatomy, chemistry, histology, pathology, and physiology. Evenings from suppertime until dusk were spent in the dental laboratory learning to refine and alloy precious metals, fashion artificial teeth from porcelain and gold, and make dentures from the newly patented vulcanized rubber. Finally, from dusk until dawn, the students were free to relax and study for the next day's work. Most nights, though, John Henry fell asleep at his reading and woke in the early hours to find the gaslight still burning and his back aching from slouching over his books.

Though he'd started out the fall session with confidence in his abilities and hopes of good marks, he was finding the schoolwork to be more difficult than he'd expected and most of the students better prepared for the material than he was. Two of his classmates were doctors, planning to add dentistry to their medical practices. Three were dentists already, hoping to expand their knowledge in the field. Six were the sons of dentists who'd already spent years working in their fathers' practices and studying their fathers' textbooks. But none was better prepared than a soft-spoken young man who stunned the class by interrupting one of the professors on the first day of the session.

"Excuse me, Sir," Jameson Fuches said, raising his hand. "I believe you mean the mesial, rather than the distal. Or if you do mean the distal, perhaps you are discussing the adjacent tooth."

The fact that the error was certainly just a slip of the tongue, and no cause for embarrassing correction in front of the class, made the student's comment seem like a criticism, and the lecturer answered with sharpness.

"And I suppose you are an expert in dental terminology, Mr. Fuches?"

"No Sir," the student replied, "but my preceptor is: Dr. Homer Judd of St. Louis, Missouri. He is a student of classical languages and fluent in Greek. It was he who invented the dental nomenclature now in use."

"Yes, Mr. Fuches, I am aware of the work of Dr. Homer Judd. But the question which begs answering is why, with Dr. Judd as your preceptor, you would make the journey all the way here to Philadelphia? I understand that he is dean of his own dental school in St. Louis, the Missouri Dental College."

"Yes, Sir, he is. I attended that school for one session, but Dr. Judd sent me here to learn the most modern techniques and bring them back to share with the other students. Dr. Judd believes that the Pennsylvania College of Dental Surgery is the finest school in this country, Sir." And though the young man had rudely interrupted the lecture, there was surprisingly little arrogance in his manner.

"Well, indeed," the lecturer replied, seeming somewhat mollified. "Now, may I get on with my own lecture, or would you like to take over as professor for the day, and finish up for me?"

A ripple of laughter went around the room, and Jameson Fuches blushed bright red right up to his fringe of pale blonde hair.

"No Sir," he said politely, "you'll do adequately." And that made the class laugh out loud, and even the lecturer seemed amused.

After that, everyone at the school called him "Professor Fuches," though Jameson was never so bold as to correct a lecture speaker again. But he took pages of notes and the rumor was that he was planning to write his own textbook on dentistry someday and dedicate it to his preceptor, Dr. Homer Judd.

The other rumor about Jameson Fuches was that he was a German, though he had no foreign accent, but his surname was certainly of Germanic origin and that made him suspect. For in a city where immigrants filled most of the working class, it was unusual to find a German attending professional school. Germans ran the restaurants and hotels and boarding houses that professional men frequented, but they didn't often rise to the professions themselves. They even had their own section of the city, Germantown, and their own German-language newspapers. But when one of the other students questioned Jameson about his family background, he only blushed red again, and said that he'd been born in New York City where his father had settled after sailing from France. Still, his scholarly aloofness and his uncertain heritage left him out of the circle of prominent young men at the dental school.

John Henry wasn't sure what to think of Jameson Fuches, though they sat only one chair apart in the alphabetical seating assigned by the dental school. He was German looking, that was true, with his pale skin and paler blonde hair – tow-headed, they would have called him back home, though the Georgia sun would certainly have turned his fair complexion ruddy red. But other than his unusual looks, there was little about him to draw attention. He was quiet, studious, and impeccably polite, and though he rarely initiated a conversation, when John Henry asked him some dental question or other, his answers were always clear and concise. So if the studies got too hard, Professor Fuches might just be a good substitute as a tutor – if John Henry ever got that desperate. For he was well aware of the social structure in Philadelphia that found its way even down to the dental school: Northerners before Southerners, Americans before foreigners. John Henry was one of only six Southern students at the dental school that session, so his standing among his classmates was shaky enough without associating himself with the likes of Jameson Fuches.

Besides, keeping himself in favor with the right people had its rewards. One of those Yankee students, a New Yorker named William DeMorat, had an uncle in Philadelphia who owned a photography studio, and the uncle, as a kindness to his nephew's friends at the dental school, had offered to make portraits of each student. John Henry's had turned out well, he thought, the sepia-toned print showing a fashionable young man wearing a vested wool suit with velvet lapels, his sandy hair slicked down and darkened with macassar oil, his blue eyes looking clearly into the future. Only the thin new mustache above his resolute mouth showed that the subject was still young, not yet twenty-years old, in a school filled with mature men – though none of them were more determined to succeed than John Henry.

The photograph had turned out so well, in fact, that he thought he might give it to Mattie as a Christmas gift – and hoped she wouldn't mind too much that it came from the camera of a Yankee. He owed her a photograph in exchange for the one that she'd sent to him. It had come carefully wrapped, a small leather-framed daguerreotype of a young woman with a delicate heart-shaped face and luminous dark eyes, her hair swept up in tendrils, silver earbobs dangling close to her slender neck. And staring at the photograph, John Henry could almost hear her gentle laughter, welcoming him home.

~~~~~~~~~~

She wrote often that autumn, her letters coming by the twice-daily Philadelphia home postal delivery service established by Benjamin Franklin. Home mail delivery was another of the luxuries of living in Philadelphia, since back home in Georgia the mail came only twice a week and had to be picked up at the post office. The only problem with old Ben's innovation, as far as John Henry was concerned, was that with the mail coming twice daily, he had two chances a day to be disappointed if an expected letter did not arrive.

But he wasn't often disappointed, for Mattie was a good correspondent and rarely a week went by when he didn't receive a long letter from her, filled with news from home. She told him how the family was doing, how her younger sisters were turning into young ladies and how little Jim Bob was growing taller every day. She told him about her students at the Jonesboro High School, and how proud she was of their progress. She even told him about the weather, and how the fall leaves were turning to yellow and gold and making a patchwork of color on the country roads.

The one thing she didn't tell him though, and the one thing he wanted most to read, was that she loved him. But Mattie was a proper young lady, he reminded himself, and too well-bred to trust her passions to paper and ink. Besides, with all that family around, how would she find the privacy to say such things, anyhow? So he consoled himself that her constancy in writing reflected her feelings clear enough, without the tender words he longed to read. And as long as those letters kept coming, one a week and sometimes more, he had no reason to doubt her feelings for him.

There was nothing tender about the letters from his father. Henry's words were as spare as his affections, written on thin paper sheets crisply folded around John Henry's monthly allowance money. The Valdosta City elections were coming up, and the contest was still a close one. The cotton crop in Lowndes County was looking better, though not as good as it had looked before the War. The buggy business was steady, and he was thinking of starting up a nursery farm on the property at Cat Creek. But mostly, his father's letters were reminders of John Henry's duty to do well in Philadelphia, with so much invested in his schooling. Rachel, he said, sent her love.

John Henry was proud to reply that he was, indeed, doing well. After the first difficult September session of medical lectures and exams, the class was moving into the clinical work in which John Henry excelled, and he was beginning to feel more at home in Philadelphia, riding the street cars for a seven-cent fare, and finding his way around without getting lost too often. He didn't add that he'd even taken himself up to Fairmount Park on the Schuylkill River to see a sculling race, in case Henry should consider that diversion a waste of good study time and chastise him for it. For though his father was a thousand miles away, buried in the small-town life of south Georgia, his good opinion was still something John Henry hungered for.

The good wishes from Rachel he simply ignored.

The first snowfall came at the end of November with a short fifteen minutes of flurries followed by a brilliant blue sky and a stiff northeast wind. By midnight the temperature was below freezing, and the next morning the ponds around the city were covered with thin ice. But while most of Philadelphia seemed unimpressed by the change of weather, John Henry was jubilant. He had never seen a real snowfall before, only the occasional ice storm when a winter rain turned to freezing sleet, and the sight of the snow falling, like so many bits of fine white paper drifting down from the clouds, dazzled him. So when William DeMorat and some of the other students suggested that they celebrate both the first snow and the last class of the fall session with a visit to the Arch Street Opera House, John Henry readily agreed. Although the theater was right across the street from the dental school, he'd never taken the time to see the varieties acts there.

"Well, it's high time!" DeMorat said incredulously. "Aren't you interested in culture?"

"You can't exactly call the Opera House culture. Looks like mostly minstrel shows and varieties acts, judgin' from the playbill. I doubt they've ever played Verdi."

"Who wants to hear Verdi?" DeMorat said with a bored yawn. "Give me Andy McKee, or Lew Simmons playing the banjo. Or better yet, show me an actress in skin tights, dancing a fandango — now that's what I call entertainment! It's about time we taught you some debauchery. You're far too pristine for Philadelphia."

Though DeMorat had a risqué way of talking, John Henry suspected he wasn't too far from pristine himself, as he spent most of his time in the dental clinic when he wasn't studying and never showed up late or drunken. It was just his New York sophistication talking – an easy worldliness that John Henry admired.

"So what time does the show start?" John Henry asked. "I'd hate to miss any of my first night of debauchery."

"Who said anything about nighttime?" DeMorat chided him. "We'll start with the matinees, and go on from there. For in addition to being a patron of the Opera House, I am also a valued client at several of the finer taverns in town. And you, my young protégé, will soon become one too."

~~~~~~~~~

The interior of the Arch Street Opera House was as grandly ornate as its façade, with a velvet-curtained stage and a crystal chandelier hanging from a stamped tin ceiling. Around the stage, seventeen rows of wooden benches were set in a horseshoe bend, while two balconies balanced on eight pairs of Corinthian columns. And though there were no private boxes for wealthy patrons, the admission price still seemed steep: two-bits for the balcony and seventy-five cents each for a seat at the front of the orchestra, but well worth it to get a good look at the dancers – though they'd have been hard to miss, even from the back of the balcony.

The dancers seemed to be wearing little more than their underpinnings, their arms and legs bared and their bosoms impolitely exposed. But John Henry's astonishment didn't mean that he didn't enjoy the show, and he had to work hard to find a balance between polite applause and the cat-calls some of the men in the audience were making. The girls didn't seem to mind the attention though, twirling flirtatiously close to the gas footlights at the edge of the stage and giving the men in the front row an even better look at those bared bosoms. And seventy-five cents, John Henry quickly decided, had never been better spent.

But the thing that John Henry most remembered about that evening was the thrill of ordering his first drink across a saloon bar. For much as he had done his share of youthful drinking, he had never actually walked into a drinking establishment and ordered a glass from a barkeep before. His liquor drinking had been pretty much limited to borrowing some of his father's whiskey from beneath the sideboard or sharing a stolen bottle in the back room of Griffin's General Store with the other boys in town. So it was with a feeling of both adventure and accomplishment that he joined DeMorat and the others in standing up to the polished wood bar at the Broad Street Saloon, put one foot on the brass foot-rail like a practiced sporting man, and asked for a shot of Bourbon – and never had liquor tasted better.

After the shots of whiskey, the dental students stopped at the Dublin House Hotel and Restaurant for a light supper and a glass each of French champagne wine. Then they moved on to the Volks Halle Hotel to play ten-pins and shuffleboard and ease their thirst with some foamy lager beer. The Thistle House came after that, where they drank dark Dublin Porter and heavy English ale, and some of the other students said goodnight and left the rest to their entertainments. By the time they reached the St. Bernard Sample Room and got back to the Bourbon, it was just DeMorat and himself, and John Henry was feeling peculiar.

He'd never been drunken before, only a little tipsy from time to time. But he was well beyond tipsy now, with his head pleasantly spinning and his thoughts all loose. He was witty, he was dashing, he was having trouble keeping his balance as they walked along the brick streets of Philadelphia. And even that was amusing, laughing at the passersby who turned away in prudish disdain as the two young men stumbled from one saloon to the next. But what did a chastising glance from strangers matter, anyhow? They knew themselves to be true gentlemen and bon vivants. DeMorat said so himself, looking serious over a glass at a Front Street groggery by the river.

"Did you notice that fandango dancer looking down off the stage at me? The one with the dark-siren eyes?"

John Henry took a sip, wiped his mustache clean, and tried to focus on DeMorat's face.

"I wasn't payin' too much attention to their eyes," he said earnestly.

"Well, she was looking at me, all right," DeMorat said. "The last girl on the left in the chorus line. The one with the shapely thighs."

"Why, Mr. DeMorat!" John Henry said in pretended surprise at his companion's coarse language. "You know ladies don't have thighs, they have limbs. Which we, as gentlemen, are not supposed to notice. Like their bosoms," he said properly, then hiccoughed.

"Breasts," DeMorat corrected, lingering on the word. "Which we do, of course, notice. Why else would they pad themselves with ruffles and such to add to their natural, wondrous dimensions?"

"They pad themselves?" John Henry asked in amazement. "How do you know?"

"I know," DeMorat said with a self-important air. "Really, it is amazing how innocent you still are. Well," he said with a sudden determination, putting down his glass and standing shakily, "we must remedy that."

"What are you talkin' about?"

"We must introduce you to some women and let you study human anatomy for yourself — thighs and breasts and every other delightful aspect of femininity. I did promise you a night of debauchery, didn't I?"

John Henry couldn't argue the point, and he couldn't say that he wasn't tempted. But he was also beginning to feel a little queasy, the pleasantly euphoric spinning of his head beginning to turn into downright dizziness.

"I believe I'll have to decline…your gracious…offer," he said, his words suddenly sliding together. "Perhaps someother night…"

"You are beginning to look peaked, Holliday," DeMorat said with a laugh. "And we still have so much yet to do: billiards, bagatelle, several hands of poker…"

He didn't wait around to hear the rest of DeMorat's catalogue of gambling games, as the dizziness turned to nausea and he pushed himself to his feet and ran from the tavern, retching into the brick gutter.

He had only vague recollections of what happened after that: DeMorat hailing a horse-drawn cab and helping him up the stairs to his boarding house room; gaslight flickering on the ceiling as he lay across the bed, his head spinning; waves of nausea that made him run to the wash basin, heaving until his whole insides ached. And sleep at last.

~~~~~~~~~~

He had thought that the nausea would be the worst of it. He was wrong. The worst came next morning, when he awoke with the first hangover of his life. The giddiness of the night before was gone, and in its place was a piercing pain that made the daylight streaming into his window seem like fireworks going off in his head. And when DeMorat knocked on the door to see how he was faring, the noise sounded like a canon salute.

"You look like hell, Holliday!" DeMorat said cheerfully, clearly not suffering any himself from the night's intemperance. "Have you seen yourself in the mirror?"

He hadn't even thought to look at himself, since opening his eyes at all was a torture. But when DeMorat held a silvered shaving mirror to his face, he had to agree that he did, indeed, look hellish. His face was still peaked with a purplish cast about his mouth, his nose was red and running, his eyelids were swollen over teary bloodshot eyes.

"And you smell even worse than you look," DeMorat commented. "Morning-after vomit, I suppose. Though I take some of the responsibility myself for not watching better how much you were drinking, being a novice at this still."

DeMorat's half-hearted apologies didn't help John Henry's mood any, only serving to remind him of his complete failure at debauchery. The sporting life, it seemed, was not meant for him, and he said something to that effect.

"Nonsense," DeMorat countered, "everyone starts out that way. You'll get over the liquor sickness soon enough. You just need to toughen yourself up a bit, keep drinking regular until it doesn't bother you so much. Why, I had an uncle who could down a quart of hard liquor a day like drinking water, and never have it show. Just takes practice, that's all. And as for the rest of it, well, there's plenty of time yet. We've still got all of Christmas vacation ahead of us, after all."

"Christmas," John Henry said, then he lay back down and closed his eyes against the thought. He had hoped to go home to Georgia for the three-week winter break, maybe even getting a chance to see Mattie while he was there. But the cost of the trip – forty dollars for a round-trip steamboat passage – was a needless expense, according to his father. Better to save the money for his room and board for the next session of school than squander it on vacation travels. But being away all those months still, clear until June, seemed like forever. Especially now, with every moment a long painful eternity.

"It'll pass," DeMorat said as he picked up his hat and headed for the door. "And when it does, I'll be ready to finish your training. We've still got all that gaming to do, you know – and the ladies to meet, of course. Then he turned from the doorway and pulled something from his coat pocket, tossing it to John Henry: a silver flask with a stopper chained to it.

"What's this for?" John Henry asked.

"Hair of the dog that bit you," DeMorat replied. "The only known cure for drinking too much liquor is drinking a little more. Cheers."

As his footsteps echoed down the wooden stairs like pistol shots ringing off the walls, John Henry pulled the stopper from the liquor flask. The smell of the whiskey made his stomach grow queasy again, but he held his breath and took a sip anyway. Nothing could make him feel any worse than he already did, and he'd try anything that might make him feel better. Then he dropped the flask to the floor, groaned, and pulled the bed pillow over his head. Debauchery, he thought, wasn't near what it was made out to be.

~~~~~~~~~~

The whiskey helped some, lessening the pain in his head and settling his shattered nerves. But the queasiness stayed through supper and into the next morning, and the very thought of drinking more than a sip at a time was repulsive. So when DeMorat came back around a few days later offering to show him more of Philadelphia's night life, John Henry nearly declined – and only went with trepidation. He would never go on a binge again, he told himself, gingerly nursing the same one glass of whiskey all night. But drinking it slow like that, one careful sip at a time, was enough to give him the pleasant liquor light-headedness without the humiliation of puking in the street or the pain of the hangover the next day.

Moderation also left him with enough wits about him to enjoy the variety of pastimes the Philadelphia taverns advertised. Billiards came to him easy enough, and he soon became expert at the challenging table game called Bagatelle, using a cue stick to shoot small marble balls into a series of target holes on a decorated board. And though Philadelphia wasn't much known for card playing since the days when the Quaker founders had frowned on all forms of gambling, there were still plenty of card games around, including one John Henry had never seen before. It was called Faro, played on a table of green wool baize patterned with a suit of Spades where the players laid down their bets while a dealer pulled cards to see who'd won. He watched the Faro game, made a little money on Spanish Monte, and a little more when he and DeMorat found a poker game at a riverfront saloon. And as long as he went easy on the whiskey, staying only mildly inebriated, he enjoyed the nightlife immensely.

But his vacation wasn't all leisurely fun. He did study some, reviewing his notes from the fall session and looking over the winter session material to come, in case his father happened to ask how he'd spent his free time. And he made sure to go to church on Christmas Sunday morning, as his mother would have wanted him to, even though he'd been out gaming and drinking for most of Christmas Eve. But if the other members of the congregation of Old Saint George's Methodist Church smelled the whiskey still lingering on his breath, they didn't mention it. It was Christmas, after all, and the season of peace on earth and good will toward men.

~~~~~~~~~

It was hard to get back to work again when January came and the winter session of school began. He had gotten so used to staying up past midnight and sleeping in until noon that the eight o'clock clinic hour seemed more like the middle of the night. And the weather didn't help any, snowing heavily and dropping to a low of five degrees, then warming up just enough to melt the snow and leave a slippery sheeting of ice on the cobblestone streets and brick sidewalks. The river froze solid above the Schuylkill Dam, and steamships in the Delaware had to maneuver around the ice. The newspapers were filled with stories of ice injuries: sprained ankles and strained backs, broken limbs and head concussions, and the tragedy of a boy on Race Street who fell to his death while leaning out a third-story window trying to catch an icicle. Yet the locals said it was a mild winter, all things considered, and John Henry wondered what bad weather was like in Philadelphia.

But other than cursing the ice as he slipped and slid and shivered his way from his boarding house to school every morning, he didn't have time to ponder much on the climate, for his professors seemed more determined than ever to overload their students with work. There were exams at the end of every lecture week, and case presentations to be made, and the endless line of clinic patients to be treated. And come March, when the senior students would be graduated and gone, the clinic work would double.

Spring came on all at once, with the ice in the Schuylkill River thawing out overnight and the riverbanks turning floody. But the warming temperatures brought the tree-lined streets into a bloom of green leaves and flowers, and made John Henry suddenly homesick for Georgia, where the air would be lazy-sweet already with a smell of honeysuckle to it and the azaleas would be blooming pink and white and wild among the pines. And best of all, Mattie was in Georgia, waiting for him.

Chapter Nine

Valdosta, 1871

There was an old proverb that said you could never go home again, and it had never before made sense to John Henry. But as the Atlantic and Gulf Line Railroad chugged along through the Georgia piney woods and steamed to a stop at the depot in Valdosta, he suddenly understood what it meant. For though he knew that Valdosta was a small place, with its few hundred inhabitants and fewer businesses, he had never before realized how very primitive it was. There were no paved streets in Valdosta, no sturdy brick sidewalks, no horse-drawn trolley cars going anywhere, and no place to go if there were. There were no gas street lamps to light the green darkness of the country nights, and no public waterworks to bring bath and drinking water into the rustic frame cottages where the smell of the outhouses stewing in the summer heat nearly overwhelmed the scent of the honeysuckle. And as far as John Henry was concerned, Valdosta was not only miles away from anywhere worth being, it was years away, as well.

He had a hard time explaining his dissatisfaction to his father, for Henry had seen Philadelphia, too, and thought it crowded and noisy. But Henry had only been a visitor there, come and gone in a week's time. John Henry had spent ten months of his life there and had grown to enjoy the bustle of the place, with its theaters and restaurants, its music halls and saloons. And that was the problem: he'd grown up in Philadelphia. But now that he was home he was being treated like a child again, expected to obey his father's every whim.

Henry had his life all planned out for him, of course. In addition to the preceptorship he'd be serving under Dr. Frink, there was work to be done in the Carriage and Buggy business and plenty to do around the home place as well. His father wanted the horses groomed, the barn cleaned out, the buggy polished until the brass fittings shone like mirrors. There were bird droppings to be cleaned from the window sills, squirrel nests to be swept out of the attic, and loose roof shingles to be nailed down before another wind shook them free. And though there were still paid darkies around to do the hard labor, he wouldn't have been surprised if his father had asked him to clean out the privy, as well. But when he made any mention of the fact that he was halfway through dental school and practically a doctor already and ought to be above such work, Henry only gave him more to do. Responsibility, he called it, and gratitude as well, as though John Henry had never shown either.

Mostly, though, he just wanted to sleep. The long days of dental school and longer nights of studying had left him worn out, and even Rachel commented that he seemed awful tired. It was probably the change in climate that was causing it, she said, being home again where the weather was warm and languid-like. Rocking chair weather, she called it, and enough to make a body feel downright fatigued. His father just thought he was being lazy.

~~~~~~~~~~

Rachel was right about the weather being warm that summer, even for south Georgia. The temperature stayed near one-hundred degrees for five straight weeks, hardly coming down much at night, and folks slept with their windows wide open, letting in flies and mosquitoes along with whatever cooling breezes might come by. But uncomfortable as the nights were, the days were worse – especially for the town dentist and his apprentice, working all day in a stuffy dental office and properly dressed in wool suits and high-collared shirts. By the end of the day, John Henry was sweating like a field hand and wishing he were down at his old swimming hole skinny dipping in the green waters of the Withlacoochee. And imagining himself there only made him more miserable still. For the swimming hole was where he'd taken Mattie all those years ago when her family had stayed with his at Cat Creek, and thus far he hadn't yet figured a way to get up to see her, though he'd looked forward to the visit all year long.

The trouble was, he couldn't just up and announce that he was heading off for a few days to see his sweetheart, as their romance was still a secret as far as he knew. Nor could he leave his preceptorship with Dr. Frink since his attendance was a required part of his dental education. So until he could come up with a reasonable excuse for leaving work and town both, all he could do was cool his heels and curse the heat – and in the end, it was the heat that made his trip possible.

Dr. Frink and his family were originally from the town of Jasper, up towards the

Blue Ridge Mountains of north Georgia. So when the weather turned torrid and stayed that way too long, Dr. Frink decided to close down his office and remove his family back to the mountains for a spell, and John Henry was suddenly free to make a trip of his own – and he soon settled on the perfect excuse to make to his father.

"Uncle John's been wantin' to know how my dental studies are comin'," he said one evening after supper, as his father sat out on the front porch sipping at a lemonade and watching the fireflies in the yard. "I reckon I could use the time to go on up to Atlanta and tell him all about it." And stop off in Jonesboro to see Mattie as well, he thought to himself.

"I reckon you could," his father said, "but your Uncle John's not in Atlanta just now. He's taken the family up to Tennessee to visit your cousin George's wife's kin. They're havin' a big first birthday party for that new baby of theirs. A good excuse to get out of the city, sounds like to me, away from the heat and the smell both. You think one outhouse is bad in the summer? Atlanta's got thousands of 'em, and street garbage as well. Glad I live away out here in the country when the weather is steamy like this."

But John Henry wasn't happy to be stuck in the country, nor was he going to be so easily distracted from his plans.

"Well, I suppose I should at least pay a call on Uncle Rob," he said with a sigh, as though that were the last thing he wanted to do. "He was mighty good to me that summer I stayed in Jonesboro. Seems right to thank him for his generosity."

"Seems like the thanks is a long time in comin'," Henry replied, giving him a curious look. "What's got you so mannerly all of the sudden?"

John Henry shifted uneasily under his father's steady gaze. "Well, I reckon I'm just growin' up, Pa, and recognizin' my responsibilities."

He chose the words carefully, knowing that the one thing Henry couldn't deny him was the chance to be responsible. Still, his father took a little long making up his mind, not answering until he'd drunk down the whole lemonade.

"All right," Henry said finally, "I'll send a letter to your Uncle Rob, let him know you're comin' for a visit. But you make sure to be a good houseguest up there, help out around the place and all. You know Rob hasn't been doin' well since the War. I reckon he could use an extra pair of man's hands, with all those girls he's sired. Good thing he joined the Catholics when he got married. He's practically raisin' a convent up there."

John Henry smiled a reply, but it wasn't for his father's attempted humor. It was the other thing Henry had said, about his Uncle Rob needing an extra pair of hands around the place. For that was the first time, to John Henry's recollection, that his father had ever called him a man.

~~~~~~~~

His father, it seemed, wasn't the only one who noticed he was no longer a boy – as he discovered when he finally arrived in Jonesboro and Mattie's little sisters met him at their front door, giggling.

"What's that on your face, Cousin John Henry?" Marie asked. "Did a 'coon lose its tail?"

"Don't be silly," Theresa replied, "that's just a mustache. Like Pa's, only scraggly."

"Well it looks like a 'coon to me," Marie said again. "And it don't look right on John Henry."

But before he could take too much offense at their girlish chatter, Mattie stepped up behind them and said with ladylike kindness, "Why, I think it makes him look real handsome. Welcome home, John Henry."

The afternoon light coming in through the open door shone like gold on her auburn hair. And though it had been nearly two years since he'd last seen her at Cousin George's wedding in Atlanta, suddenly it seemed that no time had passed at all.

" 'Afternoon, Mattie," he said, his heart warming at the sight of her. "How've you been?"

It was a needless question, considering all the letters they had exchanged since he went away to school. But he couldn't very well say what he was feeling – that seeing her again was like coming up for air after staying under water too long – without embarrassing them both in front of her whole family. So for the time being, pleasantries would have to do.

"I've been well, Cousin," she replied politely. "And we're all so happy you could come to pay us a little visit. Why, I can't remember how long it's been since you were last in Jonesboro."

Her little sisters, however, were not quite as schooled in the social graces as Mattie was, and Catherine blurted out: "Of course you remember, Mattie. Last time John Henry was here, everybody was talkin' about him tryin' to blow up that Courthouse. His Pa made him leave town and come on up here…"

"That's enough, Catherine!" Mattie replied firmly. Then she put her hand on

John Henry's arm, "Never mind her, honey. She lives for dramatic moments and we have so few of them here in little Jonesboro. And it is, truly, very good to see you again." And the way she looked up at him, her eyes filled with more than just family affection, made him forget Catherine's careless words. "Now why don't you put your things down here in the hall and come on into supper? Lucy and Roberta and I've been cookin' a nice welcome home meal for you."

Then, as if overhearing them, his Aunt Mary Anne called from the kitchen at the back of the house, "Suppertime, children! And don't you let that front door slam behind you, John Henry!"

"Don't worry Mother, he's all grown up now!" Mattie called back, and John Henry looked at her quizzically.

"And just what is that supposed to mean?"

But Mattie didn't answer, only laughing a little as she slipped her arm through his and led him into the dining room. And John Henry decided that, whatever else was said, the only thing that mattered was that Mattie had said he looked handsome.

~~~~~~~~~~

The old Celtic cross hanging on the wall over the dining table had been given to Mattie's mother by her own mother, who'd received it as a wedding gift when she was married long ago in Ireland, and Aunt Mary Anne revered it as though it were some sort of saintly relic. Taking her place at the far end of the long trestle table across from her husband, she always stopped a moment to bow her head toward the cross, a quiet gesture of faithfulness. Then she would settle herself onto her slat back chair, skirts draped around her and hands clasped on her overturned supper plate, and lead her family in the blessing on the food.

"In the name of the Father, and of the Son, and of the Holy Spirit," she would say in her lilting Irish-accented drawl, "Bless us, oh Lord, and these thy gifts which we are about to receive through thy bounty through Christ our Lord, Amen."

The family would say the holy words along with her, then cross themselves properly before she would allow them to turn their plates over and begin the serving. But that was as far as the solemnity went, for as soon as folded hands were free to pass the bowls of rice and buttered squash and biscuits with gravy, her husband would take over as head of the table and the laughter would begin. For Robert Kennedy Holliday was as light-hearted as Mary Anne Fitzgerald Holliday was serious-minded, always ready with a joke or a funny story about someone in town – which Aunt Mary Anne tolerated with Christian patience and long-suffering.

"Now Rob, dear," she would say in gentle admonishment, "the Blaylocks are our neighbors. We mustn't talk about them unkindly."

"It's not unkindness," he would answer between mouthfuls of his supper, "just pointin' out the truth, that's all. If a man can't tell the difference between a bottle of liquor and a bottle of castor oil until he's drunk too much of one of them, I reckon maybe he's already had too much of the other. Or ought to build himself a new privy closer to the house so's he can get there before having to admit his mistake publicly. Pass the stewed prunes, please."

Though Mary Anne had tried for all the twenty-odd years of her marriage, she had never been able to temper Uncle Rob's sense of humor. So it was surprising to John Henry that his uncle seemed less jovial now, though his father had mentioned something about Uncle Rob's not being in the best of health. He did look more worn than usual, tired-out maybe, or troubled.

"So how long are you plannin' on stayin', John Henry?" his uncle asked as the family finished supper and started into dessert.

"Only a week or so, Sir," he replied, "just until Dr. Frink gets his wife and children settled up in Jasper and goes on back to Valdosta. I hope my bein' here won't inconvenience you any. My father told me you could use some help around the place, anyhow." He was careful not to add his father's comments on Uncle Rob's place being like a convent – which seemed true enough, with all the praying that went on. Once supper was over and the evening chores had been done, there'd be more praying as Aunt Mary Anne gathered the children around her for evening devotions and the long recitation of the rosary before bed.

"I reckon I could use some help," his uncle agreed. "That fence around the yard is needin' some paint for one thing, if you're willin'."

"It needs more than just paint," his Aunt Mary Anne countered, "it needs to be pulled out and rebuilt, that's what. Why, John Henry would have to spend his whole visit here workin' to fix it right. Whatever are you thinkin', Rob?"

"Hard work never hurt a body," his uncle replied with a shrug. "Besides, I know my brother Henry. He'll expect to hear I gave the boy too much to do, or he won't think I've been a good host."

Mattie's little sisters giggled at that, but John Henry saw nothing funny in it.

"I don't mind fixin' your fence, Uncle Rob," he said earnestly. "I reckon I owe you a debt of gratitude for all you did for me some years back. I hope you'll let me do whatever you need, to show my thanks."

He'd prepared that little speech all the way up from Valdosta, but only his aunt seemed much impressed by it.

"Why, isn't that sweet!" Mary Anne said with a smile. "I do believe Mattie's right about you, John Henry. You have grown up – and turned into a real gentleman, as well."

"But Mattie didn't say John Henry was a gentleman," Theresa said, eyes looking mischievous. "She said he was *handsome*," and the way she drawled out the word made it seem sweet as pulled taffy.

"Is that right?" Uncle Rob said, and shot Mattie a quick look.

But his eldest daughter didn't catch his glance, her eyes lowered and a blush rising in her freckled face.

"I suppose I said somethin' like that," she replied, then quickly changed the subject. "Is it true they really have ten libraries up there in Philadelphia, John Henry? That must have been lovely with all those wonderful books to read."

"Actually, there's eleven libraries in the city, if you count the one at the Medical School. But there's more music halls than libraries, and more taverns even than that." He regretted the words as soon as he spoke them, as his Aunt Mary Anne said with a disapproving lift of her brows:

"Oh?"

"Though I myself never visited such places, of course," he added quickly. And as the lie seemed to placate her, he was about to add that he had spent most of his free weekend time at church, when little Jim Bob spoke up.

"Pa's goin' to the city," he said. "He's gonna live on top of a store."

"*Above* a store," Mattie said, whispering a correction. *On top* would mean livin' on the roof, and that's silly, of course."

"What are you talkin' about?" John Henry asked, bewildered by the seemingly meaningless turn in the conversation.

"Jim Bob means I've takin' a position up in Atlanta," his uncle said casually. "Your Uncle John Holliday has asked me to come up and help awhile in his mercantile partnership with Mr. Tidwell. I'll be home again soon enough."

"You're leavin' Jonesboro?" John Henry asked in surprise. He could imagine his own father going off from home on business, as Henry regularly traveled to Savannah and Atlanta on buying trips. But Uncle Rob was so much a family man that John Henry could hardly picture him without them, or them without him. "What about your job at the depot?" he went on. "I thought you were Baggage Master for the Macon and Western."

"I was. But I'm gettin' to be too old for baggage work, and I used to be in the mercantile business myself once, back before the War. Seems like a good opportunity."

There was a general silence at the table, then Aunt Mary Anne said a little too brightly, "Well, look at the time! Why, it'll be past bedtime before we get these supper dishes cleared and washed. Girls, get to your chores. And Rob, do take Jim Bob upstairs and get him ready for bed. Seven-years old is entirely too young for stayin' up so late."

Uncle Rob smiled wearily. "You see how it is, John Henry? I'm a hen-pecked rooster in a hen house. Be good to get away for a while, pretend I'm a single man again. I'll let Jim Bob here wait on these women. Come on, son," he said, tousling the boy's hair, "best not disobey your Mama. And don't you stay up too late, either, John Henry. You'll want to start on that fence before the sun gets too hot."

"Yessir, Uncle Rob. And Sir?"

"Yes, John Henry?"

"Do you still have that saddle horse you used to keep? The one with the russet coat?"

His uncle nodded. "She's out in the barn if you want to take a look at her. She could use a good groomin', too, when you get done with that fence."

"Yessir," he said again, and gave a casual glance across the table toward Mattie. "Maybe I'll go out for a ride tonight, once the moon gets high. I always was fond of that pretty mare."

~~~~~~~~~~

He hadn't been riding in Jonesboro since the summer of his exile there, but it was all so familiar still: dusty Church Street that joined up with the Fayetteville Road, the green waters of the Flint River over to the west, the track that led down to Lovejoy off to the south. But he wasn't riding out of adolescent frustration this time, letting the horse take him where it would, and he had no interest in ending up at the Fitzgerald's plantation – though he did have a plan in mind. For he hoped that Mattie might have taken his hint and would be waiting for him back in the barn when he returned from his ride. And this time there would be no anger between them, only the sweetness of a few stolen moments of romance in the moonlight.

He could see just how it would be: he'd come in from the ride, feeling flushed and healthy, and Mattie would step out of the shadows with a smile that said she knew what he was thinking of. But lady that she was, she would cast her gaze aside, pretending not to see the eagerness in his face, paying attention to the horse instead.

"She is a pretty thing, isn't she?" she would ask.

"She's pretty all right, more than I remembered."

And when he slid down from the saddle and ran his hand over the horse's shining flanks, his fingers would meet Mattie's as if by accident, and hover there.

"You didn't wait up just for me, did you?" he would ask, teasing, and she would answer with a toss of her auburn hair.

"Of course not. I was just worried about the horse, that's all."

But her hand wouldn't move from under his, and when he closed his fingers around hers and turned her to face him, he would hear her breathing coming fast as a heartbeat.

"I have missed you, Mattie," he would say, whispering the words, and she would sigh and look up at him with shining eyes.

"I have missed you too, John Henry!"

And when he bent to kiss her lips she'd catch a breath and then melt into his arms. And where it went from there, only the night and the moonlight knew.

That was the plan, anyhow, and thinking of it made him feel light-headed and he raced the horse faster than he should have in the late summer heat. By the time he got the mare back into the barnyard she was working on a lather, and he had to attend to getting her brushed down and watered before he could look for his expected company. But though he waited in the barn for nearly an hour, grooming the horse until her russet coat gleamed, Mattie never did come.

Had she misunderstood his intention? Had he been too obscure for fear of being too obvious? Had something else demanded her attention when she tried to free herself of the house? Or was she simply not interested in meeting him there in the moonlight? His pride wouldn't let him consider the last possibility, and left him wondering and frustrated with his unfulfilled imagining.

But as he shut up the barn and headed back into the house, past the rows of vegetables in the kitchen garden and the heroes' graves in the flowerbed, his eyes caught a glimpse of something unexpected. In one of the upstairs windows of the house, a curtain fluttered to a close and an oil lamp went quickly out. And he was certain, with all the surety of youthful passion, that it was Mattie who had been there at the window watching him all along.

~~~~~~~~~~

But that furtive glance from a window was all the satisfaction he had for his train ride north and his week's visit in Jonesboro. For with all the family meals and family prayers and the work of mending his uncle's dilapidated fence, he had no time at all to be alone with Mattie. And if he hadn't known better, he might have thought there was some kind of conspiracy to it, the way everyone in the family seemed to work together to keep the two of them apart. When Mattie brought him a pitcher of lemonade after his long morning of pulling nails from the old fence boards, her sisters Lucy and Roberta came along to help pour. When she brought him a wet towel to wipe his brow after a hot afternoon of digging post holes, Catherine and Theresa had to help her with the water bucket. And even on his last morning there, when he boldly asked her to walk with him up to the train depot to say goodbye, young Jim Bob was sent to walk along with them.

"I like to watch the trains," he said, as the three of them trudged up Church Street toward the railroad tracks. "Did you like to watch the trains when you were little, Cousin John Henry?"

"I reckon I did, Jim Bob. I always liked to think of the places a train could take you – far-away places you only heard of."

"I like the noise," Jim Bob replied. "And the smoke."

Mattie smiled over his head at John Henry. "Jim Bob says the train looks like a dragon, the way the steam comes out its nose."

"Mama says I have a *peculiar* imagination," the little boy said. "That's a funny word, ain't it? Mama's always saying funny words like that. And what's a party-gal, anyhow?"

"A party gal?" John Henry asked with a laugh. "Why, I reckon that could mean a lot of things..."

"None of which you need to know about just now, Jim Bob," Mattie put in primly. "Where did you hear that, anyhow?"

"From Mama," Jim Bob said, absently kicking at a stone lying in the dirt. "She told Pa that John Henry's like a regular party-gal, come home again. She said it like it was somethin' nice, like a black sheep turned white, she said."

John Henry gave Mattie a glance and saw that she was smiling, too.

"So what's a party-gal?" Jim Bob asked again, and Mattie answered him patiently, like the schoolteacher she had trained to be.

"I believe the word was *prodigal*," she explained, "like the story of the prodigal son in the Bible. You remember Mama tellin' you that at bedtime when you were little, don't you? The Prodigal Son is one of the Parables of our Lord, about a rich young man who went off and squandered his inheritance, then repented of his sinful ways. And when he returned home at last, his father gave him a feast and put a fancy new cloak on him."

Jim Bob took a long look at John Henry, considering. "Are you really rich, John Henry?"

"Only a little," he replied, laughing at the boy's literal-mindedness. Of all Mattie's bothersome siblings, the inquisitive little boy was the most entertaining. But his next words took the laughter right out of John Henry's heart.

"So if you're rich and your father gave you a cloak and all, how come you have to wear sheep's clothes? 'Cause when Mama said you were a black sheep turned white, Pa said maybe you were really just wearin' sheep's clothes. What's that supposed to mean, anyhow?"

John Henry didn't answer the question and neither did Mattie, taking a firm hold of Jim Bob's hand like he'd done something wrong.

"That's enough questions, Jim Bob," she said with uncharacteristic sharpness. "Why don't you take John Henry's satchel and run ahead and see if the porter can put it on the train?" Then she gave him a push and turned to John Henry. "Don't listen to him, honey! You know how he is, always makin' things up. Why, a train's a dragon to Jim Bob. He probably just misunderstood. I'm sure my father never said anything of the sort..."

"I wouldn't be surprised if he did," John Henry cut in hotly, "the way everyone's been actin' this week, like they can't trust me to be alone with you. Your father said he felt like a rooster in a hen-house, so I reckon he thinks I'm a wolf, come to steal his chickens away. No wonder he kept me workin' so hard I never even had a chance to kiss you." He was so angry at his uncle's injustice that he didn't realize what he'd said until Mattie remarked demurely:

"You wanted to kiss me?"

"Hell, yes! What did you think I came all the way up here for, anyhow? Just to fix your father's broken fence? If all I wanted was a lot of hard work, my father's got plenty for me to do back in Valdosta. I've been waitin' for over a year to kiss you again, Mattie Holliday, and I hoped you'd been wantin' the same."

It wasn't the romantic speech he'd intended to make nor even a particularly passionate one, more anger than anything. But Mattie blushed prettily like he'd just paid her the nicest compliment in the world, and said softly, "I wouldn't mind you kissin' me."

If there hadn't been a crowd of people gathered at the platform already and no privacy at all, he would have taken her in his arms and kissed her right then. But Jonesboro was too small a town to make a public show of affection like that without word getting back to Mattie's folks even before she got home herself. So all he could do was lean down to kiss her on the cheek, like a proper loving cousin.

"I'll be back again come spring," he promised. "And then I will kiss you, if you're still willin' to have me."

Mattie nodded a reply, but her words were lost in the scream of the steam engine's whistle, as Jim Bob came running back toward them with his arms waving.

"John Henry! You better get your ticket before the train leaves. Wish I was goin' off somewhere on the train!"

And for the first time in his life, John Henry didn't feel the same way.

~~~~~~~~~~

He thought about Mattie and that unfulfilled kiss all the way back to Valdosta and for many long summer days after that, which was probably why Miss Thea Morgan became the surprised recipient of his frustrated affections, if only for a brief evening.

Thea had been one of his preceptorship patients that summer, come into the office with a troublesome toothache that ended up as six fillings and three extracted molars. And though it had been a complicated treatment, taking five office visits altogether and causing her several painful nights of recovery, Thea had borne it all bravely – a courage that impressed John Henry. For in most ways Thea Morgan still seemed the same plain and timid girl he had known during their school days at the Valdosta Institute, pale-haired and pale-eyed, with a skinny figure that womanhood had done little to enhance.

She also seemed to have the same infatuation for John Henry that she had harbored during all those school years – though he blamed himself some for that. If he hadn't taken Sam Griffin's bet those many years ago and kissed Thea at the spring barn dance, she might have gotten over him as soon as school let out. But he could tell by the way she still turned moony eyes toward him, simpering at his every word, that she had neither forgotten him nor given up her schoolgirl hope of winning him over. But though he didn't return Thea's affection any more than he ever had, he did feel flattered that she should hold him in such high esteem. So he wasn't opposed, as the time drew near for his return to dental school, to accept her invitation to supper at her family's home as a sort of farewell party for him. Besides, the Morgans still owed him twenty-one dollars for the work he had done on Thea – and the money would come in handy on his return to Philadelphia.

The Morgans lived out at the end of Troupe Street, close to the piney woods at the edge of town, and they didn't receive too many visitors – especially since Thea's father had recently passed away and Mrs. Morgan was in her widowhood seclusion. But in spite of their proper mourning, the family seemed pleased to entertain "young Dr. Holliday," as they kept calling him, even though he explained twice that he wouldn't receive that title until his graduation in the spring. And when Thea said in a meek voice that, doctor title or no, John Henry was still the best dentist in town and they would all miss him when he left for school again, he found himself enjoying the attention. It was nice to be fussed over and hear that his leaving home meant anything to anybody. For unlike the year before, when he'd left Valdosta with a shiny new set of luggage and best wishes from the whole town, it seemed that folks had gotten used to his being gone and didn't notice much that he was leaving again.

Thea noticed, though, and when supper was over and she walked him out to the front porch to say goodbye, there were even a few tears in her colorless eyes, and John Henry was grateful enough for the attention that he thought he might manage to give her a quick kiss on the cheek in parting. After all, they were old schoolmates.

But Thea seemed to misunderstand his casual intention as he bent his head toward hers, for just as his lips should have met her cheek, she turned her face and he found himself giving her a real kiss instead.

As a gentleman, he should have turned his face aside, coughed as though he hadn't noticed the unexpected intimacy, then made a hasty farewell to save them both from an embarrassing moment. As a gentleman, he certainly shouldn't have taken advantage of the situation for his own gratification. But finding himself in a sudden embrace, with surprisingly willing lips against his, he pushed all gentlemanly thoughts aside and went right on kissing her. And for a few stolen moments in the dark shadows of the Morgan's front porch, he let himself imagine that it was Mattie he was kissing and who so eagerly kissed him back.

But Thea wasn't Mattie, and beyond his brief fantasy, he was no more moved by the intimacy than he had been when he'd kissed her behind the barn at the school dance. The truth was, her lips were still too prim and cool for his passions. So once he had satisfied himself that Thea had nothing special to offer him, he stepped back, said his polite goodbye, and walked off into the Valdosta darkness.

If Thea stood smiling at his retreating figure, he didn't care enough to turn around and look.

~~~~~~~~~~

There were no fireworks to greet his arrival in Philadelphia as there had been the year before, only the bustle of the busy waterfront and the crowded cobblestone streets, and a dental clinic filled with patients waiting to be seen. He and his classmates were senior students now, supervising the clinic operations and sniggering at the mistakes made by the incoming students. But though their study load was somewhat lighter than before, they still had afternoon lectures to attend and exams to prepare for. And after the Christmas holiday there would be the doctoral thesis to present, as well, the final proof that the students had learned enough to be proclaimed dentists and be awarded their diplomas.

John Henry wasn't too concerned about the thesis. He'd always been good at composition and quick with a clever phrase, and he figured he'd have plenty of time during Christmas to get the work done. But the regular coursework was becoming more of a challenge, as his lack of preparation compared to the other students became more apparent. While the others seemed to be able to face each week's exams with only a little review of the information they already knew, John Henry had to work hard to memorize everything. If it hadn't been for the humbly offered help of Jameson Fuches, the bright young man the others still called "The Professor," he might not have passed the exams at all, and he counted himself lucky to be one seat down from the best student in the class. But not until the weather turned wintry again did he know how lucky he really was.

~~~~~~~~~~

The year before had been mild as far as Yankees were concerned, though John Henry had thought the temperatures less than temperate. But that winter of 1871 was too cold even for the hardy people of Philadelphia who complained that it was the worst season they had ever seen. For a boy from south Georgia, used to lazy humid summers and pleasant sunny winters, the cold was nearly deadly.

It started with a heavy rain that November, causing a three-foot rise in the level of the Schuylkill River where the waters turned turbid and the channel was choked with tree limbs and debris. All across the city, fences collapsed and awnings came down, taking out the telegraph lines and leaving Philadelphia deaf and mute for a week.

By Thanksgiving Day, when the Yankee General George Meade made a show of reviewing the troops at Fairmount Park, the rain had turned to sleet, freezing the shallow ponds around the city and filling the street gutters with ice. But the glistening streets didn't stop the throngs of promenaders from taking their traditional stroll in front of Independence Hall, nor did it dampen the spirits of the laughing children who played in the congealed standing water at the excavation site of the new City Hall. It was early winter, that was all – and only the frozen fire hydrants seemed any real cause for concern.

But when Thanksgiving passed and December began, the weather turned more bitter still. With the temperature hovering just above twenty degrees, the gutters froze over and water pipes burst, flooding the cobblestone streets with ice and mud. The Schuylkill River froze over, too, the ice forming so rapidly that boats were bound fast in it. Even the Delaware was closed above the city, the channel between Philadelphia and New Jersey filled with floating ice.

For the first time since John Henry had arrived in Philadelphia, the streets were nearly deserted of traffic as everyone not needing to venture out stayed indoors enjoying the warmth of Franklin stoves and tight-shuttered windows. But the stuffiness of the overheated rooms made John Henry even more uncomfortable than the cold did. He wasn't used to so much dry heat, as the hot air parched his lungs and left him with an irritating sore throat. And by the end of the fall session and the last clinic day before Christmas, he was anxiously looking forward to spending an evening walking from one tavern to the next breathing in the stiff cold air and sipping whiskey until his sore throat was numb.

But one night of whiskey didn't help much and the next morning he woke feeling achy all over, the irritating sore throat turning into a raspy cough. And though he needed to get started on his vacation work of researching, writing, and polishing his doctoral thesis, he couldn't seem to find the energy to do it. He opened his books and tried to focus on the pages of dental pathology and therapeutics, but his head felt so heavy that he could hardly keep reading. And he was sweltering, even with the window shutters thrown wide open. If only he could get cooled down, wave away the heat that was rising up inside of him, he might be able to get to work...

Outside, the thermometer on the wall of the Merchant's Exchange registered a noon high of ten degrees while Chestnut Hill reported a temperature below zero. It was the coldest December day on record and John Henry slept with his head on his books and the freezing air filling his open-windowed room. But with the fever that raged inside of him, he didn't feel the chill at all.

~~~~~~~~~

It was the pneumonia, his landlady said, when she came in to bank the fire after dark and found him half-conscious there. But when he tried to answer that he really wasn't ill, just suffering from a sore throat, his words were lost in a fit of coughing that tore at his chest.

He'd never felt such a pain before, like a knife in his side when he breathed. And without Mrs. Schrenk's helping hand to steady him, he might not have made it to his bed to lie down, though once there, he couldn't move without the coughing coming on again, leaving him breathless and teary-eyed. She would send for the doctor, she said, as she pulled closed his window shutters and turned down the gaslight. But whether or not one would come out on such a night, and so close to Christmas, she didn't know.

The doctor came, held a stethoscope to his chest, prescribed a regimen of Tartar Emetic and boiled turpentine vapors for the congestion, then left him to his own nursing. There were pneumonia cases all over the city, he said, and the old folks and babies needed his tending more than a young man who would probably recover just fine on his own. But if the pneumonia should happen to take a turn for the worse, there was always the sick ward at the Medical College – though that thought didn't give John Henry much comfort. Beneath the Medical College, deep in the dungeon-like basement, was the pit where the anatomy lab cadavers were thrown. And feeling as weak and fevered as he was, he wouldn't be surprised to find himself there among them soon.

Mrs. Schrenk scoffed at the doctor's medicines and brought out her own home remedies of Comfrey tea, a fried onion plaster, and a liniment made of camphor and lard rubbed onto his chest and covered by a flannel cloth to ease his breathing. But even her charitable attentions did little to ease his pains and he lay for long days shivering and sweating in his sleep, then waking with a racking cough that brought up rusty-green sputum.

He had odd dreams in those feverish days and nights. He was home again in Georgia, a little boy with a head cold, and his mother was gently tending to him. He was coming in from a long horse ride, breathing hard, and finding Mattie there waiting for him. He was walking into a hot and crowded tavern, where DeMorat kept insisting he finish a tumbler of whiskey.

"One sip, for now. Then we'll get the rest of it down," DeMorat said, but as John Henry took a taste of the bitter liquor, he sputtered and choked.

"What is that?" he said aloud, his words waking him from the troubled dream.

"Rat poison," DeMorat answered. "But it has some efficacy in curing pneumonia."

John Henry forced his fever-bleary eyes to open and focus, and realized that it was not DeMorat who was pouring the deadly drink down him after all, but pale-haired Jameson Fuches.

"Good," Jameson commented. "It'll be easier to take if you're awake. One teaspoon now, then another every two hours. But no more than two teaspoons at a time, or you'll end up dead like the rats."

But John Henry closed his mouth against the poison, shaking his head. "What are you doing here?" he mumbled through pursed lips.

"I came by to wish you a happy New Year. I expected to find you deep into the study of salivary calculus for your thesis, but found you ill instead. Your landlady seemed pleased when I offered to take a look at you. Seems her poultices weren't working, though better old-wives poultices than the prescription that quack doctor left. Tartar Emetic! Do you know what that is?"

"No," John Henry answered weakly.

"High doses of ingested antimony potassium tartrate. Induces blood-letting by vomiting. You'd think in a city with four medical colleges there'd be some decent doctors around. Now be a good patient and drink your medicine down."

But John Henry turned his head aside. "I'm not takin' rat poison." What did he know of Jameson Fuches, really? Only that he was brilliant and peculiarly reserved. Maybe his quiet demeanor covered a mind murderously deranged…

"I'm not trying to kill you, John Henry," Jameson said, as though reading his thoughts. "I'm trying to save your life. And blue as your lips are, I'd say you're cyanotic already and ought to be glad I came along when I did. This particular poison is also an excellent cardiac stimulant and bronchodilator, if taken properly. It's called Squills, from the bulb of a Mediterranean blue lily. You may recall our Chemistry professor giving a rather thorough description of its properties, first session."

"All right," John Henry replied, too tired to keep up the fight. Besides, Jameson had never been wrong about anything scientific so far. He opened his mouth to the medicine, and coughed as it went down.

"Now go back to sleep," Jameson ordered. "I'll wake you in two hours for another dose."

"And what are you gonna do until then?" John Henry asked as he closed his eyes.

"Sit here and work on my thesis. I figure I'll have to get it done early so you can borrow my notes for your own. It'll be another week or two before you're well enough to even think about working again, and that won't give you much time to finish up."

John Henry only nodded a reply as he drifted back into his exhausted sleep. If Jameson Fuches really were a murderer, at least he killed with kindness.

~~~~~~~~~~

The rat poison worked and he began to breathe easier from that very afternoon, though Jameson was right about his recovery. It was weeks before he was able to do more than drag himself out of bed and to school every day, then drag himself back home to collapse in sleep again. And the weather didn't help any, the bitter cold of that hard winter holding on with long icy fingers that seemed to reach right through his heavy wool overcoat and tightly wrapped neck scarf. Both the rivers were frozen over and the snow was piled so high on the city streets that there was hardly room for single buggies to pass by. And with the cold came a fresh outbreak of house fires around the city as people left their hearths burning too high against the frigid nights. The fire alarms would sound, the fire engines would race to the scene with hoses opened to vainly spray water that turned to ice as soon as it hit the chilled bricks. It was a bad time for Philadelphia, and for anyone recovering from the pneumonia in particular.

But he did recover, and even managed to complete his doctoral thesis on time – thanks, again, to Jameson Fuches. For good as his word, Jameson loaned him his own carefully detailed notes on the various diseases of the teeth, so that they both ended up presenting essentially the same paper. If the professors noticed the similarity, they didn't make any comment on it, only commended John Henry for having the fortitude to finish the session in spite of his prolonged convalescence. Any other student might have asked to be allowed a sabbatical from the coursework, and finished another year. But then, no other student had the devoted friendship of Jameson Fuches – though why John Henry had earned the honor, he wasn't quite sure. Until that fortuitous New Year's visit, he and Jameson had never done any more than study together a little. Since his illness, they seemed to have become true confederates.

But even more than Jameson's support, John Henry had his father to thank for inspiring him to finish school successfully. For he knew that if he returned to Georgia without having completed his work, his father would never forgive him, and even the very real excuse of illness would not have softened Henry's displeasure. Illness was weakness, in Henry Holliday's philosophy, and weakness could never be accepted. So John Henry struggled along and ignored the tiredness that continued to plague him, giving up sleep for long hours of study and finishing the session with such high marks that even Jameson was impressed.

There was more to be done than just a doctoral thesis, of course. There was a specimen box to be delivered to the College Collection, a denture of carved ivory set in vulcanized rubber to be presented to the Professor of Mechanical Dentistry, a completed patient treatment case to be approved by the Professor of Clinical Dentistry. And all of that had to be finished before he would be allowed to stand for a final examination by the entire Faculty. But by the end of February, as the winter finally let loose its icy hold and melted into a muddy early spring, John Henry had finished up with all of it and was ready to become a graduate of the Pennsylvania College of Dental Surgery.

The only challenge he had remaining was his age.

"You knew our policy, of course," the Dean said apologetically, when John Henry stopped into his office to pay the required $30 graduation fee. "It's stated clearly in the college handbook: *The Candidate must be twenty-one years of age.* From your birth date as printed on the application, you are still only twenty years old."

"But I'll be twenty-one in just a few months, Sir," he explained. "My birthday's August, that's only six months off."

"Admittedly," Dean Wildman replied. "But the rule remains, and for good reason. Most of the states, including Georgia I believe, have now passed dental acts requiring a practicing dentist to be of legal age. It would be pointless for this institution to graduate doctors who could not practice. I'm sure you understand."

But John Henry didn't understand and he felt his heart stop cold in his chest.

For though he had indeed read the college handbook, somehow he'd thought the age requirement would be waved with all his other work considered. "You mean I won't be allowed to graduate?"

"Not technically, no. You will, of course, be allowed to participate in the Commencement ceremony and have your name printed on the graduation announcement in acknowledgement of your fulfilling all the other requirements. For which, may I say, you have gained the admiration of this faculty. You have proven yourself a fine student, Mr. Holliday, and will be a benefit to the profession, I am sure. And you ought to take no small pride in the knowledge that you are one of the youngest students we have ever trained here. But we are constrained as to awarding the diploma. At the ceremony you will be presented with a provisional certificate, with the official document being forwarded on to you after you have reached the age of majority. I trust this will cause you no undue difficulty."

"No, Sir," he said heavily, "there'll be no difficulty." Nothing that the college would have to worry about, anyhow. For his professors wouldn't have to write Henry Holliday and tell him that his son would only be participating in a ceremony and not receiving the long-awaited diploma. And a ceremony alone would not be enough to make Henry spend the money to travel all the way to Philadelphia when he had his own business to attend to. So after all of John Henry's long two years of study and sacrifice, he seemed to be getting very little in return.

"But it's only six months," Jameson said, trying to console him. "Come August, you'll be a full-fledged doctor and ready to do some good in the world."

"And what am I supposed to do until then? Go back to Dr. Frink? Then the whole town will know I've failed."

"I hardly call coming-of-age failing," Jameson remarked. "You should appreciate your youth, enjoy yourself while you can. You'll be old and stolid like me soon enough." For all his quiet ways, Jameson had a humorously sarcastic streak in him, but John Henry wasn't in a mood for smiling.

"You've never been to Valdosta, Georgia," he replied. "There's not a lot of entertainment goin' on out in the country."

"Then why don't you come to St. Louis with me instead?" Jameson asked. "I could use an extra pair of hands in my office. Besides, you know everything I do about the diseases of the teeth."

It was another of Jameson's quiet sarcasms, and one that John Henry couldn't help but smile at, and suddenly the thought of having a few free months seemed appealing.

"All right," he said, "I accept your invitation. Hell, my father won't want to see me home again for a while anyhow, once I write and tell him about the graduation. I reckon I might as well have a little adventure until then."

"Well, I don't know if I can guarantee you adventure exactly," Jameson said with a smile, "but at least St. Louis has some of the best beer around. And that's worth something, I suppose."

~~~~~~~~~

The Sixteenth Annual Commencement of the Pennsylvania College of Dental Surgery was held on the first of March at Musical Fund Hall. And though there'd been another week of wintry weather blowing through, by eight o'clock in the evening when the graduation ceremony began, the snow had ended and the sky was bright with stars. The rivers had finally thawed and with the news that steamboat traffic had begun again, John Henry almost expected to see his father appear in the commencement audience. But that was just a hopeful folly, he knew, for in answer to his letter about the situation of his graduation, Henry had sent only a short note of congratulations, with nodding approval of John Henry's plan to make a visit to St. Louis before returning home.

"We will, of course, be looking forward to the final receipt of your diploma," Henry said in closing, as though he looked forward more to that than to the arrival of his son.

But John Henry was determined not to let his father's cool correspondence detract from the glory of his final night of dental school. And it was a glorious night, with the Germania Orchestra playing a rousing overture while the faculty, alumni, and graduates marched into the Hall and took their places in rows of seats on the gaslit stage. There was an invocation by the Reverend William Blackwood, and a reading of the impressive accomplishment of the graduating class: 5,036 patients treated in the Clinic and 1,591 cases mounted in the Dental Laboratory. Then, one by one, the students stood and walked across the stage to shake hands with Dean Wildman and be awarded the Doctor of Dental Surgery Degree. And though John Henry's diploma did indeed have the words *Provisional Certificate* printed where the date should have been, at least his name was written properly, and as it would be known forever more – Dr. John Henry Holliday.

His mother would have been proud.

Chapter Ten

St. Louis, 1872

He had expected the river to be bigger, after all he'd heard of it. But here where the ferry crossed the muddy waters, the Mississippi was hardly wider than the Savannah River back home in Georgia. It was a quarter of a mile across maybe, not much more, and flat as a fishpond. Yet for all its seeming calm, the Mississippi flowed swiftly southward, carrying a crowd of river commerce along its three-thousand mile run from Minnesota to New Orleans.

On the western bank of the river, midway on its course, the city of St. Louis rose in smoky splendor, the stacks of its factories thrusting up into the coal-gray haze that hung overhead. Along its crowded, cobblestoned levee, teamsters maneuvered delivery wagons, stevedores unloaded freight, mud clerks checked shipping lists, and roustabouts threw down gangplanks from riverboats moored so close together that they could have scraped paint from each other's hulls. In the shadows of the Ead's Bridge pier, a curious group had gathered to poke sticks at an old alligator, while nearby one man was beating another man with a spade so hard it looked like he might kill him. The St. Louis riverfront was less of a grand entrance than a back door, flanked by those rows of factories and warehouses and the requisite saloons and gambling parlors along Levee Street. The city proper turned its face westward, toward the prairies and the wild frontier.

But it was no frontier town that Jameson and John Henry entered as they made their way from the river and Levee Street up the long hill of Market Street. Though St. Louis was less populous than Philadelphia, it was civilized enough to have horse-drawn streetcars on its graveled macadam roads, and rows of tall brick business buildings and fine new hotels. On the south side of the city, where Jameson lived, the shops and restaurants gave way to homes and boarding houses, livery stables and schools. It was a comfortable city, like a big Atlanta, John Henry thought as they made their way to Fourth Street. At least, he thought so until Jameson knocked on the paneled door.

"*Ja? Was wollen Sie?*" A small gray-haired woman stood in the doorway and peered at them, her eyes appraising John Henry first before turning to Jameson. Then she let out a squeal of delight. "*August! Liebchen!*"

"*Tante!*" Jameson answered back as the woman's arms were flung around him.

"*Ich habe dich sehr vermisst, mein kleiner August!*" the woman exclaimed. "*Bleibst du diesmal hier? Dein Zimmer ist schon fertig.*"

"*Ja, Tante, ich bliebe jetzt fuer immer.*"

Then the woman turned those appraising eyes back to John Henry.

"*Und wen hast du hier mitgebracht?*"

"*Das ist ein Freund von meiner Schule aus Philadelphia. Er ist auch ein Doktor, John Henry Holliday. Ich hoffe du hast auch Platz fuer ihn.*"

John Henry guessed that to be an introduction, and when Jameson gestured toward him he quickly pulled off his hat and swept it down into a bow. The woman smiled and curtsied, then to John Henry's surprise, she flung her ample arms around him as well.

"*Ach! Jeder Freund von unserem August ist hier willkommen.*" Then she nodded and said in heavily accented English: "Doctor, come in, come in. We are all family here," and she pulled both young men into the house, baggage and all.

"Who is she?" John Henry whispered as the woman took their things and bustled away into an adjoining room. "What does she mean 'we're all family'?"

"She's my mother's cousin," Jameson whispered back. "We all call her *Tante* – that's German for Aunt – in respect for her age. She owns this house and takes in borders to help make ends meet."

"German? But I thought you said your family was French. I thought you were born in New York City..."

"I was born in New York," Jameson said defensively, "and my Father was born in France, as I said. But his parents were German, like my mother and her family. My full name is Auguste Jameson Fuches Junior, after my father. Everyone here calls me Auguste, like him." Then he added in a lowered voice, out of his aunt's hearing. "I only used Jameson in Philadelphia, because it seemed so much less..."

"German?" John Henry said, completing the unfinished thought, and Jameson's fair face reddened right up to his pale-blonde hair.

"My family is still only one generation off the boat," he explained apologetically, "and you know how those Philadelphians are about society and all. One has to have the right background to be considered really American..."

John Henry knew just what Jameson was talking about. He couldn't count the number of times he'd been called "Johnny Reb", mostly in jest, but often by way of an insult, as well. But finding out that his friend was something less than he seemed still didn't sit well with him. Being Southern was one thing, but being so close to foreign was something else again...

"Well, here in St. Louis, everyone is German!" Jameson said proudly. "There's Prussians, and Saxons, and Bavarians – it's the water they all come for. Not the muddy Mississippi, but the artesian water from caves under the river. Best beer-making water outside of Germany! And Tony Faust's restaurant has some of the best beer in St. Louis. We'll be having dinner there tonight with Dr. Judd to celebrate my graduation from dental school. *Tante!*" he called to the old woman. "*Kannst du uns ein Bad einlassen?*" Then he turned back to his friend. "We'll have to wash off some of this road dirt before we meet with Dr. Judd. Though as you'll see, our city water isn't as pure as the artesian springs. As Mark Twain says, 'There's an acre of soil in dilution in every tumblerful of St. Louis tap water.'"

"And who is Mark Twain?" John Henry asked. "Another German relative?"

Jameson answered with a laugh. "He's just a journalist who used to live here abouts. He's got a sense of humor and a clever way of writing about things. Maybe you've heard of a book he wrote: *The Innocents Abroad*? It got some good reviews. But it seems to me that what he ought to write is river stories. That's what he really knows."

~~~~~~~~~~

Tony Faust's famous beer was supplied by the brewery of Eberhard Anhauser, a former soapmaker who won the beer business in a poker game and gave it to his son-in-law Adolphus Busch to manage. After several trips back to Germany looking for a good malt recipe, Adolphus had finally found one in the little village of Budweis. "The Beer of Kings" the Budweisers called their lager, but Adolphus turned the name around to "The King of Beers," and it was making the family brewery a small fortune back home in St. Louis. But it was dentistry, not beer brewing, that Dr. Homer Judd wanted to discuss as he met his former student Jameson Fuches and young Dr. Holliday at Tony Faust's restaurant that night.

Dr. Judd was a quietly serious sort of man, his eyes as solemn and gray as his neatly-trimmed gray goatee. He seemed bookishly brilliant but otherwise dull, as he and Jameson discussed the merits of higher dental education and how Dr. Judd had devised the Greek nomenclature that identified the surfaces of the thirty-two teeth in the adult mouth. For anyone other than a dentist, it would have been a deadly boring conversation, and even John Henry was only halfway listening. With a whole new city to explore, discussing dental terminology seemed like a shameful waste of time.

So when Dr. Judd mentioned that he'd spent some time in the California gold fields back in the rush of '49, walking away from a prosperous medical practice in Ohio to go off fortune hunting, John Henry was suddenly paying attention.

"Of course, packing up my medical office didn't require much but a medical bag, as I had already bought a portable head-rest and Pocket Dental Office in case I should need to make house calls in Ohio."

"A Pocket Dental Office?" John Henry questioned. He knew, of course, of the portable headrests which itinerant dentists used, attaching them to any convenient armchair to turn it into a dental surgery chair. But the other was something he hadn't encountered.

"A tiny box," Dr. Judd replied, "only as big as a daguerreotype case, holding a boned handle and attachable instruments: miniature-sized probes, lancets, carvers. There's a company in Chicago that manufactures the cases, custom-fitted. I thought the traveling tools would come in handy when I reached California. If I didn't make my fortune right away, I could practice a little medicine or dentistry on the miners in the gold camps. I soon discovered that a miner with a toothache and a little gold dust in his pocket would gladly part with some of the latter to relieve some of the former."

"And did you make your fortune, Sir?"

Dr. Judd took a sip of his beer before answering. "I learned a fortune's worth about the world," he replied. "But no, I didn't bring home any gold. Just a back worn from bending over a sluice run all day taking up panfuls of Sacramento River water. That and a heart disillusioned with the nature of mankind."

"How is that, Dr. Judd?" Jameson asked.

"It was the greed of gold that drew me across the plains. Crossing the plains was an adventure in itself in those days, but for myself, as for so many thousands of others, it was the greed of the gold that made the trip seem worthwhile. Though somehow, personal greed is easy to justify. I needed the riches that California

172

would bring, I told myself, so that I could establish a school where I could share my knowledge of medicine with others. I reasoned that my desire for gold was good, unlike the ugly greed I saw all around me there in the gold fields. The others only wanted the riches to buy themselves fine clothes, or fast horses, or more liquor than they already had. I didn't see, at first, that we were all after the same thing: personal gratification. It matters little what the end of the journey brings, if the journey itself has been poorly made."

He was silent for a moment, staring down into his foamy beer, and something made John Henry push for more.

"And how did your journey go, Dr. Judd?"

"Not well," the doctor said quietly. "Not well at all." Then he looked up and the sorrow in his solemn gray eyes sent a shiver through John Henry's soul. "I shot a man there, in California. It was over nothing, of course; the right to a particularly profitable stretch of the river. We were all armed, as one is in frontier territory, and when I disputed the man's claim, he pulled his weapon on me. I didn't even think before reaching for my own. I didn't expect it to go off, really, only to point it at him in my own defense. But I hadn't understood that self-defense is also offense; that as soon as the weapon is drawn, the end is inevitable."

"What do you mean?" Jameson asked, his pale face growing paler still in apprehension.

"I killed the man," Dr. Judd said quietly. "I pulled the trigger and shot him through the heart. But there's something somehow disconnected between the pull of a trigger and a bullet slamming into an enemy, as if the two actions aren't really cause and effect. I shot in self-defense; I didn't mean to shoot him down. I watched him fall and couldn't believe what I had done. I still can't believe it. And only because we were in the wilderness with no law at hand did I escape retribution. But I pay the price, nonetheless. I live everyday with that man's death hanging on my soul."

"But you had to pull on him, Sir," John Henry said quickly. "That miner might have killed you..."

"Then the blood would have been on his hands, not mine. He died innocent, at least of my death. Pray you never have to live with a thing like that, young Dr. Holliday."

~~~~~~~~~~

Jameson was shaken by his preceptor's confession and worried over it for days after, as if the Dr. Judd he had known before and the one he knew now were two different men entirely. But John Henry found the story daring. He'd have drawn his pistol too, under the circumstances, and likely have fired the shot as well. There wasn't much sense in having a firearm for protection, after all, if one didn't plan to use it. The real lesson of the story, in his opinion, was that a man had to choose his companions wisely and not find himself at odds over a mine claim.

But there wasn't much time for the two young men to discuss the tale, as they saw to the patients in Jameson's newly opened dental office. Tante had given up her parlor for his use and he'd turned the small space into an efficient operating arena, with an old dental chair positioned near the front windows to catch the sunlight and a long table to serve as a laboratory. A chair in the narrow downstairs hallway served as a waiting room, and as soon as Jameson hung out his shingle, that chair was rarely empty. The neighborhood was glad to have a local boy practicing dentistry, and it seemed like half of his Fourth Street neighbors had been nursing toothaches and broken teeth, just waiting for their own Dr. Fuches to return from Philadelphia. There was even enough work for John Henry to handle some cases, and for the first time in his life, he had some pocket money of his own, money his father knew nothing about and couldn't control. It was fine feeling to be a young man of means in an exciting new city.

The spring was sultry, the sky hazy with humidity carried on the warm wind from New Orleans. Cyclone weather the locals called it, though there was not so much as a rain cloud in sight. A little rain would have been a welcome relief, clearing the air and watering down the gravel and macadam streets that seemed dusty all the time. Even the horses that pulled the Fourth Street rail cars were dusty-maned, billowing brown clouds with every shake of their heads. John Henry wondered idly if the brick buildings that crowded the downtown streets got their distinctive ruddy-red color from the brickmaker's clay, or from the cloud of dust that rose up so endlessly from the streets below and came into Tante's parlor along with the patients.

When the two young dentists weren't working, they took in the sights of St. Louis: restaurants and beer-gardens, steamboats plying the muddy waters of the Mississippi, horse-drawn rail cars and the new horse racing track on the outskirts of town. But the biggest amusement in St. Louis was the theater – because of the city's favored location as the gateway to the west, every traveling show in the country passed through town, from P. T. Barnum's Great Traveling Museum Menagerie billed as the "Greatest Show on Earth," to Buffalo Bill's Wild West Show starring the Indian fighter William Cody and a lot of shooting and roping and riding, along with real wild Indians.

But not everyone in St. Louis appreciated such extravaganzas. Jameson's Tante did not approve of the theater, and did her best to stop her nephew and his friend from taking in a traveling equestrian show at the Comique Variety House the last afternoon in March.

"*Ach!* Full of lewdness!" she exclaimed. "You boys stay home tonight. I cook for you something special, *ja*? *Apfelkuchen,* maybe?"

"Whatever you cook is special, Tante," Jameson said fondly. "But John Henry will only be here for a few weeks and he wants to see some entertainment before he goes. Don't you want me to be a good host and show him a good time?"

"A good time is the Beergarten in the park on Sunday. You sing some, you drink some beer. You meet nice girls there, too. Good German girls who will make fine wives for you both. You go to the Beergarten for a good time, Auguste," she said, calling him by his German name.

Jameson put his hands on her shoulders, smiling down into her motherly face. "*Ja*, Tante. We could meet nice German girls there. But John Henry isn't German, so what good is the Beergarten to him?"

"But the Variety Theater!" she exclaimed. "Better you should go to the Opera House and see some Wagner. Even Verdi, that Italian. No varieties, with those dancing girls and lewd tales. Better you should stay home."

"Now Tante, if I didn't know better I'd think you were jealous! But don't you worry, I'll bet none of those dancing girls can cook like you! My vest is already getting tight since coming home to St. Louis. With your cooking, soon I'll be so fat not even the Beergarten girls will want me!"

Tante laughed with pleasure at that, then her smile turned to a frown as she looked at John Henry, her matronly eyes sizing him up and down from sandy blonde hair to polished leather boots. "*Ja*, Auguste, you are getting nice and fat, like a good German man, but your friend..."

"I've always been a little lean," John Henry said defensively, though he knew the old lady meant no harm.

"You look too thin to me, Dr. Holliday," Tante said, addressing him formally as she always did. "And you cough too much in the night."

"It's the river air," he replied quickly, uncomfortable with her sudden attention. "I'll be fine once I'm back in Georgia."

But Tante shook her head again. "You boys stay home. There is bad weather coming, I think, a storm maybe. And the Comique Theater is so far, eighteen blocks on the horse rail cars. Better you should stay close and go to the Beergarten around the corner. And this one," she said, looking John Henry over once again and laying her hand on his arm, "I am afraid he will be carried away in the storm. You be careful," she said, "you watch out for the Valkyrie."

"Tante!" Jameson said with a laugh, "you have too much of the old country in you. Or too much Wagner, maybe! Now stop your worrying and start baking that Apfelkuchen for us. We're only going for the matinee. We'll be home again before you know it."

"Valkyrie?" John Henry whispered as he reached for his hat and headed for the door. "What's she talkin' about?"

"It's nothing. Just the old stories my family grew up on: legends of the Valkyries – lady spirits who ride the storm and carry away the souls of dead warriors. Richard Wagner wrote an opera about it. Haven't you seen it?"

"There's not a lot of opera back in Valdosta," John Henry replied, "and not much of anything else, either."

~~~~~~~~~~

The rain began even before they reached the theater, coming with a cold edge from out of the north. The wind that carried it was fitful, indecisive of which way it wanted to blow, so that the black umbrellas of the theater-goers were useless against it. Even the sky seemed undecided, changing color by the moment from blue to gray to mackerel green. But the inclement weather didn't dampen the spirits of the audience, happy to pay thirty-five cents for a matinee ticket for the best varieties show in town.

The Comique Theater still had an air of elegance left over from its days as DeBar's Opera House, with faded red velvet stage curtains and torn leather upholstered seats. But the mostly male audience didn't seem to mind the tattered décor – all a good burlesque house really needed was a solid lineup of entertainment, and the Comique always offered that: song and dance men, clog dancers, trapeze performers, even ballets with plenty of dancing girls. And on this afternoon, the Comique hosted the opening of a touring show about a Russian prince and a spell-casting sorceress, with an actress named Kate Fisher and a horse named Wonder sharing top billing.

"And now," the stage manager announced as the house lights faded and the gas lamps at the edge of the stage flickered into brilliance, "I give you *Mazeppa!*"

And there before them, painted on canvas but looking as real as imagination would allow, were the Steppe Mountains of Russia, home of the wild Tartar horsemen. In front of the mountains, stretching clear across the stage, lay a lake of some shimmering blue material, and in front of that, close to the gas lamps, stood a rocky cavern where two tethered horses grazed.

"Behold, the cavern of the Tartar prophetess Korella!" the stage manager went on, setting the scene for what would be played out in that fantastic setting. 'Tis said that she awaits the return of Mazeppa, grandson of the ruling Khan, last of his line and rightful heir to the throne of Tartary. Although some say Mazeppa perished when an infant in the invasion of the Polish frontier, the prophetess believes that he escaped from death and dwells in slavery. How real her prophecy is will soon be seen, for Mazeppa is not dead, but held a slave in Poland, across the river. And for the crime of falling in love with the Polish princess, he has been stripped naked and tied to the back of his wild Tartar horse to wander 'till death on the deserts of Tartary. Will he return alive to his homeland? Will he succeed to the throne of his ancestors before another usurps his birthright? The play will tell all!"

Then in a swirl of dark robes, the prophetess Korella appeared from her painted cavern, her stage voice carrying to the back of the rapt audience.

"Omens of woe!" she proclaimed. "On Poland the storm cloud driven by the hurricane – my brain is burning! Oh, this night's wild and wondrous visions! Warnings from the skies!"

John Henry sat entranced. He'd never seen anything like the play that unfolded before him with Tartar chiefs in furs and horned headdresses and the prophetess with her omens and incantations, all underscored by stage thunder and streaks of lightning made by blasts of gunpowder in a tin pan somewhere in the wings. The assembled cast gave out appropriate expressions of terror and the thunder rolled again, this time loud enough that the walls of the theater itself seemed to shake.

"How'd you reckon they make the thunder sound?" John Henry asked Jameson.

"Drums, I suppose," Jameson whispered his reply. "Though I've never heard it done so effectively. Sounds like a real storm, doesn't it? Now watch for the lightning," he said. "Mazeppa is supposed to appear in the midst of the storm." Then another flash of gunpowder drew their attention back to the stage, where Korella shrieked as the stage thunder rattled the walls of the Comique.

"He comes!" Korella cried, pointing her robed arm toward the painted Steppes. "He comes! I saw him in a hurricane of dust! He flies hither from the mountains bordering on Poland. He rides a wild horse which scours the desert like a tempest. He comes!"

There was another shriek of horror from the onstage cast, then the storm seemed to break loose in all its fury. Lightning flashed across the stage; thunder crashed and echoed through the theater, and in the midst of it all a wild horse came galloping onto the stage, a half-naked rider tied to its back. The horse, a gleaming black thoroughbred with a streak of a white blaze, dashed from curtain to backdrop, rearing and wheeling around, seeming to throw its captive rider at any moment to a brutal death. But the rider, all bare legs and streaming dark hair, somehow caught control of the wild animal, and in a breathtaking show of equestrian skill wheeled the horse around to a stop, then pulled the animal to a stand on its hind legs.

"Set me free!" the captive rider cried. "Oh, release me! In mercy set me free!"

And in perfect timing with the horse rearing up once more, the thunder rolled again and lightning illuminated the entire stage. The cast of aides and vassals cowered at the amazing sight, and even the great Khan seemed overcome. Only Korella had the courage to speak.

"See the royal star on a chain around the rider's neck," the prophetess exclaimed. "The royal emblem of Tartary..."

"Can it be?" the Khan asked, stepping forward. "Can it be my own lost grandson, my own – Mazeppa!"

And with that the stage thunder roared again, like a living thing this time, and the audience exploded with applause. And yet the sound of the thunder grew louder still, its howling louder even than the ovation, louder than anything John Henry had ever heard inside a building.

"Sounds like a train comin' through..." but before he could finish the thought, the doors of the theater were blown wide open by a blast of wet wind, and all at once the storm was everywhere.

"Cyclone!" someone hollered, and the wind whipped at the gaslights at the edge of the stage, blowing them out. But one lamp held onto its flame long enough to catch on the billowing velvet curtain, and in a moment the whole stage was on fire.

The actors screamed and pushed past each other for escape, and in the fiery light Mazeppa and his horse took one perfect leap off the front of the stage, flying over the orchestra pit and coming down hard in the main aisle of the theater. And it wasn't until that blazing, fiery moment that John Henry finally saw the actor close enough to see that Mazeppa was no man at all, but a woman. And more than that, she was a woman in trouble, for her thoroughbred's tail had caught fire, and the horse was running like a demon was after it.

He didn't even stop to wonder what would become of Jameson, as he shoved his way past the other theatergoers and pushed up the aisle heading straight into the wind, following after the actress. At the entrance door the rain hit him hard, slanting sideways from the green sky, and he had to hang onto the doorjamb to keep his balance. Before him on what had been the dusty streets of downtown St. Louis, all hell had broken loose along with everything else not securely fastened down. The dirty rain was whirling in every direction at once, flinging aside everything in its path – wagons, trolley cars, uprooted trees, shutters, glass window panes, a dog still tied to the post that should have kept it safe in some shaded yard.

"John Henry!" he heard Jameson shouting after him. "What do you think you're doing?"

He couldn't have explained it to Jameson – he could hardly explain it to himself. But chasing after the actress had something to do with honor and gentlemanly gallantry – something his father had drilled into him long ago when he'd taught him that a man's duty was to protect his womenfolk. Not that the actress was his, but she was a woman who needed help and, for the moment, that seemed all that mattered.

He pulled his hat down low on his head, put one arm up against the wind-blown debris, and stepped out into the storm. Though the wind was lessening some, it was still so loud that it nearly drowned out the sound of the thunder, and the rain was coming down in sheets. If he were going to follow that wild horse through the maelstrom he'd need a horse of his own, so he didn't think twice about untying a saddled mount from the horse rack outside the theater, and the horse seemed grateful to be at a run instead of tethered in the wild wind.

The actress was a good rider, all right, for even in the storm, dodging debris and jumping muddy potholes, she and her horse, Wonder, were a graceful pair. Though the animal's fiery tail had gone to a smolder in the rain, it was still running wild enough to give John Henry a good race. If he hadn't been such a well-trained horseman himself, he'd have lost them both in the wind and the rain. But he pulled his hat from his head and used it to whip the horse to a run, trailing the actress by a long city block.

He paid little attention to the landmarks they were passing, keeping his eyes fixed on the horse and rider ahead of him, but he could tell they were heading southwesterly away from the heart of the city. Then the wind suddenly settled, the green sky above turning back to blue and the torrential rain changing to mist. Yet ahead of him the horse still ran hell-bent-for-leather, and as John Henry finally drew close enough to see clearly through the misty sky, he had a shock – the mount ahead of him was running not from fright, but because the rider was whipping it to a run. And more amazingly, through the growing quiet of the evening he heard that she was laughing.

"Well, I'll be damned!" he said aloud, as he finally came head to head with her, her horse rearing to a sudden stop in front of a Ninth Street livery stable. "What the hell do you think you're doin'?"

"Going for a ride!" she answered with a wild laugh.

"But you were in trouble," he said, "the storm and all..."

The actress turned brilliant blue eyes on him and laughed again. "I like the storm!" she said, then she slid from her horse and led it into the livery.

John Henry bounded down from his own horse, grabbing the leather reins as he followed her into the brick stable building.

"But your mount was on fire..."

"That's why I took him out in the rain."

"But he kept on runnin' wild..."

"He wasn't running wild," she said, turning back toward him, "he was running home. This is where I board him. He knew the way. And what business is it of yours?" Though she stood before him bedraggled, her long dark hair hanging limp and wet around the wreck of her scanty costume, there was something almost arrogant about her. "Well?" she demanded. "What are you doing here?"

He stared at her a moment longer, then he shrugged. "I just came in to dry off this horse. I guess we've both had a soakin'."

And for once his sarcastic sense of humor didn't go unappreciated. "You're funny," she said, her mouth curving into a smile. "I like that in a man."

It wasn't a comment he expected, unfamiliar as he was with being countered, and he hardly knew what to say next. But something about the arrogant way she stood there, looking up at him like she was really looking down, felt like a challenge to him.

"So now what?" he asked, feeling somehow that there was more.

"Now you tell me why you really followed after me."

"I came to save you, like I said."

She tossed her hair, imperious, and drops of water flew from the dark strands.

"Well, I don't need saving. I'm not some damsel in distress who can't mount a horse without a hand up. There's no man who can ride better than me, storm or no."

"I'll give you that," he nodded. "You gave me a race, and I'm better than most."

"You're not bad, for a horse thief," she replied, glancing toward the quarter horse he still held by the reins. "And where did you steal this one?"

He could have lied to her, told her it was his own horse and demanded that she apologize for insulting his integrity. But he didn't really care what she thought of him. She was only an actress after all and hardly worth the time he was taking to talk to her – though talking to her was stimulating.

"I found it in front of the theater. But I didn't steal it, only borrowed it for a bit. I'll be returnin' it shortly."

"Silas is going to be jealous," she said, her voice softly accented with something exotic. "He doesn't like anyone else sitting his favorite mount."

"Who's Silas?"

"The man whose horse you stole – he's an admirer of mine. He comes to see all my shows, always sits in the same first row seat, always rides the same blood bay gelding, always makes the same advances when he comes to the backstage door. Sometimes I let him take me out for a ride after the matinee, so he can pretend we're lovers."

"And you're not?"

She stared up at him again, haughtily. "I may be in the theater, but I have more refinement than that. Silas is handsome, but he's not near smart enough, or rich enough, for me." Then she added, almost as an afterthought, "Besides, he's married."

"So why do you keep leadin' him on?"

She shrugged her shoulders, turning away from him to hand her horse to a stable boy. "He flatters me. He buys me things. What's wrong with that?"

"It's a lie," John Henry said. "You're as good as stealin' from him, if you tease him that way."

And once more, she gave him that arrogant, blue-eyed stare. "From one thief to another," she said. "Why do you care what Silas thinks? I don't."

"So you're heartless, then?"

"That's not true. I am all heart. I'm just saving myself for the right man."

"Sounds like you're sellin' yourself to the wrong man, more like."

"Oh? And who are you to judge what's right or wrong for me? I don't even know your name."

He paused a moment before answering, then said with a sarcastic shadow of a bow. "Dr. John Henry Holliday. And you're Kate Fisher."

"Doctor?" she said quickly, turning back to face him once more.

"At your service, Ma'am," he said with an affected air. "Newly graduated from the Pennsylvania College of Dental Surgery."

"Dr. Holliday," she repeated, then looked him up and down appraisingly. "You do dress better than the usual varieties follower. What's your background? Your accent sounds Southern."

"And what business is that of yours?" he asked, mimicking her own earlier question.

Her reply shocked him. "I just like to know something about a man before I take him around to my room. You didn't really follow me just to save me from the rain, I think."

He had never met a woman like her before: arrogant, worldly, unapologetically greedy, and surprisingly self-righteous all at once. He smiled down at her, flattered by the offer, then drawled out an answer: "I wouldn't want to make Silas jealous, sittin' his favorite horse. Besides, he'll be needin' a ride home by now. Looks like the storm is about over."

"Ah, a virtuous horse thief!" the actress said approvingly, as though he'd just passed some sort of test. Then she added with a smile, "Maybe you should come around and take me to supper sometime after rehearsal. The restaurant at the Planter's Hotel is excellent."

And looking into those challenging, captivating eyes, somehow he knew that the storm wasn't over yet.

~~~~~~~~~

He could have gone on back to Fourth Street then, tried to explain to Jameson's Tante how he'd left his friend in the middle of a cyclone and how he'd come to have a dinner engagement with a varieties actress, but he was too elated from it all to be done with the day just yet. So as long as he still had a horse under him, he thought he might as well take a ride around St. Louis to see what kind of damage the storm had done before having to face any more damage at home. But he'd no sooner rounded the corner of Ninth and Washington, headed back toward the theater, than he near collided with a man running toward him down the middle of the red-brick street.

"Thief!" the man shouted, his face registering relief and anger together. "Robber! Give me back my horse! I'll have you arrested, or worse!"

Then the man looked from John Henry on the horse toward the Ninth Street Livery behind him, and his anger turned to suspicion.

"What is this?" the man said quickly. "Are you stealing my horse and my woman, too? What are you doing at Kate's place?"

So this was Silas, Kate Fisher's admirer: he was younger than John Henry would have thought for a would-be adulterer, not much older than himself. But just because the man was a cad didn't mean John Henry couldn't be a gentleman.

"I was just escortin' a lady home," he replied, looking down coolly from his height on the horse, taking advantage of the altitude. "And what are you doin' here, Silas? Shouldn't you be home seein' if your wife is safe?"

If Silas were surprised that the stranger on his horse knew something about him, he didn't show it. "I came to check on Kate. I saw her leave the theater, and figured she'd be heading home. I guess you beat me to it, thanks to my horse."

"It was available," was all John Henry offered by way of explanation. Then he made the mistake of dismounting, throwing the reins over to Silas. "But I'm done with her now. You can have her back."

But Silas had already lost interest in his missing horse, and let the reins fall as he pulled back one meaty fist and threw it into John Henry's jaw.

"That's for stealing my horse," Silas said, as he drew back again, "and this one's for Kate."

John Henry was dazed from the unexpected assault, but the taste of blood at the corner of his mouth brought out the Irish in him. Silas was a bigger man, but John Henry had always been fast. He dodged and brought up his own clenched hand so swiftly that he caught Silas by surprise, landing the blow square in the bigger man's eye. "And that one was for me," he said with a smile.

Silas gasped and grabbed at his face, then swung around and flung his fist out, nearly catching John Henry again. The man seemed bent on destruction, keeping up the fight even with one eye bleeding and fast swelling closed. His blow unlanded, he curled his fist and flung it out again, though this time John Henry ducked neatly and then stepped out of the way.

His inclination was to make some smart remark, but knew that his voice would only give the man a better target. So he silently backed away while Silas wiped at the blood that dripped from his battered eye and tried to get his bearings back.

Behind John Henry the horse stood untethered, waiting for a rider, and in one swift move he was mounted again, sliding the reins into his hands and kicking the animal into a run. He was only borrowing the horse again, he told himself, and would return it to Silas soon enough. For no matter what Miss Kate Fisher had called him, he was sure that he was no horse thief.

~~~~~~~~

The cyclone had left a rubble of fallen chimneys and tree limbs and broken window glass, making for a slow ride through the darkening evening light. On every street corner, crowds had gathered in the dusk to share their stories of the storm, counting losses and blessing the fact that so little human damage had been done. The worst of the storm seemed to have blown right over St. Louis proper, across the Mississippi and on into Illinois, taking the smokestacks of the steamboat Henry G. Yeager with it along the way.

Intrigued, John Henry picked his way along Washington Avenue and down to the levee to see the damaged steamboat for himself. Sure enough, the twister had torn the massive stacks right off the boat deck and thrown them overboard like they were nothing more than matchsticks. The salvage activity wasn't going well, what with the weight of the stacks and the swift current of the river, and the boatmen's little poled rafts circled around the half-submerged smokestacks like so many minnows around a throw of bait. It would take daylight and a couple of good tugboats to pull those heavy smokestacks up from the sandy bottom of the swift-flowing Mississippi.

Farther down Levee Street, where the saloons and the bordellos faced the river, business was going on as usual, with scantily clad ladies leaning out of second-story windows, calling out their prices for the evening and barkeeps in the drinking rooms down below pouring drinks for the rivermen. It wasn't a place for a gentleman, surely, and John Henry almost turned back toward Market Street and the ride home, but the hanging tavern sign above the *Alligator Saloon* intrigued him. Painted in garish colors, the sign depicted a sailor wrestling an alligator, and the alligator appeared to be winning. One drink in the place, he told himself as he tied the horse to a rack outside the saloon, one drink and maybe a quick hand of cards, and then he'd be on his way.

"Two bits for a stranger, mon?" a voice spoke out of the shadows of the saloon's eaves, where a lanky colored man lounged. "Two bits for a riverman to buy hisself a drink, mon?" The accent was unusual, lilting and musical.

"Where are you from, boy?" John Henry asked, naturally assuming the superior tone he'd been taught to use with the house servants and field hands.

"I ain't no boy, mon, never was. I be a free Negro from Jamaica, workin' on this river. Workin' hard enough, but not gettin' paid near enough. You can spare two bits for a drink, for a friend from Jamaica?"

"I don't remember us bein' friends," John Henry drawled. "And liquor is the last thing I'd buy for a darky. Get out of my way, boy, and let me about my business."

But the Jamaican took no offense, letting out a musical laugh. "Business? You say you got business in dat place? Ain't nobody got business in there, mon, 'cept for Hoodoo. That place be full of his black magic. You only think you' doin' business when you in there. You be better off givin' your money to me, and let a riverman buy hisself a drink."

"Out of my way!" John Henry said angrily, and pushed past the man and into the musty darkness of the riverfront saloon, trying not to hear the Jamaican's laughter from behind him.

Though afternoon was only half-over, the saloon was as dark as night, lit only by a few hanging oil lamps and wall-sconces of smoky candles. But the darkness didn't seem to darken the spirits of the rivermen inside who were gathered noisily around a gaming table at the shadowy far end of the room. John Henry ordered a drink, then listened with growing interest. "Bets down!" a dealer cried, "Place your wagers for the second card turned, copper a bet to turn it around. And the lady shows her hand!" Then he slickly pulled a card from a silver dealer's box.

There were cheers from the winning punters and curses from the losers, but the wagers went down again all around. And intent as John Henry was on the game, he only vaguely noticed the smartly dressed sport who came to stand beside him, smoldering cigar in hand.

"You look a little out of place in this establishment," the sporting man commented, as he tapped his cigar ash onto the oiled plank floor. "You look more like the society gentleman type than these river rats."

"You look a little overdressed yourself," John Henry replied, glancing at the man's fancy brocade vest and sparkling finger rings, his black hair slicked back and glossy with macassar oil. He wasn't a riverman, that was for sure.

"I'll take that as a compliment," the man said with a mocking bow. "So what brings you into the Alligator Saloon?"

"Just a drink," John Henry said, "and maybe a little game." Then he nodded toward the noisy playing table. "That's Faro, isn't it?"

"The ubiquitous saloon standard," the man replied. Then he added with something of a gleam in his eyes, "Have you never played it before?"

"Spanish Monte is my game," John Henry said, not quite answering the question. "But I hear they're somethin' alike."

"Well, Monte's one thing," the man said. "Faro is quite another. Any child can play a Monte hand. It takes grit to buck the tiger."

"Buck the tiger?" he asked.

"Play the Faro odds, especially in this dive. The dealer's as crooked as they come. Only the real sports can beat him. And as you can see, this saloon is sadly lacking of good sporting men."

"Like yourself?" John Henry asked, a trace of sarcasm in his voice. The man was not only rude, but arrogant as well.

But the stranger just smiled. "I don't have to play to win. Allow me to introduce myself: I'm Hyram G. Neil, owner of this rat-hole, along with several other doggeries along the levee. All I have to do to win is find monied dupes like yourself and point them toward the table. The dealer takes care of the rest. So how would you like to try your hand?"

John Henry didn't know whether to feel flattered that the man had recognized him as gentleman, or offended that he had called him a dupe. But mostly, he felt the sting of a challenge slapped across his face.

"I don't mind tryin'," he replied, "but I don't much like losin'."

"Win or lose, that all depends on you," Hyram Neil said. "As long as you've got the cover charge you can learn all you like, wagering or not. One dollar, please."

John Henry hesitated only a moment before reaching for his money purse and a silver dollar piece, tossing it to Neil who caught it neatly in mid-air.

"In God we trust," the gambler said, reading the motto on the coin. "What a charming new sentiment the government has chosen to add to our coinage! As for myself, I prefer to trust in Lady Luck. Have a good time, Sport!"

John Henry ignored Neil's parting laughter as he turned his attention to the game. The layout table looked much like the ones he'd seen in Philadelphia: a long rectangle covered in green wool baize with a suit of Spades lacquered to it. The cards were laid out in two rows, left to right: Ace through Six on the lower row, Eight through King on the upper row, the Seven nudged in between. The players placed their bets on the layout, then watched while the dealer slid the cards one at a time from a spring-loaded dealer's box, the first card being deadwood, the second card taking the wagers. Bets placed on that card went to the house, bets placed on any other card went to the player. Coppering a bet meant that a penny was placed on top of another player's wager, betting on the deadwood instead of the second card drawn.

The wagering rules of Faro were easy. Keeping track of which cards had already been drawn and which might still appear in the dealer's box was a little more challenging, though the dealer's case keeper kept a running record of the draws. The hard part of the game was guessing which card of those remaining would come up next, or next after that – especially since Hyram Neil had already proclaimed it a brace game. If the wagers ran too high on a particular card, the dealer would just play a little slight-of-hand to make sure that card didn't appear as expected. So the real trick of the game was not just in wagering on the right cards, but in watching what the dealer was up to.

But John Henry had always been good at watching people, having learned as a child not to speak until spoken to and keeping a guileless look in his wide blue eyes. And on that night at the Alligator Saloon, his pretended inattention paid off. In spite of the crooked dealer, he came out having won enough to hire a boy to take Silas' horse back home as well as pay his own street car fare back to Fourth Street.

For a first evening at the Faro tables, it was a promising beginning. Even Hyram Neil thought so, giving him a grudging congratulations as midnight drew near and he declined another game. "Though it's probably just beginner's luck," Neil commented. "Next time around maybe you'll leave me a little more in the bank."

So John Henry was feeling smug by the time he stepped out of the saloon and into the bright night. The storm had blown away the haze that had hung over the city for the past week, and the air was so clear that the river reflected the stars above like a silvery rippled mirror. What a day he'd had, and what a night! Why, if a passing steamboat had moored up to the levy just then to take on passengers he might have hopped aboard and wagered himself all the way to New Orleans. Or maybe he'd take his winnings and make his way back to Ninth Street to pay a visit on the actress Kate Fisher...

The Jamaican's laugh broke his pleasant musings.

"So you won something tonight, mon? So you think you be a winner, 'cause you leave that place with coins in your pocket?"

"You still standin' around, boy?" John Henry said, irritated at being confronted by the riverman again. "I'm still not buyin' you a drink."

"No, mon, I ain't after nothin' from you now. You got Hoodoo money now, and that be bad luck for you and me both if I drink what it buys."

"What are you talkin' about? What the hell is 'hoodoo'?"

"Ah, mon, hoodoo be black magic. I seen it before, in Jamaica. And that man in there, he be hoodoo, too. He be bad luck, mon."

John Henry laughed derisively. "You mean Hyram Neil? He's not hoodoo – he's not even all that much of a gambler. I beat his dealer nearly every turn. I reckon he's been good luck for me."

"Good luck with that man *be* bad luck. Hoodoo, he is. Bad medicine."

He'd had enough of the riverman's superstitious talk, and just to buy his quiet John Henry threw him a coin after all.

"There's your drink, boy. Now move aside and let me pass."

The man did as he was told, stepping back into the shadows. But as John Henry swept past, he heard a clink as the coin hit the cobbles of the levee, and he felt a shiver run over him. Though he knew the Jamaican's talk was nothing but ignorant superstition, he'd been raised on such superstitions himself. And for a moment, he felt like he was back in a Georgia piney wood, where haints and bogeymen peered at him from out of the green darkness.

The Jamaican's laugh followed him home like a haunting.

~~~~~~~~~

It was no wonder that he had bad dreams that night, after all he'd been through. For if the cyclone and the drinking and the Jamaican's strange superstitions weren't enough, he'd come home to find Jameson worriedly waiting up for him and Tante sure that the Valkyries had carried him off. He made what apologies he could, considering how he'd rudely run off and left his friend to fend for himself in the midst of the storm, then pled a headache and went quickly to bed. But he found it hard to fall asleep and when he finally nodded off in the early hours of the morning, his sleep was nothing but a series of nightmares, one after the other.

The dreams were as stormy as the evening before had been. One moment he was an actor on a gaslit stage, riding a wild-spirited horse, and the next moment he was the horse itself, racing through darkening clouds. There was a raven-haired girl somewhere ahead, beckoning to him, but a dark man stood between them, laughing like the Jamaican and shuffling an endless deck of cards. And while John Henry's dreaming-self watched, the card-player turned into an alligator, its monstrous mouth opened to devour him. And then, most disturbing of all, the girl became an alligator too.

But the most troubling part of the dreams was that Mattie was nowhere in them. Since he'd left Georgia, almost every dream that he remembered had her sweet presence somewhere in it. In this troubled nightmare night, there was no sweet Mattie to calm him or chase away the darkness.

He awoke more tired than he'd been when he fell asleep, and in no mood to deal with Jameson's chastisements.

"It's not your town, of course, so you don't have to worry so much about your reputation," Jameson said as they prepared to open the dental office for the day. "But if word were to get out that my houseguest was a sporting man..."

He didn't look at John Henry as he spoke, but went about the business of pulling up window shades and hanging out the sign that read *Auguste Fuches, Zahnarzt.*

"I don't see how word could get out," John Henry replied, concentrating his own gaze on organizing a tray of instruments, "unless you spread it. You're the only one who knows I spent last evening down on the levee." He'd been careful not to share that information with Jameson's superstitious Tante, letting the old woman think he had indeed been carried off by her Valkyries and gotten lost in the storm – and strangely, that had seemed to satisfy her. But to Jameson, he'd been obliged to tell all.

"You took a mighty big chance, John Henry, gambling against Hyram Neil. He's famous around here, and not in a good way. Everybody knows he's the slickest gambler on the river..."

"Not all that slick. His dealer does all the playin', and I beat him every turn without hardly tryin'. Wait till I give him some real card playin'..."

"You're not thinking of going back to the levee!"

"Thinkin' about it and plannin' on it," John Henry shot back. "I can't afford not to play another game or two. Besides, it's gonna take some cash to treat Miss Fisher to dinner at the Planter's Hotel. I hear they've got a fine eatin' establishment there..."

Jameson turned blue eyes on him, aghast. "What are you talking about? You can't

189

really mean to take that woman up on her offer! Gambling in public is bad enough, but escorting an actress? She's not nearly your equal, nor your station..."

"That's funny, comin' from you," John Henry said with a rush of irritation.

"What do you mean?"

"Pretendin' to be French to fit in better in Philadelphia. I reckon bein' German was beneath your station, back then."

Jameson's jaw tightened but he held his words back, and when the jangle of bells at the door signaled the arrival of the first of the day's patients, the conversation was forced to an end.

He hadn't meant to say such hard words to Jameson, didn't even know he'd been thinking them. But he hated being told what to do — especially when he knew that his friend was right. Kate Fisher wasn't equal to his station in life. But he wasn't marrying her, wasn't even courting her, really, so what harm could come from his having a little supper with her? He had to eat, after all, and might as well do it in pleasant company.

As for his apology to Jameson, he was already planning the right words to say. His mother would have been ashamed of how cruelly he'd spoken, and she would have agreed that an actress wasn't lady enough for a gentleman like himself.

~~~~~~~~~

The Planter's Hotel had somehow escaped any damage from the storm, which was a wonder as the building filled a whole city block. Though its neighbors had lost roofs and chimneys, its four stories of white-washed brick façade and rows of arched windows only sparkled all the more after being washed by the rain. The interior sparkled as well, lit by flickering gaslights that reflected off the gilded cherubs on the grand staircase, the gilded picture frames on the papered walls, the gilded chairs set around gilded tables in the main salon. It wasn't surprising that the 1870's were being called *The Gilded Age*, with stylish establishments like the Planter's putting a superficial layer of gold on everything, making even ordinary objects seem ostentatious. And with all its glitter and gold, the Planter's seemed a perfect setting for a supper engagement with the dramatic Kate Fisher.

She'd accepted John Henry's invitation to dine, but declined his offer to collect her from the theater at the end of her rehearsal — preferring, he supposed, to make her own grand entrance with him as her waiting audience. Although he'd never known an actress before, he knew his Shakespeare from school well enough to understand that all the world was a stage and all the men and women merely players. So he played his own part, arriving early at the Planter's, then taking a seat in the dining room until Kate Fisher was ready to make her appearance.

In the center of the room, surrounded by tables covered in white linen and set with fine china and shining silverplate, stood a rosewood grand piano where a pianist played music for the diners. But John Henry was only half-listening until the pianist started into a song that captured his attention and brought a swirl of memories to his mind. *Dream of Love*, it was called, the song he and Mattie had first danced to, long ago in Georgia...

"It's lovely," a voice said, interrupting his thoughts, and he looked up into the captivating eyes of Kate Fisher. "Franz Liszt is one of my favorite composers," she said with a smile.

"You know of Liszt?" John Henry asked in surprise, quickly standing to offer her a chair.

"Liszt is from Hungary, like me," she replied. "You're surprised I'd recognize fine music? Did you think I was so common?"

But as she settled herself across the table from him, John Henry couldn't help thinking that there was nothing at all common about her. Though he'd expected that she would seem somehow coarse here in the elegance of the Planter's Hotel, an actress only playing the part of a lady, Kate Fisher seemed surprisingly at home, as though she were bred to such places. She seemed, indeed, an altogether different creature from the one he'd tried to rescue on the night of the storm a week before.

Now, instead of a mane of damp hair and a bedraggled boy's costume, she wore a gown of wine-colored silk trimmed in wine velvet at the high collar and tightly-fitted cuffs, and fastened modestly from neck to waist with buttons carved with tiny flowers. From her earlobes hung golden earrings that caught the lamp light, swaying and sparkling as she spoke. Her skin was the color of golden honey, her eyes a startling blue beneath dusky brows, her dark hair swept up at the back of her head and balancing a nose as proud as the Roman goddesses he'd read about in school. But if her looks made him think of Latin verses and Greek dramas, her voice was even more intriguing, rich and seductive with a trace of something foreign.

"It's the Hungarian," she explained as they ordered and ate the expensive fare of the Planter's House dining room: brook trout and oysters, asparagus soup and sweet breads, fancy sugar cakes. "But I've lost most of my accent, traveling around on the theater circuit. You pick up a little accent here and a little there, and soon you sound like everyone – or no one, depending on the role."

"Fisher doesn't sound Hungarian to me," he commented, though he wasn't sure just what a Hungarian name would sound like.

"I was born Maria Katharina Haroney. Americans couldn't pronounce it properly, so I took Fisher as my stage name. A serious actress needs a name people can remember."

"And is that what you aim to be, a legitimate theater actress?" He was well aware that the varieties theater was not the same as serious stage acting, though it was wildly more popular.

"It's what I've always wanted, ever since I was a child in Budapest. The theater was the center of the cultural world there and actors were considered the elite. Not like here. America is so puritanical still. Theater people are scorned in polite society. My own family are Magyars, the ruling class of Hungary before the Austrian invasion. We were the privileged people, my father one of the leading doctors in the city. I grew up visiting the theaters and the art museums, walking through the gardens of the old royal palace..."

"A palace..." John Henry said, imagining the wealth and power of royalty. That accounted for what he'd taken as haughtiness, no doubt.

"But things changed when the Austrians came. My father decided the American frontier would have better opportunities for him, so he bought land up the Mississippi, in Davenport. The city was just being settled then, and booming in spite of the War."

"And does he come to visit you here when you're performing?"

"He doesn't know anything of it," she said quickly. "But why talk about me? Tell me of yourself, Dr. Holliday."

The swift change in her caught him off-guard, and he found himself telling her more than he might otherwise have done, recounting his life growing up as the son of a Confederate officer.

"A little Rebel!" Kate said with a laugh that made her golden earbobs dance in the gaslight. "And what of your mother?"

His words came out in measured tones. "My mother died when I was just turned fifteen."

And again, there was a sudden change in her, as though she had dropped her acting mask, and a look of pity – or sympathy – came into her eyes. "I am so very sorry..." she said softly, and reached out across the table to lay her hand on his.

192

It was such a simple, human gesture that he almost told her more – about how lonely he'd been when his mother had died, about how his father's sudden remarriage had shattered his childish faith. But before he could bring himself to speak, the actress in her returned and so did the laugh. Quicksilver she was, mercurial. "And now here we both are, on our own in this wonderful, dirty city! Tell me, what brought you to St. Louis? Did you tire of the fallen South?"

"I had a classmate in dental school from St. Louis; he invited me to visit him here for the spring. I've been helpin' him in his dental office."

"And how do you find St. Louis?"

"I find it very entertaining," he said honestly. "Horse races, melodramas, cyclones – women who masquerade as men. I reckon I don't know when I've been so entertained."

"And are you being entertained now?" she asked, leaning her chin on her hand and staring at him with dazzling blue eyes. And again her gaze struck him as it had when they first met, like a jolt of something electric that seemed to pass across the table between them.

"I am indeed, Miss Fisher."

He was so entertained, in fact, that the evening seemed to slip away too soon, as they talked and laughed and shared stories of her travels and his life in Philadelphia, of her dreams of fame and fortune, of his plans for a brilliant professional career. And before he was ready for it to end, the evening was over.

"Well then, Dr. Holliday," she said, gathering her beaded purse and her gloves, "I do thank you for a most enjoyable supper. I'll see myself home, if you don't mind. I'll be out riding most of the day tomorrow, training with my horse, and I'll need my rest."

It was such a ladylike statement, and so out of character with the taunting way she'd parted with him at their last meeting, that he almost laughed. Instead, he gave a polite bow from waist and said:

"I hope you'll do me the honor of allowin' me to call a cab for you?" Then he offered her his arm as they walked from the dining room to the door of the hotel, looking like as fine a couple as ever graced the Planter's Hotel.

He hailed a horse-drawn buggy, paid the driver, and gave instructions on where the lady should be delivered, then stood and watched her ride away. It had all been so proper – polite conversation over a perfectly served supper, the lady dressed like one of society's best, and himself acting the gentleman at all times. Yet there had been a sense of something between them that went past politeness, and left him feeling unsettled and unsatisfied – and hungry for more.

~~~~~~~~~~

He didn't have to do much sleuthing to discover when she went riding, and where. A tip to the livery man at the Ninth Street stable where she boarded her horse got him all the information he needed, as well as a hired horse for himself. So on the next fine afternoon, he rode out to the empty fields a mile past town where the stable boy said she liked to ride. The place was called Forest Park, a tall stand of trees around a natural spring that watered hundreds of acres of grass. There was talk around town of turning the undeveloped tract into a fancy new neighborhood, but for now it was just empty, rolling countryside perfect for riding.

He saw her as soon as he came through the tree line, running her horse in the clearing ahead. And though he should have called to her as soon as he dismounted to let her know she was no longer alone, he couldn't bring himself to break the magic of the moment, for the proper Victorian woman with whom he'd shared supper was gone and the wild gypsy-girl he'd met in the storm had returned. This was no dainty gentlewoman, riding sidesaddle with fingers on the reins. Kate Fisher rode astride like a man, her skirts pulled up to show shapely legs, her strong hands guiding the horse through its paces. And as she rode, she laughed, throwing back her head until her raven hair came loose around her.

As she finished the exercise, leading her horse to water at the spring, John Henry stepped out of the shadows and applauded.

"Bravo, Miss Fisher! A fine show, indeed. And a fine day for a ride, as well."

He had thought only fleetingly of what her reaction might be to his sudden appearance at her training session: surprise, perhaps, or even pleasure at seeing him again. But as always, her response was unexpected.

"Is it?" she asked lightly. "I thought you liked riding in the rain."

Her flippant reply put him off for a moment, but having gone to all the trouble to hire a horse and follow her here, he would not be so easily dissuaded.

"I like watchin' you ride," he replied honestly, as he led his horse to the spring beside hers.

"And where did you get this one?" she said, nodding to his hired horse. "Is he stolen like the last one?" Again the sarcastic tone, but he was equal to it.

"Unfortunately not. I had to pay good money to hire him for the day. I figured it was worth it, for the show."

She raised her dark brows. "And you paid this good money just to come watch me ride?"

"Actually, I was hopin' we might ride out together. Borrowin' Silas's horse reminded me how much I've missed ridin'. I didn't get the opportunity very often in Philadelphia."

"And you think you can keep up with me? Wonder is no hired horse, you know."

"And you're no Tartar Prince," he said, letting his gaze travel down to her immodestly bared legs. "I'm surprised your audiences ever believe you're a man."

"They know I'm not a man. They don't come for the prince. It's the naked lady they want to see. I'm not naked though, the costume just makes me look that way — it's flesh colored skin tights. But the audience wants to believe that I've left my clothes off, so that's what they see."

"Well, I can't blame them for wantin' to believe, but it's a shame that's all they see. For my own self, I find the equestrienne even more interestin' than the actress. I never did see a woman ride the way you do."

Kate smiled at that, and he had the feeling that he had again passed some sort of unspoken test. She was challenging all right, and not just when she was outrunning him on a horse. Even talking to her seemed like a horse race of sorts, the way she made him jump through hoops.

"Well?" she said as she slung the reins over her animal's head and stepped up into the stirrups. "Shall we give that hired nag of yours a try? I'll give you a run for your money."

"I reckon you will, Miss Fisher."

She took off like something was on fire again, and it was all John Henry could do to keep up with her. And once again, she had the clear advantage over him. She knew these green fields well – where the hills fell away unexpectedly, where the spring broke through the grass into rivulets that the horses had to take at a jump. But though she could surely have outrun him and lost herself in the trees, she gave him enough slack to let him stay close behind. And when she finally crested a last hill and reined up near the tree line, she was breathless and laughing.

"You're not bad, for a horse thief!" she said, taunting him.

"I told you, I'm no horse thief. But if I had somethin' worth runnin' for, I'd make this mount put your Wonder to shame."

"Is that so?" she asked as their horses drew close, saddle leather creaking together. Then unexpectedly, she leaned across her saddle, smiled, and kissed him quickly on the lips. "That's something to run for," she said, "if you can catch me!"

And with that she was off again, her dark hair streaming down her back, her riding crop slicing the air as she whipped her horse to a run with John Henry fast after her. There was no slack in her race this time. She ran full-out as she had that night of the storm. But John Henry wasn't about to lose to a woman – especially this woman. He leaned down into his horse, one hand on the reins and one slapping at its haunches. And hired mount that it was, it rode well.

He caught up to her at the far reach of the meadows where the grass gave way to trees again. And maybe it was the way she slid gracefully from her horse and gazed up at him with that gypsy fire in her eyes, or maybe it was just the exhilaration of the race, but before he could even think what he was doing he had swept her into his arms.

"I am no horse thief..." he said, bending his head to hers.

"Yes, you are a thief," she whispered as his kisses found her lips, "for you are stealing my heart..."

And though he had never meant for it to happen, the flirtation had become a romance.

~~~~~~~~~~

They met together often in the weeks that followed, sometimes riding out in the park, sometimes sharing a late supper after her rehearsals at the theater ended, though Jameson quietly disapproved of the relationship. Seeing a variety show had been daring enough; courting a varieties actress would be scandalous in his close-knit German community. But John Henry wasn't German and didn't much care what Jameson's neighbors might think, for he found Kate Fisher to be good company, more world-wise than her twenty-two years, and full of interesting conversation. Besides, their romance would be fleeting, for come the month of May she'd be leaving on tour with *Mazeppa* and he'd be heading back home to Georgia – and Mattie. Kate Fisher was, after all, nothing more than a diversion along his way.

Truth was, he couldn't afford a long-term romance, with the hotel suppers he had to buy and the horses he had to hire and what was left of his school allowance and his money from Jameson's office running out fast. So before long he found himself back down at the levee and Hyram Neil's Alligator Saloon where he was certain to find a Faro game going. It would be a brace game, of course, but he figured he could beat the dealer as he had his first night there, and wager his small savings into something more.

Hyram Neil had other plans for him, however, as John Henry discovered when he stepped into the saloon and found the gambler holding court at a corner table. As before, Neil was elegant in a snow-white shirt and brocade vest, a gaudy stickpin in his silk tie and even gaudier gold rings on his well-manicured fingers. It was the classic sporting man's garb, fancy duds that could be put in soak at the pawnbrokers if the gambling ran thin.

"Ah, the gentleman returns!" Hyram Neil said with a smile. "Back so soon? I thought you made out pretty well last time – long enough to hold you for a while, at least."

The voice was sarcastic, though the white-toothed smile looked welcoming enough.

"I've had some expenses lately," John Henry said with a shrug. "I thought I'd try my hand at pickin' up a little cash if there's room at the Faro layout."

"There's always room at Faro, for the dupes. But a gent like yourself shouldn't waste his time playing children's games."

"So what do you suggest?" John Henry replied warily, though his pride was already rising to the gambler's challenge.

"Poker," Hyram Neil said. "And not penny ante. It'll take twenty dollars to get into the game tonight. Are you good for it?"

Again the feeling of wariness came over him. Anteing up twenty dollars would mean dipping into his ticket home money, but he was sure to win that back, and more, once the game got started. It was only poker, after all, a game he'd been playing for years. So he pushed the wariness away and answered easily, "I'm good for the twenty."

And with no more thought of caution, he reached into his money purse and pulled out two gold eagles, dropping them easily onto the green baize of the poker table.

"And you're in," Neil said with that same slick smile. "Gentlemen?" he said to the crowd of rivermen and drunkards who inhabited the place – other than John Henry, hardly gentlemen at all – "shall we begin?"

And so started the most profitable evening of cards that John Henry had ever played, with a dealer playing for the house and Hyram Neil sitting off to the side, watching with casual interest while he fingered the rings on his bejeweled hands.

Jewels won in other profitable games, perhaps, when his own luck was running.

But luck was against Hyram Neil and his Alligator Saloon on this night, as his dealer gave up winning hand after winning hand to John Henry, the draws bringing him ever better cards. He opened with a small pair that became three of a kind and brought him the first pot, then went on to a straight and then a full house, as the other players wagered and raised, then raised again, bluffing until they had to show or fold, leaving him the winnings. And when he picked up his cards and found the beginnings of a royal straight and only two players besides himself left in the game, he went all in and won the biggest pot of all.

"Well played!" Hyram Neil said admiringly as John Henry reached out to gather his winnings, enough to wine and dine Kate Fisher and her whole theater company along with her. "It's a pleasure to watch a man who knows his cards the way you do, driving all the other players out of the game, very nearly breaking the bank."

"Nearly?" John Henry said, pausing over the pile of poker chips and coins and looking up at Neil. If he'd nearly broken the bank, how hard would it be to break the bank entirely?

"We have to keep something back to reinvest, of course. That's the business, and a good thing you're out of partners. We couldn't afford you much longer. But maybe, just this once…" He leaned closer, his black eyes glittering in the lamplight.

"Just this once, what?" John Henry asked warily.

Neil smiled. "Because you are such a fine player and such a pleasure to watch, not like these stupid rivermen, I believe I'll sweeten that pot with something of my own and let you keep playing a little longer, going against the house." Then he pulled off two of his finger rings and dropped them onto the pile of John Henry's winnings, shining like pirate booty in the lamplight.

He had no reason to believe the jewels weren't real, and if they were – he was suddenly facing the possibility of winning more money than he had ever had at one time. Enough money to entertain Kate Fisher for as long as he'd like, and to outfit his own dental office as well. Enough money to be a man of means, independent of his father or anyone else. And all he had to do was play a few more lucky hands of cards. How could he resist such an offer?

"All right," he said with a grin, "I'm in."

But Neil's next words quickly ruined his golden dreams.

"So now that I've raised the stakes, what do you have to offer? This is poker, after all. See my wager and raise it, or lose the pot and refill my bank."

"But I don't have anything else. It's all there already, all my money, along with my winnings."

"Come now!" Neil said incredulously. "You must have some other resources, a gentleman like yourself with such fine clothes, such fine manners. Surely you can come up with something? A bank draft, perhaps? I'd be willing to let you play on credit, for the chance of winning back some of my money. I've put my own property in, to show my good will. There must be something you can add."

But he had nothing to add to the pot, no bank account on which to draw a draft, no jewels or stashes of hidden coins. He had only the money he'd made working with Jameson, along with what was left of his dental school allowance, and it was all on the table already.

Neil watched him, waiting, then said with a dramatic sigh, "Ah well! Such a shame! And it would have been so amusing to play against a real opponent for once. But at least there's this…" And he stretched out his arm to sweep up the pot, all of John Henry's winnings, all that was left of his own money he'd wagered away.

"Wait!" he said quickly, putting up a hand to stop the looting. "There is something. I'll gain an inheritance this summer when I turn twenty-one. I'll see your wager with that."

"And who's to say your inheritance is a match for my jewelry? My wager is there on the table for all to see. You're wagering something you don't even own yet. What proof is there that you really have an inheritance at all? What if turns out to be nothing but a mess of potage?"

"It's more than enough to match your baubles," John Henry said proudly, his ire rising at the challenge, "it's good Georgia land and some money as well…"

"Land?" Hyram Neil cut in. "What sort of land?"

"What difference does it make?" John Henry said haughtily, covering the fact that he wasn't sure himself what his inheritance would bring him. All he really knew about it was that when he turned twenty-one he'd inherit some kind of McKey land, along with his share of the proceeds from the sale of the old Indian Creek Plantation. His mother had mentioned it once, but John Henry had never thought much of it. In truth, he'd tried not to think of it at all, as the inheritance came down to him from his Grandfather McKey's estate through his mother's last will and testament, and thinking of it had only reminded him that she was dead.

"Land," Hyram Neil said with relish, a smile sliding across his cunning face. "Very well. Dealer, you may proceed."

Hyram Neil was no casual observer, hoping to win back some of his banking money. Hyram Neil was the slyest sporting man on the river, waiting like a gator in dark water to gobble up an arrogant country boy who thought he knew how to play cards. And from that deal on down, John Henry watched his winnings disappear before his very eyes.

What luck he'd had before had turned – if luck it had ever been at all. More likely Neil's dealer had been handing him winning cards so slickly that John Henry hadn't even noticed. It was a game he'd never considered – letting an opponent win hand after hand to woo him into wagering more than he dared lose. In all his years of playing cards, he'd only thought of how he could beat the other players, not how he might get another player to lose. But he was losing sure enough now, and faster than he had earned that golden pot, he had lost his inheritance.

"You look surprised," Hyram Neil said as he collected the last of the pot and pulled out paper and ink pen. "You had to have known my reputation. Surely you didn't think that Hyram G. Neil could be so easily bested. Sign here, please," he said, and handed the pen across the table.

"What's this?" John Henry asked, his eyes too dazed by his stunningly swift demise to even read the words Neil had scrawled on the paper.

"It's a promissory note. Standard legality in this sort of business. You wagered your land and lost. This promises me the right to come and claim it."

"But you can't!" John Henry exclaimed. "You can't just come and take my land. It's McKey land. It'll always be McKey land!"

"What it was doesn't concern me. It's mine now, wagered and won. Sign please."

And though John Henry had an impulse to tear the paper in two and throw it back in Hyram Neil's cunning face and walk proudly from the saloon, he didn't dare. Neil was waiting for his signature, one hand on the paper and the other on the pearl handle of the derringer that he placed beside him on the table. He meant what he said and he wanted what was his – what had been John Henry's until this night.

"Of course, this is a promissory note only," Neil said as John Henry slowly took the pen in hand, dipped it in the ink well offered, and put his signature to the note. "You'll send the actual deed as soon as you return home. And you said there was money in a bank in Georgia? You'll send a bank draft for the money as well."

Home – it seemed far away now. Farther away than ever, since he had no money left to buy a train ticket. And even if he did, home would never be the same again, now that he had squandered his inheritance on a hand of cards.

But Hyram Neil was smiling as he read the signature John Henry had written. "So you're a doctor, are you? Well, that makes this even more entertaining. It isn't often I get to ruin a professional man. But don't look so glum. What's a little land between sporting men? It's the game that counts, the thrill of the win. I am thrilled at any rate. You'll be thrilled again soon enough, once you've gotten back on your feet."

"And how am I supposed to get there?" John Henry said bitterly. "You just took everything I had – every penny and more. I don't even have hack fare home, let alone enough to get to Georgia. It's gonna be a long time before I can send you anything at all."

He hadn't said it to gain any sympathy, and certainly expected none from a man so professional in his thievery. But Neil suddenly seemed to take a sympathetic turn, smiling again with his shark-white teeth.

"I suppose you're right. Your lack of funds could pose an obstacle to my collecting on the debt. I'll tell you what: I'll make you a loan of sorts, an advance from what you've so kindly gifted me with tonight. Say your original twenty-dollar ante? You can pay it back with the bank draft – and interest on the loan, of course."

"You're loanin' me my own money back?" John Henry asked incredulously.

"No. I'm loaning you some of my money," Neil corrected him. "Money I happen to have in a bank in Georgia, along with some land. My money," he said again. "And you are in my debt."

He might as well have said in hell instead of debt, for that was where John Henry felt he'd suddenly landed. This stuffy, smoky saloon reeking of rotting fish and the smell of the river was hell enough for him, and Hyram Neil could easily pass for the fallen angel of that dark world.

But devil's pay or not, John Henry put out his hand and took back his coin purse, now filled again with gold coins from the pile Hyram Neil had won. He had to eat, after all, and he had to get home again. And once there, he'd put this all to rights somehow. He had to put it all to rights.

"Well, Dr. Holliday, it's been a good night's work. Now, if you'll excuse me."

Hyram Neil swept out of the saloon leaving John Henry to follow into the darkness alone. And standing in the dank night air, stars overhead and the river lapping against the cobbled levee, he could almost hear the Jamaican's warning echoing in his memory:

"*Hoodoo*, that man be, black magic. Good luck with that man *be* bad luck."

There was no laughter in the warning tonight.

~~~~~~~~~~

There was no more thought of courting Kate Fisher. Thinking of her at all only reminded him of the nightmare he'd stumbled into, losing his land and his money – his whole inheritance all at once. And though he had no intention of making good on the debt, he was sure that Hyram Neil would try to hold him to it. His only hope lay in getting out of St. Louis fast, before Neil learned any more about him, for he couldn't chance that the gambler would come looking for him, finding him at Jameson's house and making threats, or worse. Tante's fears of the Valkyries had been just so much German superstition. The real danger was a gambler cheated out of his due.

But how to excuse himself on such brief notice? He didn't dare tell Jameson and Tante that he had gone down to the levee, and the disastrous results that had come of it. That would mean disgrace at the very least. Yet he had to have some reason for suddenly packing his bags and buying a train ticket home, so he settled on the plausible story that an elderly relative was ill and wanted him home immediately. And though he never said just who the relative was, Tante's guess that it was his dear Oma, the way he dropped everything to run to her side, wasn't too far from the truth. Though both of his grandmothers were already dead, it was his McKey grandparents' fortune that had created his inheritance, and losing it was indeed the cause of his hurrying home.

He let Tante believe what she wanted, and tried to avoid Jameson's questioning eyes. All he really cared about was taking the ferry across the Mississippi and getting on an eastbound train. And it wasn't until the Vandalia Line Railroad had steamed its way from East St. Louis across Illinois and into Indiana that he began to relax a little, though not enough to stop looking over his shoulder. He had miles to go still, south through Kentucky and Tennessee and Georgia and nearly to the Florida line, and he wouldn't stop until he got there, not even to pay a visit on Mattie. For until he was buried back in south Georgia, far from the greedy reach of Hyram G. Neil, he wouldn't feel safe again. But he only meant to stay home long enough to turn twenty-one and collect on his nearly-lost inheritance money. Then he'd move to Atlanta where he could open his own practice and be close to Mattie at the same time. And St. Louis, and Kate Fisher, would be forgotten forever.

Chapter Eleven

Valdosta, 1872

His father, however, had other plans for him.

"I hope you've had your fill of big-city life," Henry Holliday said over supper on John Henry's first night home. "Time you got back down to the business of things, started pullin' your weight around here. Dr. Frink has generously kept a position open for you. You'll start tomorrow as his assistant until that diploma arrives and he can make you a partner. Rachel, pass the greens."

And that was the end of the conversation, if it could be called that. Henry didn't say another word and Rachel sat silent as well, and the only sound at the table was the clatter of china and silver as the plates went around and were instantly refilled.

It was all he could do to sit through the rest of supper without shouting out his feelings. He wasn't the same boy who'd left home two years before, hot-headed and anxious to find something he couldn't name, nor was he a struggling dental student dependent on his father's continued good will. He was a man now, well-educated and well-traveled, and he knew what he wanted: freedom and space and some say-so in his own life. And he didn't want to go into partnership with Dr. Frink.

But until he came into his inheritance, arguing with his father wouldn't do any good. So he kept his troubles to himself, then escaped to the quiet refuge of the front porch as soon as the last plates were passed and cleared away. And as he had been the year before, he was struck again by how empty the country nights were. There was no noise of horse-drawn cars on cobbled streets, no raucous piano music coming out of corner saloons or street vendors hawking their wares in a crowded market place. Looking across the yard toward dusty Savannah Avenue, he could hear nothing but the chirping of katydids in the trees and the stifled beating of his own restless heart.

The creak of the door opening and closing behind him was startling in the silence, but Rachel's voice was surprisingly soft, as if she didn't dare disturb the darkness.

"Mind if I stand here awhile?"

"Suit yourself," he answered, not bothering to glance her way. He didn't have to look at her to know she was still wearing her white serving apron. She still smelled of cooking grease and cook stove smoke – homely smells that might have made him feel welcome, but only reminded him that he was home where he didn't want to be.

Rachel stood in silence for a while, then said: "Thea Morgan's been asking after you."

"What's she want? I fixed those bad teeth of hers last summer. She can go see Dr. Frink if she's got more trouble."

"Well, I don't 'spect it's tooth trouble she's got. More like a sweet tooth, I reckon. Looks to me like she's sweet on you, John Henry. Been that way, so I hear, ever since you sparked her last summer."

"Sparked her!" he said with a laugh. "I never sparked Thea Morgan! All I did was kiss her a little. And it wasn't even all that much of a kiss, as I recall."

"It don't take much of a kiss to get folks talkin'. But it's good talk, mostly. The Morgans are well-thought of around here. And your Pa thinks it's a good match. He's been talkin' it over with Mrs. Morgan…"

"I am not gonna marry Thea Morgan!" he exclaimed, loud enough for all of Savannah Avenue to hear.

"I'm not sayin' you are," Rachel replied calmly, "but it wouldn't do you no harm to go on up and pay her a visit. Folks'll be expectin' the Major's son to make a showin', anyhow. He's been tellin' everybody how you're comin' home and goin' in with Dr. Frink…"

"Well, I'm not goin' in with Dr. Frink," John Henry said hotly, "so he can stop tellin' the whole town that I am. And I've got better plans for myself than Thea Morgan! I'm aimin' to marry my cousin Mattie…"

He hadn't planned on saying all that, of course. But Rachel had got him so riled that it just seemed to come out on its own. And once out, there was no taking it back.

"Oh, John Henry!" she said in a hushed voice, "you mustn't even think such things! Why, your Pa'd never let you marry that cousin of yours, if you was to ask the rest of your life. He don't approve of in-marryin'. Says it's bad for the bloodlines, like when cows breed too long in the same lot."

If Rachel had been a man he would have hauled back and hit her. How dare she compare the sweet love he shared with Mattie to something as base as animal husbandry? But it wasn't her comparison, after all, but Henry's. So he kept his temper under control and his hands clenched tight against his sides.

"I will pretend you didn't say that, Rachel."

"Pretendin' don't make it so," she said, undaunted by his cool reply. "That's the way he thinks, and you ain't changin' it. So you'd best start lookin' around elsewhere for a wife. If Thea Morgan don't please you, there's other girls around town."

"I told you, I am not goin' in with Dr. Frink. And I am not stayin' here in this town, either. As soon as I come into my inheritance I'll be leavin' here for good and goin' to Atlanta."

She looked at him quizzically. "And how's your inheritance gonna make you free as a bird?"

"Why, I reckon I'll use what's in the bank to pay my way, set up my own dental practice." It sounded perfectly reasonable, but Rachel's laughing reply was disconcerting.

"What's left in the bank won't pay your way out to Cat Creek! Don't you know your Pa had to use that money up sending you to dental school?"

"What are you talkin' about? That was my money, from my mother..."

"And you got it, one way or another. Your Pa was trustee. The bank didn't fuss with him over it. 'Course there's still the land left, whatever good that'll do you. You don't seem to like farmin' much. And you know those McKey relatives of yours won't ever let you sell it off. So looks to me like you're stuck right here, inheritance or no. 'Cause your Pa's only payin' for you if you stay put. If you leave here, he won't give you nothin', that's what he says. And you know he means what he says."

He had never liked Rachel less than he did at that moment, though she wasn't to blame for any of it. But after all his worries about getting out of St. Louis before Hyram Neil found him, it was maddening to find that his inheritance had turned out to be nothing but a mess of potage after all.

~~~~~~~~~

There was little choice but to do what his father had determined. Henry had things all arranged with Dr. Frink and had even paid money to have a second dental chair brought in and a second cuspidor installed in the dentist's Patterson Street office. Under other circumstances, John Henry should have been grateful – having a partnership ready-made was a blessing for a new dentist just starting out. Instead, all he felt was trapped and angry.

Valdosta had never seemed more provincial than it did that summer. Even the people seemed provincial, though they'd all come from somewhere else originally and should have been more interested in things outside their own little county. But news from the outside barely caused a ripple, even when it was something as thrilling as a photographic wonder reported in the *Savannah Daily News*.

"Would you look at that," John Henry said, as the headline grabbed his attention away from the rest of the mail. "A movin' picture!"

"What's that?" the postmaster asked, reading over his shoulder.

"It says right here: *The president of the Central Pacific Railroad, Mr. Leland Stanford, has asked a photographer to prove that all four feet of a running horse are off the ground at the same time at some point in the animal's stride. The photographer, Englishman Edward Muybridge, has done so by taking a sequence of photographs showing a horse running. When viewed in rapid succession, the photographs show the horse's motion, and prove Mr. Stanford's claim. Science once again amazes."*

"I don't see what's so amazin' about a horse runnin' on four legs," the postmaster commented. "Seems like the natural way."

"It's not the runnin'," John Henry tried to explain. "It's the horse havin' all four feet off the ground at once, flyin' more than runnin'. And more than that, this man's got photographs that show it happenin' – a picture that moves. I reckon I'd like to see that!"

"I'd rather see that horse that can fly," the postmaster said, missing the point entirely, and proving once again that Valdosta was a small world unto itself. But to John Henry, the story only reminded him of the exciting world beyond Lowndes County. In Valdosta there wasn't any kind of photographer at all, especially not one who could make moving pictures.

"You got a letter here," the postmaster said, interrupting his reading.

"I do?" he asked, putting the paper down. "From Jonesboro?" He'd been waiting a week or more for a letter from Mattie after writing her of his return to Georgia. But so far, no letter had arrived, and he was beginning to wonder if she were ill. Surely, there could be no other reason for her lack of correspondence.

"Not Jonesboro," the postmaster replied, handing him the ivory envelope. "Another one of them letters from St. Louis, looks like. Been forwarded here by a A. J. Fuches. Looks like it's from that lady again, judgin' by the handwritin'." He smiled knowingly as he handed the letter across the counter to John Henry. "Looks like you got yourself a lady friend out west."

John Henry made no comment as he reached for the letter. It was just another

206

in an embarrassing barrage of correspondence from Kate Fisher. She'd written him a half-dozen times already, the letters arriving almost as soon as he got back to Valdosta. Every letter was the same, her words filled with angry emotion. How could he have left her without even saying goodbye? Hadn't their time together meant anything to him? Surely, he must have cared for her, the way he led her on...

He never answered the letters. Writing back would have meant joining in her emotion, and he had no intention of ever going that way again. And though he had indeed had some feeling for her – how could he not, with all her fire and passion? – the whole affair had left him with a bad taste in his mouth. When he thought of Kate Fisher, he remembered how courting her had almost lost him whatever was left of his inheritance. So the letters from Kate came and were read, and then burned in the fireplace.

But he couldn't burn the memory of her. And though the memory of their time together was distasteful to him, it also seemed to symbolize the freedom he had lost. He'd been a grown man in Philadelphia and even more so in St. Louis. Here in Valdosta he felt like a child once more, Henry Holliday's boy come home again to stay.

~~~~~~~~

When Mattie's letters finally arrived, they only made matters worse. The reason her correspondence had been delayed, she explained, was that she was no longer living in Jonesboro, having moved up to Atlanta where she was living in their Uncle John's home and working as a teacher at a private school. The move had been necessitated by her father's continued ill-health, as he'd left his clerking position at Tidwell and Holliday and had gone back home to recuperate. So the responsibility of supporting the family fell to Mattie as the oldest child. But she'd been fortunate in being offered a good position in Atlanta where schoolteachers were paid more than at the High School back home in Jonesboro. She'd even be able to keep working when the school year ended in June, as many of her students' parents had asked her to stay on as a summer tutor.

Her letter would have seemed like good news, if only John Henry had been free to move to Atlanta himself. But trapped as he was in Valdosta, her letter only made him feel all the more restless. And it didn't ease his mind any when she went on and on about how kind Uncle John's family had been in helping her get settled there – especially dear Cousin Robert. For it was Robert who had first suggested that she move to Atlanta, and Robert who had arranged for the teaching positions. Why, without Robert, she wrote, she wouldn't have known what to do with herself in Atlanta. The way she talked about him, Robert was a regular knight-in-shining armor, and John Henry began to wonder if Cousin Robert was being more than just accommodating. What if Robert had feelings for Mattie, too, and she were beginning to feel the same for him? But as long as John Henry was stuck at home, there was nothing he could do but worry about it.

He had another worry right there at home as people were beginning to talk about all the mail he received – not the few letters from his cousin, but the undiminished flood of correspondence from the lady in St. Louis. Word was beginning to go around town that he did indeed have a lady friend out west – talk that he didn't want getting back to Mattie somehow. Spending time with a woman like Kate Fisher while on a visit to St. Louis was one thing. Bringing the story of the scandalous actress back to conservative Georgia was another entirely. So to throw off the speculation, he decided to follow Rachel's advice, after all, and stop by the Morgans' home to pay a visit on his old school-friend, Thea.

But word traveled faster than thought, it seemed, and by the time he arrived, hat in hand and hair neatly pomaded into place, the whole Morgan family was standing on the front porch waiting for him. There were a few neighbors outside as well, as though the whole end of Troupe Street had heard that a circus was coming, and had stepped outside so as not to miss the parade. That was life in Valdosta, he thought irritably as he opened the gate and walked toward the waiting family – everybody knew everybody else's business, so nothing was ever a surprise.

But Thea did seem surprised, or the blush of her cheeks made her seem that way, anyhow.

" 'Afternoon, Mrs. Morgan," John Henry said, nodding to Thea's mother.

" 'Afternoon, John Henry," the widow replied. Though she was still in mourning, her black widow's weeds had been traded for less dour purple and gray. Thea, he noticed, was out of mourning entirely, and wearing a pink dress that almost matched the color of the blush in her cheeks. Unfortunately, the pretty dress didn't disguise the fact that she was still as thin and pale-eyed as ever. And for a fleeting moment he had a memory of Kate Fisher, and how she'd filled every thread of the wine-satin gown she'd worn at the Planter's Hotel...

"And how are your folks?" Mrs. Morgan asked, as though she didn't see or hear of them every day.

"Just fine, Ma'am," he replied. But though local etiquette required that he say something more, commenting perhaps on his father's business or his stepmother's garden, he let his comments end there. He had no interest in discussing his father or Rachel, or in satisfying Mrs. Morgan's curiosity. He'd only come up here to calm the talk around town, after all.

"Well then," Mrs. Morgan said, as though they were finishing a conversation that had never really begun, "I'll be going in now. Thea, you stay out here and entertain Dr. Holliday." And with that she turned back into the house, the rest of the family following obediently.

"Yes, Mother," Thea said, the blush rising even higher in her cheeks.

John Henry gave a quick bow as the older woman departed, then turned a bland smile to her daughter. "You're lookin' well, Thea."

"Why, thank you," she said, blushing again as though he'd made more than the prescribed polite remark. "You're lookin' well, too, John Henry."

Her reply didn't leave any room for further conversation, and for a few moments they stood together silently.

"Looks like it's gonna be a rainy summer," he said at last, nodding toward the horizon where the hazy sky was turning dark with clouds.

"Yes, I reckon it does," she replied. "Be good for the crops, though."

And with that the conversation ceased again, and he had to think hard to find something more to say.

"Do you see any of our old school friends much?" he asked, though he already knew the answer. Albert Pendleton was gone off to Augusta to continue his education. Constantia Bessant was married already, but not to Sam Griffin who had been so sweet on her. Constantia had married a newcomer by the last name of Crewe, and was already mother to a baby boy. And Sam himself, John Henry's pal from those younger days, had gone off to Charleston and never written home. The other boys, the Vigilantes, had scattered to the winds after their release from the military prison in Savannah. It was good that John Henry already knew all that, because Thea, with her timid voice, gave him precious little news.

"No, I don't see much of anyone. Mother keeps me busy here at home, most days." And again the conversation ended, as she looked up at him with adoring, expectant eyes as though waiting for him to say something momentous.

"So how are those teeth doin'?" he asked at last, the only important thing he could think to say. "Any trouble since I filled them?"

And as if embarrassed by the mention of the dental work, she put her hand to her face and said in an even quieter voice.

"No," she said. "They're just fine now, thank you."

And as the conversation died again, they stood in uncomfortable silence. For a girl who was supposedly sweet on him, Thea had mighty little to say to him. And again, he had a flash of memory: Kate laughing and taunting him with her worldly conversation. Then another memory flooded past thoughts of Kate – Mattie, brown-eyes staring deep into his, soft words soothing his restless soul...

He looked down at Thea Morgan and couldn't remember for the life of him why he'd bothered to walk all the way out there to see her. Sweet on him or not, she was still as uninteresting to him as she'd been back in school. At least then she'd held the fleeting promise of a first kiss. Once that was accomplished, he'd lost any more interest.

"Well, I reckon I'll be goin' now," he said abruptly. "Give my regards to your family."

Thea looked flustered and glanced toward the front door as if someone might be listening to her from there. "Wouldn't you like to stay to supper?" she asked. "I'm sure Mother wouldn't mind..."

"Not today," he said, putting on his hat and heading for the gate.

"Then maybe some other time?" she asked hopefully.

He stopped for a moment and looked back at her, all dressed up to wait for his visit, her blushing face showing how happy she was to have him there. There was something pathetic about how a woman could be so set on a man who returned as little interest as he did.

"Sure, maybe some other time," he replied, making the blush spread all the way into her pale hair.

His mother would have been ashamed at how easily he lied.

~~~~~~~~~

It had been too long since he'd been to see her, since before he'd left for dental school, but visiting her was always too painful. The stillness of her resting place and the quiet shadows of the overhanging trees only reminded him of how empty his life was without her. And even now, nearly six years since her passing, there was still a hole in his heart that had never seemed to mend. Yet suddenly he was hungry to see her gravesite again, to be close somehow to the mother he had lost.

Sunset Hill Cemetery had hardly any hill to it at all, as Valdosta was built on the sandy flatlands between two rivers: Alapaha River to the east, Withlacoochee River to the west, and nothing but piney woods in between. Still, the name of the cemetery was only partly figurative. While sunset seemed an appropriate name for a place where the light of mortality passed into the darkness of death, the mounds of fresh made graves did give a hilly aspect to the burying ground. One day, perhaps, the mounds would be covered by grass and ringed with flower bushes and greenery. But for now, Sunset Hill was just a dirt graveyard, one plot after another holding the remains of the first settlers of Valdosta.

His mother's grave was near the center of the cemetery, and as he came close upon it, his mouth opened in astonishment. He'd been expecting the site to be unkempt, forgotten as his mother was seemingly forgotten by everyone but her still-grieving son. But instead of mounded dirt or scattered rocks as covered the other graves, Alice Jane's grave was covered with flowers. Someone had made the plot into a flower garden, ringed with smooth river stones, and marked with a freshly-cleaned headstone and footstone.

"Well, I'll be..." he said aloud, as if anyone there could hear him.

He stood staring in amazement a moment, then took off his hat and bent to his knees at the foot of the grave.

"Ma..." he said, "I've been gone away awhile..."

She knew that, of course, looking down on him from her certain place in heaven. For if anyone deserved a seat with the angels, keeping watch over the world below, his mother surely did. In his memory of her she'd always been an angel, too ill for most of his life to reprimand or raise a harsh voice. Most of their quiet conversations had centered around God and his mysterious ways. Most of their time together had been spent in study of the holy word or prayers at her bedside. And though those times had seemed constraining to him as a child, they seemed now like sacred hours spent in the company of one too good for the earth.

"Too good for my father," he said, speaking out loud again. "Oh, Ma! If you only knew!"

And though, of course, she had to know that her beloved husband had brushed her memory aside to marry his young mistress, John Henry couldn't bring himself to say the words.

"Well, she's nothin' like you, anyhow, nothin' at all! And she won't ever take your place, not with me. I'll always be your boy, Ma. I'll always be Alice Jane McKey's son..."

And that was when he realized that her tombstone was missing something elemental: her maiden name had not been carved into the stone. The inscription read only: *Alice Jane Holliday ~ September 16, 1866.* And to his mind, that seemed a disloyalty almost as great as Henry's hasty marriage to Rachel Martin. For Alice Jane had always been proud of her heritage, eldest daughter of William Land McKey, the master of Indian Creek Plantation. It was her McKey heritage, after all, that made John Henry as much of an aristocrat as upcountry Georgia could claim. It was her McKey inheritance, brought to her marriage as dowry, that had made Henry Holliday a landed gentleman. And now her McKey name was as good as gone.

"Except for Uncle Tom," John Henry said aloud, "and Uncle James, and Uncle Will..."

And all at once he knew what he would do. South of Valdosta, just over the Florida line in Hamilton Country, was his McKey uncles' place, Banner Plantation. He'd only been there once, on a brief visit after his mother's death, but suddenly he had a yearning to be there again. Maybe there, in the midst of his mother's people, he'd feel her close again. Maybe there he'd find some peace from the pain of living in Rachel and Henry Holliday's house.

He stood and brushed the cemetery dirt from his trousers, still holding his hat in his hand. "I'm goin' to see your kin, Ma. I'm goin' to see the folks who still love you like I do." He didn't stop to wonder who had planted all those flowers on her grave.

~~~~~~~~~~

But going wasn't as easy as simply deciding to go. His weekdays were obligated to Dr. Frink; his weekends were obligated to helping out with his father's businesses. Henry still had the profitable carriage and buggy business in town, and had brought in a stock of furniture to be sold at Zeigler's Hall as well, and both shops needed tending on Saturdays when the county folk came into Valdosta to do their shopping. Then on Sundays, John Henry was expected to help out with the nursery farm his father had started on the family land out at Cat Creek. Where Henry had failed as a cotton planter, he was having some success as a horticulturist and seller of Scuppernong grape rootlets, pecan tree seedlings, and McCartney rose cuttings.

But even with all the work that needed to be done on the farm, it was still only proper that John Henry be excused to pay a call on his mother's folks after having been gone away so long. And because it was the proper thing to do, Henry let him

212

have a few days off to make the visit. So on a hot June morning, John Henry saddled one of his father's horses and rode off for the forty-mile journey into Hamilton County, Florida. There was no train to take – that part of the country was still so remote, even the rails of the Valdosta-Florida Line ran away from it. But John Henry didn't mind the ride. He'd walk all the way to Banner Plantation, if he had to, just to get out of Valdosta.

There wasn't much of anything to mark the change from south Georgia to north Florida. It was all pretty much the same terrain: sandy soil and scraggly piney woods, brackish ponds, palmettos with their trunks bare to a crown of fan shaped leaves. And off to the east, the Suwannee River flowing slowly through the tangles of the Okefenokee Swamp. Nor were there any real towns along the way where he could stop for some refreshment in the summer heat. Even Belleville, the closest post office to the McKey place, was hardly more than a mail drop, with no hotel or general store where he could buy a drink. So by the time he found his way to Banner Plantation, he was breathless from the heat and drenched with sweat right through his cotton shirt and woolen riding vest.

"You look like you've been through it, boy," Tom McKey said as he opened his front door to find his nephew standing on the doorstep. "Rough ride down from Valdosta?"

"Rough enough. I feel like I've been eatin' bugs all the way. The gnats are bad this time of year."

"The gnats are always bad down here. You get used to ridin' with your mouth closed. Good to have you. Plan on stayin' long?"

"Only a couple of days. I just needed some time away..."

Tom nodded as if he understood without hearing any more. John Henry was family, after all. It was Southern tradition that he was free to visit whenever he liked and stay as long as he liked with few questions asked.

"Well, this place is about as away as you can get," Tom said. "I'm surprised you found us, all alone."

"I asked around," John Henry said as he led his horse to the barn out back of the main house – calling it a plantation house would have been too grand. Even with nine hundred acres in cultivation, Banner Plantation was still just a struggling farm, with a farm house and outhouse the only buildings between the dirt road and the barn. But it looked like paradise to John Henry, since there would be a bed and a washbasin inside and a pitcher of cool water from the well.

"So where is everybody?" John Henry said, coming into the house and seeing no sign of Tom's brother Will, who was a partner in the farm, or his unmarried sisters who lived there as well.

"Will's taken the girls off to visit with your Uncle James and Lorena. Won't be back 'til Sunday, so I guess it's just you and me this trip. Hope you don't mind bein' entertained by a bachelor."

"I don't mind," John Henry said. "You know you were always my favorite McKey uncle, anyhow."

Tom smiled back at him, and John Henry was struck as always by how much Tom favored the McKeys – and Alice Jane in particular. For though he had his own bright red hair and fair skin, he had his older sister's deep blue eyes, her gentle smile. John Henry was right to have come here looking for some bit of his mother remaining. And there was more than just the family resemblance; Tom was a great collector of photographs, and had a wall full of them. There, gazing out from silvery frames, were Tom's brothers and sisters: Martha, Margaret, Helena, Ella, and Eunice, Alice Jane and Henry on their wedding day, James Taylor and William Harrison in their Confederate uniforms – and Jonathan Leval, the oldest son who'd gone west to Texas years before. John Henry stared at the photograph of that handsome young man and studied the face, familiar McKey features and a stranger's eyes.

"I never knew Uncle Jonathan much," he said to Tom. "What was he like?"

"Jonathan? I guess you could say he was adventurous, always lookin' for the next big dream to follow. He heard about all that land goin' for nothin' out in the Republic of Texas and there was no keepin' him home. He headed for that Brazos River country and never looked back. Last time we heard from him, he was growin' cotton on a big spread in Washington County, makin' a fortune, I reckon. 'Course the way those Texans talk, everybody out there is livin' in high cotton, gettin' rich."

"Texas sure sounds good to me right now," John Henry said heavily, "just pack my bags and head on west as far as I can go…" Then a sudden thought came to him. "Hey Tom, let's go west! Just you and me! Have us some adventures, maybe go all the way to that gold country in California! Just think of it: the whole wide open west just waitin' for us, and all we have to do is get on a train and keep on goin'! How does that sound to you?"

Tom laughed. "Sounds like a nice dream, John Henry. But I've had enough adventures in my life already, what with the War and all. Besides, I've got other plans." And surprisingly, Tom looked suddenly bashful. "I've made a proposal and been accepted. It's someone you might know, a piano student of your mother's, Miss Sadie Allen."

John Henry let out a whistle. "Sadie Allen! Why, I went to school with her brothers. Isn't she kind of young for you?"

"I'm not so old, John Henry. Only nine years older than you. But the wedding won't be for a while yet, anyhow. I've got the plantation to think about right now. And I've got to get a place in Valdosta for us to settle into. Sadie doesn't want to be this far off from her family. But that's the nice part about having a young sweetheart – gives me time to get myself all set before I tie the knot. And what about you, John Henry? I always suspected you were sweet on your cousin, Mattie Holliday."

"I was," he answered glumly. "Still am, for all the good it will do me. But my Pa's dead-set against the match, so Rachel says. She claims he doesn't believe in relations marryin'."

"That's funny, comin' from Henry," Tom replied. "I hear the Hollidays were mostly inbred from the start. They've got cousins married to cousins and uncles married to nieces clear back through the line. You should have a talk with him about it."

"Talk to my Pa? We don't have conversations. He just gives orders and expects me to follow, that's about the size of it. Tell you what: if I had my way, I'd be out on my own and never have to take his orders again."

"So what's stoppin' you?"

"Money mostly. Rachel says that's what's keepin' me in Valdosta. My Pa's got things all figured out that as long as I stay around, he'll pay my way. If I leave, he won't give me a penny. I had planned on goin' up to Atlanta to open my own practice, but it looks like that won't be happenin' now."

"So what do you need your father's money for? You're comin' up on twenty-one this summer. Soon it'll be Henry who'll be askin' you for a handout."

"What are you talkin' about?"

"I'm talkin' about your inheritance, of course. Soon you'll be a landed gentleman yourself, and near equal to your father."

"Oh that," John Henry said heavily. "I reckon there really isn't all that much inheritance after all." From what Rachel had said, there was precious little left.

Tom looked at him quizzically. "How much do you know about the inheritance, John Henry?"

He shrugged. "There's some land, maybe a building somewhere too. My mother tried to tell me about it once, on my birthday. I wasn't payin' all that much attention.

There was some cash money put aside that I was countin' on, but I hear it's gone now..."

"The cash is gone, all right," Tom said. "Your father used it to put you through dental school. But that wasn't the bulk of it, anyhow. It's the land that counts. And the Iron Front especially."

"The Iron what?" John Henry asked, though there was something familiar about the name, something his mother had told him long ago...

Tom's voice changed a little, as though he were about to share something he'd kept close for a long time. "Sit down, John Henry," he said, and motioned to the dining table, then waited until they were both seated before going on. "Do you remember much of what happened after your mother died, I mean after your father remarried?"

"Some. I remember the talk around town. I tried not to believe it..."

"And do you remember the trial?"

"You mean up in Savannah, over the Courthouse trouble?"

"No, not that," Tom said with a shake of his head. "I mean the trial down here in Lowndes County, over your inheritance."

John Henry's mind rushed back to those turbulent days in the aftermath of his mother's death. He'd kept himself away from home as much as possible, staying out late nights, playing cards and drinking with his Vigilante friends. There was only a vague recollection of his father fuming over some legal matter, but then Henry fumed a lot. He shook his head, "I reckon I wasn't payin' much attention to anything but myself back then."

Tom leaned forward, pulling the oil lamp close until it made a circle of light on the dark wood table.

"There was a court case over Alice Jane's inheritance. When she died, her share of my father's estate passed on to Henry, at least the portion that wasn't left to you. But when Henry married Rachel Martin, my family wanted to get that inheritance back. We'd heard some talk around the town about him and Rachel, and my brothers and I weren't pleased about havin' McKey property go to support Henry's new wife, under the circumstances. The thing finally came to trial at the Courthouse there in Valdosta: McKey versus Holliday. And I'm the one who brought the suit."

John Henry took a quick breath, stunned. Tom McKey was the most mild-mannered of men. It was hard to picture him fighting any kind of a fight, let alone taking on the hot-tempered Henry Holliday. And with a disheartening realization, John Henry knew that the town talk about his father and Rachel must have been

216

true after all. Tom never would have made a public spectacle of the family if there weren't something to it.

"The biggest point of contention was a business house back in Griffin, the Iron Front Building on Solomon Street. Our family wanted that building back and Henry wouldn't agree to give it up, so the judge found a novel solution. He ordered us to cut the building in half, one side for each family."

"The Wisdom of King Solomon," John Henry said, remembering the Bible story his mother had recited to him. "Divide the baby in half and see who the real mother is. The judge must have had a sense of humor, seein' how the building was on Solomon Street."

Tom nodded. "And that's just what happened. We built a partition wall right down the middle of the whole thing, one half for McKey, one half for Holliday."

"Half Holliday, half McKey," John Henry said, "kind of like me." Then he remembered something else his mother had said: *Good and bad sown together, like the wheat and the tares. Until the harvest, when the reapers come...*

"So your father deeded over the eastern half of the building to my sisters and me, like the judge ordered. But Henry still has the western half, actin' as your guardian until you come into your inheritance on your twenty-first birthday. That Iron Front building is your inheritance from your mother, John Henry. It's full of renters now, shops leasing out space. Your father has been collectin' rents on it in your name all these years, but now you'll be turnin' twenty-one, those rents will be comin' to you."

"You mean I'll be a landlord?" he asked in surprise.

"If you want to keep leasin' it out. As long as you keep the property in good condition, it'll keep turnin' a nice little profit every month. It may not be enough to set you up in your own practice, but it's an income, anyhow. And it sounds to me like an income is all you need to pay your way out of Valdosta."

~~~~~~~~~~

He stayed on in Florida for a few more days, long enough to have a good visit with Tom – and to write a letter to his Uncle John Holliday in Atlanta. Might he beg his Uncle John's hospitality for an extended visit there? He hoped to settle in Atlanta himself, once he came of legal age, and would need somewhere to stay while he found a partnership arrangement.

Uncle John's reply arrived soon after John Henry returned to Valdosta. Of course he was welcome to come and stay for as long as he liked at his uncle's home in Atlanta. The family was looking forward to visiting with him and hearing all about his recent graduation from dental school. But why wait until his twenty-first birthday? Uncle John's own dentist, Dr. Arthur Ford, was planning to attend a dental convention at the end of July and was looking for someone to attend to his patients while he was gone. And if John Henry did well in that situation, he might be offered something more permanent.

His father thought him foolish for throwing away a perfectly good position with Dr. Frink in hopes of making a place for himself in Atlanta. But he couldn't very well forbid the trip, what with his brother's kind invitation and an offer of temporary employment tendered. So Henry gave his grudging approval, along with a warning that Dr. Frink couldn't keep the place in his practice open forever once John Henry came to his senses and decided to come back home.

But John Henry had no intention of ever coming back to Valdosta, though he didn't put it quite so bluntly to his father.

"I appreciate all you've done for me, Pa. But I reckon it's time I made my own way in the world. Valdosta may be fine for some folks, but I've got bigger plans for myself."

If Henry had a criticism to offer, he kept it to himself.

Chapter Twelve

Atlanta, 1872

His uncle's home had seemed so grand in his memories of it, with its lace-curtained double parlors and dark-paneled study, its carpeted hallways and gleaming brass light fixtures. But after the elegance of Philadelphia and the excitement of St. Louis, Uncle John's house on Forrest Avenue seemed merely comfortable in comparison – though comfort was all John Henry needed, as long as Mattie was there. And being able to sit with her on the curve of the veranda after his welcome home supper, sharing the evening together, made his uncle's house seem like paradise.

Mattie made a pretty picture, sitting there on the porch swing and smiling up at him. She was dressed all in white, in a soft cotton gown that clung to her legs as she pushed the swing back and forth, her slender little feet wearing leather slippers as simple and white as her dress. Against all that pristine whiteness, her auburn hair shone like a dark fire.

The only thing wrong with the picture was that they weren't alone. Cousin Robert was there as well, sitting comfortably beside Mattie on the porch swing, and John Henry had to look at them both together from where he sat balancing on the porch rail. But Robert was only being a good cousin, he reminded himself, showing polite interest in his plans and asking all the proper questions.

"And after Dr. Ford comes back from his convention trip, what then? Will you open your own practice here in Atlanta?"

"Not right off," John Henry said. "I'll have to partner for a while first, until I can save enough money to outfit my own office. I have my hand-tools from dental school, but you'd be astounded how much equipment it takes to practice dentistry these days. Things aren't as simple as they used to be, back when your father pulled teeth in his medical office."

"I'll remember to take that as a warnin'," Robert replied, "and study hard in dental school myself."

"What are you talkin' about?"

"Robert wanted to surprise you," Mattie said with a smile. "He's been talkin' to Uncle John about followin' in your footsteps, and goin' into dentistry as well."

"Father says he can manage the tuition all right," Robert added, "and with my own cousin as my preceptor, I ought to do well enough in Philadelphia."

"But I don't even have a practice yet – how can I be your preceptor?"

"Oh, I won't be goin' for another year at least, so you've got time to get yourself settled first. Father needs my help in the store awhile longer, as Mr. Tidwell is sellin' his half of the business to us. But when I do get my degree, you can take me into your practice as a partner. Think of it: *Holliday and Holliday, Dentists.* Has a ring to it, doesn't it?"

"But what changed your mind from medicine? I always thought you'd take over your father's practice one day."

"Same thing as changed yours, I suppose: too many sick people and too many late nights. There's not many dentists who have to make house calls in the middle of a good night's sleep." Then he smiled in his old taunting way. "Or maybe it's just that old family rivalry – I never could stand to have you beat me at anything!"

John Henry's eyes narrowed with the challenge. "Then you're gonna have a mighty miserable life, Robert Holliday, 'cause there's nothin' I can't beat you at!"

"Listen to you two!" Mattie scolded. "Does everything always have to end up a competition?"

John Henry looked up at her from under his sandy lashes, a smile playing at the corners of his mouth. "Seems like you were the one who turned things into a competition, Mattie, jumpin' out of windows, and all, and darin' us to follow."

She started to blush, remembering, and Robert laughed.

"You sure did look pretty, Mattie, sittin' underneath that tree with your skirts up around your waist."

"Stop it, both of you! That was a long time ago, and I was just a child!"

The pink flush ran across her face, and John Henry thought how little she had changed since those childhood days – still as tiny and delicate as ever, her fragile figure a lovely counterpoint to that stubborn Irish spirit – and yet somehow she had changed completely. There was a light in her eyes now that John Henry had never seen before, a soft new expression when she smiled. And when she leaned forward to laugh, there was a gentle hesitation, a shy flutter of dark lashes against ivory skin that set his head spinning. He'd thought he was in love with her before, but that was nothing compared to the way she made him feel now.

"What did you miss most about home?" she asked, turning the attention away from herself and toward John Henry.

His voice caught in his throat and for a moment he couldn't speak. He wanted to answer: "*You, Mattie. I missed you more than anything. I missed seeing your face and hearing your voice and having you close to me like this.*" But he couldn't tell her that – not in front of Robert, anyhow – though as he thought of it, there wasn't much of anything else that he had missed. "I reckon I missed my name," he said, settling on something at last. "Those Yankees couldn't even take the time to say the whole thing out. Just called me plain 'John,' like they couldn't wait to get it over with and get on to somethin' else. It didn't even sound like me to me."

"John Henry Holliday," Mattie said slowly, his name sounding sweeter than anything, coming from her mouth.

"Well, I don't care what they want to call me up there," Robert said, "as long as I can get a good hot meal every day and a good warm bed every night. You two are just plain short on common sense." Then he yawned and stood up, stretching his long arms. "I am fallin' asleep out here, listenin' to your nonsense. Time I went on to bed. You comin' up, John Henry?"

"Not just yet," he answered as he stared into the night, avoiding Mattie's eyes.

"Then don't wake me when you come to bed. Father needs me in the store early." Then he bent down and kissed Mattie's cheek. "G'night, honey. Don't let him keep you up too late."

Mattie tipped her face up for his kiss on her cheek, smiling. "G'night, dear Robert."

John Henry tried not to let their easy intimacy bother him – Mattie and Robert were only fond cousins, after all – but feeling as he did about her, he couldn't help feeling a little proprietary jealousy, as well. If Mattie hadn't left the swing just then, coming to stand by his side at the white-painted porch rail and looking up at him with tender eyes, he might have had to make an issue of it. But her gentle words calmed his worry.

"It's so good to have you home again, John Henry! Seems like old times, havin' the three of us back together again. Almost like old times, anyhow," she said as her voice took on a sudden sadness. "Except that things aren't well back home. I wrote you about my father's troubles, didn't I?"

"You mentioned he was feelin' poorly. What's the matter?"

"Nothin' in particular. But he gets worn out so fast and has such a hard time workin'. He's been that way, on and off, ever since he came home from that awful

221

prison camp. Oh, how I hate the Yankees, John Henry! They didn't have to be so cruel, just to win the War! Was it just awful, livin' up there in the North?"

"It was hard at first," he admitted, "like livin' in a foreign country, almost. They don't understand anything about us or what we were fightin' for. They all talk about the 'Emancipation of the Slaves,' like that's all the War was about. Keepin' a slave isn't somethin' worth dyin' for! But the right to choose what you will do – now that's a cause. Seems like we've lost our own freedom, when the government can tell us how we ought to live our lives."

Mattie gave him a long look, like his words were the solution to a puzzle she'd been working over. "I guess I never understood what you were so angry about, that summer your father sent you to Jonesboro. I thought you were just a hot-headed boy lookin' for somethin' to fight about. You used to slam the door every time you came in, like you needed to hit somethin'."

"I reckon I was hot-headed, back then, but I wasn't lookin' for a fight. But when there's one I believe in, I can't just stand back and stay out of it."

"I was so worried about you that summer. You were so very unhappy."

He stared at the woods across the way, dark shadowed in the moonlight. "I wasn't altogether unhappy, Mattie – you were there. And now, you're here," he said, turning to look into her eyes, and smiling.

It should have been the perfect moment for the conversation to take a more romantic turn, but instead, she said:

"Thanks to Robert. He arranged the whole thing after my father had to go back home. Robert has friends all over town and found me the teachin' positions, and the summer tutorin' as well. Wealthy folks are always lookin' for tutors. Then he insisted that I come live here instead of stayin' with my students. Most tutors take room and board in their employers' homes, but Robert wouldn't hear of it."

"Cousin Robert sounds like a real hero," he said slowly, watching her face.

"He's been wonderful! I don't know what I'd do without him."

And seeing the tenderness in her eyes, John Henry felt something tearing at his heart. Then he started to cough, that same troublesome cough that had plagued him on and off ever since his bout with the pneumonia.

"John Henry, what's wrong?" Mattie asked in sudden concern.

It took him a moment to catch his breath, the wheezing leaving him dizzy. He put his hand to his forehead and felt the cold perspiration that always came with the coughing fit. From somewhere in the folds of her dress, Mattie pulled out a handkerchief and started dabbing at his face.

"Oh honey, you look awful! What's the matter? You didn't tell me you were ill. Here, hold onto me until you get your breath back," and somehow tiny Mattie was steadying his whole weight and helping him to the porch swing. Then she sat beside him wiping his brow until his breathing came slow and regular again.

"I've had the pneumonia..." he started to explain.

"I know. But that was last winter."

"It's hard to get over. The doctor warned me to watch out for relapses." Her touch was so gentle, her nearness so comforting.

"That's nonsense. You don't relapse all of a sudden on a warm summer evenin'. Has this coughin' happened before?"

"I don't remember," he lied. "Maybe once or twice. But I'm fine, Mattie, really. It's just that leftover cough, that's all. I am not sick." Although he was enjoying her attentions, he had never forgotten his father's philosophy that illness was weakness. He was not weak; he would not be ill.

But Mattie peered into his face, her head to one side, not believing him. "I never heard anybody cough like that who was altogether healthy. We must have Uncle John listen to that cough first thing in the mornin'."

"I don't need Uncle John to examine me. I am a doctor now myself, and I tell you I'm just fine."

"And still as stubborn and arrogant as ever! I don't believe your dental degree makes you a physician, not like Uncle John. You may be a wonderful dentist, but you are not a medical doctor."

It was good to have her attention, even though she was fussing at him. And since she was still holding his hand in hers, stroking it while chastising him, he couldn't let the evening go completely to waste.

"Mattie, do you remember what I told you last summer in Jonesboro?"

"I remember you sayin' you were in a bad way for some lemonade after mendin' that fence all day," she said, smiling. "I never saw anyone drink a whole pitcher full down so quick!"

"You know what I'm talkin' about. I told you I was gonna kiss you when I came home again. Well, I'm home now. And I still want to kiss you, if you'll let me."

She dropped his hand and looked away bashfully, just the way a lady should, and said softly, "I don't mind."

But when he put his hand under her chin, lifting her face to his, she suddenly turned her head, giving him her cheek instead of her lips.

It was such an unexpected rebuff that he didn't know what to do but kiss her on the offered cheek like a good cousin. Had she misunderstood his intention, as Thea Morgan had misunderstood in a different way? Did she think that all he felt was a brotherly sort of affection for her? Or worse, was a sisterly affection all she felt for him?

But before he could ask her to explain her sudden aloofness, she looked up at him with glistening eyes, and whispered:

"Oh, I have missed you, John Henry!"

Then she slipped off the porch swing and ran into the house, leaving him alone with his unanswered questions.

~~~~~~~~~

The dental office of Dr. Arthur C. Ford occupied a second-floor suite of rooms above a confectionery shop at the corner of Whitehall and Alabama Streets, right in the middle of Atlanta's business district – which meant that it was in the middle of Atlanta's railroad business, as well. Whitehall might have been more properly named Railroad Avenue, with the tracks of the Atlantic Rail and the Macon and Western Railroads running alongside each other down the middle of the street. Crossing Whitehall during the business day was an act of faith and fortitude, dodging wagons and buggies and listening for the warning whistles of oncoming locomotives, and it wasn't unusual for an incautious pedestrian to be hit by a train. Only then did the traffic on Whitehall Street slow while an ambulance came around to carry the victim off to the hospital or the morgue. Then as soon as the road was cleared, business started up again right where it had left off. Atlanta didn't have time to stop long for anything.

Any other dentist might have found the constant noise of Whitehall Street distracting. But John Henry had spent two years in bustling Philadelphia, and he found the commotion less of a bother than the uncomfortable heat rising up from the big candy stoves in the confectionery shop below, though all in all, Dr. Ford's office was a pleasant place to work. The two small rooms were well-appointed with velvet upholstered cast-iron dental chairs facing toward the light of the long windows overlooking the street, fancy brass cuspidors beside the chairs, and a carved rosewood cabinet for the instruments. Dr. Ford had even installed a Morrison Dental Engine, the new foot-pedal powered machine that drove the dental drill, as modern as anything at the dental school. And with all that, it was likely the best-equipped office in Atlanta, and a far sight better than Dr. Frink's crowded little storefront where John Henry might have had to spend his professional life.

Dr. Ford's fine office seemed a reflection of the man himself, for in a society in which birth and breeding still meant something, Dr. Ford had the best of pedigrees: English by birth, trained in his profession by an eminent New York dentist, and a Southerner by choice and service to the Confederacy. His manners were impeccable, his grooming flawless, his speech cultured and refined. And compared to him, John Henry felt like a county rustic, although Dr. Ford had been impressed enough by his own credentials to offer him a temporary position. Young Dr. Holliday was, after all, not only a graduate of the Pennsylvania College of Dental Surgery, but also the nephew of Dr. John Stiles Holliday, and thereby kin to Dr. Crawford Long whom Dr. Ford had known in Jefferson, Georgia, his home before moving to Atlanta. Birth and breeding, it seemed, had worked in John Henry's favor as well.

Dr. Ford announced their association in the professional card section of the *Atlanta Constitution* of Friday, July 26th:

CARD

I HEREBY inform my patients that I leave to attend the session
of the Southern Dental Association in
Richmond, Virginia, this evening, and will be absent
until about the middle of August, during which time
Dr. John H. Holliday will fill my place in my office.
Arthur C. Ford, D.D.S.
Office 26 Whitehall Street

It wasn't the first time John Henry had seen his name in the newspaper, as there had been a brief article in the *Philadelphia Ledger* listing the graduates of the dental school there. But it was the first time a newspaper had printed his name with the title of "Dr." preceding it, and seeing it that way made John Henry feel he'd already made a success of his professional life. And just in case he might never see his name in the papers again, he cut out the advertisement and tucked it away inside one of his dental textbooks, as a memento of his coming-of-age.

~~~~~~~~~~~~~

Aunt Permelia had her own idea of how a coming-of-age ought to be celebrated. So on the Sunday afternoon before John Henry's twenty-first birthday, she had Sophie pack a lunch and the stable boy hitch up the phaeton, then instructed her husband to carry them all out to Ponce de Leon Springs, the popular resort just outside the city limits, where mineral waters bubbled up out of the rock and flowed into Peachtree Creek. It was a lovely picnic spot, and quite fashionable for social gatherings, though John Henry had to laugh at the way his aunt mispronounced the name of the place, slurring the Spanish syllables together until they came out sounding something like "pons-da-lee-on," and barely recognizable as the name of a famous explorer. Her brief history lesson, taught as they rode out to the park, was almost as amusing.

"They named the springs after the gentleman who went lookin' for the fountain of youth," she explained. "But he got lost and found Florida instead. The real fountain was back here in Georgia all along, and now we have a nice park built around it."

In spite of its adventurous history, Ponce de Leon Springs was civilized recreation, well-mannered and well-dressed. Ladies in bustled gowns strolled along the stone paths with gentlemen in light summer jackets and wide straw Panama hats, the woodland quiet only occasionally disturbed by the rumble of a passing train on the trestle of the Air Line Railroad or the sound of waltz music drifting down from the bandstand where the old 5th Georgia Regiment band played. And every leisurely idyll ended with a stop at the springs, where the little colored boy in attendance dipped an iron cup into the mineral water and passed it around – health and happiness for only a penny a drink.

Picnics in the park were elegant affairs, and Aunt Permelia was not to be outdone. Her table under the trees was spread with linen and set with bone china and the family silver, and even the sweet tea seemed like something special when it was poured from a cut crystal pitcher. But though John Henry should have enjoyed all the fuss the family was making over his birthday, he found that he didn't have much of an appetite for dinner, what with the August heat and humidity and the insects buzzing all around, and Mattie drawing Robert like she was some sweet summer flower. And worse: Mattie seemed to be overly enjoying Robert's attentions, laughing at all his jokes and not paying nearly enough attention to John Henry.

But no one else seemed to notice Robert's flirtations, as they all chatted around the table discussing business and politics and family matters as the afternoon slid by.

Then, over a dessert of lemon cake, Uncle John tapped a silver table knife on the tea pitcher, and the crystal made a pretty tinkling sound as he announced:

"As y'all know, your cousin John Henry here will be turnin' twenty-one years old this week, the age at which a young man takes his proper place in society and comes into his inheritance. And as John Henry has always been a special nephew to me, bein' my namesake and myself havin' had somethin' to do with his comin' through infancy safely, it seems fittin' that I should bequeath him somethin' of my own as an inheritance in honor of his comin'-of-age. George, reach me that gun case, please."

Aunt Permelia smiled and nodded approvingly as Uncle John opened the polished mahogany gun case to reveal a glint of dark metal and a pair of matched pistols resting in black velvet.

"I ordered these revolvers when the War started," Uncle John went on, "standard issue for the Army in those days: Colt's Navy Model 1851, single action, .36-caliber, blued steel barrels with walnut grips. Happily, I never had to use them, except for target practice. But these pistols bein' manufactured the same year that both Robert and John Henry came into the world, I thought they'd be appropriate comin'-of-age gifts, sharing a shared birthdate so to speak. I've already gifted one of these pistols to Robert, when he turned twenty-one. Now I'm givin' the other to you, John Henry," he said, carefully lifting one of the guns and handing it to his nephew.

John Henry was near speechless at his uncle's offering, that fine pistol being the best present he could ever remember receiving, although his gratitude was a little diminished by the fact that Robert had already received its twin. Robert was always first in everything. Still, it was a very generous gift.

"Sir, I'm honored," John Henry said, as he took the heavy revolver from his Uncle John's hand. Then he added admiringly, "They say Colt's 1851's the very same model that Wild Bill Hickok uses."

"If you can believe what Harper's Magazine writes!" Robert said with a laugh, taking his own revolver from the box. "And who cares what Hickok uses? You'll never do anything but target shootin' with that pistol, anyhow."

"Maybe Robert and John Henry can have a contest over at the shootin' range," said young Cousin Johnny eagerly, "to see which pistol's the fastest."

"Where mine will win, of course," Robert replied, challenging as always. "Not because it's a better firearm, but because I've been better trained."

It was true that Robert had good training, having learned marksmanship among the other gentlemanly subjects taught at the expensive private school he'd attended on Atlanta's Peachtree Street. But John Henry knew a thing or two about shooting himself, and was proud of his skills. "I reckon I can beat you at draw and fire, Robert, even without your fancy trainin'. I've done my share of shootin', livin' out in the country."

"Well, the way I was taught, it's not good form to try and take the target by surprise the way you do. A gentleman shouldn't have to lower himself to actin' like the animal he's stalkin', sneakin' up on it."

John Henry was about to say something cutting in reply when Aunt Permelia, seeming to sense a growing tension in the air, drew the conversation in another direction.

"I expect your father will have a nice birthday gift for you, as well," she said. "Henry's done just fine in business, with his carriages and his rose farms. And now he's growin' pecan trees, isn't that right?"

"Yes, Ma'am," John Henry replied, reluctant to turn his attention to his father, always a sore subject for him. "He says pecans are the next cash crop of Georgia."

"Uncle Henry always did have a mind for business," Cousin George commented approvingly. "I reckon we'll see him as a wealthy planter yet."

"And how is your stepmother?" George's wife Mary asked, looking up from tending to her new baby. "I haven't heard you say anything of her."

Having to talk about his father was bad enough, but making pleasantries about Rachel was beyond him on any day, and especially on the day of his birthday celebration. Instead of answering the question, he dropped his linen napkin on the table and said quickly, "Will you excuse me, Aunt Permelia? I believe I've had enough for one afternoon." And with a stunned silence following him, he pocketed his new pistol and walked away from the picnic table, heading toward the wooded grove at the stream's edge.

He stood there fuming, trying to get his angry thoughts under control. He'd been unsettled enough by Cousin Robert's attentions to Mattie without having his father and Rachel brought into the conversation, as well. He still remembered too clearly the words Rachel had repeated about his courtship plans – that cows didn't breed well in the same lot. Why, if she'd been a man...

"Would you like someone to talk to?" Mattie asked, and John Henry turned in surprise to see her picking her way through the leaves to join him in the shade of the trees.

"Won't Robert be missin' you?" he said sharply, but Mattie seemed not to catch his meaning.

"The rest of the family's all goin' off to try the mineral water," she said, sitting down on the thick summer grass and spreading her skirts out around her. "You know Mary didn't mean to offend you, askin' about Rachel. She's still new to the family. You can't expect her to understand about your stepmother."

"Rachel is no mother of mine," he replied bitterly.

"Well, she's your father's wife, isn't she? And that does make her your stepmother."

"I don't want to talk about it, Mattie," he answered, but she ignored his protest and went on.

"I know what a hard time that was for you when your father remarried, but it was so long ago. Can't you forgive him? You know you'll never be happy if you're not at peace with your own family."

He sat down beside her then, caught up a clump of wet grass and flung it aside. "I don't feel like I have a family anymore. Rachel ruined that. And my father..." his words broke off angrily. "Sometimes I think I hate him, Mattie!"

"You don't hate him, John Henry. You love him, and that's the trouble. Can't nobody hurt you that you don't care about. Why, I remember when you used to just idolize him."

"He used to be my hero," he agreed sullenly, "the great Major Henry Holliday. I used to look at that sword of his hangin' on the parlor wall and wish I could be like him someday. Even when he came home, so sick and all, I imagined it was like a battle wound. But then my mother passed and he brought Rachel home, and there was all that talk..."

But he couldn't tell her what the townsfolk had said. Such things weren't fit for a lady's ears, and he shook his head and looked away.

"I thought he was a hero, Mattie, but I was wrong."

"And do you have to have a hero?" she asked gently.

"I reckon I do..." he replied, and had to blink back unexpected emotion.

"Oh honey!" Mattie cried, looking into his eyes and somehow seeing everything that he was feeling. "It just breaks my heart to have you hurtin' so!"

At the touch of her hand on his, the anger and the pain in him started to melt away. It was amazing how someone so small could have such a powerful effect on him.

"Sweet Mattie!" he said, a sudden urgency in his voice. "You know how much you mean to me, don't you? How much I care for you?"

Her mouth opened as if she were about to speak. Then she looked away, a sudden hesitation, a quiet pulling away from him. "Of course I know how much you care.

I'd be a fool not to know. But there is nothin' in it, John Henry, not the way you want it to be. I can't ever care for you like that." Although her words were earnest, there were tears glistening at the edges of her lashes.

"Is there someone else, then?" he asked, but she looked down and didn't answer, and he pressed the point. "Is it Robert, Mattie? Hell, anybody but Robert..."

Then she looked up past him, a flush on her face, and John Henry realized that they were no longer alone.

"Did someone mention my name?"

Robert strode toward them, hat in hand, and John Henry was struck by the unhappy notion that they still looked enough alike to be brothers.

"Well, honey," Robert said, smiling broadly, "you missed a mighty fine walk. But that mineral water – I think it's the awful taste that chases the disease away!"

He bent over and gave Mattie a quick kiss on the cheek, then sat down beside her on the grass, his long legs brushing the edge of her cotton skirt.

"So what do you say about tryin' out that new pistol, John Henry? I mean, if you're still any good at that sort of thing."

John Henry glared at him. "I am still damn good at that sort of thing!"

"No need for that kind of language, Cousin," Robert chastised. "We've got a lady present. Though I suppose we can't expect someone who's been livin' in the North to remember his manners all the time. But don't you worry, Mattie honey," he said with a wink, "we'll turn him Southern again, soon enough!"

If Mattie hadn't been sitting right there between them, John Henry would have slapped him across the face. "Are you callin' me a Yankee?"

Robert laughed out loud. "I never saw a Yankee with a temper as quick as yours! What's got you so riled today, anyhow?"

There was no explaining it without confessing his feelings for Mattie, and he wasn't about to do that in front of Robert. Instead, he forced a smile and answered:

"I believe I would enjoy doin' a little shootin' this afternoon. But why don't we make it a real contest, with a prize for the winner?"

"I'm game," Robert replied. "But what shall we have for a prize?"

John Henry looked up at Mattie and said with a slow drawl, "How 'bout a kiss from our favorite cousin for the champion?"

Mattie started in surprise, but Robert laughed. "Well, what do you say, honey? Shall we make you our Helen of Troy and give you to the winner?"

"I never heard of anything so ridiculous!" she said, tossing her auburn hair.

"Come on, Mattie," John Henry said. "It's just a little wager to add some excitement to the game. Unless, of course...you're scared."

He knew just what to say to taunt her. Mattie had never been afraid of anything in her life, courage being the Holliday birthright, and she put up her little chin and gave him a steady, solemn gaze.

"All right, if that's what you boys want."

"Well, then," Robert said with a smile, pushing himself to his feet and brushing the grass from his linen summer trousers, "gauntlet thrown and challenge accepted. And may the best man win."

"Oh, indeed," John Henry repeated coolly, "may the best man win."

~~~~~~~~~~

The shooting range was already crowded with curious spectators by the time Robert and John Henry had loaded their pistols and taken their places facing the paper targets. But John Henry wasn't paying attention to anything except the competition, and Mattie who would be his prize. He was certain to win, but not so certain of what her reaction would be.

On the toss of a coin Robert was the first to shoot, using the twin of John Henry's new Colt's Navy. He bowed to the crowd, then turned sideways to the target in a classical shooter's stance, back hand on one hip and pistol raised, and taking careful aim he slowly pulled back on the trigger. The pistol jerked as he fired, and a moment later the target shuddered with the impact.

"Bull's eye!" he called out proudly, and the crowd answered with applause. "Your turn, John Henry. See if you can beat that!"

John Henry squinted into the sun, studying the targets. "Be a mighty fine trick if I can. I reckon I'd just about have to blow that target to pieces to beat your shot."

Robert smiled in triumph and called to Mattie, "Got my kiss ready, honey? He's practically concedin' defeat."

But Mattie's face was unreadable, her gaze set on the distant targets. John Henry shrugged and took a deep breath, preparing to make his shot, then he paused to consider. He'd always been ambidextrous, almost as good with his left hand as he was with his right, and he had the sudden urge to show off. He switched the pistol over from his right hand to his left, and smiled at the spectators. Then in one fluid motion he spun around and fired, left arm flung out and pulling off five fast shots from the revolver. The target jumped at the first hit and exploded, then shattered into the air. He watched it, staying crouched as the smoke rose up thick and acrid around him. It wasn't the fine classical style that Robert's school had taught, but it always seemed to work – and it gave him pleasure to know that he could beat his cousin even left-handed.

There was a startled hush from the crowd, no one quite believing that lightning fast shooting or the quick destruction of that paper target. Then there was a smattering of appreciative handclaps that grew into a full round of applause, and John Henry stood and slowly turned around, cool and arrogant.

"There, I win," he said, casting a contemptuous glance at Robert. "And I believe I'll take that kiss now, Cousin Mattie."

He walked toward her, the pistol hot in his hand, and reached for her with his free arm, pulling her close.

"You are makin' a fool out of me," she whispered. "Everybody's watchin'."

"But you are the prize, and I have won you fair and square."

"Then get it over with and let me go," she said, turning her head to the side and waiting for his kiss on her cheek.

But John Henry slid his hand under her chin and tipped her face up toward his.

"Nothin' so chaste as that, dear Cousin. I'll have a real kiss this time or none at all." Then he bent his head to her face, his lips close to hers, and spoke under his breath. "Unless you'd rather have my cousin Robert kiss you."

"Stop it!" she said, yanking her arm free. "You don't know what you're talkin' about!"

"Are you in love with him, Mattie?" he said, his voice rough with emotion. "Are you in love with him?"

But Mattie raised her eyes and spoke with a resignation he did not understand. "What difference would it make?" Then she walked away toward the rest of the family, and left John Henry standing there alone.

~~~~~~~~~~

It had all gone wrong, from start to finish. Yet John Henry could not believe that he had misread Mattie's feelings for him. She had always cared for him, had always been so tender and loving and full of understanding. And what of the promise they had made to each other, before he went away to dental school? He had been so sure of her love then. He had lived on the certainty of it all these years, and his stubborn pride wouldn't let him believe that she might not love him after all – stubborn pride and the powerful need to have her with him.

But as the carriages pulled into the gravel drive after the ride home from the Springs, Robert held him back from following after her into the house

"Let her go, John Henry. You've done enough damage for one day."

John Henry looked at him sharply. "What are you talkin' about?"

"I'm talkin' about the fool way you've been actin' all afternoon, fussin' and fumin' and teasin' poor Mattie like some lovesick school boy."

"And what are you doin' with her, Robert?"

"I am not stealin' her away from you, if that's what you're askin'. I know you care a great deal for Mattie. There's always been somethin' special between the two of you, even back when we were children. But that doesn't mean she wants you to romance her."

"I don't reckon that's any of your business," he said angrily.

"It is if your plans are gonna make her unhappy. And I think they might, if her father still feels the same as he used to about you."

"You're talkin' in riddles, Robert."

"I'm just tryin' to talk some sense into you. Do you remember the boy who went to stay with Mattie's family that summer after the War, the one whose father had to send him away before the Yankees came after him? Well, Uncle Rob does. Hot-headed, he called you back then, and he cautioned Mattie against gettin' too close to you. And you should understand Mattie well enough to know that she would never disobey him. She adores her father."

"But that's not the way I am now. You know I've changed!"

"Have you? And what was all that show at the target range today? That wasn't a friendly shootin' match, and you know it. That target you shot to pieces was me, and you were damn proud of it."

"A man's got a right to fight for what is his!"

"Mattie is not yours, John Henry. And no fightin' with me will ever win her for you. No fightin' with anybody will. If her father considers you a bad risk, then that's the end of it. I reckon you sealed your own fate with her back in Valdosta when you tried to take the law into your own hands and run the Yankees out of town. Forget tryin' to win her, John Henry. You lost her long ago."

He had no reason to doubt Robert's words, but his heart still railed against them. What did it matter if Mattie's father disapproved of him? It was Mattie's opinion of him that counted, and she had always loved him and thought the best of him. Indeed, it was Mattie's good opinion of him that had helped him to get where he was now, starting out on a fine professional career. Without her constant letters and loving support, he might have wasted more time in dental school, taking up DeMorat on his offer of a life of debauchery in Philadelphia. He might have taken up Kate Fisher on her unspoken offer as well, and had a real affair with the varieties actress in St. Louis. But knowing that Mattie trusted him, he had kept himself from it. Surely she wouldn't turn away from him now on account of the troubles of his youth. But Mattie had hurried into the house after their return home, obviously unwilling to talk to him, so he'd have to find some other way to calm his anxious mind.

What he needed was a drink, something more bracing than a crystal pitcher full of sweet tea or his Aunt Permelia's prized peach wine. And then he remembered that the streetcars ran into town clear into the night, and he could be downtown in no time at all. And downtown he could find a drink and clear his mind enough to sort everything out.

It was already dusk by the time he got into the city where the plate glass windows of the Maison de Ville Saloon were shining in the light of the gas street lamps, welcoming him. The Maison was a first-class drinking establishment, owned by a longtime friend of the Holliday family from Griffin, Mr. Lee Smith. The finest men of Atlanta society played cards there, while the deposed leaders of the Democratic party planned their political comeback over drinks at the bar. So no one could fault John Henry for celebrating his upcoming twenty-first birthday in such a friendly masculine atmosphere, or for drinking more than he might otherwise have done as Lee Smith poured him free drinks in honor of his coming-of-age.

By the time he was on his way back to Forrest Avenue, walking as it was past the hour for the streetcars to be running, he was feeling relaxed and almost cheery again and even Robert's warnings didn't seem to trouble him anymore. It was wonderful what a little whiskey could do when life got difficult, and he'd had more than a little at the Maison. Then as he rounded the corner of Pryor and Decatur Streets, he stopped. From somewhere up above, a voice was calling out, a friendly female voice offering flattering words.

"Hey, handsome!" the voice called, and John Henry looked up into the open windows of a Decatur Street bordello. "Lookin' for some fun?"

Decatur Street was an interesting mix of businesses, with warehouses and proper saloons standing side by side with discretely shuttered bordellos. Except on this hot summer night, when one dark-haired girl was daring to flaunt propriety and call to potential customers down in the street below. But John Henry wasn't interested in a prostitute, and he told her so.

"I'm just out for a birthday drink, that's all," he said as politely as he could.

"Well, happy birthday," she replied. "Kind of a poor party, though, celebratin' all alone."

"What makes you think I'm alone?"

She leaned a little farther out of the window and took a look up Decatur Street one way and then the other. "I don't see anybody down there but you. Shame to be alone on your birthday. Why don't you come up and share a drink or two with me? No charge, bein' as it's your special day. Business is slow tonight, anyhow."

It wasn't quite a proposition, but still he hesitated. Stopping into the Maison de Ville for a round of drinks on the house was one thing, but having a nightcap in a Decatur Street bordello would be quite another, if anyone saw him.

But who was there to see, in the dark lamplit hours past midnight? And she was a pretty thing, with a tangle of dark curls falling over a bosom indiscreetly exposed. Dark hair, he thought with a sudden stir of memory, like Kate Fisher's...

"Well?" the girl asked as he stood a moment longer in the street. "Are you comin' up or not?"

He took a quick breath and gave her his most gentlemanly smile. "I believe I am."

Her room was at the end of a dark little hallway, but he found it fast enough, though once there, he wasn't quite sure what to do with himself. He'd only come up for a last drink of the night, after all, and there was only one chair for the two of them to share. The only other piece of furniture one could sit on was the bed, occupying most of the rest of the shabby chamber. And though he'd already had plenty of liquor for one night, he said uncomfortably, "You had a free drink for me? I'd prefer whiskey if you have it."

"Whiskey it is," she said cheerily. "Whatever the gentleman prefers."

She brought the glass to where he stood, hat in hand. "Come now! At least let me take that nice hat of yours so you don't spill your drink on it. Shame to spoil a nice expensive felt like that."

She pulled the hat out of his hand and brushed it off gently, then laid it on the dressing table. She knew how to treat fine things, anyhow.

He finished the whiskey faster than he should have considering the amount of liquor he'd already downed that night, but the girl was already refilling his glass. She was a sweet and attentive little thing, bringing him his drinks like that and not expecting anything in return. Why had he hesitated before coming up? Then she startled him by reaching to touch the blue silk of his necktie.

"Pretty color," she said, "just like your eyes. You have real nice blue eyes." And in a moment the tie was loose and in her hand. "Silk is so soft, and mighty expensive too. You must be rich as well as handsome."

He nodded, not sure what to say, but her pleasant chatter ran on like music in his liquor-filled mind. "A shame to do nothin' but drink on your birthday," she said as she moved closer to him, deftly unbuttoning the high starched collar from his shirt bosom, her fingers brushing over the blonde stubble on his neck, and she laughed when he jumped at the unexpected intimacy.

"Now don't tell me this is your first time, a handsome thing like you! Must have been plenty of other girls ready to go for a tumble with you."

He couldn't answer her, his head dizzy with whiskey and his senses warming at her touch. He wondered if there was any liquor left in the bottle and if he could reach it easily from where he was standing. But he wasn't standing anymore, as the girl took his hand and led him toward her bed.

"We're gonna have a real nice birthday party together, just you and me. And when we're done, you can pay me what you think it's worth."

What better way to celebrate his coming-of-age?

~~~~~~~~~

By the time he got back to Forrest Avenue, the dawn was breaking, the sky already beginning to thin out and turn from deep black to a misty early morning blue. The house was quiet, except for the ticking of the grandfather clock that stood sentinel in the front hall. Thank goodness it was still too early for the maid Sophie to be up getting breakfast. He couldn't face anyone right now. He could hardly face himself.

"*Johnny*," the girl had called him, like he was young as his young cousin. "*Johnny*," she had murmured against his neck, and even the memory of the sound of it gave him chills all up and down. He could still feel that silky black hair of hers falling over his skin, still smell the perfume she rubbed down the long white curve of her throat. He hadn't realized that sin could smell so sweet. He stood there letting the memory run across his skin and cursed himself for it. This must be what hell was like, he thought – trying to forget and relishing the memory all at once. If only he were a Catholic like Mattie and could attend confession! For surely God would understand how a woman like that could make a man forget his moral duty. In the future, he would be sure to do his drinking in a proper saloon.

He stepped lightly as he made his way up the stairs, glad the family was all still asleep, glad he'd spent most of the evening at the Maison de Ville where Lee Smith would surely keep his confidences. But as he snuck into the second-floor bedroom that he shared with Robert, he found his cousin still awake, sitting reading by the light of an oil lamp.

"You're out late," Robert commented, closing his book. "And you've been drinkin', by the smell of you."

"I was celebratin' my birthday," John Henry replied. "I reckon comin'-of-age means I'm man enough to do as I please. More of a man now than you are, anyhow –"

"And what's that supposed to mean?"

"It means my life is none of your business!" he said, the anger of the afternoon and the shame of the evening running together. He was sure that respectable Robert had never spent a few lost hours in a woman's bed, on Decatur Street or anywhere else.

Robert studied him a moment, then sighed and shook his head. "You haven't changed at all, have you? You're still just as selfish and thoughtless as ever. I wasn't the only one waitin' up for you. Mattie stayed up past midnight herself, worried over where you'd gone."

"Mattie waited up?" John Henry said sharply, his heart growing cold. Mattie had waited up for him, while he was spending himself in a bordello?

"She had a birthday present for you and wanted to give it to you privately. Poor thing cares for you more than she should. And if you cared about her half as much as you care about yourself…"

"She had a present for me?" he asked as his heart slowly warmed again. If she cared enough to wait up, to bring him a gift, then there must still be hope…

"Take it," Robert said, tossing a small paper-wrapped bundle into John Henry's hands. "She asked me to give it to you as soon as you got home, so now I've done my duty. I won't tell her how late you came in, or how much liquor you've been drinkin'. She deserves better than that."

But not even Robert's chastising words could hurt him, as he opened the package .
and found the gift that Mattie had brought for him: A little leather notebook, the
pages blank as if she meant for him to fill them with his own words, the inside front
cover inscribed in her delicate and feminine handwriting:

To my dearest cousin, J.H. Holliday –
Happy birthday!
Love always, M.A. Holliday

~~~~~~~~~~

It had all been so easy, once he knew that she still cared, to set things back on course
again. He'd simply taken her into the parlor of his Uncle's house and lied a little,
telling her that he had no intentions toward her other than friendship, so there was
no reason to worry her father over his past or his future.

"But what about that talk we had, before you went off to Philadelphia?" she
asked as they sat together on the hard horsehair sofa. "I thought you wanted..." she
stopped, too well-bred to make such assumptions out loud.

He reached for her hand and held it lightly. "Of course I had intentions, Mattie.
How could I not? You are the finest girl I know. Who wouldn't want to win your
heart?" That part came easily enough; he meant every word. Then he took a breath
and went on. "But after Robert told me the situation with your father, of course my
intentions no longer matter. I will never again press you for somethin' you cannot give."

"And we can still be friends?" she asked.

"Oh Mattie!" he said, with unfeigned emotion, "haven't we always been friends?"

But alone with her there in the quiet of the parlor, with just a breath of space
between them and her face tipped gently up to his, he had a sudden yearning to
bend his head and kiss her, after all.

"Don't look at me that way, John Henry," she said softly.

"What way?" he asked.

"That way," she said, pulling her head away from his shoulder, though she kept
looking up as though his eyes had some kind of hold on her. "It makes me feel funny."

"Funny good or funny bad?" he asked, teasing her a little, and enjoying the sudden
discovery that he did still have some effect on her.

"Just funny, that's all," she said, giving a small quiver with her shoulders. "Just don't
do it anymore."

But still she didn't look away, and all at once he knew just what she meant. He had that same funny feeling too, flushed and breathless, and for a moment he didn't know who had a magical hold over whom, or if they were both caught in the same thing.

Chapter Thirteen

Atlanta, 1872

That was the summer that baseball fever came to Atlanta, and not since the War had there been such a thrilling spectator sport. The hometown team was called the Osceolas, named after a tribe of southeastern Indian braves, and the game they played was fast and physical. It wasn't unusual for a player to be knocked clean senseless by a wild ball or a carefully aimed bat, and in the crowds watching the game ladies fainted at the show of violence, but the fans still yelled for more. But there were other, gentler pleasures to fill those languid summer days. There was rowing on the lake at Oglethorpe Park, and roller-skating on the rink at the bottom of Forsyth Street. And with church barbecues and county fairs, slow sultry afternoons and firefly nights, it was a perfect summer for courting and sparking and falling in love.

It was also the summer that Mattie's cousin, Annie Fitzgerald Stephens, moved to Jackson Hill, right around the corner from Forrest Avenue. Annie was second of the seven daughters of Phillip Fitzgerald, and had been the belle of Clayton County before she ran off and married Captain John Stephens during the glory days of the War. She'd been only eighteen-years-old at the time and her elopement with the dashing Confederate officer had been the talk of the county, until Gettysburg and Vicksburg overshadowed everything else.

Captain Stephens was stationed in Atlanta in 1863, and the newlyweds made their home there, living in a rented boarding house room and taking their meals in restaurants. It was a fashionable way for a young couple to live in a city full of soldiers and the excitement of the War. Annie thrived on life in Atlanta, feeling a kinship with the city that had been founded in the same year she was born – she liked to think that they were both of them young women, full of passion and vibrantly alive. Then Sherman's army came to Georgia, and Annie watched the city she loved go up in flames.

With the Yankees in Atlanta and Captain Stephens back at the front, Annie refugeed south to live with her sister Mamie in Macon. But that elegant old citadel on the bluffs of the Ocmulgee River wasn't much safer than Atlanta for a beautiful young War bride and her unmarried sister. Macon was full of the riffraff that followed Sherman's destruction: swaggering Yankee soldiers and freed Negro slaves, drunken Confederate deserters, and ladies of ill repute. So brave Annie marched right through the Yankee camp to the General's headquarters and demanded that a guard be placed upon her home for her protection, and the Yankee general was so impressed by the fiery Irish lass that he sent not one guard but four, a day shift and a night shift, to stand post at Annie's house as long as she remained in the city. She was something of a legend in Macon after that – the Rebel girl who had dared to challenge the Yankees, and won.

After the War ended Annie returned to Atlanta where she and Captain Stephens set up housekeeping in a pretty home on Peters Street, close to the downtown. John Stephens had been trained as an accountant and found plenty of work keeping books for the new businesses that were turning Atlanta into a boomtown. He brought home $200 dollars a month in gold, a fortune during the Reconstruction, and his wife had everything she wanted – except a child.

By the time Annie was twenty-three years old she had birthed and buried four babies – two sons and two daughters. Then finally, one little girl survived. Annie named her daughter Mary Isabelle after two of the blessed Saints, but Captain Stephens said that was too much of a name for a baby and he shortened it to Maybelle, and as a baby gift to his wife he bought a new house, one where there were no memories of dead children to haunt the nursery. And that was when the Stephens family moved to Jackson Hill.

Mattie was thrilled to have her cousin living so close. They hadn't seen much of each other since Annie had run off to Atlanta to be married, but they had long memories of growing up together in Jonesboro.

"Oh, John Henry, just think of it!" Mattie exclaimed when she first heard the news. "Real family livin' right up the street, close enough to walk to whenever I want to visit!"

"Aren't we real family?" he asked with a little envy, seeing Mattie with her eyes dancing and her cheeks all in a blush at reading the calling card that Annie had left for her.

"Well, of course you're real family," she answered. "But Annie is from Jonesboro, and her father is my mother's very own Uncle Phillip. We practically grew up together. Why, it'll be like havin' my own sisters here with me, with Annie so close!"

John Henry didn't understand why a woman always wanted to have other women around. Aunt Permelia was the same way, spending time at her sewing circles and literary parties where the ladies sat for hours and talked about babies and such. It wasn't like they had anything really important to discuss, not the way men did, debating politics and business over a drink and a friendly game of cards. He smiled benignly and said as if he didn't care one way or another:

"I could walk you over there now, if you wanted to go for a little visit." A half-hour alone with Mattie, walking her up to Jackson Hill and home again, would be worth an hour or two of sitting while she chatted with her cousin. Besides, she couldn't go out unescorted. Forrest Avenue was safe enough, but just over the crest of the hill was the wooded ravine called Buttermilk Bottom, where all sorts of ruffians lurked in the green shadows.

"I suppose, if it wouldn't be too much trouble..." Mattie said. And though she seemed a little unsure still, she was already reaching for her bonnet. "Well, I'm sure Annie will enjoy meetin' you. She was already married and gone to Atlanta when you came to Jonesboro for your little visit."

John Henry smiled as he followed her out into the heavy afternoon heat. Mattie always referred to his summer of exile as his "little visit," as though he'd been there for pleasure instead of punishment. She was always trying to see the good side of everything and everybody. Heaven help her, if she ever met the Devil face to face she'd find something polite to say.

A gust of hot wind whipped across the front porch, fluttering Mattie's skirts and blowing John Henry's hat right off. He grabbed after it, looking up into the clouding sky. On the western horizon, a thin veil of gray was gathering and turning dark.

"Looks like there's a storm comin'," he said, nodding toward the clouds. "We sure could use a good rain."

~~~~~~~~~

By the time they arrived at the Stephens' elegant new home, John Henry was actually looking forward to meeting Mattie's married cousin. He knew from the stories he'd heard that Annie was a feisty little thing, full of enough gumption to face down that Yankee general. But though he knew she was still young when she'd had those War adventures, he somehow expected that marriage and five babies would have aged her past her twenty-something years.

There was nothing matronly, however, about the beautiful Annie Fitzgerald Stephens. Her black Irish looks were still stunning enough to put any Southern Belle to shame. Her hair was thick and dark with just a hint of curl in the tendrils that fell against her sleek white neck, her smooth black brows arching over cat-green eyes. Her skin was as fair as her hair was dark, her lips a bright blush of berry red against magnolia white. She rose to greet Mattie and John Henry in a sweet scented rustle of taffeta and silk, and smiled just enough to show off her dimpled cheeks.

"Mattie, darlin'," she said in a honeyed drawl, "you look just lovely! Why, I simply adore that sweet little dress you're wearin'!"

It was generous of Annie to make such a fuss. Standing by her cousin, Mattie seemed suddenly plain by comparison, with her red-brown hair and innocent brown eyes and that dusting of freckles that made her look like a schoolgirl. Mattie's neat little figure had no voluptuous curves hiding behind bustle and bodice, her ladylike smile didn't tease and pout and dimple seductively. She was no Southern Belle and never had been, and John Henry thought with a little guilty envy that Captain Stephens was one damned lucky Rebel, having a woman like Annie to call his own.

But Mattie showed no jealousy, happily throwing her arms around her cousin. "Oh Annie!" she said, "I'm so glad to have you livin' close by! It's been so lonely up here in Atlanta without my sisters."

Annie kissed Mattie lightly on the cheek, then stared across her shoulder at John Henry, her eyes sweeping over him approvingly.

"And who is this fine lookin' gentleman? Shame on you, Mattie Holliday for not tellin' me you had a beau!" She reached her hands out to John Henry and looked up into his face with a practiced tilt of her head, showing off those green eyes to perfection. It was easy to see why that Yankee general had given her four guards instead of one. Annie had enough feminine charm to put a whole army into a lather.

Mattie blushed and stammered, "Why, he's just my cousin, John Henry Holliday. He's not my beau."

"John Henry," Annie repeated, still holding his hands. "Where have I heard that name before?"

"He stayed with us one summer in Jonesboro," Mattie explained, "after you moved away-off to Atlanta. Maybe the family mentioned him to you?"

"No," Annie said, and pursed her lips prettily. Then she smiled, and John Henry felt she knew more about him than she was admitting. "Why yes, I do recall somethin'.

You're the boy from Valdosta who was so good with a gun. I believe my sister Sarah mentioned your name."

"John Henry's just graduated from dental school. He came up to Atlanta to work for the summer in Dr. Arthur Ford's office, and now Dr. Ford has invited him to stay on until he's ready to open his own practice. It's quite an honor."

"Well, how delightful," Annie said, finally letting go of his hands, but still looking up flirtatiously into his eyes. "We shall have to make sure he feels welcomed. There aren't nearly enough handsome men in Atlanta, now the War is over." It was a brash kind of compliment for a married lady to make, but coming from Annie's pretty lips it sounded sweet as anything.

John Henry smiled and said something polite in return, but his mind felt a little fuzzy, looking back into those intoxicating eyes.

Annie had always had that effect on men. Half the boys in Clayton County had sworn to kill Captain John Stephens for taking her off the way he did. But it was probably just as well that Annie had run away and gotten married to someone from outside the county. If she'd stayed in Jonesboro, those hometown boys might have taken out their frustration by killing each other instead. As it was, she had an adoring husband who was smart enough to know that Annie meant nothing by her flirtatious behavior. She couldn't help being beautiful or liking men the way she did.

"Now do sit down, Mattie honey," she said, finally turning her attention back to her cousin. "You must tell me all the news from home. It's been ever so long since I had a nice visit in Jonesboro."

"I haven't been there in awhile myself," Mattie answered, obediently sitting next to Annie on the slick brocade sofa.

John Henry sat across from them in a heavy carved wood chair that was even less comfortable than it appeared. The furnishings in Annie's expensively decorated home were obviously made to be seen and not sat upon. But like Annie herself, they were lovely to look at.

"Your father is doin' well," Mattie went on. "He's done a wonderful job of makin' the plantation profitable again. Most of the planters in the county couldn't do a thing without slaves to work the land, but Uncle Phillip is just amazin' at gettin' folks to work for him."

"That's what Father calls 'Irish Diplomacy'," Annie said with a smile. "He says it's a special talent, bein' able to tell people to go to hell and have them look forward to the trip."

John Henry had never heard a proper lady use profanity before, but Annie was only quoting her blustering father, after all, and the Irish were experts at swearing.

"Most of our hands stayed on at Rural Home," Annie went on, "even after the Emancipation. Mother makes such a fuss, you know, treatin' them like they were part of the family. I remember how she used to make us girls go out to the little house and teach our darkies how to read and write so they could learn their Bible and be baptized into the Faith. I do believe that most of the Catholic population in Clayton County is made up of my father's slaves. He even brought some of them up here to Atlanta to be confirmed at Mass. You should have seen how proud he stood there, watchin' them write their own names in the parish register."

"That's not the picture of planter life they have up in Philadelphia," John Henry said, giving up his struggle to get comfortable on that monstrously charming chair. "They think we're all a bunch of demons down here, beatin' our people and enjoyin' it."

"Well, I feel sorry for our colored folk!" Mattie said with sudden passion. "Poor things never had to take care of themselves before! I think it's just a sin the way they've been set free. It's like turnin' little children loose with no one to watch over them."

"Well, they're the Yankee's problem now, aren't they?" John Henry drawled. "Let that damned Federal government of theirs figure out how to take care of them."

"And are your people planters too, John Henry?" Annie asked.

"My father is, but he's raisin' grapes and trees now, instead of cotton."

"Trees?" Annie asked with a raise of those finely arched brows. "And how does one raise a tree?"

"Just like raisin' cotton, Mrs. Stephens. Plant 'em in rows and watch 'em grow. Looks like a forest, except that the trees are all lined up nice and neat."

"How very fascinating," Annie answered with growing interest. "And what made you leave the tree plantation and come to Atlanta? Surely there were plenty of folks in Valdosta who could use the services of a trained dentist like yourself."

"Valdosta's not all that much of a town, Mrs. Stephens. Not compared to Atlanta, anyhow. I reckon I've already spent enough of my life in the woods. And there were some...opportunities here I wanted to pursue." Though he didn't look at Mattie as he spoke, he could feel her eyes on him.

"Well, Valdosta's loss is our gain, I'm sure," Annie said politely. "Mattie, darlin', wouldn't it be fun to have Sarah come up for a little visit, now that you and I are livin' so close? Maybe your cousin John Henry would be sweet enough to escort her around town."

John Henry hadn't even seen it coming, he'd been so busy staring at Annie's maddening good looks. But it wasn't too surprising. Of course Annie would try to arrange a match between her unmarried sister and a single gentleman of some means, especially when that gentleman had already made romantic overtures in the past. His mind was racing, searching for some good reason why he would not be available to escort Miss Sarah Fitzgerald on her visit to Atlanta, when Mattie spoke up:

"Oh Annie, you know what a homebody Sarah is, she never likes to go anyplace! Used to be, she wouldn't even go into Jonesboro for Court Day, on account of all the crowds. I don't think she'd have a bit of fun in Atlanta!"

John Henry looked at her with astonishment. Mattie was sitting there just as sweet and demure as ever, her little face showing nothing but concern for her cousin Sarah's welfare, but there had been an unmistakable trace of something like jealousy in her voice.

"Why, Mattie," Annie said with a lift of her brows, "if I didn't know better I'd think you didn't want Sarah to come visit. Don't tell me you're tryin' to keep your handsome cousin all to yourself!"

John Henry looked from Mattie to Annie and back again, waiting for Mattie's answer, but before she could open her mouth to speak an ominous roll of distant thunder interrupted the conversation. Annie started and looked up sharply, forgetting all about Sarah's visit.

"Sounds like a storm comin' on," she said with a shudder. "Thunder always reminds me of artillery fire. I was here, you know, in Atlanta, durin' the siege."

She didn't have to explain. They all knew about that summer of 1864 when Sherman had held Atlanta captive, raining his artillery fire down on the city. At first the citizens had tried to go on with normal life, ignoring the screaming of the minié balls that sailed in from the Yankee strongholds just past Peachtree Creek. But then the solid shot was replaced with canister and the whole sky was filled with flying death, the charges exploding in the air and sending shrapnel everywhere, and the people of Atlanta were forced to take cover underground in bombproofs dug into the hilly ravines that ran through the city. But there was no place to hide from the awful sound of those big guns going off all day and night, rocking the earthen shelters and rumbling over the ground.

The thunder rolled again, rattling the windows of Annie's house, and she bit her lip and said nervously:

"Well now, y'all will just have to stay to supper! I can't send you out in a storm, can I?" She made the invitation with a strained smile, but the coyness had fallen away from her and it was clear that she was truly frightened by the coming storm.

"We can't stay," John Henry said firmly. "It'll be gettin' dark soon, and the family will wonder where we are."

A flash of lightning tore across the windows, lighting Annie's pale face, and the rain followed after it, coming down hard. It was going to be a devil of a storm, all right, and it didn't look like it was going to let up any time soon.

Mattie slipped her arm around her cousin's shoulder and looked up beseechingly at John Henry.

"Do we have to go just yet? Can't we wait just until Captain Stephens comes home?"

He was just about to insist on their going when Annie looked up again, and John Henry was surprised to see those taunting green eyes filled with tears.

"I know it's childish," Annie said, "but I am just terrified of storms. Won't you please stay?"

There was no denying her wish with that sweet feminine way she looked at him, like he was all that stood between her and the memory of the War itself. And by her side, Mattie sat stoically sheltering her from the storm. He couldn't fight them both, and he suddenly realized something of what that Yankee general must have felt, bowled over by the gentle force of Southern womanhood.

~~~~~~~~

It was past supper by the time the storm had calmed to a late summer shower, and without the little note Annie had written to Uncle John, explaining why they were so late getting home, there would have been all hell to pay. What would people think, seeing Mattie and John Henry out together after dusk, walking in the rain? Captain Stephens still hadn't returned from the city, so there was no buggy available to drive them home, and all Annie could do was apologize prettily for the inconvenience and give them her own dainty ruffled parasol for protection. But it wasn't much help against the drizzle that still fell, catching on the wind and coming up under the umbrella in wet gusts.

All that rain had turned the dirt road of Forrest Avenue into a mire of red mud, and Mattie's long skirts dragged heavily as she tried to stay out of the deepest of the puddles. John Henry wasn't much help as her escort, busy holding that little umbrella over their heads as if it were really doing any good at keeping them dry. They were both a pitiful sight by the time they arrived at their uncle's drive, and Mattie stopped to push her dripping hair out of her face and straighten her skirt.

"Don't bother, Mattie," John Henry said. "You don't look any worse than I do."

She glanced up at him and grimaced. "That's not much comfort. You look just awful."

He was as wet as she was, his sandy hair clinging against his neck, his fine pastel summer shirt spoiled and his starched collar unbuttoned and hanging loose, his trousers splattered with mud and his soft leather boots standing an inch deep in the muck.

"There's no need to insult me, Mattie. If I hadn't been gallant enough to agree to stay and keep your silly cousin company, neither one of us would be such a mess."

"She's not silly, John Henry. She's really very brave, except for storms, and that's only because of the siege and all. I'm sure I wouldn't have had half her courage, facin' up to the Yankees."

"Well, I'll give her that. She did show some gumption down in Macon, though I doubt it was just her famous courage that won her that honor guard."

"What do you mean by that?"

"I mean that a woman who looks like that could get just about anything out of a man, even a Yankee."

Mattie pushed at her wet hair again and looked up at him sharply. "Did you really think she was all that beautiful?"

There was something in her voice that warned him to answer carefully. If he lied and said that he hadn't really paid much attention to Annie's looks, Mattie might be insulted that he didn't appreciate her cousin's charms. If he told the truth and said that he had never seen a more beautiful creature in all his life, she was sure to be jealous. So he decided to err on the side of jealousy.

"Annie is pretty, in her way," he said evenly. "I guess some men might find her type attractive."

"And do you find her attractive?"

She was staring at him steadily, waiting for him to give whatever answer it was that would satisfy her. And while she waited another gust of wind came up under the umbrella, blowing warm rain all over both of them.

John Henry took a quick breath and said smoothly: "I found her very attractive. And if I weren't already in love with her cousin, I might just be foolish enough to fall in love with a married woman. But I am no fool, and I am in love with you, Mattie Holliday."

He waited for her to fuss or look away or stomp her little foot in the mud for being so direct about his feelings again. But she just stood there looking up at him in the rain, and all at once he knew what she was waiting for, and he leaned down and kissed her.

It was the first time in three years that they'd kissed, since the night of Cousin George's wedding. But this time, she had actually encouraged it, and knowing she was suddenly so willing made him hungry for more. He closed his eyes and was about to kiss her again and with more feeling, when she spoke softly:

"You are a terrible liar, John Henry Holliday! I saw how you looked at Annie. You were as infatuated as any poor country boy!"

He opened his eyes wide and stood back, bewildered. "Then why did you let me kiss you?"

"I was just wonderin'..." she said, half smiling.

"Wonderin' what?"

She bent down to gather up her muddy skirts, and smiled again. "Just wonderin', that's all..."

Then she turned away and trudged up into the house, leaving John Henry standing holding that useless umbrella, and wondering some himself.

~~~~~~~~~

Annie really had been frightened by the storm and was sorry for the inconvenience of delaying their return home — or so she said in her prettily written thank you note. And to prove her thanks, she had included a little gift of two tickets to the upcoming production of Shakespeare's *Hamlet* at DeGive's Opera House for Mattie and her cousin. Of course, they would make a foursome for the evening as it would be inappropriate for a single young woman to go out at night with a single young man, even if the couple in question were first cousins and dear friends as well. But the Stephens would be pleased to act as chaperones and would come calling for them in their new carriage. It was only a shame that her sister Sarah was still in Jonesboro, Annie wrote. Sarah just loved all that Shakespearean melodrama.

But it wasn't Sarah Fitzgerald that John Henry was thinking of as he stopped by the Southern Shirt Manufactory on Alabama Street to buy a new collar and cuffs for his best dress shirt. He was hoping to impress Mattie, and all dressed up in dark trousers and Robert's borrowed frock coat, with that crisp new collar tied around with his blue silk scarf, he thought himself quite the dandy.

Mattie's costume, however, overshadowed any fine outfit that John Henry could put together. Annie had dressed her for the evening in a bustle-backed gown of black silk trimmed with jet passementerie, tiny glass beads that sparkled around the low neckline of the tightly fitted bodice. Below the short puffed sleeves of the dress, her arms were covered to the elbow with long gloves of white suede trimmed with rows of tiny buttons. Her thick auburn hair was curled all over in finger-puffs, with small bunches of artificial flowers strewn in the glossy tendrils.

She came down the curving stairs of their Uncle John's house looking like every fantasy that John Henry had ever had about her, and his hands almost trembled against her skin as he draped a black lace shawl around her, the musty scent of perfume permeating the air between them. Annie Stephens had an eye for fashion, and she had turned pretty Mattie Holliday into a beautiful woman. Not that Annie was to be outdone, of course. She and Captain Stephens arrived in full dress themselves – he trim and handsome in a dark tail coat and trousers, she stunning in a deep ruby-red dress that set off her black Irish looks to perfection. Annie certainly wouldn't have to worry about losing her place as the center of attention at the Opera House.

But it was Mattie who held John Henry's eyes. There was a glow about her that went past the expensive silk and the elegant hairstyle, and in the dusky light of their private box hanging just above the stage, she let John Henry take her hand in his and whisper words against her perfumed neck. So it took all the control he could muster to keep his attention on the play, even though it was one of his favorites, committed to memory in those drafty schoolhouse days back in Valdosta. There was something poignant about young Prince Hamlet's struggle to make reason out of his father's death and his mother's hasty marriage to the king's brother. The story had haunted John Henry as he was growing up, and watching the stage now, forcing himself to listen to the measured lines of Shakespeare's verse, he found himself suddenly caught up in the story again:

> *O God! A beast that wants discourse of reason*
> *Would have mourned longer —*

O most wicked speed! To post
With such dexterity to incestuous sheets!
It is not, nor can it come to good.
But break, my heart, for I must hold my tongue.

And as Hamlet agonized over his mother's disloyalty, John Henry remembered his own painful adolescence. His father had been a widower barely three months before welcoming a new wife into his bed while his son was still grieving in the room next door. And John Henry had watched it all in silence, acting the part of a good son while his heart was breaking. When the curtain came down on the fifth act, the stage gory with blood-red paint and dead royalty, he was still leaning over the edge of the theater box, his hands clenching the rail, and Mattie laid one of her little gloved hands over his.

"Are you all right, honey?" she whispered.

"I'm fine, Mattie. It's just...I've never seen *Hamlet* acted out before, only learned it in school."

"It's quite different as a play, isn't it?"

He nodded, "It's very sad."

"Why sad?" Captain Stephens asked as he stood and straightened his tail coat. "They all got what they deserved in the end, didn't they?"

"But Hamlet shouldn't have been killed," John Henry said, "he didn't do anything wrong."

"Just plotted murder and committed it!"

"But it was revenge!" John Henry objected. "Don't you believe, Sir, that revenge is more honorable than murder?"

"I believe that you are both takin' a little play far too seriously," Annie chided. "The theater is supposed to be entertainment. And did you ever see such a glittering crowd? I am sure I saw the Governor himself sittin' in the box across the way."

Captain Stephens laughed at her indulgently, "So that's who you were flirtin' with, my dear. I wondered why your attention kept strayin' from the stage!"

"Don't be silly, darlin'," Annie drawled, slipping her arm through his, "you know you have my everlastin' devotion!" Then she smiled over her shoulder at Mattie, "The Captain still thinks I'm just an empty-headed country girl, out to collect an armful of beaux!"

But as she spoke, she threw one last look across the theater and received an appreciative nod from a gentleman in the Governor's box. Then, guilelessly, she pulled a lace handkerchief from her bag and fanned herself with it for a moment before slipping it down into the low-cut bodice of her ruby-red dress.

The Governor, of course, was watching.

~~~~~~~~~

There was a chill in the air that autumn evening, a quick wind gusting through the gaslit streets of Atlanta. Outside DeGive's Opera House, Mattie and Annie stood chatting together, waiting for Captain Stephens to bring the buggy around while John Henry stood close by, keeping a clear space at the curb and ready to lift the ladies into the buggy as soon as the Captain pulled up. He was looking forward to the long ride home, sitting in the back of the buggy with Mattie huddled close at his side for warmth, his arm around her to protect her from the wind. And if he were lucky, he might even find a chance to kiss her again in the dark shadows of the trees that overhung the road along the way.

Although the hour was late, Atlanta was crowded with theater goers and revelers enjoying the season, and across the street from the Opera House a noisy group of Yankee soldiers was gathered, passing around a bottle and laughing too loud. They had some fancy-dressed girls with them, sharing the bottle, and every few minutes one of the girls would squeal as though she'd just been pinched, and the soldiers would laugh a little louder. There was a pleasant sort of ribaldry to it and John Henry watched them for a moment, enjoying the show. Then one of the girls stepped toward the edge of the curb and looked across the street. She was a pretty little thing, not more than eighteen-years old or so, with a mane of black hair blowing around her, and as she gazed at the crowd in front of the Opera House, John Henry felt a sudden hot flush of memory sweep across his skin. It was the girl from that bawdy house down on Decatur Street, and she was staring right at him.

His first impulse was to turn and run, disappearing into the theater crowd, but his legs were frozen under him like a sleeper's in a bad dream. Then the girl raised one soft white arm and called out across the street: "Hey, Johnny! Where' you been?"

It was just a voice in the crowd, but to John Henry it sounded like all the wailings of hell. And when he didn't answer her, she called out again: "Johnny! Don't you remember me?"

And worse, the girl had pulled away from the noisy group and was walking right toward him. Then one of those Yankee soldiers reached out and grabbed her, giving her a quick slap on the backside, and she turned to her friends and laughed – and for the first time in his life, John Henry was grateful that the Yankees had come to Georgia.

He breathed a sigh of relief and turned back toward the ladies still waiting by the theater door, where Mattie's attentions were blessedly occupied in greeting some acquaintance or other. How close he'd come to having his sins uncovered and his romance ended before it had even begun! But then he noticed Annie's cat-green eyes watching him, her knowing look saying that she'd lived in Macon and Atlanta both during the War, and she understood all about those Yankee soldiers and the kind of lewd company that they kept. And she knew that it was no coincidence the girl had been calling his name.

Chapter Fourteen

Atlanta, 1872

He was fearful at first that Annie might share her suspicions with her cousin, but Mattie never seemed to waver in her affections or doubt John Henry's affections for her. If anything, she seemed to favor him more than ever, smiling at him across the supper table, laughing at his stories, spending whole evenings willingly listening to him talk about his work at Dr. Ford's dental office. And when she needed a ride to Mass on Sundays, it was John Henry she wanted to take her there, driving Uncle John's runabout into town to the Church of the Immaculate Conception.

So when a letter arrived for John Henry inviting him away from Atlanta to pay a visit to his father's Mexican serving boy, Francisco Hidalgo, he was loathe to go. Surely, the birth of the Hidalgo's new baby required nothing of him but a congratulatory letter in return, or perhaps a wire. It had been years since he'd seen Francisco, after all, making them barely even acquaintances anymore, though they'd lived in the same household years back. But Francisco's letter was adamant: *Please come to Jenkinsburg as soon as you can. I need to speak to you personally.*

Having Mattie say she'd miss him every day while he was gone almost made the trip worthwhile.

~~~~~~~~~~

He took the train south to Griffin on a bright November morning and hired a horse to carry him the ten miles out to Jenkinsburg. The autumn had been unusually cool, the trees turning early from green to yellow and brown, and the ground was covered with a blanket of golden leaves that scattered across the road with every stride of the horse. Overhead, the sky was a brilliant, cloudless, perfect blue.

Jenkinsburg wasn't much more than a general store and a Baptist Church with a few farms scattered into the surrounding countryside. Francisco's fields should have been laid fallow by now like his neighbors' fields were, the neat rows of carrots and beans all harvested, the red dirt planted in a cover crop of winter grass. But as John Henry reined the horse to a stop in front of the place, he saw that there were still too many plants in the ground, the cornstalks dried and bending over, the greens going to flower. He'd heard that Francisco had been ill, and the place showed his lack of care.

"Rueben and Dickens have been tryin' to keep things up," Martha Hidalgo explained as she met John Henry at the door and ushered him into the cabin that faced the farmland. "We even kept John and Finney out of school this fall to help, but it's awful hard to get all the work done. We'll have to hire a man next year, I fear, and where we'll get the money, I don't know."

"Francisco wrote that he needed me to come right away?" John Henry questioned. Considering Martha's comments, he was afraid that what Francisco wanted was an extra hand on the farm. He'd left Valdosta to get away from one farm; he wasn't about to start plowing and planting on another one.

Martha nodded. "We appreciate you comin' so fast. Francisco's got it in his head to take care of family business all of the sudden. Guess he's had too much time to think, bein' in bed so much this fall. You know how he is, though, always has to be doin' somethin'."

"Is he still feelin' poorly?"

"You don't know?" Martha said. "It's the consumption. He's likely had it for years, so the doctor says." Then she stooped to a cradle on the brick hearth of the kitchen fire, gently pulling back the blanket to show a sleeping infant. "This is our newest, Exa Elon. Francisco named her after his sister he hasn't seen since he was orphaned in the Mexican War. But I call her Nita. She'll be one month tomorrow."

John Henry bent to look at the child, and without thinking, reached a hand down to touch its honey-colored face. Then the baby opened its eyes and looked up at him, and for a moment he had the eerie feeling that the innocent child was somehow wiser than he was.

Martha took the child from the cradle. "She'll be wantin' to nurse, now she's awake. Why don't you go on over to the Springs and see Francisco?"

"The Springs?"

"The Indian sulfur springs, out past Jackson. He's been seein' Doc Whitehead over there. Rueben drives him over a couple of times a week, so he can do the baths and the water. The Indians used to say the spring water could cure anything. 'Course,

256

they believed it was healin' spirits that did it, not the sulfur." Then she looked down lovingly into her baby's face. "The Indians wouldn't let children nearby though, for fear of the cryin' scarin' the healin' spirits away. Savage superstition. There's nothin' more healin' than havin' a new baby around." Then she looked back up at John Henry, and this time there were tears in her eyes. "Go on over to the Springs and see Francisco. He has somethin' he needs to talk to you about."

~~~~~~~~~~

It was five miles from Jenkinsburg to the county seat of Jackson and another five miles from there to Indian Springs, and although the weather was still lovely for riding, John Henry's thoughts were no longer on the pleasant Autumn day. Francisco was dying the slow death of consumption and leaving behind eight children and a wife who was already mourning for him. If they were having trouble making ends meet now, things were only going to get harder after he passed on.

Beyond Jackson, the road narrowed and led down into the wooded Ocmulgee River bottoms where the streams the Indians called the Abbothlacoosta and Hopoethlelohola converged from two directions to form Big Sandy Creek, and where cold sulfur springs rose up right out of the ground. By the time the half-breed Chief William McIntosh built a hotel there, the Indian Springs were already famous. "The Saratoga of the South," folks called the place, and visitors came from hundreds of miles around to try the healing Indian waters. But the Indians were gone now, driven out on their Trail of Tears to the Oklahoma Territory, and only McIntosh's Indian Springs resort remained in what was now a white man's town.

John Henry found Doc Whitehead's shingle hanging just past the Wigwam Hotel, and he tied his horse to a rack outside the doctor's office and pulled on the bell chain. A moment later, the door was opened by a gentleman in dark trousers and shirtsleeves, a stethoscope hung around his neck.

"Dr. Whitehead?" John Henry asked.

"Yes," the man replied. "Emergency or appointment?"

"Neither. I'm just lookin' for someone, and hoped you might be able to help me. I believe he's a patient of yours – Francisco Hidalgo?"

"Hidalgo?" the doctor queried. "You mean E'dalgo? From over near Jenkinsburg?"

So Francisco had changed his name for something a little more sophisticated – and a little less Mexican, John Henry mused.

257

"I reckon that's him. His wife said he was here at the Springs, takin' the treatment. Do you know where I might find him?"

"Same place he always goes," the doctor replied. "He'll be down at the bath house, soakin' in the sulfur water."

"I hear it can cure the consumption," John Henry said.

"I've seen some cures come out of the Springs. Even seen some when the patient was farther gone than Mr. E'dalgo."

"And what about Francisco?" John Henry asked. "Is the water doin' him any good?"

Of course it was improper for him to even ask such a question, considering the confidence between doctor and patient. But the grief in Martha Hidalgo's face that morning made him ask anyway.

"Are you family?" the doctor inquired.

"I reckon you might call us kin."

"Then you should know that I don't hold too much hope. Mr. E'dalgo is far along, I'm afraid. Has been for some time. There must have been symptoms for years, of course, but they can be deceiving: the lack of appetite, the loss of weight, the tiredness, the night sweats, the chronic cough. But many illnesses cause the same conditions. It's only when the lung tissue begins to come up that we know for sure, and then it's really too far gone. As I said, Mr. E'dalgo is very ill. He's a good man, a good father. Hard to see his family left alone like that. I'm glad to hear he's got kin. They'll be needin' you."

John Henry wanted to answer that he was only kin by association and not really responsible for Francisco's dependent family, but the sympathy in the doctor's face struck a guilty chord within him. If he wasn't family to Francisco, who was?

He left the doctor's office feeling as heavy-hearted as if it were his own life that was ending too soon, instead of that of a Mexican orphan boy who was lucky he'd had any kind of life at all.

~~~~~~~~~

The bathhouse stood on the high ground above the rocky shoals of the Big Sandy, close by the Indian Springs. The place was easy to find; you just followed the steam and the stench. If the sulfur water smelled of rotten eggs when it was cold, it smelled even worse when it was pumped from the springs to the bathhouse and heated over the big wood fires. It was no wonder the Indians had thought the Springs to be possessed by spirits – with the steam rising up from the roof of the bath house and the awful smell of the heated sulfur water, there was something almost supernatural about the place.

Francisco was in the bathhouse, as the doctor had said he would be, reclining on a wicker settee and wrapped from head to toe in Turkish towels.

"It's the treatment," he whispered hoarsely. "Pull up a chair."

John Henry took a seat on a wicker stool and pulled off his hat, stunned speechless at the change that had come over Francisco. He was only a shadow of his sturdy brown-skinned former self, a thin cadaver of a man with dark eyes sunk deep into an ashen face. Swathed as he was in toweling, he looked like he was already wrapped for the grave.

"They have me soak in the tubs until I can't stand the heat," Francisco said, pausing to catch his breath, "then they wrap me up like this and let me sweat awhile. Supposed to bring out the poisons. Feels like they're draining the life right out of me."

John Henry took a moment before replying, unsure of what to say. "I saw your new baby," he remarked at last.

Francisco managed a weak smile. "Seems strange to have life coming and going all at once, doesn't it? But life is *milagro*," he said, lapsing into the Spanish he'd spoken as a boy.

"A miracle?" John Henry said, translating without thinking. He'd learned a little Spanish from Francisco when he was growing up, and some of it still came back to him.

"Who knows? Maybe I will live long enough to see this new one grow old," Francisco said, coughing weakly as he shifted on his settee, trying to sit up. "It's about the baby that I needed to talk to you – the baby and the other children, as well." His words came slowly, as he paused to take careful breaths. "Cisco Junior is seventeen now, near a man. But the others – Rueben, Dicken, John, Finney. They need guidance still. They need a strong hand. Maggie is just a toddler. And the baby..."

"Martha seems like a good mother," John Henry said, hoping the reminder would somehow soothe Francisco's worries. But his words seemed to have the opposite effect, making Francisco speak too quickly again.

"Martha has too much on her. I should be home seeing to the farm instead of here." He coughed again, then fell back against the settee, moaning.

"Shall I get the attendant?" John Henry asked, but Francisco shook his head and went on.

"No, it's you I need right now," he said.

"But what can I do? I'm no medical doctor."

"Not for me," Francisco said painfully, "for them. For the children. For Martha. I need you to act as guardian for me, as your father would if he were closer. But Valdosta's too far away, should they need something. You are just up in Atlanta..."

"But I'm too young to be a guardian!" John Henry protested. "I've just turned twenty-one myself!"

"And your father wasn't much older when he took me out of Mexico. But he raised me anyway, as best a bachelor could do. Of all the things he did in that War, that was the bravest."

"Brave?" John Henry asked. "What was so brave about that?"

He stopped himself before saying anymore, though the words were waiting to be said: what was so brave about Henry Holliday bringing an orphan boy back from the War? He was used to having slaves take care of him, after all. Now he had a Mexican orphan boy as a valet. There wasn't all that much difference. And yearn as Francisco might to be a member of the Holliday family, he'd never been more than household help. But John Henry couldn't say all that, not now when Francisco was so sick.

"There wasn't anything brave about takin' you in, Francisco," he said carefully. "You worked plenty hard for your keep. My father was lucky he found you. But I still wouldn't be all that good as a guardian. Atlanta's a half-day's train ride away, and I have my work at Dr. Ford's office..."

But his easy words froze when Francisco reached out one thin, cold hand to his, like a touch from the grave.

"*Hermano*..." he said, the Spanish word coming out in a broken whisper.

"What?"

"*Hermano*," Francisco said again. "I know I'm not blood relation to you, but you're the closest thing I have to a brother, John Henry. And as my brother, I beg of you, please don't let my children be orphaned as I once was..."

There was such pleading in his whispered words that John Henry could not deny them.

"So what do you want me to do?" he said heavily.

"Watch over my family for me when I die, as your father would have if he were here. Take care of them as he once took care of me..."

"But Martha must have kin. Surely there's some real family close by?"

260

It was a reasonable enough question, but somehow it brought a new look of pain to Francisco's face, and John Henry regretted the words.

"She has family," Francisco replied heavily, "but you are all I have close. You are all I have to stand in stead for their father..."

"All right," John Henry said with quiet resignation. "All right."

Francisco lay back on the settee, a faint smile on his pale lips. "*De tal palo, tal astilla*," he said, lapsing into Spanish. "Like father, like son..."

Francisco's gratitude did nothing to lighten the weight on John Henry's heart, for the last thing he wanted to be was anything like his father.

~~~~~~~~~

He was enough like his father, however, to take care of business matters. So before his return to Atlanta, he stopped by the Spalding County Courthouse in Griffin to record the deed to his newly inherited property, still fearful that somehow Hyram Neil had beat him to it.

The Courthouse stood across Broad Street from the railroad tracks, a solid building of red brick and white arched windows with iron-barred jail cells. John Henry remembered it well from his childhood days, when the Courthouse had seemed to him like a great red palace where all the important men of Griffin gathered: the cotton planters and cotton merchants, the slave brokers and mill owners, the bankers and railroad stockholders. And standing tall in the midst of them, his father was one of the most important men of all. Henry Holliday had been Clerk of the Spalding County Court back then, which gave him inside knowledge of all that was going on. He knew who was buying and selling property and for what profit, who was losing property to foreclosure, who might be willing to sell at a loss to avoid the embarrassment of a sheriff's sale. The great men curried his favor in hopes of gaining profitable information, and Henry used the favor to make connections that might one day win him real political office.

Of course, all that was before the War, and now Henry Holliday's political aspirations were confined to the smaller world of Valdosta. But his legacy, it seemed, had remained in Griffin.

"Holliday?" the court clerk said, as John Henry handed him a copy of the deed paperwork, his father's birthday gift to him that had come folded inside a letter reminding him of his duties as a guest in his Uncle John's home.

"That's right. John Henry Holliday."

"Any relation to Henry Holliday?" the court clerk asked, peering at him through wire-rimmed glasses.

"He's my father."

The man looked him up and down and shook his head. "I don't recall Henry Holliday having a boy as big as you."

"I've grown now, Sir," he replied. "I've come of age."

"I reckon. I served with Henry Holliday in the War with Mexico, you know – Fannin's Avengers. Fought under Winfield Scott after he took over from Zach Taylor. Too bad Scott went Yankee. He was a helluva commander."

John Henry had heard it all before, a hundred times at least.

"Will this copyin' take long?" he asked, as the clerk went about his slow labor of transcribing each long legal sentence into the heavy deed book.

"Only if you want it done right," the man replied without looking up. "You don't want to have me make a mistake and find yourself in a legal battle someday. That's what started that War with Mexico, you know, a dispute over who owned what. I try to keep us peaceful here in Spalding County by recordin' everything proper. Your father ever tell you about Veracruz? That was some fight, the last one for the Avengers before we got mustered out. We were twelve-month recruits, started up right after the War got going. But we only went as far as Jalapa with Scott before they sent us back to Veracruz to take ship to New Orleans. That's where Henry found the boy, as I recall."

"The boy?" John Henry asked. "What boy did he find in New Orleans?"

"Not there. Back in Veracruz, while we were waitin' on the ship. His folks had been killed in the siege the spring before. He must have been livin' alone there all that time, 'til Henry found him. Warn't more than a child, livin' in the rubble of our bombardment from the spring. We had artillery on that city for near three weeks, land and navy both. There wasn't much left to live in, but he'd lived somehow. Henry found him hidin' in the horse barn behind a church, sleepin' in the hayloft. Like the baby Jesus, some of the men said. But other'n said, 'Shoot the dirty little Mexican.' But Henry said No. He was Second Lieutenant, so his word meant somethin'. He kept the boy with him, in case the men got it in their heads to do some shootin', anyhow. Don't think he really meant to take the boy home, just keep him from gettin' killed. It was the boy's idea to go along."

John Henry's disinterest in hearing the man's ramblings had changed to fascination. His father had never told the whole story of how he came to be guardian for a Mexican orphan boy, and Francisco had always spoken as if his life had begun on American soil. He'd even adopted the birthdate of July 4th in honor of his new country.

"What do you mean, it was the boy's idea?" John Henry asked, urging the man on.

"Well, you couldn't blame him for wantin' to go," the man said. "Henry was good to him, shared his rations, found him somethin' decent to wear. The boy was so grateful, he'd do anything for Henry, fetch his drinks, carry his bags..."

"Be his valet," John Henry said, and the man nodded.

"I reckon you could say that. Henry never asked him, but the boy did it anyhow. I figure he was tryin' to make himself so useful that Henry couldn't do without him. Anyhow, time came for us to board ship for New Orleans, and Henry figured to say goodbye to the boy there at the dock, but he couldn't find him anywhere. 'Too bad,' was all he said about missin' that goodbye, 'he was a good boy.' I was surprised he didn't show more feelin' about it, close as the two of them had got to be, but I guess that wasn't the Lieutenant's way. Cool, folks called him, and I reckon he was. Still, that boy had been mighty attached to him..."

"So what happened?" John Henry asked, caught up by the story, though of course he knew how the thing ended. Francisco came to Georgia and Henry kept him on as his serving boy.

"The boy stowed away," the clerk replied. "That's why we didn't see him at the dock. He knew Henry wouldn't take him home, so he hid himself away with the horses and the munitions, and didn't come out 'til we docked at New Orleans. Closest thing I ever saw to a smile on Henry Holliday's face, I saw that day. We were off the ship and headin' to the muster office when along comes the little Mexican. 'Carry your bags, Señor?' he says to Henry, about all the English he knew. And Henry just nodded to him. Not a word, only a nod, but almost a smile at the same time. I wasn't surprised when he brought the boy home after that. Francisco was his name, as I recall. He lived with Henry a few years, then he went to work and moved on. Had a barbershop here in Griffin for a while. Haven't heard much of him lately. Do you know how's he's doin'?"

"He's dyin'," John Henry said. "He took the consumption."

"Now that's a shame," the clerk replied. "Well, your deed's all copied and legal. You can pay the cashier for the registration."

His business taken care of, John Henry paid the registration fee and left the

263

Courthouse, his mind filled with thoughts of a stowaway boy and the American Lieutenant who had taken him home.

~~~~~~~~~~

The Iron Front was an impressive piece of property, two-stories tall and made entirely of red brick, with fancy iron façade work and long twelve-paned windows facing the street and letting the morning sun stream into the shops inside. On John Henry's western side of the building, the liquor and tobacco store of N.G. Phillips occupied the entire downstairs space, and the proprietor looked up with a smile when a well-dressed young gentleman came into his shop, setting the door bells jangling.

" 'Afternoon, Sir!" Phillips said in greeting. "What can I do for you?" He seemed the jovial sort one often found in establishments that sold liquor, and as he leaned forward on the counter, his paunch strained at the buttons of his plaid waistcoat. "Can I interest you in some of my fine stock today? Old corn whiskey, old Holland gin? Apple brandy, Virginia leaf tobacco?"

John Henry straightened his lapels and said with a purposely superior tone: "I am Dr. John H. Holliday. I am here to meet my tenants."

"Is that a fact? Well, you look mighty young for a landlord."

John Henry tried to ignore the insult and glanced around as if he really were inspecting the place. "This is a sturdy building," he said approvingly, "good high ceilings." Though he didn't really know all that much about architecture, he did like the look of the place. The ceiling was covered with embossed tin panels and edged all around with a heavy molding of the same design. One sidewall was brick, but the other was a curious combination of fluted beams and covered arches – likely the court-ordered partition wall between his half and the McKey's side of the building.

"It's a real nice place," Phillips agreed. "I'd be interested in expanding into the other rooms, if you're lookin' to sell the place."

"I appreciate your interest, Mr. Phillips, but the truth is, I only own half the building. My Uncle Thomas McKey owns the other half."

"I know, I know, already got in touch with him about it, and he's not ready to sell just yet. But I'm willin' to buy one half at a time. I'd be willin' to pay good money for it – cash money."

Though John Henry had no intention of selling his inheritance before he'd even taken possession of it, he was interested in knowing just what it might be worth. "What kind of money are you talkin' about?"

Phillips smiled and cleared his throat, obviously sure he had an impressive offer. "Eighteen-hundred dollars, Dr. Holliday. Top dollar for the place!"

John Henry had to stifle his surprise. Eighteen-hundred dollars! That was more money than he'd ever seen at one time. It was no wonder his mother had considered the Iron Front the true prize of his inheritance.

"Like I said, Dr. Holliday, top dollar. So what do you say? Are you interested?"

"I'd be lyin' if I said I wasn't impressed by your proposition, Mr. Phillips. That's good money all right. And I can't say I'm not tempted. But I'm not in the market to sell."

Phillips sighed. "Well, you let me know if you ever change your mind."

"I will certainly do that." He eyed the shelves lined with bottles, amber and brown and full of choice liquors. "And I believe I will have somethin' to drink, after all. A bottle of Tennessee whiskey, if you have it."

"My pleasure," Phillips said with a smile, "and for my landlord, somethin' special." He reached under the counter and pulled out a small silver flask and flipped open the stopper. "Just right for a young gentleman. Holds enough for a day's ride or an evenin' by a lady's side." Then he opened a bottle of whiskey and filled the flask. "Call it a down payment, in case you change your mind."

~~~~~~~~~

There was one more thing he had to do while he was in Griffin, and he rode up Hill Street to Taylor, whipping the horse to a gallop and heading east out the McDonough Road. There hadn't been a hard rain for weeks and the dust of the road rose up in a cloud and trailed behind him. Then from out of the haze and the dust, he saw something else rising up: an angel hovering in the air, outspread wings reflecting the afternoon light. He reined the horse to a stop and wiped the dust from his eyes, and peered ahead again. There was indeed an angel poised there before him, bent with sorrowful face, and below it, row upon row of grave markers, stark white against the green hills.

The Confederate Cemetery had been established after the Hollidays left Griffin, with acres of burial plots for the soldiers who had died during the battle of Atlanta.

Griffin had been headquarters for the Confederate hospital, with thousands of wounded soldiers coming in every day on the train. Soon the schools and churches were full to overflowing with the sick and the dying, and the army commandeered private homes for hospital space as well. And still the wounded kept coming, more men than the medical officers could treat, more dead than the townspeople could bury. When the fighting ended, the corpses remained, and the country was covered with the bodies of the dead, rotting in the hot Southern sun.

The ladies of Griffin lost no time in forming the Ladies' Memorial Association, setting aside land for a new cemetery. They paid for headstones for the graves, bearing the name, company, and state of the fallen, though too often the inscription was only *Unknown*. And to watch over the fallen heroes, they placed an angel of Italian marble standing on a tall marble shaft. They claimed it was the first monument ever erected to the Confederate dead; it was certainly the first angel John Henry had ever seen face to face. He must have heard and then forgotten what lay out the McDonough Road, and it was an eerie feeling to find himself suddenly surrounded by the silent dead, riding through the remains of all those lost young lives.

He rode up the hill to the top of Rest Haven, trying to remember just where his sister was buried. There was a tree nearby the spot, he was sure – he remembered playing under it while his mother had fashioned her flower wreaths. But the trees had grown and changed in ten years, and the place looked very different than he remembered it. He slid out of the saddle and led the horse, walking along between those graves until something at his feet caught his attention. A patch of granite showed through the grass, a sliver of a headstone peering out from under a tangle of weeds. He bent to brush away the overgrowth and saw his own name carved into the stone: *Holliday.*

He caught his breath and pulled away, then laughed at himself for his foolishness. It wasn't his own name, of course. It was his sister's grave he had stumbled upon, somehow remembering better than he knew how to find the place. He bent back down and pulled the rest of the weeds aside, reading the inscription:

In Memory of Martha Eleanora
Daughter of H.B. and A.J. Holliday
Who Died June 12th 1850
Aged 6 Months 9 days

Alice Jane had made sure that her baby's exact age was recorded – 6 months and 9 days, precious short little life. Ellie would have been twenty-two years old now, if she'd lived, likely married and with children of her own, children who would have called John Henry their uncle. He'd lost a whole part of his own life when his sister had died so young. He took off his hat and bowed his head, thinking a prayer, and felt a sudden rush of emotion.

He'd lost his sister before even knowing her. He'd lost his mother too soon. He'd lost his father as well, when Rachel had come along. But he wouldn't lose Mattie, and he'd do what he had to do, whatever he had to do, to keep her. He'd speak to Uncle Rob and win him over, show him how he'd changed since his reckless youth, how temperate and steady he'd become. He'd find a way to fund his own dental practice, being a man of respect in the community. He'd become a Catholic even, if Mattie wanted him to. He'd do anything he had to – but he wouldn't wait any longer.

~~~~~~~~~~

He pondered a plan all the way back to Atlanta, knowing that the hardest part would be changing Mattie's father's mind about him. For how could he do that if he couldn't talk to him man to man? And how could they have such a talk when Uncle Rob was down in Jonesboro and John Henry was in Atlanta? He couldn't very well just show up on his uncle's doorstep uninvited, the prodigal black sheep returned, asking for Mattie's hand and expecting a warm welcome.

When he arrived in Atlanta, he found the house on Forrest Avenue empty except for the servants who greeted him then scattered to their work. His Uncle John and Aunt Permelia, they said, had taken the family off to a social at Wesley Chapel Church. His cousin Mattie was visiting with her Fitzgerald kin over on Jackson Hill, but was expected home again soon. So with nothing else to do but wait, he wandered into the parlor to pass the time, sitting down at the grand piano and running his hands over the ivory keys.

The piano had been a housewarming present to Aunt Permelia, but she'd insisted she was too old to learn to play and her boys had never taken to it. So the piano stood there decoratively, deep rosewood shining with careful polishing and covered with lace doilies and fussy little knickknacks, adding a cultured air to the room and regularly tuned, but never played.

John Henry hadn't played a piano in years himself, not since his mother had died and his father had sold the parlor spinet to make room for Rachel's new furniture, but his hands still had a feel for it. There was a small stack of sheet music on top of the piano, laid under the paws of one those Chinese dogs his aunt collected, and he leafed through the folios reading familiar names – Schubert, Chopin, Liszt. He opened the Liszt and began to play, one finger finding the melody, then haltingly adding the chords, then right hand and left hand slowly remembering together. He knew he wouldn't be able to accomplish the arpeggios, out of practice as he was, but he thought he could manage most of it. And intent on the music, he didn't notice until she spoke that Mattie had come quietly into the room.

"I remember that piece," she said, her voice as sweet as music to his ears. "Your mother was playin' it that Christmas in Valdosta, at your Aunt Margaret's wedding."

She'd left the parlor doors open behind her, and the gaslamp in the hallway beyond cast a halo of light around her, making her look like an auburn-haired angel.

"And I remember you teachin' me to waltz that night," he replied, pausing over the keys while the music hovered in the air. "I was sure there wasn't a more beautiful dancin' partner in all of Georgia."

"You were just a boy, John Henry," she said with a smile, "you hadn't been to many dances. And you were very reluctant, as I recall."

"I was a lot of things then that I'm not now," he said deliberately, remembering her father's disapproval. "But I've changed, Mattie."

"But I don't want you to change! I just want you to be your best. I like you fine the way you are, mostly."

"Mostly?" he asked, and his heart faltered. Did she know what she shouldn't know? Had Annie shared her suspicions? But surely, Mattie wouldn't be so comfortable talking with him if his sins had come between them. And the fact that she went on without a blush put his fears at rest.

"Well, you are hot-headed sometimes," she said.

And knowing that she wasn't talking about more important transgressions, he asked :

"And arrogant? I remember you accusin' me of that, years back."

"A little arrogant," she agreed.

"And selfish?"

"Often selfish," she said with a small nod.

"And vain?"

"Always vain!" she said with a laugh. "But John Henry, you can be awfully sweet when you try!"

And taking advantage of the light-hearted moment, he stood quickly from the piano and turned toward her with open hands.

"Well, at least I'm not reluctant anymore. Dance with me, Mattie?"

"But there'll be no music if you don't play."

He didn't answer for a moment, gazing into her eyes. Then he said quietly, stepping closer: "There will be if you dance with me."

There was a world of meaning in her hesitation, there was a struggle in her heart that played across her face, in those lovely eyes that could never lie. She loved him but she loved her father as well, and she couldn't please them both at the same time.

"It's only a dance, that's all," he said softly, reaching for her hands. "Waltz with me, Mattie, like we did when we were young."

She hesitated only a moment longer, then answered by putting her hands in his. And as they turned together around the room, waltzing in the silence of the parlor, he knew they were both hearing the same thing: the music of their shared memories, the sound of two hearts that would always beat as one. When the music came to an end they were still standing together, arms circled around each other.

"Come home with me for Christmas!" she said suddenly, "home to Jonesboro. Oh, John Henry, let's be together again the way we used to be!"

"Dear Mattie, there is nothing I would like better!" he said with a smile. For Christmas in Jonesboro would be the perfect time to speak to her father.

Chapter Fifteen

Jonesboro, 1872

The old Macon and Western Railroad was still the main route south to Jonesboro, heading past East Point and rolling through the new towns of Forrest Park and Morrow's Station. But other than those little mail stops along the way, there was nothing much to see outside the thick windows of the rail car but the heavily wooded countryside of north Georgia.

It had been raining again, on and off, ever since the beginning of December, and now a cold wind was blowing the rain into an icy sleet that froze on the trees and frosted the red-brown earth. There had never been such a cold spell so early in the winter, and folks said it looked like there'd be snow by Christmas, for sure.

Inside the crowded rail car the little potbellied stove was stoked with a hardwood fire, putting out too much heat for the nearest rows of passengers, who perspired and wiped sweating faces, and not near enough heat for anybody else. At the far end of the car where John Henry and Mattie sat, huddled in heavy woolen overcoats, the air was cold enough to turn breath to a fog. But with Mattie by his side and a mind filled with visions of the Christmas to come, John Henry hardly felt the cold at all.

Mattie was being especially tender to him these days, calling him "honey," and letting him hold her hand the way she had when they were young, and laughing at his talk about the other passengers who shared their car. He'd always liked watching people, trying to guess by their dress and demeanor what their circumstances in life might be – the fussy old woman with an unruly grandchild alongside; the traveling salesman with his carpet bag full of overpriced wares; the lonely old maid with her nose in a book and her spectacled eyes looking about the railcar, wondering, "Is that one a bachelor? Is that one? Have any of them noticed me?" John Henry had an eye for those little things that gave away a person's character. And as he watched those other passengers, he knew that they were watching him as well, leaning his face

271

close to Mattie's, holding her hand to keep it warm. Was it obvious to everyone that they were a courting couple now? Mattie had never said anything to acknowledge that they were, but surely her actions were acknowledgment enough. And with Mattie's obvious affection to give him confidence, he imagined his soon-to-come conversation with her father:

"Uncle Robert, Sir, I know you've had some misgivings about me in the past, but I hope that you will put them aside. You see, Sir, I love your daughter, and I want to marry her..." Should he say which daughter, or wasn't that obvious? No, better to use her name. "I want to marry your daughter, Mattie, Sir..." That sounded a little more personal. "I have a promisin' professional career, and as you know, I've recently come into some inheritance, as well..." Better to ease over that part, since there wasn't really much money in owning that property, but it did sound good. "So I hope, Sir, that my proposal may meet with your approval..." Then, finally, Uncle Rob would nod and shake his hand, and on Christmas Eve John Henry would make his proposal to Mattie. Of course she would accept, once they had her father's approval.

They hadn't brought much baggage with them, only Mattie's train case and traveling bag and John Henry's valise, and he gathered those together as they stepped down from the train and onto the open platform of the familiar gray granite station. He remembered that stone too well from the hot summer long ago when he had worked for his uncle on the railroad, helping out at the depot. But just look at him now: a fine young gentleman returning to Jonesboro with a bright future and a pretty lady on his arm. His railroad days were behind him, for sure.

~~~~~~~~~~

They hired a buggy for the short ride to Church Street and Mattie's family home, the iron-rimmed wheels crunching on the hard icy ground, and were greeted by a fluttering of curtains at the windows and Mattie's younger sister Lucy stepping onto the porch.

"Oh, Mattie! Thank goodness you're here!" she said, shivering in her knitted shawl. "I wanted to send you a wire, but Mother said no, it was too expensive."

"Send a wire about what?" she said with a knowing smile. "Have you and Fred Young made wedding plans already?"

"No, it's not that. It's Pa. He's awful sick. Mother's afraid he's failin'..."

272

Mattie caught her breath and reached for John Henry's hand, but her voice seemed calm in the face of this unexpected emergency.

"Well, I'm home now, Lucy. Where is he?"

"In the parlor, in front of the fire. Mother had him moved in there since the bedroom is so cold. There's a roof leak that needs mendin'..."

"We'll worry about the roof later, Lucy. What does the doctor say?"

"Pneumonia, a bad case, both lungs. And he's so weak...."

"Damn the Yankees!" Mattie said quickly, "they're gonna kill him yet!" It was the first time John Henry had ever heard her swear, and even Lucy seemed surprised. Then she took off her bonnet and coat and handed them to Lucy, smoothing her hair with her hands.

"I am goin' in now, Lucy. You put on my coat and help John Henry get our things settled." Then she reached her arm around her sister and hugged her close, whispering against her face, "It's all right now, honey, Mattie's home."

Lucy did as she was told and slipped into Mattie's heavy coat and bonnet without bothering to tie the ribbons. She looked almost ill herself, her dark eyes circled with shadows of worry and too little sleep.

"And how are you, Lucy?" John Henry asked, as he pulled the luggage down from the buggy. "You look mighty tired."

"I haven't slept much since Pa got so sick. Mother's busy takin' care of him, and I do what I can to help, and watch the little ones, too." Lucy certainly had her hands full with all those children of Aunt Mary Anne's still living at home. There should have been a colored girl to help out around the house, but Uncle Rob had never had the money to hire help once he lost his businesses during the War and went to work for the railroad to make ends meet.

"Where shall I put our things?" John Henry asked.

"Upstairs," she said, nodding. "Mary and the other girls are in Jim Bob's old room now, but Mattie still shares with me when she comes home. I reckon you can share with Jim Bob again, next door to us."

"Is that quite proper?" he asked, surprised that Lucy would even suggest that an unmarried man would sleep so close to single young women. Aunt Permelia was always so careful about such things, keeping a discrete distance between the sexes in her Atlanta home.

"The roof is leakin'," Lucy answered simply. "There isn't any place else. But it is good to have you here, John Henry. Merry Christmas."

Then she turned and went back into the house, and he followed her up the stairs to that leaking second floor, where the chill of winter filled the rooms and Christmas seemed like something already long gone.

~~~~~~~~~~

For most of a week the family waited, hovering around Uncle Rob's bedside while the fever of the pneumonia raged on. There would come a crisis point, they knew, when the fever would finally break. But whether he would live through that crisis or not, only God knew.

The doctor came every day, listening to Uncle Rob's breathing and tapping on his chest trying to loosen the congestion. But his efforts never seemed to do any good, and Uncle Rob still labored for breath, wheezing so loudly that the rattle of it could be heard in the next room. The only blessing was that he was too feverish to know how ill he really was. In his poor deluded mind he seemed to think he was back in that Federal prison camp, and kept crying out for water from some merciless Yankee commander.

Mattie cursed the Yankees more than once during those days, her face strained with anger and exhaustion as she stayed up nights watching at her father's side. Until she'd come, Aunt Mary Anne had refused to leave the sickroom and take any rest at all, and the strain had nearly made her sick as well. But now that Mattie was home, Mary Anne gave up her night vigil and went to her own bed to cry herself into a fitful sleep.

During the days, Mattie helped Lucy tend the younger children, staying patient with them somehow though she was fading from lack of sleep herself. And John Henry could do nothing to help lighten her burden but put his arms around her and let her rest her head against him for a few peaceful moments during the day. And knowing that Mattie, who had always comforted him, should come to him for comfort now, touched him more than any loving words she could have said.

Then, three days before Christmas, Uncle Rob's fever finally broke and the Christmas celebrating began. Uncle Rob had always loved Christmas — the "Holliday's holiday" he called it, as Christmas was for children and he had more children than anyone else he knew.

He was still very ill, of course, and unable to be moved from his bed by the parlor fire, so the family gathered there around him, singing Christmas songs with extra

274

joy, with Mattie's pretty voice sounding the sweetest of all. She had come so close to losing her beloved father without even getting to say good-bye, and now she had him back again. But John Henry found it hard to share in the happiness. He had watched his mother die, and there was a look about Uncle Rob's pallid, blue-cast face that reminded him of life slowly slipping away.

~~~~~~~~~~

The day before Christmas Eve dawned thin and cold, and John Henry woke up shivering under the old quilt in the upstairs room next to Mattie's. At first he didn't know what it was that had awakened him so early. Most mornings he had to drag himself out of bed to get ready for work, a tiredness left over from his own bout with pneumonia the past year. But now with only the gray light that came before the sun, he was wide awake and listening. To what?

Then he heard it again, the sound that must have brought him out of his sleep. There was a groaning in the thin winter air, and then a crash like glass shattering on a hardwood floor. He leaped from the bed and pushed open the shutters at the window. In the yard outside, the heavy limb of an old pine tree had broken away from its trunk and fallen to the frost-covered ground, weighed down with a mantle of ice.

It was the first tree to bend and break that ice-storm morning, but there would be others to follow. As far as John Henry could see, the woods that surrounded the homes along Church Street were glistening, trees turned to glass with the ice. And before he could turn away from the window, there was another deep moaning and a shattering roar as another tree limb bent and fell to the hard icy ground. And off in the distance there were more tree limbs falling, laying heavy on the wires of the telegraph line, and cutting off Jonesboro from the rest of the world.

By noon of that day, it was clear to John Henry that his uncle hadn't long to live. The fever was gone, but Uncle Rob's breathing had gotten slower and heavier until his chest was hardly moving at all. But Aunt Mary Anne insisted that he was just resting, getting his strength back after the illness, and when John Henry suggested that they ought to send for the doctor soon, she turned on him angrily and ordered him from the room.

Mattie stood by her mother, believing along with her that their prayers had been answered and her father was getting well. She went in and out of the sick room with a kind of manic joy, smiling and chattering away as if by the very force of her hope she could make him be well again. And even when the doctor finally arrived for his afternoon call and shook his head sadly, they refused to give up hope.

John Henry waited outside the parlor sickroom, listening to the whispered voices behind the closed door. He could hear the doctor, trying to explain in calm tones what was to come, and Aunt Mary Anne's voice, hoarse from sleepless nights and the strain of holding onto her husband's life, and, softer, Mattie's voice, comforting, trying to find hope in the doctor's dim prognosis. And waiting in the darkness there in the hall, John Henry felt as helpless in the face of this passing as he had felt when he was a child, waiting outside in a dark hallway while his mother died a slow suffocating death.

The doctor came out of the room a few moments later, medical bag in hand, shoulders hunched with resignation.

"They won't listen to me, either one of them," he said. "I'm afraid Mrs. Holliday may lose her mind with grief if she won't accept the inevitable."

"Are you sure he's dyin'?" John Henry asked.

"Son, I have seen a lot of life and too much of death, and I think Captain Holliday hasn't the strength to live any longer."

"Then...how long?"

"Tomorrow, or maybe the day after. But no longer."

"But that's Christmas!" John Henry said. "Surely on Christmas..." He still held onto some hope too, and a little faith in the kindness of God.

The doctor shrugged again and reached for his overcoat. "I don't believe God much cares about Christmas, one way or another. It's just another day for livin' and dyin'. I am sorry about your uncle. Try to be a strength to those ladies. It's going to be a terrible shock to them, I'm afraid."

~~~~~~~~~~

It was coming on dusk when Mattie finally left the sickroom, taking a little rest before starting the night watch. She stepped out of the dim, hot parlor and into the dimmer light of the hallway, wiping her brow with the corner of an old apron, and John Henry called to her from the dining room just beyond. He'd been waiting there for her, hoping that she would see the truth before he had to explain it to her.

"How's he doin', Mattie?"

"About the same. He's sleepin' again, but restless. At least the fever hasn't come

276

back. His skin feels very cool." Then she smiled weakly. "He may be able to join us for Christmas dinner, Mother thinks, if we have it in the parlor."

"And what do you think, Mattie?"

"I am too tired to think," she answered heavily. "I've never been so tired in all my life." Then she sank down into a chair and put her hands in her lap while she stared unseeing at the old Celtic cross hanging on the dining room wall.

John Henry watched her, gathering his courage, then he said quietly: "He's dyin', Mattie. You've got to face it, and prepare yourself."

"Oh no, you're wrong!" she protested. "We've been prayin' so hard for him, Mother and I have, kneelin' by his bed. Mother says..."

"Your mother is beside herself, Mattie. It's clear to the doctor. It's clear to me, too. Can't you see it, and do somethin' to help her?"

Mattie shook her head slowly, still staring at the cross on the wall, "But we have prayed so hard."

"I know, we've all been prayin' for him. But he's failin', Mattie." Then he laid his hand on her shoulder. "Wouldn't it be worse to be unprepared for what's to come?"

"Unprepared? Yes, yes, you're right," she said absently, almost too tired to talk, "It would be worse to be unprepared... unshriven..." But then the distant look on her face disappeared, and she cried out, "Oh no, not unshriven! Please God, not unshriven too!"

"What are you talkin' about?" he asked, afraid that the strain had already been too much for her and she was delirious.

"Not like my grandfather, not again! Please, Holy Mother, not that again!" But when she turned her face toward John Henry he saw no delirium there, only cold fear. "My grandfather Fitzgerald died unshriven, without the priest, condemned to dwell in Purgatory for all eternity. He took ill on a ride into the countryside past Fayetteville and died before a priest could come to give him final rites. My grandmother mourned out the rest of her days, prayin' for his poor lost soul. He was forty-four years old when he died, John Henry – just like my father is now."

"But that was long ago, Mattie."

"Don't you see? It's like my grandfather all over again, and without the priest, my father will die unshriven, too! Condemned to Purgatory!" There was a sound like a keening wail in her voice. "Oh, John Henry, if he dies this way – for my poor mother to lose her father and her husband both!" Then she reached for his hand, holding it with a strength he didn't know she had. "You must go and send word for the priest to come down, right away! You must send a telegram to Atlanta. Tell the priest at the Immaculate Conception that Captain Holliday may be dyin', and must have his final rites. Please, please, you must hurry!"

"I can't," he said, his heart sinking.

"Why not?"

"The wire is down, Mattie. There is no telegraph. The ice storm's broken the lines."

Her mouth opened in speechless horror, her lips moving noiselessly. Then she shook her head and started to cry and John Henry put his arms around her, holding her while she sobbed as though her heart were breaking.

"Shh, honey, shh," he murmured against her hair, "it's all right. It's gonna be all right."

"Never," she moaned, "never! Nothin' will ever be all right again!" and she shuddered against him, overcome with grief.

Then a glimmer of hope appeared, and John Henry almost laughed with the relief of it. "Then I'll go to Atlanta myself and get the priest!"

"But how can you?"

"I'll take the train," he said reasonably. "I'll be in Atlanta by midnight and go wake the priest if I have to, and send him here. You see? I said it would be fine!"

But Mattie just shook her head and sighed despondently. "The train to Atlanta doesn't run this late. The last one left at noon."

He had never felt so useless in all his life, bearer of bad tidings and comfortless cheer. But he couldn't sit back and watch Mattie's heart break this way, not while he still had half a heart left himself, and suddenly he knew what he had to do. He bent his head and quickly kissed her hair, then pulled his arms from around her, and stood.

"I'll bring the priest, Mattie. Tell your mother, if she comes to her senses." Then he strode out of the room and took his overcoat and hat from the coat hook in the hall, swinging the front door open and letting it slam behind him. The icy rain had almost ended but a sharp cold wind was picking up, and it cut across his face as he headed around the house toward the barn out back.

"Where are you going?" Mattie cried after him, running out of the house with her own coat thrown around her shoulders and her hair coming undone in the wind.

"I told you. To Atlanta to get a priest!"

"But there is no train runnin'!"

He kept walking, his leather boots crunching on the ice-hard ground. If he stopped to talk to her he might lose his resolve and change his mind, and there was no other way. "I'm gonna ride, Mattie. I'm sure your father won't be needin' the horse tonight."

"You can't! Not in this awful cold! It's a day's ride to Atlanta, even when the roads are good!"

"Then I'll ride day and night."

Mattie stood watching him, unbelieving as he brought the horse out of its stall, bridling it and hefting the heavy saddle over its back. But when he slipped his foot into the stirrup and swung up into the saddle, she gasped and ran to his side, grabbing onto the reins as if she could hold him back.

"Please don't do this! It's madness, you know it is!"

"What else can I do, Mattie? Tell me that. What else is there to do?"

"You'll kill yourself. You'll freeze to death out there!"

"We all die sometime, don't we?" he said flippantly, but his heart was racing from emotion and a brooding fear. If he didn't get the priest down to Jonesboro in time to grant safe passage to Uncle Rob's soul, Mattie might be lost to a lifetime of melancholy. She was near enough to mad exhaustion already, but thinking of her father spending eternity in Purgatory would be damnation for her soul, too. So, for Mattie, he had to make this reckless ride.

"Please, honey!" she said again, crying now and hanging onto John Henry's arm as he pulled at the reins. "I can't lose you, too!"

The pleading in her voice and the pain and terror in her eyes tore at his heart, but he couldn't let it stop him. He leaned down from the saddle, reaching his arm around her and holding her to him.

"I'll be back, Mattie, I swear I will! And I will bring the priest, as I have said. And you will never, never lose me!" Then he bent his head and kissed her, tasting tears and sweetness all at once before he let her go and rode off into that cold, darkening night.

~~~~~~~~~~

It was the worst weather for riding he had ever seen. The weeks of rain had turned the rutted dirt road to mud that froze into furrows and ridges when the ice storm came, and the horse stumbled and lost its footing again and again. The trees that crowded alongside the road were ice-covered too, their heavy limbs bowing down toward the ground and reaching out to snare a rider in the dark. And gusting out of the north, the winter wind was bringing snow with it, sending clouds scudding across the moon and making the moonlight seem to shimmer and glow off the icy fields. Then the road dropped down through river bottoms where the moonlight disappeared entirely, and the horse clattered across icy wooden bridges over silent, slow moving streams.

Folks said it was a haunted road, that track that wound north from Jonesboro toward Atlanta. And riding alone through those dark woods with only the horse's heavy breathing to keep him company, John Henry shivered and tried not to remember those superstitious stories.

But there were ghosts. He could see them rising right up out of the icy fog, the phantom figures of Confederate soldiers marching endlessly toward Jonesboro, pale eyes staring toward cold heroes' graves, and mute voices crying out, *"Too late! Too late to save Jonesboro! Too late!"* And behind their ragged, straggling columns, the caissons creaked noiselessly along, canon gleaming in the cold, cold moonlight. Shades and shadows, apparitions on a lonely, haunted road.

By the time he got to the tavern at Rough and Ready, halfway to Atlanta, he was numb from cold and tiredness, his arms aching from holding onto the reins and his chest heavy from breathing in the icy air. He looked longingly at the glowing windows of the tavern, the spirals of smoke that rose up from the twin chimneys of the old log building and spoke of warmth and comfort inside, but he couldn't stop. The horse was warm, breathing hard and taking the ride well, and he couldn't risk having her cool down now. So he turned north again, to where the track joined the McDonough Road and headed toward East Point.

He kept riding, pushing himself to go on when he thought he could go no farther, remembering Mattie's desperate pleas, the agony in her voice: *"If he dies unshriven, too..."* And that gave him strength to stay in the saddle, keep racing the horse over that long difficult road, past the quiet farms sleeping in the moonlight, past the old crossroads church at Mount Zion.

It was nearly dawn when he finally rode into Atlanta, the clatter of the horse's hooves on cobblestones shaking him to wakefulness as he came onto Peachtree Street. Across the tracks that divided Atlanta in two he could see the unfinished towers of the Church of the Immaculate Conception rising up against the dark, cloudy sky. But not until he had tied his horse at the gate and stumbled up the steps of the church did he really believe that his nightmare ride was over.

He slammed his hand against the heavy wooden door that led to the sanctuary, his whole body shaking from cold and exhaustion. There was a long, empty silence, then finally the door opened and a small woman glared up at him suspiciously.

"What is it you're needing, then, so early as it is?" she asked in a thick Irish brogue.

"I need...to see the priest," he answered, struggling to stay standing, leaning against the heavy wood doorframe.

"Father Duggan is sleeping now, if it's penance you're asking. Come back in the daylight when the drink is worn off a bit, and make your peace with God then."

"I am not drunk!" he said, swaying toward her, his eyes wild, and then he started to cough, his chest giving way all at once. But there was no liquor on his breath, and the woman waited until he could speak again.

"Are you sick, then? Are you needing a place to stay?"

"Please! The priest, I need the priest!" And as the last bit of energy left him and his legs started to slide out from under him, he coughed again and whispered between gasps, "Tell him...tell him...Captain Holliday is dyin'." Then the world went black and he collapsed on the hard stone pavers of the sanctuary steps.

~~~~~~~~~~

The next hours slid by him in a fevered blur, the frantic message to Father Duggan and another to his Uncle John, then the hurried train ride south again hoping that they were not too late, after all. And when they arrived, Mattie's face was full of joy and relief, until she threw her arms around his neck and felt the stinging touch of his skin.

"You're burnin' up with fever!" she cried, pulling away from him and peering up into his face.

"I'm fine, honey," he said weakly, trying to smile, but his voice was just a whisper and he had to cover his mouth to hold back a rasping cough.

"Oh, how could I have let you go off like that?" she said, laying her hand, cool and comforting against his cheek.

"You didn't let me go, Mattie," he protested, "you tried to stop me, remember?" Then he started to cough, and had to hang onto her until his breath came back again.

"I knew this would happen! Oh, I knew that ride would come to no good!"

"But I did bring the priest, as I promised. And I did come back, didn't I?" But when he tried to smile again, the room swayed crazily around him, and Mattie's face blurred before his eyes. "Now, I think, I need to get some rest. Will you help me... get upstairs?"

But she had already run ahead of him, throwing open the bedroom door, tearing quilts off the other beds to lay on top of him. He stumbled up the stairs after her, feeling more tired than sick, and falling gratefully into Jim Bob's bed while Mattie fussed over him, pulling off his boots and loosening his shirt. And the last thing he remembered before he sank down into a deep, exhausted sleep was Mattie's face against his, kissing his cheek, and crying as she pulled the blankets close around him.

~~~~~~~~~~~

Mattie's father died just before midnight on Christmas Eve, after receiving all the last rites of Holy Church. He was buried two days later in the Catholic family plot in the Fayetteville Cemetery, on a bleak winter afternoon.

It was a long, slow funeral procession that followed the coffin-laden wagon the ten miles from Jonesboro to Fayetteville, over roads that were still slick with ice and a dusting of new-fallen snow. The horses and wagons jostled along, crossing the wooden bridges at Flint River and Camp and Morning Creeks, then heading up the long grade toward the higher ground where the cemetery stretched across its windswept ridge. Yet in spite of the difficulty of the journey, the cemetery was crowded with mourners come to say good-bye to husband, father, brother, and friend.

Father Duggan had stayed on for the funeral, and his lilting Irish accent added warmth to the stately Latin words of dedication on the grave:

"*In manus tuas, domine, commendo spiritum meum,*" he said, then crossed himself and touched holy water to the coffin before it was covered over with clods of cold Georgia clay. Then came the recitations: the Benedictus, the Kyrie Eleison, the Pater Noster, and prayers for the family left behind.

And, finally, Captain Robert Kennedy Holliday was at rest, lying near his wife's father and mother, with an empty space left beside him for his beloved Mary Anne to follow one day. And standing around his grave, his family embraced and wept and could not be consoled.

John Henry stood alone outside the circle of mourners, his shoulders hunched and his collar turned up against the cold. His fever was down but his chest was still aching, and he felt as fragile as the sparrows that scattered into the winter wind. Mattie had tried to persuade him to stay home in bed until he was stronger, but he had stubbornly refused. He needed to be here sharing in the grief of her loss, and his own.

In this cemetery, surrounded by the graves of his relatives, he felt his own mortality weighing heavy on him. In front of him, the Fitzgeralds lay in neat rows – Mattie's grandfather and grandmother, aunts and uncles, cousins who had died young. Behind him, past the curve in the road that separated holy Catholic ground from plain Protestant graves, lay his own grandfather and grandmother, Robert Alexander Holliday and Rebecca Burroughs. And with them the row of little Holliday sons, his uncles who had died in childhood.

He didn't notice soft footsteps on the path behind him and was startled to hear a voice speaking his own thoughts.

"It's like Tara, isn't it? The seat of the high kings in Ireland, and the place where they were buried as well. I reckon this is like Tara, too, holy Irish ground, consecrated with the bones of our Irish ancestors. Like our own little bit of Ireland."

He turned toward the voice and looked into the bright blue eyes of Sarah Fitzgerald.

"Hello, John Henry," she said, a wistful smile on her face. "It's been a long time since you came for a visit."

"I've been away-off at dental school, in Philadelphia," he said quickly, feeling an uncomfortable need to explain himself. The last time he'd seen Sarah, she was waving him a sweet good-bye from the front porch of her father's plantation house as he was riding away vowing never to return.

"Yes, I know about your becomin' a dentist. We're all so proud of you. Your letters from Philadelphia were wonderful."

"You read my letters?"

"Well, not exactly. Mattie read them to us, when she and her mother and the girls came callin' at Rural Home. She was always so excited to tell us how you were doin'."

He knew it was common practice for families to share their correspondence, sometimes even giving letters up for publication in the local paper as public interest. But his letters to Mattie had been meant for her alone, to be read in private.

"Did she...did she read everything?"

"Well, she may have skipped over some things, I suppose. She never actually let me read them myself." Then she paused and lowered her eyes, "I kept hopin' maybe you'd write a letter to me, too. I waited for you to come back, you know, like you promised you would. But when you didn't come, and didn't write..." Then she looked back up at him, and John Henry was struck by how very blue her eyes were, like sapphires when she smiled. "Well, I realized that it was probably Cousin Mattie you'd been sweet on all along."

"I am sorry for the way I behaved that night, Sarah. It was ungentlemanly of me."

"Oh, please don't apologize!" she said swiftly, laying a gloved hand on his arm. "You didn't do anything wrong! I – I was hopin' that you would kiss me that night. I reckon I thought that if you did, maybe I could steal you away from all the other girls."

"What other girls?" he asked, bewildered.

"Don't tell me you didn't know! Why, you were the talk of Jonesboro that summer, John Henry Holliday! It about broke all our hearts when you went on home to Valdosta. Of course, all the girls were jealous of Cousin Mattie, mostly. It was so obvious that she had your heart." She paused a moment, studying his face. "And does Cousin Mattie still have your heart, John Henry?"

He glanced up toward the circle of mourners at the graveside and Mattie's sweet tear-stained face trying to smile at well-wishers. Had there ever been a time when she didn't have his heart?

"You know she'll be in mournin' cloth for a year," she said, in answer to his silence.

"What do you mean?"

"For her father, of course. She'll be wearin' black for the first six months of deep mournin' with a long crape veil on her bonnet, blockin' out the world. Then it'll be half-mournin' for another six months when she can start wearin' gray and go without the veil. It's the proper attire for mournin' a father. She won't be able to accept any social engagements for a whole year. Anything less would be unseemly."

"No social engagements at all?" he asked, suddenly seeing past the present grief to what lay ahead. No courting, no marriage proposal. Another long year of waiting.

"Of course, you and I will only be in mournin' for three months. Mattie's father was only your uncle, after all, and not even that close to me, only my first cousin's husband. So we'll both be out of black and ready for social engagements soon. And you know you are always welcome at Rural Home, John Henry, anytime you want to stop by."

There was such a sound of hope in her voice that he almost felt obliged to promise another visit, until she added wistfully:

"I'd hoped to make a visit to my sister Annie in Atlanta and maybe see you while I was there, as well. She talked about invitin' me up, last summer. But she hasn't mentioned it in a while…"

And without her saying anymore, John Henry thought he knew why Annie's invitation hadn't been forthcoming. She'd changed her mind about arranging for a meeting between him and her sister Sarah after what she'd seen that night at the Opera House, deciding he was unworthy of her sister's attentions. It was sad for Sarah, who still seemed to be seeing moonlight when she looked at him, like she had that night on the porch at Rural Home, but just as well. For it was Mattie he had loved then and Mattie that he still loved. And as long she needed him, he knew where he would be.

I hoped to find a way to involve them again in the tribal and other societies with
I was there as well, she added, about it getting all the attention. But she later
mentioned and apologies.

And when I went to wine sessions after Elena, that did the trick why Anna?
was rather unobtrusively within the session, should have become more apparent to
the meeting between him and herself as he came after what I said somehow off at the
start of one occasion, she was annoyed and they meant something. It was not for
Sam, who still deep inside seemed incompatible, who came look. Coming like me
had that night on the porch, a small frame I was carrying... he is wonderful be
had loved Elena and Marie that he was loved. And so, as far as I can see, I too, he was
eternally would be.

Chapter Sixteen

Atlanta, 1873

The Twelfth Night Carnival came to Atlanta in a blaze of bonfires and fireworks that first week of the New Year, with a fancy masque ball at the Kimball House Hotel and a gaslight parade through the streets of the city. But for good Catholics like Mattie's family, Twelfth Night was also a holy day of obligation, honoring the arrival of the wise men in Bethlehem twelve days after Christmas. "Epiphany" they called it, and spent the day in prayer and oblation, and though Mattie could have been excused for missing Mass so soon after the bereavement of her family, she wanted to offer her prayers in church. With all the rush to find the priest before her father's death and the hurried burial after, there had been no time for a proper requiem mass to be spoken. So with John Henry as her traveling companion, she hurried back to Atlanta to take her place among the communicants at the Church of the Immaculate Conception that Epiphany morning, attending mass in honor of her beloved father.

It was an odd atmosphere for a church service, John Henry thought, with the noise and the revelry in the streets outside and the hushed reverence of the sacraments inside. As the main sanctuary of the church was still being completed, mass was held in the chilly basement chapel and the parishioners stayed bundled in coats and scarves and tried not to notice the stone paver floor, hard and cold against reverent bended knees. Along the brick foundation walls, heavy candles in brass sconces gave off a shadowy, flickering light and filled the room with smoke that mingled with the incense on the cloth-covered altar to make a pungent perfume. There were no stained-glass windows in that dark basement chapel, no soaring vaulted ceilings as there would be when the rest of the church was completed, yet there was something supernal about that little gathering of worshippers sharing the Eucharist in dark simplicity. They seemed to John Henry like a congregation of early Christians, hiding in the catacombs while all of Rome made merry outside.

But there was nothing merry in Mattie's prayerful worship that morning. She was still crying over the loss of her father, her voice breaking as she repeated the words of the prayers:

"Pater Noster qui es in caelis, sanctificetur nomen tuum, adveniat regum tuum, fiat voluntas tua, sicut in caelo et in terra..."

John Henry repeated the words along with her in a voice still hoarse from his recent illness. He was proud that he'd learned enough Latin in school to understand the Lord's Prayer, at least, though there would be much more to learn when he converted to Catholicism, as he would most certainly need to do to marry Mattie. He'd convert right away if that would make her happy. He would do anything to make her happy again, but he felt helpless against the tide of her grief. Her mourning was as dark as the black crepe that veiled her face, like a shadow that separated her from him. Deep mourning, Sarah Fitzgerald had called it, and there would be six more months of it before he saw the light of her smile again.

With the chill and smoke of the basement chapel and the cold of the January morning outside, his cough started back up again, and by the time he and Mattie returned to Forrest Avenue following Mass, he was ready for a rest. But rest would not be allowed him, for before he could even take off his heavy wool coat and hat, Sophie handed him a telegram.

"Just arrived," she said. "Hope it ain't bad news. Seems like this family's had nothin' but bad news, lately."

The telegram was from Martha Hidalgo, and the words were tragically simple: *Francisco dying. Come soon.*

~~~~~~~~~~

There was no *milagro* for Francisco. The cold winter had brought the pneumonia with it, like it had to Uncle Rob, and Francisco's consumption-ravaged lungs couldn't overcome the effects of two diseases, though in the end it was the consumption that killed him. John Henry had never seen the final hours of a consumptive, having been too young at his mother's death to be allowed into the sick room. But he saw more than he wanted to now. Francisco's lungs, scarred by the disease, slowly filled with water from his own breathing, and the lack of oxygen left him delirious as he slipped in and out of a pain-ridden consciousness. He called for Martha, then didn't know her. He asked for water, then couldn't drink. He struggled against the end, tossing and moaning and gasping for breath. And at the last, his breath gurgled out as he lay drowning in his own bed. John Henry had seen wounded animals struggle to live, downed by his own gunshot, though after the struggle there seemed to be an accepting peace in the death. But there was no peace here. Francisco died with his eyes wide open, sheer terror in them, more awful than the death of any hunted animal.

John Henry would have been happy to leave right then, going back to Atlanta and forgetting the whole awful ordeal. But Francisco had asked him to watch over the family, and he had an obligation to fulfill. So while Martha Hidalgo prepared for the laying out of her husband's body and the funeral and burial that would follow, John Henry rode back into Griffin to deliver the news of his death. If Francisco had been a man of substance, instead of a struggling farmer, there would have been etiquette to follow: funeral announcements printed on vellum paper edged with black ink, notices written to the local papers, telegrams sent to distant family and friends. As it was, the best John Henry could do was make calls on the businesses along Hill Street and Solomon Street, inviting all who had known him to pay their respects to Francisco Hidalgo at his funeral at County Line Baptist Church in Jenkinsburg. It was amazing how many said they would attend; Francisco's years working as a barber in Griffin had earned him many friends. And though John Henry knew that his father wouldn't come, he sent a wire to Henry as well – Francisco would have wanted it that way.

But there was one last thing that Francisco would have wanted that wasn't so easy to accomplish. Francisco had asked him to watch over his children, to make sure they were not left orphaned as he had been, and John Henry had promised that he would. He had made the promise lightly, not understanding until later how Francisco had suffered as a child and how much he wanted to save his children from the same suffering. But lightly made or not, a promise was a promise, and he was bound to keep it. And now that he saw the state into which Francisco's death had flung his family – husbandless, fatherless, close to hopeless – he knew he had to do whatever he could to help. But how? He was too far away, living in Atlanta, to make more than occasional visits, and even so, all the traveling back and forth was wearing him out. There was no other choice but to leave his Uncle John's house and move to Griffin where he could practice dentistry, yet be a reasonable ride away from Francisco's family in Jenkinsburg should they need him.

Of course, moving would mean leaving Mattie behind, but in her state of mourning, being near her was almost harder than being without her. Living down the hall from her, spending his nights so close without being able to be closer, was tormenting. Moving away for a while was clearly the right thing to do, but funding such a move would be a problem. His monthly rents from the Iron Front Building would only be enough to pay for a boarding house room, not to purchase the dental equipment he would need to outfit an office. But the Iron Front could yield enough for all that and more – if he sold it.

He was chilled already from hours of walking through downtown Griffin in the icy January afternoon, and with the thin light fading into dusk, he was only going to get colder. A drink would help to warm him some and bolster his courage enough for what he knew he had to do, and there was one place where he could probably find a drink and sell his property, too. But before he pushed open the door to N.G. Phillips' liquor store, he stood back to take a final look at his inheritance. It was a fine house, the Iron Front Building, red brick all around and solidly built to last a lifetime. With care, it would still be standing in a hundred years, long windows looking out onto Solomon Street. But at least with his inheritance property turned into cash money, the gambler Hyram Neil could never come find it. He took a deep breath, coughing on the cold dry air, and stepped into the store.

"Mr. Phillips," he said slowly, letting his eyes adjust to the even dimmer light inside. "I'd like to reconsider your offer to buy my building."

"Reconsider? Why, Dr. Holliday, I thought you had your heart dead set on holding onto it!"

"I had my heart dead set on a lot of things. Is your offer still good?"

"Eighteen-hundred dollars."

"Then why don't you open us up a bottle of that Tennessee and we'll get down to business."

Phillips pulled two glasses from under the sales counter and popped the cork off an amber whiskey bottle. "Mind if I ask what changed your thinkin'?"

"*Mi hermano,*" John Henry said, though he knew that Phillips would never understand.

~~~~~~~~

County Line Baptist Church had been founded just after the start of the War, with Martha and Francisco Hidalgo among the nineteen original members. And though the church had grown some since then, services were still held in the old schoolhouse that was the congregation's first chapel. The building was set in a grove of pine and sweetgum trees just past the main road of Jenkinsburg, and if it hadn't been for the rows of gravestones in the churchyard cemetery, the chapel would still look like nothing more than a schoolhouse. But that was fine with the members of the County Line congregation. Church was a school, after all, where God-fearing Christians learned from the Good Book and sinners were taught to repent.

The funeral was as simple as the little church building in which it was held. The plain wooden coffin stood at the head of the main aisle, unadorned with flowers or even the usual black crape drapings – Francisco's family had no money for such a show of bereavement. But the family's mourning was clear enough to see, even without yards of crape and arrangements of funeral flowers. Martha, her face veiled, was surrounded by her six older children all dressed in their most somber clothing and sitting huddled together on the first row of the straight-backed pews. The four boys were solemn-faced, but the girls were weeping out loud, a sound made even more pitiable by baby Nita's happy cooing. She was just three-months old and would never know the father who had worried so over her future.

But desolate as the family was, they were far from deserted. The little church was full to overflowing with Francisco's friends and acquaintances from as close by as Jenkinsburg and as far off as Fayetteville. Even Doc Whitehead, the physician from over at Indian Springs, had closed his office for the day to pay his respects. It seemed that, for a poor man, Francisco had been rich in some ways.

All those mourners must be some consolation to Martha Hidalgo, John Henry thought – but they were no consolation to him. He'd had too much of dying and burying in the past few weeks, and even Pastor Kimbell's hopeful obsequies couldn't lift his own mournful spirits.

"*They that wait upon the Lord shall renew their strength,*" the pastor quoted as he read from the Holy Book, "*they shall mount up with wings as eagles; they shall run, and not be weary; they shall walk, and not faint...*"

The familiar cadence of the scripture reminded John Henry of his mother and the way her musical voice had made the ancient words come alive.

"*In the world ye shall have tribulations; but be of good cheer; I have overcome the world...I am the resurrection, and the life; he that believeth in me, though he were dead, yet shall he live...*"

But there was no cheer in the words for John Henry today; his mother was gone, his uncle was gone, and now Francisco was gone, too. And as far as he could see, the resurrection was a long ways off.

It wasn't until the funeral service ended and the congregation moved outside for the burial that he saw his father standing solemnly just inside the church door. He shouldn't have been surprised to see his father there, as he sent the news himself. But he'd never really expected Henry to make the long journey up from Valdosta just to watch Francisco's remains go into the ground. It was, after all, a three-day's train ride with the usual stopovers for food and sleep, and Henry would have had to ride straight through to get to Jenkinsburg to be in time for the funeral. There was no figuring him out, that was for sure. He hadn't been around to bury Uncle Rob the month before, his own younger brother, but now he appeared out of nowhere for a servant boy he hadn't seen in years. But there was no avoiding him either, now that he was here, and John Henry made his way to his father's side.

"Mornin', Pa," he said under his breath as the mourners shuffled past. "I reckon you got my wire."

Henry nodded. "I had some business up in Atlanta, and figured I'd stop by to pay my respects."

John Henry didn't comment on the fact that his father's business seemed surprisingly convenient, demanding his arrival in North Georgia just when Francisco was being eulogized. But then, irony was not one of Henry's strong points.

"And how did you happen to be around to send the wire, anyhow?" Henry asked.

"Martha sent me word that Francisco was dyin'. Helpin' out with the funeral seemed to be about all I could do. She's had her hands full with that new baby of theirs."

"Fool thing to do, bringing a new baby into the world, sick as he was," Henry commented.

"I reckon they were thinkin' more of life than death," John Henry replied, remembering Francisco's hope for a miracle.

"Well, they should have been thinkin' about who'd be needin' food and shelter when Francisco passed. I don't suppose those boys of his are big enough yet to run a farm alone. Rueben's not sixteen yet, and he's the oldest. And little Finney's only six, for hell's sake."

It wasn't his father's language that surprised John Henry, even within the sacred walls of the church house, but the fact that he knew the ages of Francisco's children. Who would have thought that Henry would even remember their names?

292

"Martha's figurin' on hirin' some help until the boys get bigger," John Henry said. "But it's not all that much of a farm, anyhow."

It was the wrong thing to say, he discovered too late.

"And what makes you a judge of a man's farm, John Henry?" his father said in an angry whisper.

"I was just makin' an observation..."

"Francisco had two-hundred acres on that place, all turned over by himself and those boys. Slave work, in the old days, but they done it. And likely more work than you'll ever know."

And all at once, John Henry felt like a child again trying to please his hero-father. "I know farm work, Pa," he said, defending himself. "I grew up at Cat Creek, remember? And I worked in the Pecan orchard, too, before comin' up here."

But Henry turned steel-blue eyes on him, and said coolly:

"I remember workin' the farm while you practiced your piano lessons. And as I recall, you only spent a couple of weekends in the orchard before you took a sudden notion to make a visit to Atlanta. I don't believe you ever worked hard enough in your whole life to wear a callus on your hand, John Henry."

He couldn't have been more hurt if Henry had slapped him across the face, humiliation and pain altogether. Try as he might, he was never good enough for his father. But he wasn't a child any longer and he couldn't let Henry see the anguish his words had caused.

"No, Pa, I don't believe I ever have. But that doesn't mean I don't work hard, anyhow. Why, there's been days I've left Dr. Ford's office so tired I can hardly walk home..."

"Your home, John Henry, is in Valdosta. But that is another matter. Right now, I've got a boy to bury."

And as his father turned on his boot heel and walked out into the graveyard, John Henry watched him in stunned silence. For there was such an unexpected sadness in Henry's words that instead of calling Francisco "boy," he might as well have called him "son."

~~~~~~~~~

In the little graveyard next to the church, the mourners were already gathered around the open chasm of Francisco's waiting grave. The formal religious service was over and all that remained were the singing of a final hymn and the last prayer before the red dirt was shoveled over the lowered coffin. The placing of a proper gravestone would come later. For now, the only grave marker would be the new mound of freshly turned red Georgia clay.

Tara, John Henry thought, remembering Sarah Fitzgerald's fanciful words. This, too, was Tara, except that Francisco was Mexican, not Irish, and this was no consecrated Catholic plot. But Francisco had loved the Georgia soil that was soon to be his final home, and maybe that was enough to make this a Tara for him.

Then the hymn singing began and John Henry's thoughts turned sharply from Irish legends. The song was so familiar that he could almost sing the words from memory.

Abide with me: fast falls the eventide;
The darkness deepens; Lord with me abide!
When other helpers fail, and comforts flee,
Help of the helpless, O abide with me.

He had sung that song in church services when he was just a boy, sitting restless by his mother at the old Presbyterian Church in Griffin. But there was something more than restlessness in his memory of it, something more like sadness and shame mixed together...

And then he remembered when he'd last heard that song. It was on the long road from Fayetteville to Griffin, riding home from his Grandpa Holliday's funeral, as his mother sang and he sat in the back of the wagon, holding the heavy knowledge that he knew she was going to die.

Swift to its close ebbs out life's little day;
Earth's joys grow dim, its glories pass away;
Change and decay in all around I see;
O Thou, who changest not, abide with me...

He looked up at his father, standing beside Martha Hidalgo at the head of the grave, and had a sudden longing to reach out to him, to put aside the pain of the past and somehow grab ahold of the childhood he had lost. He sniffed back a surprise of unmanly tears, took two steps toward Henry, put out a hand to touch his father's shoulder...

Then Henry's words made him freeze in his tracks.

"There's an inheritance, Martha," Henry was saying. "It came from his mother's folks, a business house over in Griffin. I'll see what I can do about having him deed it over to you, for the children. He won't be needin' it. He's got a position waitin' for him back in Valdosta, and God knows he's got no sense for handlin' property. I should have arranged for it to go to Francisco years ago. He'd have appreciated it more than John Henry ever will. He was a good boy, Francisco. He was always a good boy..."

Then Henry stopped to clear his throat and wipe something from his eye, and Martha smiled and nodded.

"I know, Major, I know. And Francisco always did love you, too. He always thought of you as a father."

Henry cleared his throat again and said in a voice hardly audible: "Well, I'd have been proud to have had a son like him..."

John Henry drew a quick hard breath of the cold January air, barely noticing the pain as it filled his aching lungs. There was a bigger ache inside of him, buried deep in his chest, where his heart felt like it was breaking.

"Your father loves you," his mother had said, *"more than he even knows..."*

But he'd loved Francisco more.

Chapter Seventeen

Griffin, 1873

He'd expected cursing when he told his father about selling off his inheritance and he got plenty of it, even though there was nothing Henry's chastisement could do to change things. The Iron Front building was sold and gone and Mr. Phillips had no intention of giving it back. What he hadn't expected was his father's grudging approval of his plan to open a dental practice in Griffin where he could keep himself close to Francisco's family. Henry said it was the first grown decision John Henry had ever made, and about time he took responsibility for himself and his career – not a compliment exactly, but better than the criticism he'd been prepared for.

Mattie, however, was not as happy about his move to Griffin. She would miss him terribly, she said, and made him promise to come back to visit as often as he could. And when she cried at his leaving, John Henry felt a bittersweet mix of emotions – sorry to be causing her any pain, glad to know that she cared about him so. But until she was out of mourning there was nothing much he could do about his feelings, or hers. So he kissed her on the cheek, like a good cousin, and took himself off to Griffin.

While the money he'd made from selling the Iron Front was no great fortune, it was enough to support him and outfit his office. And since he'd arranged with Mr. Phillips to leave a portion of the upstairs floor of the building available for his own use, his office rent came free. There was some expense in getting the space ready for dentistry, however. He had to hire a carpenter to put up board walls to enclose his corner of the second floor, separating it from the main room where Phillips planned to have his saloon. He had to hire a brick mason to turn the west window of the space into a doorway, with a narrow iron staircase going up from the alleyway beside the building to make a private entrance. But once completed, his little office was more than adequate to his professional needs, with two long windows facing south across Solomon Street to let in sufficient light. When the furnishings were ordered and delivered, he had a respectable dental office, though he still couldn't afford the expensive equipment he was accustomed to using in Dr. Ford's office. Instead of the heavy cast-iron dental chair, he had to make do with a headrest attached to a wooden armchair, and his tools were stored in something less than a glass-fronted rosewood cabinet. But he did have enough money left to buy one of the new belt-driven Morrison Dental Engine drills, a box of gold foil, and jars of porcelain powder – and even to have his name painted in large black letters on the window overlooking Solomon Street, and *J.H. Holliday, D.D.S.* was in business at last.

There were several nice boarding houses in Griffin and two first class hotels, but as he had relatives who owned property in town, he didn't have to spend much on his living expenses. His Uncle Tom was part owner of a little cottage on Broad Street, just across from the tracks of the Macon and Western Railroad. The cottage happened to be vacant at the time, so John Henry had the good fortune of getting a house to himself for less than the cost of a boarding house room. Of course, a house didn't include meals the way a boarding house did, but some of the saloons near the depot had lunch counters so he was able to keep himself fed and watered at the same time and play a few card games as well. But he was careful not to drink or wager too freely in public. He had a reputation to make in Griffin if he expected to build a profitable dental practice.

As he had promised Francisco, he visited in Jenkinsburg often, spending nearly every Sunday with the Hidalgo family. He'd arrive just after they returned from morning services at County Line Baptist Church, then stay on for dinner and sometimes supper as well. Martha and the children seemed to appreciate his visits, and he enjoyed the rides out from Griffin so much that the obligation actually became pleasant. For though he still refused to consider himself a farm boy and declined to help with the plowing and planting, he was country boy enough to love the freedom of riding across that quiet countryside.

There was another ride he made often while living there in Griffin, and another promise he had to keep, so when he wasn't working or visiting with Francisco's family, he rode out past town to Rest Haven Cemetery, where he pulled the weeds from his sister Martha Eleanora's grave and made sure her small gravestone was swept clean.

It was a solitary life he had fallen into, but he found he didn't mind it all that much. After sharing a room with his cousins in Atlanta, the privacy was refreshing, giving him space to think and breathe again. For much as he enjoyed the excitements of a city, he was discovering that he needed his quiet, too. When he and Mattie married, they might even live away out in the country like the Hidalgos did – though he had no intention of actually farming the land. He should have been born in the plantation days of his Grandfather McKey, when slave labor did the farm work and the master of the house spent his days riding and shooting and making love to his wife.

The thought of lovemaking had become something of an obsession with him, having to hold himself back as he was from his plans of marriage, so it wasn't surprising when his circumscribed thoughts turned themselves into dreams from time to time, and he awoke knowing that he'd spent the night imagining Mattie in his arms and in his bed. As long as the dreams were dreams of Mattie they didn't bother him too much. But now and then, he dreamed it was a girl with a tumble of black hair who took his kisses and returned his caresses, a girl who called him "Johnny" and told him that she'd done this plenty of times before. And sometimes the girl would turn into someone else, a wild gypsy-woman with eyes like the ocean and a voice that sounded like music.

His dreams of Kate Fisher left him feeling guilty on awakening, as if he had any control over what he dreamed. But did he need to enjoy the dreams so much, waking with a hunger to be asleep and dreaming all over again? He'd left her in St. Louis and never looked back, and it was unsettling to find himself thinking of her again when he had no conscious desire to be. But once Mattie's mourning was over and they were finally wed, those dreams would be gone, he knew. It was only the waiting that was causing his dreams to be so confused, putting Kate where Mattie ought to be.

~~~~~~~~~~

In April, he received a wire from Dr. Ford inviting him to attend the annual meeting of the Georgia Dental Society to be held at the Rankin House Hotel in Columbus. Dr. Ford himself would be the featured speaker, demonstrating the new Morrison Dental Engine, and he could use the help of an assistant familiar with the equipment. John Henry wrote back that he would be honored to attend, and he was.

Columbus was the westernmost city in Georgia and the northernmost port city on the Chattahoochee River. Paddle-wheel steamboats plied their way up from the Gulf of Mexico, along the Apalachicola River in Florida to the Chattahoochee, carrying cotton from the inland plantations to the Columbus textile mills where fabric and finished clothing were made. At the height of the War, Columbus had been home to the largest cotton mills in the South and supplier of uniform materials and iron works to the Confederate Army. Since then, business in the city of 20,000 had dropped off some, but the riverfront was still smoky with the stacks of cotton mills and crowded with cotton warehouses.

John Henry knew something else of the place from the stories his father had told him of the Creek Indian Wars in the early decades of the century. Columbus had been called Coweta Town then, chief city of the Creek Nation that stretched from the Atlantic Ocean across the Chattahoochee and into Alabama. The Creeks had been a peaceable people at first, trading with the white men who came to settle in their green paradise. But as more and more white men came, the Creeks grew defensive of their land and war erupted. Henry Holliday had been a young man then, and eagerly left his Fayetteville home to go fight against the Indian threat, sending the Creeks on their Trail of Tears into the Oklahoma Territory. For his gallantry in service, Henry Holliday was made a Second Lieutenant, and started out on the proud military career that had taken him across the continent and back.

The Indians were gone from Coweta Town now, and Columbus had risen in its place: a white man's city of neatly laid out streets and soaring real estate prices. The Merchants and Mechanics Bank, one of the first to be organized after the war, had just opened its doors and helped to fund grand new building projects like the Rankin House Hotel that filled half a city block with fifty sleeping rooms, private baths, and a skating rink and ballroom on the second floor. With its spacious lobby and wrought iron balconies, its excellent restaurant and indoor plumbing, the Rankin was a popular resort for guests from all around the South. It was one of the most elegant hotels John Henry had ever stayed in and he hoped his studied nonchalance wouldn't give him away. As the youngest and least experienced dentist at the meeting, he felt a little overwhelmed by the company and the accommodations both.

Dr. Ford, however, seemed right at home at the Rankin House and the Dental Society meeting being held there, and his proper English accent somehow made others defer to him, which John Henry found both amusing and irritating. The bellboys and busboys had only to hear Dr. Ford say something trivial like, "I dare say, could you take that for me?" and they jumped to do his bidding, whereas John Henry's drawled "Y'all carry those on up now," hardly got any response at all.

Even the other members of the Georgia Dental Society deferred to Dr. Ford, giving him the floor whenever he had a comment on the long and tedious business proceedings. John Henry was surprised to find that there was so much business to conduct. He'd assumed that the meeting would be more like his days at the Pennsylvania College of Dental Surgery, mostly lectures and clinical work. But for the better part of two days, the dentists read and discussed the new Georgia Dental Practice Act, elected a Board of Examiners, voted in a new constitution and by-laws for the Society, and debated whether to endow a southern dental college. Then came the reading of scholarly papers, and by the time the final session came to a close, John Henry was bored and restless. If he'd wanted to be a lawyer or a legislator, he wouldn't have bothered going to dental school in the first place. It was the art of dentistry he enjoyed, the meticulous handwork in gold and porcelain, and not the business end of things. So on the last evening of the convention he excused himself, saying that he was feeling a little under the weather and needed some air after the long indoor meetings. Let Dr. Ford carry on with the business proceedings; he wanted to find what Columbus offered in the way of amusements.

The new Springer Opera House, just across the dirt street from the Rankin Hotel, was billed as the finest theater between New York and New Orleans, though from the looks of it there was more than theater going on there. The first floor shared space between an open-air market, indoor shops, and a first-class saloon. The only problem with the Opera House Saloon was that there was no card playing allowed.

"No Sir," the bartender told John Henry as he slid a shot glass of whiskey across the polished wood bar. "The Springer is a fine establishment, as you can see by them black and white marble floors in the lobby. The theater's up on the second floor. Third floor's the hotel. But there's no gamblin' goin' on, no Sir. Not that I'm opposed to a little wagerin' myself. But Mr. Springer's anti-gamblin', so he keeps it out of his house. Plenty of other entertainment here, even so. Mr. Springer's talking about bringin' in Buffalo Bill Cody and his Indian show, maybe even Mr. Edwin Booth one of these days. But if it's cards you're after, there's a couple of places I know about. The Villa Reich, down by the waterfront, usually has a game goin', but it's local gentry mostly, and hard to get into. Your best bet's across the river, over into Alabama. City fathers try to keep the sporting men out of Columbus, so most of the gamblin' dens and bordellos are over there across the Chattahoochee, in Girard. The 'Sodom of the South' they call it. Don't suppose they ever considered that makes us Gomorrah, and near as bad."

There was a lingering chill in the air that April evening, and the wind gusting over the river felt more like winter than early spring. Even with the wide collar of his wool suit coat turned up against the cold, John Henry couldn't stop shivering as he wandered down to the waterfront, past the Columbus Iron Works building and the cotton warehouses to the low bluffs of the Chattahoochee. The river was only four-hundred yards wide at the Dillingham Street covered bridge, the green waters skimming over rocky shoals and flowing slowly down towards Florida. Upriver from the bridge, where the fall line turned the water turbulent, rose the smokestacks of the Eagle and Phoenix Cotton Mill. Downriver, where the Chattahoochee widened between wooded banks, were the brick and stone wharves of the paddle-wheeled riverboats. As the bridge divided the river north from south, it also connected the two riverfronts of Georgia and Alabama: the Georgia side bustling with the business of cotton and iron, the Alabama side busy in its own less reputable way.

He heard Sodom calling to him before he was halfway across the Dillingham Street bridge. The raucous sound of saloon pianos and women's laughter floated across the river like a siren song and echoed eerily through the tunnel of the covered bridge. But as he came out on the Alabama side, he was struck by how dark things remained. There were no gas lamps in Girard to light the narrow alleyways, no oyster shell sidewalks like there were in Columbus. The whole town was only a block or two across in any direction, with more saloons than any other business establishment. Other than one general store, the town's only commerce seemed to be debauchery.

As he'd already had that one shot glass of whiskey at the Opera House Saloon, getting into the rhythm of Girard didn't take him long. The liquor was bitter but cheap and the games penny-ante, so between the whiskey and the cards, he just about broke even on the evening.

It was past midnight when he started back toward Columbus, the stars reflecting off the dark waters of the Chattahoochee. In the distance, he could hear the blast of a riverboat's horn, and the slap and spill of its paddle-wheel churning the water. Intrigued by the sound, he stopped at the river's edge and stood waiting for the steamer to pull out of the shadows and into sight as it neared the stone wharves. It was a big boat, with a wheel that looked to be nearly thirty feet across and with the fitting name of *The Wave* painted across the starboard side. But as he watched the riverboat drift near to the wharf, the motion of the paddle-wheel seemed to seize him and all at once his head started spinning like the wheel. Around and around, reflecting off the water, spinning, turning again...

He swayed on his feet, reached out to grab ahold of something to steady himself, but found nothing but the night air. Then the swaying turned into a burning in his chest, and he started to cough and was overtaken by a fit of vomiting, throwing up whiskey and everything else he'd downed that day. He should have known by the taste of it that it was nothing but root whiskey they sold in Girard, made with slop water from behind some Alabama outhouse. But he didn't have time to ponder on the thought before another fit overtook him and he fell to his knees in the dirt, retching like a sick animal.

It was awhile before he could push himself to his feet again, wipe the filth from his mouth onto his linen handkerchief, and drag himself back across the covered bridge toward Columbus. The four-hundred yards felt more like a thousand now, the way his chest burned with every breath, and he had to keep stopping to steady himself while he wheezed. The fact that his handkerchief was stained with a smear of blood didn't bother him nearly as much as the stench of vomit that clung to it. His whole insides felt like they'd been torn apart, between the retching and the burning of the rot gut as it came back up, so it was no wonder there was a little blood. And as he stumbled along Front Street toward the Rankin House Hotel, he vowed he'd never trust himself to cheap liquor again.

~~~~~~~~~~~~

His sleep was troubled that night, full of strange dreams. There was a river with dark waters and tangled undergrowth, grasping at him and trying to pull him in. There was a girl with golden eyes, reaching out to rescue him. Then the girl's eyes turned liquid as the water, and she laughed with the sound of saloon pianos, taunting him. And hovering somewhere on the edge of his dreaming was a pain that made him moan in his sleep.

He finally awoke with such a hangover that he had to excuse himself from the closing session of the dental meeting, staying in bed past noon and only getting up in time to meet Dr. Ford for the train ride back north. But sick as he was, the sudden illness had given him a new determination to speak his mind to Mattie. If she'd been there with him, he would never have been tempted to stray across the Chattahoochee. If she'd been there, he would never have been so restless in the first place. And though it would still be some time before they could marry, he had waited long enough to ask for her hand.

Chapter Eighteen

Atlanta, 1873

It had been four months since he'd moved to Griffin, and going back to Atlanta for a weekend visit felt like a real reunion, especially when Mattie was smiling so happily at seeing him again. And even though she was still in mourning for another month and limited in her social relations, she was no longer swathed in somber black cloth and heavy veils, and the muted grays and mauves of half-mourning flattered the delicacy of her own coloring, making her cheeks seem rosy and her eyes glowing. But it wasn't just seeing John Henry again that was cheering her up. Her family was thinking of moving up from Jonesboro too, now that her father was gone.

"Mother says she could let the house for rent, and find a place to live here in Atlanta close to Uncle John and Aunt Permelia. She's not used to doin' without a man around to help out, and Jim Bob needs someone to be a father to him. And it would be wonderful to have the family all back together again – all except for my father, of course."

Her eyes misted over as she remembered him, but the constant tears were gone.

"And how is Francisco's family doin'?" she asked, as she and John Henry sat together in the parlor of Uncle John's house, catching up on the news.

"Better than he thought they'd do, I reckon. Martha does have some family out that way, and between them and me, we keep an eye on things. But I doubt I'm the father figure Francisco hoped I'd be. The boys treat me more like an older brother or an uncle, like Tom McKey was to me. But it's somethin', I suppose. And I have enjoyed bein' back in Griffin again, though it's mighty quiet livin' alone..."

He could solve his loneliness, of course, by marrying Mattie. All he needed was some sign from her that she was ready to entertain a proposal of marriage, and he would offer one. The setting was right for it, he thought, with Mattie sitting prettily on the horsehair sofa. All he had to do was slip down on one knee, look up at her with earnest eyes...

"Are you sure you're feelin' well?" she asked him, and he realized that he had been silent in his thoughts.

"I'm fine, Mattie, just thinkin', that's all." Now if she would just ask what he'd been thinking about...

"You're lookin' a little peaked to me," she said, ruining the moment. "You haven't had that fever back, have you? I have worried over you every day, since you took so sick in Jonesboro."

"Aw, Mattie," he said, touched by her concern, "don't you worry. I'm just fine, as I said. You know I've had a hard time since I took the pneumonia up in Philadelphia, and this past year hasn't helped any, what with all the travelin' on trains and movin' around. But I have an idea of what might help put an end to all the travelin'..."

He was just about to take his place on one knee and make his pretty proposal before she could pull him off the subject again, when Sophie put her head in the door.

"Suppertime, Miss Mattie, Mist' John Henry. Don't be slow."

Mattie nodded and smoothed her skirts as she stood. Then she turned to him and smiled. "Was there somethin' else you wanted to say to me, honey?"

She was looking at him so sweetly, her eyes full of honest affection, that he almost asked her to marry him right then. But Sophie was still standing in the doorway, waiting for them both.

"I reckon it can wait," he said with a sigh. It had waited for months, and years, already. Surely, another hour or two could hardly make much difference.

~~~~~~~~~

Aunt Permelia was even more interested in his health than Mattie had been, and spent most of the supper hour discussing the topic, noting that he seemed to have lost some weight since he'd been living on his own.

"Though you always were frail," she finally admitted as the dishes were being cleared away. "Of course, that was because of your difficult time as a newborn. Your mother told you about how your Uncle John and I went down to Griffin when you were just a baby, to mend that poor misshapen lip of yours, didn't she?"

"Yes, Aunt, she told me."

"And she told you how we all worked with you to learn to speak properly, after the surgery? Why, the whole family took you on as a special project, teachin' you to talk. Of course, we all lived close together back then, and could help each other out

306

more than we can now. The worst thing to come of the War, in my mind, is how we've all scattered across the country so. It seems family just doesn't mean what it used to, when everyone stayed close by for generations and generations. Why, if the Yankees hadn't made a ruin of Fayette County, we'd still be there, I'm sure, livin' in our lovely home. This one is much larger, of course, and more stylish, but that was our first, where the boys were little, so it holds special memories for me. Well, listen to me go on! Really, once I get started, I just don't know when to stop!"

John Henry didn't mind her chattering, especially when she talked of things he knew about: his family, his old hometown, the house he had spent time in as a child. Aunt Permelia, with all her talk, was a walking library of family history. What he did mind was her insisting that his uncle take a look at him.

"Just a little examination, dear," his aunt said as she led him into his uncle's dark-paneled study after supper. "Your mother would have wanted it, had she been here, rest her soul. You know how she always fussed over you. Of course she did, as you were her only livin' child and she'd lost her first baby in that awful way. Now you go on and talk to your uncle a bit. It won't hurt any, I promise!"

Uncle John smiled as he pulled the pocket doors closed, separating the study from the hallway beyond. Although he bore some resemblance to his older brother Henry, with the same strong chin and steady gaze, Uncle John had none of Henry Holliday's brusque manner, and he said amiably:

"Best nurse I ever had, your Aunt Permelia. Always made the patients happy to get in to see me, just to get some peace and quiet! So tell me, how long do we get the pleasure of your company, John Henry?"

"Only until Sunday mornin', Sir. I'm expected in Jenkinsburg for supper Sunday evenin', and it's five hours on the train and an hour on horseback between here and there. I try to visit with Francisco's family on a regular basis."

"I'm sure they appreciate that," his uncle said with an approving nod. "And how is the practice goin'?"

"It's growin', Sir. I have a good location, and that helps."

"Location's the most important thing for a professional man. I had my Fayetteville office in my home, right off the town square where I could be convenient to things. You used to like to help me there when you were a boy, always askin' questions, wantin' to know how things worked." He laughed as he remembered. "The skull drill fascinated you most of all, as I recall. You used to offer to do the drillin' for me, should the need ever arise. Not surprisin' you went into dentistry, seein' as how you loved that drill."

"Dentistry's a little different than brain surgery, Uncle John. The drill's a whole lot smaller, for one thing."

His uncle knew that, of course, having done simple dental procedures as part of his general medical practice. But Uncle John liked to tease a little, to relax his patients before an examination. John Henry had seen him do it plenty of times, as a child spying from the other room. And as if to underscore the casualness of the conversation, Uncle John settled down into his favorite leather armchair and lit up a cigar.

"Your aunt tells me she's concerned for your health, seein' how you've gotten thinner in the past few months. Not unusual, though, without a woman to do the cookin' for you."

"No sir," John Henry replied, and smiled at the thought that before too long he'd have a woman to do his cooking, and whatever else he needed.

"I don't need to tell you how important it is to eat properly, especially when you're workin' long hours indoors. If you find your appetite isn't good, try takin' some exercise, get some fresh air."

"I walk to work and back," John Henry said in his own defense, "and ride whenever I can afford to hire a horse. But my office is stuffy, I'll give you that."

"Well, it's not unusual for a young man to lose some weight, first goin' out on his own. How are you feelin', other than that?"

"Fine now, Sir, though I had another bout of the pneumonia at Christmastime, when Uncle Rob passed. I took that long ride in the ice storm..."

"Ah, yes," his uncle said sadly. "That was a fine sacrifice you made, comin' to Atlanta to let us know about Rob. Not surprisin' you took sick yourself, after an exertion like that." He took a long draw on the cigar, letting the smoke slide out in easy circles. "And since then? Have you had any more of those coughin' spells?"

John Henry took a long moment before answering. In the silence, the mantle clock seemed to tick in time to his heartbeat. Should he confess how sick he'd taken in Columbus? If he did, would he have to explain where he'd found that bad moonshine? While his uncle didn't mind a little drinking, his intemperance would surely bring a censure. But he had, indeed, been very ill...

"No, Sir," he lied. "I've been hale and hearty ever since. So you see Aunt Permelia has nothin' to worry herself about. And Sophie promises to fatten me up again, as long as I keep comin' up to visit."

"Which we hope you do often." But the conversation wasn't quite over, as Uncle

John took another draw on the cigar, then spoke with sudden solemnity. "You know your mother passed from the consumption?"

"Yessir."

"And we find that, sometimes, the consumption runs in families..."

"Yessir."

There was another draw on the cigar, another ring of smoke settling into the air before he went on. "I want you to take special care of yourself, John Henry. Make sure you get enough sleep, enough nutritious food. Get out of your office whenever you can and walk, or ride if you prefer. And let me know if that cough and fever of Christmastime comes back. If you start to wheezin', or ever cough up anything red, you let me know. I'll take a listen to your chest, just to make sure everything is clear in there."

And hearing the concern in his uncle's voice, John Henry almost told him the truth after all: that he'd coughed up blood with the whiskey down there in Columbus, that he'd been wheezing nearly every morning since. But he really was feeling so much better, other than the shortness of breath when he walked up the long hill to his office, that he didn't want to worry his uncle unnecessarily. He'd be in Atlanta often enough from now on, so there'd be plenty of time for a real examination if the need ever arose. But there wouldn't need to be any examination. With the summer soon at hand, there was little chance of his coming down with the pneumonia again, and surely that was the cause of his breathing trouble – that and tainted whiskey.

"I appreciate your advice, Uncle John," he said politely. "But I think it's corpulence you'll need to treat me for, not consumption, if Sophie has her way."

Uncle John laughed at that, the levity breaking the tension in the room.

"And Sophie always has her way around here, I am afraid to say. I have proven to be a poor master of my own household, the way I let the women run things. Not like your father. There's no question who's the head of Henry's home. He's a fine man, your father. You're lucky to be his son."

"Yessir," John Henry replied heavily. "I'm lucky, all right."

~~~~~~~~~~

Though he'd tried to show no trace of emotion, his uncle's words had troubled him. He knew he wasn't sick, not like his mother and Francisco had been sick, but it was true that he coughed and wheezed and felt tired much of the time. He blamed it on bad whiskey, but even on days when he hadn't had a drop to drink, the tiredness lingered on. He blamed it on overwork; he blamed it on slim meals at the Griffin saloons; he blamed it on loneliness even. But he wouldn't let himself blame it on illness. As his father had taught him, illness was weakness, and he was not weak...

He tried to push the thoughts of sickness from his mind, and thoughts of his father rushed in to take their place. He was a fine man, Uncle John had said, a man one should be lucky to count as a father. Francisco had counted himself lucky, though Henry was only his foster father. But how lucky was Francisco when he died before his time? And how lucky was John Henry if he were indeed sick like Francisco?

The thoughts swirled around in his mind, and the only conclusion he could come to was that he needed a drink, and the silver pocket flask Phillips had given him was gone dry. A little whiskey would settle his unsettled thoughts and make the sudden aching in his chest go away as well. But it wasn't his lungs that were giving him trouble, as Uncle John had suggested, but his heart, down deep inside.

Though supper was over and it was growing dusk, Aunt Permelia seemed to believe his excuse that he needed to go downtown to check on some business at Dr. Ford's office. He didn't even bother making excuses to Mattie. She would know it was something more distressing than business, just by looking at him. So without even saying goodbye to her, he put on his coat and hat and walked the eight blocks from Forrest Avenue to Whitehall Street and the Maison de Ville, where Lee Smith was pouring the drinks himself that Friday evening, and greeted John Henry by name.

"Young Holliday! Haven't seen you around in a while. Welcome!"

"I've been workin' down in Griffin, Mr. Smith. Whiskey, please."

Lee Smith pulled a tumbler from the glass shelves behind him, poured it half full of dark amber liquor, and slid it across the bar.

"Haven't been down to Griffin myself much lately," Smith said. "Been real busy here at the Maison, and plannin' my next big adventure."

John Henry picked up the tumbler and considered it a moment before holding it to his lips. Though he knew the Maison stocked only the best liquors, his experience in Alabama had made him wary.

Lee Smith, seeming to sense his hesitation, laughed out loud. "Best whiskey in Atlanta, Holliday. Straight up one-hundred-twenty proof Tennessee bourbon. A couple of those and you'll be so drunk you won't be able to walk home. But that's no problem. For a price, I can hire you a cab. You can pay now, to save yourself the trouble later, if you'd like."

310

"I won't be needin' the cab," John Henry said as he put the tumbler to his lips and let the whiskey slide down his throat, sweet and smooth as liquid fire. "I'm only in for a shot or two. So what's your next big adventure, anyhow?"

And with that, Lee Smith proceeded to tell him all about a banking deal he'd set his hopes on. It seemed the firm of Jay Cook and Company was backing the railroad boom and looking for investors. "Gonna make me some money in that deal, sure enough," Smith said. " 'Course it'll cost me a pretty penny to get into the game."

"Sounds more like a wager than an investment," John Henry commented, finishing the whiskey too fast and pushing the tumbler back toward Smith.

"Well, I reckon there's some wager to it," Lee Smith said, as he refilled John Henry's glass. "But it's not as risky as a card game, anyhow. You play cards, you've got nothin' but your own cunning to rely on. Jay Cook's a financial institution. Those bankers know what they're doin', and if they're willin' to put their own money into the pot, sounds safe enough to me. Let you young men wager on cards. I'm puttin' my money into the railroads!" Then he nodded across the room to where a poker game was just getting underway. "Looks like they could use an extra hand, if you've got the time."

John Henry had as long as his supposed errand would take, and maybe a little more, before he was expected back at his uncle's house. Enough time for a quick hand, or maybe two...

"And I believe I'll have another whiskey, as well," he said, as he pushed the tumbler across the bar again. "That's smooth stuff, all right. Best liquor I've had in months."

Lee Smith laughed. "Well, you've been away from the Maison too long!"

It was good liquor, all right, as potent as Smith had claimed, and by the end of three fast hands of poker he could hardly remember why he'd walked downtown in the first place. His uncle's worries over his health hardly bothered him at all anymore, and he let the talk of his father just slip from his mind entirely.

~~~~~~~~~~

Lee Smith offered to hail him a horse-drawn cab as the streetcars had stopped running at midnight, but John Henry insisted that he was still quite able to walk back to Forrest Avenue. Besides, the walk would help to clear his cloudy mind. Though the liquor had loosed the painful thoughts that had plagued him, it only seemed to sharpen his thoughts of Mattie, and he was intent on speaking to her as soon as possible — that very night even, if he got a chance.

He thought about his proposal all the way back home to his Uncle's house as he walked along under the gaslamps of Peachtree Street, and tried to think just how he'd say the words. He imagined himself like a player in some romantic drama, something Shakespearean perhaps, climbing balconies and flinging roses to catch his love's attention, though there was no balcony on his uncle's house and the green roses were too thorny to pick safely. And by the time he reached the long hill that led from Oak Street to Forrest Avenue, he felt like a player in some Shakespearean play himself, like the *Hamlet* he had taken Mattie to see at the Opera House.

Hamlet seemed the answer somehow, and as he stumbled along rutted Forrest Avenue, he began quoting from the play, finding himself to be very amusing. He was still reciting as he stepped out of the shadows and headed into the gravel drive, and self-absorbed as he was he didn't notice a slender white figure standing alone on the front porch.

"Who's there?" the figure asked, alarmed. "Who's that out there?"

But when she spoke, John Henry recognized Mattie's sweet voice.

"I am a poor player, madam," he answered, "here to win your heart," then he made a crooked, courtly bow.

"John Henry?" Mattie asked.

"Ah! She knows her lover's voice!"

"What are you doin' out there in the night air? You'll make yourself sick again..."

"Better die of night air than die longin' for your love, lady."

"You've been drinkin'!"

"I could accuse me of such things," he said, still quoting Hamlet. "I am very proud, revengeful, ambitious..." He stopped suddenly. "Where is your father?"

"My father is passed, John Henry, you know that. You were at his funeral."

"Oh yes, faithful old Polonius who would deny me my love. Well, rest his soul. But thou art honest, lady, and very fair."

"You are talkin' nonsense and makin' a spectacle of yourself."

"I may be a spectacle, but I am only talkin' a little nonsense. Will you miss me, my dear Ophelia, when I am off to England?"

"England?"

"Well, only Griffin, but will you still miss me nonetheless? Will you hang from willow trees, heartsick for my company?"

"I wish you would go off and stop actin' like such a fool."

"But I am not actin'. Tonight I am a fool, Mattie Holliday. Fool in love with you!"

And as she shook her head and turned to go back into the house, John Henry took four fast steps and bounded up onto the porch, amazed himself that he didn't trip and fall.

"Oh, don't go in, Mattie!" he said, breathing hard and leaning on the porch rail. "There's somethin' I have to ask you."

"All right," she said, turning back toward him. "What is it?"

He could hardly see her eyes in the darkness but her skin was glowing like moonlight, and he took a step closer and touched his hand to her face. "Say you'll marry me, sweet Ophelia, for you know how I love you."

She was very quiet for a moment. "I know you are out of your head and not thinkin' clearly."

"Thinkin' has nothing to do with it. It's here," he said, taking hold of her hand and laying it against his chest, "in my heart. In my very heart."

"Why are you playin' this game with me?"

"There is no game, my lady," he said, "I am speakin' from my heart. Look into my eyes and say you don't see the love there."

"I don't see anything but too much liquor. Your eyes are all red from drinkin'." But she kept her hand on his chest and let him pull her closer until he was gazing down into her face. And as he held her, he could feel her trembling against him.

"Say you love me, Mattie!" he said, his voice breaking with sudden emotion.

"You are talkin' crazy. Let go of me and let me breathe some clean air."

"Say it, Mattie!" he said again, bending his head and brushing his lips against her neck.

"Please, I..."

"Say it!" he whispered roughly, kissing the base of her throat and feeling the quick intake of her breath.

"It is the liquor talkin'..."

"Always, Mattie," he whispered against her skin, "I have always loved you!" Then he put his mouth to hers, unwilling to wait any longer for her answer, and she shivered in his arms and opened her lips to his kiss...

"Dear God! What do you think you're doin'?" said a sharp voice, and John Henry looked up in surprise.

Robert stood in the dark doorway, one hand on the brass knob, one hand clenched into a fist. "Get in the house, Mattie. Go now."

"You don't understand, Robert," she said hurriedly, "he's been drinkin'..."

"Yes, I can smell the liquor on him. I'm surprised you can stand to be near him. What are you doin' out here in your nightdress, anyhow?"

She pulled her white gown around her in sudden modesty. "I was just lookin' to see if John Henry was comin' home. He's been gone so long."

"Well, he's certainly home now, and disgustingly drunk. Have you no decency at all, either one of you?"

"It wasn't what you think!" she protested. "We were just talkin'..."

"Then you can continue your conversation in the daylight. Now go inside, Mattie."

"Don't tell her what to do, Robert!" John Henry said, trying not to slur his words. "She hasn't done anything wrong."

"No thanks to you. Have you lost your mind entirely?"

"He didn't hurt me, Robert," Mattie said softly.

"Surely you're not defendin' him! Look at him, Mattie, he's fallin'-down drunk."

"I'm not all that drunk, Robert," he protested, leaning back against the porch rail to steady himself. "I'm still sober enough to take you on, if you want a fight."

Robert let the door close behind him and stepped out onto the porch. "You'd like that, wouldn't you? You've been wantin' to make a fight with me for months now. Well, let's get to it then, right now. It would give me pleasure to knock some sense into you."

"Stop it!" Mattie cried, "Stop it at once, both of you!"

But Robert paid her no attention. "What was that nonsense you were saying out here? Poetry?"

"Shakespeare," John Henry answered smugly. "Didn't they teach you anything in that wonderful private school of yours? At least I know the classics, even when I've been drinkin'. Shall I do some for you?" And feeling quite proud of himself, he started into Hamlet's soliloquy:

"To be or not to be..."

Robert shook his head. "What did I tell you, Mattie? Crazy drunk."

"...To die - to sleep,
No more; and by a sleep to say we end
The heart-ache and the thousand natural shocks
That flesh is heir to: 'tis a – consummation..."

And that suddenly struck him as funny somehow, and he coughed once and started to laugh, until he saw the stricken look on Mattie's face.

"You didn't mean a word you said to me, did you?" she whispered.

314

"Oh, but I did, honey, I meant everything..." But though he felt quite sincere, he couldn't seem to stop laughing. "I do love you, Mattie!" he said between laughs, and when he took a step toward her his legs went wobbly under him and he lurched into Robert instead.

"Of course you do," Robert said, bracing him up. "Now go on inside, Mattie, and hold the door. I think Romeo here is about to pass out."

"*Hamlet*," John Henry mumbled as he leaned against Robert. "It was *Hamlet*..."

"Yes, we're very impressed. And maybe when you're sober again you can do some Gilbert and Sullivan for us, as well."

And that struck John Henry as very funny too and he started to laugh again. But Mattie was not laughing, and there was a shimmer in her eyes that looked like tears as she quietly opened the front door and stepped into the gaslight glow of the hall.

~~~~~~~~~~

It took him a full day to get completely sober again, and when he did come to his senses, the memory of the night hung on like a bad dream. It had been a fool, drunken thing to do, letting his feelings for Mattie out like that. No, not letting them out — forcing them on her. But hadn't she shivered and sighed in his arms when he'd bent to kiss her? Surely, surely she must love him too.

Come Sunday morning, he was feeling like himself again and ready to make his apology to Mattie – and to tell her that, drunk as he was, he really had meant what he'd said. He loved her and wanted her to be his wife, even if they had to wait another half a year to announce their plans to the world. But when he went out to the barn to hitch up the horse and buggy so that he could offer to drive her to Sunday Mass, there was no buggy to hitch.

"Already gone to church," the little stable boy explained. "Miss Mattie went real early today, nigh before daybreak. Drove herself on in, though I said I'd be pleased to do it. But you know how she makes up her mind. 'No,' she tells me. 'I'll be goin' alone today.' I didn't dare tell her she shouldn't ought to do that, she seemed so set on drivin' herself. Said she'd be back late, too. Guess she had some mighty big prayin' to do."

John Henry turned away in confusion. Of course Mattie knew how to handle a horse and buggy; as the oldest child in her family, she'd been trained early to a whip and reins. It was her leaving so early that concerned him, for Sunday morning Mass didn't begin until eight o'clock. What had taken her to town so early? And would she even return before he had to catch the noon train to Griffin?

"Saddle me a horse," he commanded the stable boy. "I'll be ridin' into town myself."

"Can't do that, Mist' John Henry, Sir. Miss Mattie, she took the runabout with one of the horses. And Dr. Holliday, he took the phaeton with two other horses. And Mist' Robert, he rode on in to Church on his own horse, so they ain't no more horses for me to saddle. And it bein' Sunday, they ain't no streetcars runnin', neither. Guess you'll just have to walk, Mist' John Henry."

He was in no mood for walking, though the morning was fine and warm. But walking took longer than riding, and by the time he got himself downtown, Mass would be nearly over. Still, that was where Mattie was, and he needed to see her before he left for Griffin and lost the entire weekend – or worse, left her with only his drunken proclamation as a proposal. There was nothing to be done but walk, so he put on his hat and headed out the graveled drive, cursing to himself that the Sunday shine on his leather boots would be dirtied with road dust soon. Bad enough to have to walk, without having to appear in town looking like a pauper too poor to hire a horse.

~~~~~~~~~~

He could see the Church of the Immaculate Conception for blocks before he reached it, the square towers rising on the horizon like a bastion of Catholicism in the middle of Protestant Atlanta. Even the spired sanctuaries of the nearby Central Presbyterian and Second Baptist, though they housed much larger congregations, looked like simple country chapels compared to the gothic grandeur of the nearly completed Catholic Church. Its walls were solidly built of granite and red brick, its towers twenty-two feet square, its windows filled with stained glass depictions of Saints and sinners. After four years of construction only the interior needed to be completed, with its muraled ceiling and ornate chandeliers and pews to seat a thousand communicants. It would be some time before there were that many Catholics in Atlanta, but the Church would be ready for them when they came.

If John Henry had his way, the parish would grow by one new convert soon enough. His Uncle Rob had converted before his own marriage to Mattie's mother, and they'd been a happy couple until his untimely death. In the Holliday family, it was always the women who chose the religion and made sure their husbands and children stayed faithful to it. John Henry had been a faithful Methodist for his mother; surely he could become a faithful Catholic for Mattie.

Though the new sanctuary was nearly completed, Mass was still held in the basement chapel, and John Henry stepped quietly down the stone stairs, and opened the heavy doors just enough to peer into the smoky shadows. Father Duggan, gowned in white robes and vestments, stood at the wooden altar with his hands outstretched. He was speaking in Latin, and when the parishioners joined in, John Henry recognized the words. It was the Lord's Prayer, spoken at the beginning of the Holy Communion, and he mouthed the words along with the rest of the congregation while his eyes searched the rows for Mattie. But it was impossible to tell one woman from another, with their heads all covered and bowed reverently, so he'd have to wait until the Communion service was over before he could find her.

He knew the order of the Mass, having attended church with Mattie many times before. Following the Lord's Prayer there would be the breaking of the bread, the Agnus Dei, the responses, the communion, the final prayers, the blessing of the faithful. It was always the same in some ways, always different in others, as the prayers changed with the changing of the Church calendar. And though much of it was still a mystery to John Henry, there was something comforting about the repetition of the rituals, as if this one thing were immutable.

Then, as the communicants rose to approach the altar to receive the Holy Communion, he saw her. She was dressed in her mourning gray, her auburn hair covered with a chapel veil, her gloved hands pressed together prayerfully, her head bowed as she walked. And for an eerie moment, John Henry had the impression that he was looking not at his beloved Mattie, but at some cloistered nun hidden under a somber habit and stepping forward to offer her life to God. He pushed the unsettling thought aside and stepped down into the basement, waiting until she had returned to her seat before sliding into the pew beside her.

"Mornin', Miss Holliday," he whispered when her head finally lifted from prayer, and she turned her face toward him in surprise.

"What are you doin' here?" she whispered back quickly, glancing around the chapel as if to see if anyone else had noticed his sudden appearance there.

"Goin' to church, like always. I thought we'd ride in together, but it seems you left me home without a rig, so I had to walk. Hope God forgives my bein' tardy."

Mattie looked away from him, a blush rising in her cheeks.

"I didn't think you'd be interested in church, after all that drinkin'."

"A sinner's got more reason to be at church than a Saint, seems like," he replied. "Though I reckon apologizin' to God is easier than apologizin' to you."

"Hush, John Henry," Mattie said, putting her finger to her lips, "Father Duggan is about to say the benediction."

Then she bowed her head again as the Priest raised his hands to heaven once more, reciting the final prayer: *"Benedictat vos omnipotens Deus, Pate, et Filium et Spiritus Sanctus, Amen."*

As Father Duggan made the sign of the cross, Mattie quickly crossed herself, then looked back up at John Henry. "You didn't come here to pray for forgiveness, did you?"

"Not entirely, no. Mostly I came to be with you, like I always do. Why'd you leave so early this mornin', anyhow? Were you tryin' to avoid me?"

"I had something to discuss with Father Duggan. He sees parishioners before Sunday mornin' Mass."

Though her explanation seemed reasonable, she hadn't really answered his question. It was clear that she wasn't happy to see him there, but he couldn't really blame her for that.

"Mattie," he said, trying a gentler tone, "we need to talk..."

"Not now," she whispered, as she gathered her prayer book and bag and stepped into the aisle. "Not here..."

John Henry followed her, pushing past the other parishioners to stay at her side.

"Then we'll talk as we ride home," he said.

"No," she whispered again, "Robert is comin' to meet me here, after his services at the Presbyterian Church. He'll be ridin' alongside the buggy." Then she turned to smile and greet the other members of the congregation. "Hello, Mrs. Kennedy, Mrs. Hagan. How are you, Mr. McDevitt? Mr. O'Donougho?" The whole congregation was Irish, it seemed.

John Henry had to reach for her arm to hold her back from flowing on out with the crowd. "Then when, Mattie?" he asked in frustration. "You know I'm leavin' for Griffin on the noon train. And I must tell you somethin' before I go."

She hesitated a long moment, as the crowd moved past her, then she let out a sigh. "All right," she said. "But not here. Not in front of Father Duggan."

"Then where?"

"Follow me," was all she said, as she picked up her skirts and moved with the congregation to the rear of the basement chapel. But instead of going up the stone

318

steps to the light of the street outside, she moved ahead into the shadows where another set of steps rose into a dark stairwell.

"Where are we goin'?" he asked, not unpleased to find himself suddenly alone in the dark with her.

But she didn't answer, as she led him up the narrow passageway. At the top of the stair she stopped, turned a doorknob, and the passage suddenly flooded with light.

"It's the new sanctuary," she whispered reverently. "Father Duggan showed it to me just this mornin', before Mass."

As they stepped into the light of the sanctuary, John Henry gave a gasp. The space seemed as immense as heaven itself, the ceiling soaring to more than a hundred feet. At the far end of the sanctuary, the high altar was made of gleaming white marble, ornately carved. And though the gaslight chandeliers had yet to be hung overhead, the place was filled with light and color from the stained glass windows set into every arch of the roofline.

"It's beautiful..." he said, though the word did not do it justice. While the outside of the new church seemed as formidable as a medieval castle, the interior was as light and radiant as sunlight itself. "Like heaven..." he murmured.

"To make us feel closer to God," Mattie said, finishing his thought. And as she gazed upward toward the soaring ceiling, the light from the circle window in the transept shone down on her, illuminating her face in a rainbow of lead glass color. She looked like heaven herself, John Henry thought, like some angel too transcendent to be real.

"Oh, Mattie!" he said quickly, feeling suddenly full of repentance, "I am so very sorry for how I behaved the other night. I'd been drinkin'..."

"I know," she said, her eyes still gazing heavenward.

"I had been drinkin'," he said again, "but I still meant every word I said. The liquor only make it easier for me to speak my mind, my heart."

"No," she said, "you didn't mean those things. You can't mean them."

"But I do love you, Mattie! I have always loved you. Surely you must know that. And I believe that you are in love with me, as well. I felt the way you trembled when I held you. You can't deny it. If Robert hadn't come out on the porch just then..."

A sudden flush rose up in her face, and she looked away from him. "I don't deny it. But I have repented of it."

"Repented? What do you mean?"

"It was wrong, John Henry. Wrong for you to say such things to me, wrong for me to let you say them. But I have confessed to Father Duggan..."

"Confessed what? You haven't done anything wrong! It's not a sin to be in love!"

Then she lifted her eyes again and looked at him with profound sadness. "But you are my first cousin, my father's brother's child. We cannot be together."

"That's ridiculous! Cousins marry all the time! Why, Aunt Permelia's Grandfather Ware married his first cousin, and no one thought anything of it."

"They were not Catholic, as I am. The church will not allow marriages within the third degree – no closer relation than second cousins. There is no point in discussing something that cannot ever be."

"Then we'll marry in some other church," he said, stepping toward her and taking hold of her arms, feeling that if somehow he could just pull her from that light, he could sway her to his plans. "My mother was a Methodist," he said, "we'll marry in the Methodist church..."

"But I am Catholic," she said, shaking her head. "I must marry in the faith, or the church will not recognize the marriage. It would be...living in sin. Father Duggan cannot allow..."

"Then we'll go somewhere else," he said desperately, "we'll find another priest to marry us, one who doesn't know who we are. You can use your mother's name, Fitzgerald. No one will know we're first cousins. No one will care!"

And for a moment, he thought he might be able to make her surrender to him. But at last she shook her head and said with a sigh:

"No, John Henry, you're wrong. God will know. And I will know."

He could fight a rival; he could even fight her. But he couldn't fight God, and he let his arms fall away from her, like his dreams were falling away.

"Then there is no way at all for us to be together?" he asked hopelessly, "not ever?"

"Not in the sight of God," she said, looking back up into the light. "It wasn't meant, John Henry..."

"But...you do love me, don't you?"

And when she didn't answer, he put his hand on her shoulder, turning her toward him, and he asked again: "You do love me, don't you, Mattie? Tell me the truth at least, if that's all I can ever have."

Then she nodded, and whispered between her tears, "Oh yes, John Henry! I do love you!"

And before he could think what to say to her she was in his arms and he was kissing her lips, her face, whispering endearments into her hair, forgetting everything else but the blessed knowledge that Mattie did love him after all – loved him as he loved her, needed him to be with her as he had always needed her. And for a few desperate moments he could forget that there was no future for them, that they could never be together as he longed for them to be. Then Mattie pulled herself away from him, catching her breath and trying to stop the tears that flowed unbidden down her cheeks.

"I am so sorry, sweetheart!" she cried. "I never meant for this to happen! I tried to keep from fallin' in love with you, as my father told me. But how could I help it? How could I ever not love you? And for a while I did hope – I did think that we might marry someday. Oh, John Henry, I am so very sorry!"

"Then what do we do, Mattie?" he asked, like a child again, leaning on her wisdom, believing that Mattie could make everything better somehow. "What are we to do?"

"I don't know," she said. "Go on as we have always been, I suppose. Best of friends, dearest cousins. But not lovers. Never lovers..."

"And what then? Do I stand back like a good cousin and watch you marry someone else someday, make a toast at your wedding?"

"You'll marry too," she whispered.

"And you can live with that? Can you stand to see me with another woman?" and he turned away in anger and frustration. "Damn it, Mattie!" he swore, his words shattering the sanctity of the chapel. "I can't stay here and keep goin' through this! I want you more than I have ever wanted anything. I need you, Mattie!"

Then he pulled her to him and kissed her again, without asking, without caring what she thought. He only knew that in the shimmering light of the stained glass, Mattie's skin looked like ivory silk and her eyes were dark like deep shadows on the river. And when he kissed her, she sighed and opened her lips to his.

He could have stood there forever holding her in his arms, but the silence of the sanctuary was broken by the steeple bell of the Presbyterian Church around the corner, tolling ten o'clock.

"I have to go," he said heavily, "I have a train to catch..." though he could hardly remember why he needed to return to Griffin. Without Mattie, without his dreams of the future, his life seemed suddenly meaningless.

"I know," she said, reaching into her bag and pulling out a handkerchief to wipe her eyes. And as she did, her little Irish Claddagh ring caught the stained glass light, shimmering gold.

"Like a wedding ring," he murmured, and Mattie looked up at him with questioning eyes.

"Like a what?"

"Like a wedding ring," he said again, his mind strangely focusing all at once on that tiny band of gold. "With this ring, I thee wed..."

And as if she were hearing his thoughts, Mattie slipped the ring from her finger and held it out to him.

"Then here, in the presence of God," she said, "let us pledge to love each other always, even if we can never be together. Go on, take it, John Henry, I want you to have it."

It was a ladies ring, so tiny that it hardly went onto his little finger, stopping short just past his knuckle.

"It's so small," he said. "I'll never be able to get it off again."

"Then you must wear it always, and whenever you see it on your hand you will think of me. The two hands for friendship, the crown for loyalty..."

"...and the heart for love," he said, finishing her thought. "With this ring..."

"That's Protestant, John Henry. We are in the Catholic Church."

"Then what words shall we say? Right now, before God alone?"

"Oh, sweetheart!" she cried, her face turned up to his and her eyes filling with tears, "God already knows you have my heart!"

And as he kissed her one last time, the bells in the Presbyterian Church steeple rang out, more like a mourning knell than a wedding chime.

~~~~~~~~~

He couldn't bring himself to say good-bye, even after the buggy ride home with Robert riding along beside in studied silence, and his own hurried packing and thank-yous to Aunt Permelia and Uncle John. But saying good-bye to Mattie would feel like a final farewell, after all that had gone on between them that morning, and he could never say that. Mattie, and dreams of Mattie, had been his life for as long as he could remember, and saying good-bye would leave a chasm in his heart that would never be filled, bigger even than the void his mother's death had left, and how could a young man live who had lost so much heart already?

He felt numb all over by the time the train pulled into Griffin, as though he had drunk himself into a stupor but without the pleasant whiskey euphoria to wash away his pain. And though he was expected at supper with Francisco's family in Jenkinsburg, he was in no mood to make the visit. So he hired a horse and rode through Griffin instead, trying to remember a time when his world was still in one piece and his life had some hope in it.

He rode past the little house on Tinsley Street where he'd been born and spent his first happy childhood years, past the old Presbyterian Church where he'd been baptized, past the schoolhouse where he'd learned his first lessons. He turned the horse and kept riding on out of town, past the Confederate Memorial with its angel standing sorrowfully over the rows of white grave markers, and up the hill to where Rest Haven Cemetery spread out across its lonely fields. At the far end of the cemetery, he stopped and slid down from the saddle and bent to brush away the overgrowing weeds from the small granite gravestone.

"Hello, Ellie," he said softly, calling Martha Eleanora by the name his mother had used for her. "It's your brother, John Henry."

And as if she could hear him and understand, he went on talking, telling her things he himself was only just deciding. "I'm goin' away, Ellie, I'm leaving here, goin' back to Valdosta, I reckon. I don't know who'll take care of keepin' the weeds off your grave when I'm gone..."

He was quiet for a moment, staring down at that small grave.

"Our mother used to come take care of you while she was alive. I used to come out here with her when I was a child, and watch her layin' flowers over you. She told me to always remember I had a sister, even if we never knew each other. I wish I could have known you, Ellie. It would have been nice to have had someone to grow up with – a sister, a brother, someone. You never got a chance to know our mother very well, not like I did, but she loved us both very much. I was fifteen-years old when she died. You'd have been sixteen that summer..."

He stopped talking, remembering his mother's lovely face, her grieving for the daughter she'd never raised. Was there any part of life that didn't end badly? Was there really any joy at all?

"I reckon I've just imagined you all this time, thinkin' of you gettin' older every year. But you didn't get much of a real life, did you, Ellie? Six months – hardly any time. Well, shall I tell you about life? Would you like to know what you missed? Life is lonely and cold, like that grave of yours. Until you find someone to love, and then for a moment, for just a moment, you think that life is wonderful. Then your mother dies, and your father leaves you, and your only love says – she can't love you anymore..."

His voice broke as he choked back angry, anguished tears. "That's life, Martha Eleanora Holliday," he said bitterly. "I guess you didn't miss much, after all."

And in the quiet emptiness of the still evening air, he could almost hear his mother's voice again, and she was weeping too.

Chapter Nineteen

Valdosta, 1873

Henry Holliday sat in the parlor of his Savannah Street cottage, smoking a cigar. To any other observer, he might have seemed contentedly reposed, letting out long puffs of smoke then tipping the ash of his Havana into a waiting china ashtray. But John Henry knew his father's calm exterior covered an anger barely restrained.

"To say that I am disappointed in you, John Henry, would be a lie. I am far more than disappointed. I am chagrined. What am I to say to all these good people in Valdosta who thought you were doin' so well in Griffin?"

Though father and son were nearly of a height now, Henry was still heavier, more sturdily built than John Henry, and looked all the larger for it. His high cheekbones were sun-reddened, his forehead showing deep lines from working out of doors. His silvered hair was still as thick and wavy as a young man's, his clean-shaven face still square jawed and handsome. And, under a heavy brow, his light blue eyes were still as cool as steel.

Looking into those eyes, John Henry felt like a boy again, in trouble for yet another hotheaded misdeed. "Tell them I changed my mind about Griffin," he said uneasily, "and came back here to practice instead."

"A man doesn't change his mind, just like that. Not about business. You build a business, you stand by it, you stake your reputation on it. You don't just walk out on it. Irresponsible, that's what they'll say you are. Foolish."

John Henry didn't have to ask if his father thought him foolish too.

"I didn't just walk away, Pa," he said in his own defense. "I packed up my equipment and put it on the train. I closed the business, that's all. I'll just open up again down here, or go in with Dr. Frink, if he'll have me."

"He may wonder why you took such a sudden notion to leave Griffin. Did you get yourself into money trouble there, take on some bad debts? He won't look kindly on that."

"No, Pa, it wasn't money trouble. I was makin' out all right."

"Carousin', then? Did you spend too much time in the saloons?"

He couldn't deny that charge as easily as bad finances. He had indeed spent more time than he needed to in the saloons in Griffin and Atlanta both, but that was just loneliness, not bad business.

"I did some drinkin', but nothin' to shame you."

Henry took another draw on the cigar but blew it out fast, impatient for answers.

"Then what the hell brought you home like this? After all that talk of bein' a man, makin' your own way in the world and seein' after Francisco's children, I thought you'd finally managed to grow up some. Hoped you'd finally got some goals in life."

John Henry took a slow breath before answering, trying to steel himself for his father's coming rage. For surely, Henry would have something to say about his reasons for leaving Griffin.

"I did have a goal, Pa," he said at last. "That's what took me up to Atlanta in the first place. I had a plan to marry my cousin Mattie, and I reckoned bein' close to where she was would make it easier..."

He had expected Henry to curse out a response or turn that cold stare on him in disbelief. But his father's sudden laughter set him back more than any cursing could have done.

"Marry Cousin Mattie! Absurd! Close relations don't breed well, John Henry. You should know that from livin' on the farm."

It was an echo of Rachel's words the year before, and that only made his own anger rise. "We're not animals, Pa!" John Henry answered hotly, feeling the color rise in his face. To debase something as beautiful and pure as the love he and Mattie shared...

But Henry laughed again, loud and hard. "We're all animals, son. Especially men. The sooner you realize that, the better off you'll be. Once you get a good woman in your bed, one who understands about things, you'll forget all this foolishness over Rob's little girl."

"Like you forgot about my mother once you married Rachel?" He never would have spoken so rashly, but his father had goaded him into it.

"That is none of your business," Henry answered quickly, and for a moment the clear steel blue of his eyes shadowed over. "You will watch what you say in regards to your stepmother, if you plan on livin' under the same roof with her. So what happened to these fine plans of marryin' your cousin? Did she have the good sense to turn you down?"

"She turned me down, but not for lack of wantin' it. It's her religion. The Catholic church won't allow first cousins to marry."

"Catholicism," Henry said with disdain. "Your Uncle Rob had to convert to marry your Aunt Mary Anne."

"As I would have done, if it came to that."

"Catholic? You'd have turned Catholic? That would have broken your mother's heart."

John Henry flinched, then he said without thinking, "And since when did you ever care about breakin' my mother's heart? Marryin' your lover before your wife was even cold in her grave…"

And in one muscular motion Henry rose from the chair and turned on him, hitting him hard across the face, and John Henry staggered under the blow.

"I could kill a man for less than that," Henry said, his eyes cold with anger. And for a moment, John Henry believed that he might try. Then Henry drew a slow breath.

"Go to see Dr. Frink, then," he said, and might as well have said *Go to hell…* "But don't expect any help from me."

John Henry almost broke then, feeling again like that boy who could never be good enough, cowering in the shadow of the great hero, Henry Holliday. Then he put his hand to his stinging face, took a breath and put his shoulders back, raising himself to his full height, and he looked Henry square in the eyes.

"I don't expect anything from you, Pa. I don't need anything from you."

Henry nodded. "Then that's what you'll get, son. Nothin'. Find yourself another place to live. You're not welcome in my house any longer." Then he turned and walked from the room and never looked back.

~~~~~~~~~~

Brave as John Henry's words had been, there was nothing brave about the way he felt as he walked out into the shadows that steamy summer evening. For the first time in his life he was truly homeless, though his father's house was only a few steps behind him. But Henry had thrown him out, and there was no turning back. So he stood in Rachel's flowered yard, between the white-painted porch and the whitewashed fence, and wondered where he would go to now. Certainly, he couldn't beg refuge of any of the townsfolk in Valdosta. Henry Holliday was a hero to them, a fine and prosperous member of the community. If Henry wouldn't take his own son in, why should they?

He had never felt so alone, deserted by his past and his future both. So when the front door creaked open and Rachel stepped down from the porch to join him, he almost welcomed her company.

"He's hot-headed, sometimes," she said. "But I reckon you were always a little hot-headed, too."

John Henry didn't answer, though he had to agree with what she said. They were both of them hot-headed, stubborn men.

"Much alike as you are," she went on, "seems like you'd get along fine. Maybe someday you will."

John Henry shook his head. "Be hard for us to get along, now he's put me out of his house."

"So where you goin' to?" she asked.

"I don't know," John Henry answered. "You got any suggestions?"

Of course he didn't expect a reply. Common as she was, Rachel knew a wife's place and wouldn't go against her husband's wishes. If his father meant him to be homeless, then homeless he would be. So he was surprised when Rachel took a breath and said in a voice hardly above a whisper:

"Your Uncle Tom McKey's moved up here, you know. He's come to be near his Sadie Allen, seein' as they're plannin' on marryin' and all. He took up that family land over on the Withlacoochee, down the old Troupville Road, built himself a nice little cabin there. I reckon you remember the place."

He remembered it all right. He'd been there plenty of times, swimming in that bend of river near where the Withlacoochee and the Little River met. He'd been there with Mattie even, when her family had stayed with his during the last days of the War. That land had seemed like a green refuge to him then, far away from the troubles of the world. Maybe it could be a refuge for him again...

"I'd need a horse to get there before full dark," he said aloud, thinking of the four miles between Valdosta and there. And once again, he was surprised by Rachel's words.

"I reckon your Pa wouldn't notice if one of his horses was to spend the night elsewhere. Not once I give him a glass or two of that bourbon he keeps under the sideboard. He'll rant and rave awhile about you, then settle down for the night after that. If that horse was to be back by mornin', I don't reckon he'd notice it was ever gone."

John Henry looked at her in astonishment. With her unruly waves of yellow hair and her untidy house dress, she still looked much like the young farm girl his father had taken to wife, and whom John Henry had spent the better part of seven years despising. Yet here she was, acting amazingly like a woman with a real concern for his welfare.

"Why are you doin' this for me, Rachel? You know my Pa wouldn't take kindly to it."

"I ain't doin' it for you, John Henry, nor for your Pa, neither," she said. "I reckon I'm doin' it for your Ma."

Then she turned and walked back into the house without bothering to explain what she meant.

And though he didn't stop to ponder on her words just then, he couldn't help remembering them as he rode his father's horse out the old Troupville Road toward the Withlacoochee River. Had he been wrong about Rachel all these years? Had she been more, after all, than just his father's mistress, stealing away his mother's husband and home? Then another memory came to his mind and stayed: his mother's grave at Sunset Hill Cemetery, ringed with river stones and covered with flowers like a garden plot. Someone had watched over it all these years, washing the gravestone and turning the sad burial place into something beautiful. Someone had tended to the memory of Alice Jane, when even her husband seemed to have forgotten her. Rachel, he thought...

And for the first time, the thought of her didn't make him feel sick inside.

~~~~~~~~~~

Tom welcomed him without question, as he always had, and John Henry let him think the unexpected visit was nothing more than a social call. Bad enough to be thrown out of his father's house without having to admit as much to anyone else – even family as close as his Uncle Tom. And thankfully, there was so much to be done on Tom's new place that there wasn't much time to ask or answer many questions, anyhow.

The homestead was a stone's throw from the Withlacoochee, near the bend in the river that John Henry had called his swimming hole. Tom had cleared an acre or so of the woods away and built his cabin facing the water. Behind it was a well-house and outhouse, a kitchen garden already in cultivation, a nearly completed barn, and even the start of a buggy house, though John Henry couldn't see the need for something as fancy as a buggy out there in the woods. Wouldn't a spring wagon be enough for trips to the general store in Valdosta?

"The buggy's not for bringin' supplies around," Tom told him. "It's for Sadie, once we get married. She likes to be up and doin' all the time, restless like. With the buggy, she can go off visitin' in town whenever she likes."

"So why live away out here then? Why don't you buy a place in town instead?"

"I like the peace and quiet out here. I like bein' close to the water. I'd like my boys to grow up swimmin' in that swimmin' hole someday — and we're hoping for a houseful of 'em, eight or nine maybe."

"Then you're gonna need a bigger cabin, Tom."

"This one'll do for now. But I sure could use your help gettin' this buggy house finished up. The runabout arrives next week, so I'll be needin' a place to put it."

"But why buy the buggy before you even get married?" John Henry asked, as Tom had told him the wedding was still a year or two away.

"Your Pa got me a deal on it, before he sold the buggy business and opened the furniture store. Glad I went ahead and ordered it when I did. Took seven months to get here, as it was, but I expect it'll be worth it. It's a pretty one: black with a gold stripe down the side and real Morocco leather upholstery. Set me back a bit, I can tell you."

"I guess that explains the straw mattress on the bed. Won't Sadie be expectin' feathers?"

"She will, and she'll get 'em, too. Now your Pa's got that furniture business, I reckon I'll be orderin' a bedroom suit next. But for now, you and I will have to share what's there – I'll put the mattress on the floor for you and sleep on the ropes myself. Best I can offer company for a while."

"It's plenty, Tom, and I appreciate your hospitality," he said, though it was hard to hear Tom's happy plans for the future when his own plans had come to nothing. So he was glad when the talking stopped and he could pour himself into work instead. Though John Henry had little experience as a builder, Tom was a patient and able teacher, and they worked well together. Still, he wondered if Tom's building techniques were a little out of the ordinary: where another man might have used a handsaw to cut the soft pinewood for the buggy house, Tom sliced into it with the monstrous knife he'd carried off to War with him.

"The Hell-Bitch has her uses still," he said with a grin as he handed the knife, swamp oak handle first, to his nephew. "As I recall, you figured she was for throwin'. But fifteen inches long and two inches wide don't throw well. You just cut with her."

John Henry took the knife in his right hand and turned it over, feeling the weight of the thing and admiring how both sides of the blade were still sharpened to a shine.

"Shame you only use her for slaughterin' hogs and cuttin' wood," he said. "Your Hell-Bitch is a fightin' weapon if I ever saw one."

"She is, but I'd rather not be in any fight where I'd have to use her. Hand-to-hand is dangerous fightin'. Mostly, both men get hurt. If it came to a fight, I'd rather pull a pistol than a knife, anyhow. And I'd rather aim a shot-gun than a pistol."

"You can't aim a shot-gun," John Henry remarked, "unless you're aimin' at a deer. The pellets just scatter all over, you know that. Better stick with the pistol, if it comes to a fight."

It was just conversation to pass the time while they worked together, but it was pleasant enough talk, and kept his mind distracted from his troubles. But when Tom called the day's work to a halt and darkness gathered around the homesite, John Henry's misery came racing back.

The nights were the hardest, out in the woods. While Tom slept on a blanket thrown over the ropes of his single bed, too tired and content to be uncomfortable, John Henry tossed and turned on the straw mattress pallet on the floor. Mattie! Mattie! His heart cried out for her, his whole being ached to be with her. How could he live with this emptiness? How could he live and watch her with some other man someday, some good husband who would love her and hold her and give her children...

The thought of it turned his stomach, made him want to scream and flail at the awful fate that had made his only love his own cousin, closer to him than any other woman could ever be, too close for them to ever be together. And then that cruel fate took a name and he cursed God for making them cousins, for making Mattie a Catholic so that she could not marry him. Cruel, contemptuous God who sat in holy judgment against the dearest, sweetest emotions John Henry had ever felt. Did it please God to see him suffer so?

Then he remembered that simple faith that Mattie had always had, childlike belief in God's grace. Without that faith, she wouldn't be his beloved Mattie, and he almost laughed at the awful irony of it. If her faith didn't mean so much to her, if she could turn away from it and marry him without the blessings of the priest, he would have loved her less. It was her strength that made him lean on her, made him love her so desperately. It was her strength that denied him her love.

He hardly slept at all, those nights at Tom's cabin, and each new day as Tom arose rested and ready to start to work again, John Henry was more tired than the day before. The tiredness brought back the cough that had plagued him in the winter and spring, and the cough made it even harder to sleep. And by the time the buggy house was nearly done and Tom was ready to ride into town and collect his long-awaited runabout, John Henry was worn down to exhaustion.

"Why don't you stay here and get some rest?" Tom said as he packed a saddlebag and put on his town clothes. "I'll be gone overnight. I usually try to stay over and go to church with Sadie whenever I get into town. And I don't suppose you'll be wantin' to pay a visit on your Pa, anyhow..."

He didn't need to say more, for like his sister Alice Jane, Tom had a way of knowing what was troubling John Henry without ever being told.

"I don't reckon Pa would appreciate my comin' around," John Henry replied. "I don't reckon I'll be visitin' with him ever again, if you want to know the truth."

"Only if you want to tell it," Tom said. "I know there's been bad feelin's all around, ever since your Pa remarried. And it don't help that Henry's not one for talkin' much. But that don't mean he don't love you, John Henry. Some things just take time, I reckon."

"I reckon," John Henry said, though he took no comfort in the thought. Time hadn't fixed anything with Mattie, only made matters worse. He didn't see how an evening's visit with his father would repair the rift between them. "I guess I'll stay here and get some sleep, like you said. You go on and have a good visit with Sadie, show her that pretty new buggy."

But as Tom rode away down the old Troupville Road, headed toward Valdosta, John Henry had a sudden urge to run after him. Tom had been his comfortable companion these hard days, and without him the woods were going to seem mighty lonely. For while he had never minded being alone before, now the quiet seemed to settle down on him like a pall, and he feared he was about to become melancholy. There was a medicine to ward off the melancholy of course, the same *spiritus fermenti* that doctors prescribed for coughs and such, and Tom happened to have a bottle or two tucked away in his dish cupboard. And though John Henry knew that drinking alone was a sign of a weak will, he didn't see how he had much choice. Under the circumstances, he could either drink alone to try and push away the despair, or succumb to his misery completely. Besides, a little whiskey might help him to sleep...

But sleep was long in coming that night, even after he'd emptied his little silver pocket flask and downed most of one bottle and contemplated starting onto another.

Filled with whiskey as he was, he lay on the straw mattress pallet on the floor in a drunken half-wakefulness remembering all the sorrows of his life. In his twenty-one years, he'd lived through more than most men would see in a lifetime, and now it all seemed to come back to him at once: the horror of War and the humiliation of Reconstruction; the frustrated anger of the boys who called themselves Vigilantes and the murder of their hero, the Captain; the failed retribution of the Courthouse bombing; the arrest and imprisonment of his friends and his own unworthy escape from punishment; the long, awful death of his mother; the disloyal remarriage of his father. And round and over and through it all, his doomed love for Mattie who could never be his. When he finally slept, the memories turned to nightmares.

He woke in a sweat, the summer sun glaring in through the cabin windows and turning the place breathless as an oven. It was late morning, maybe, or early afternoon, and hot as hell already, but it wasn't the heat that had awakened him. From somewhere outside the cabin came sounds that shouldn't be there: voices talking, getting closer.

He rolled over and reached for his valise, pulling out his pistol, the walnut-gripped Colt's Navy revolver Uncle John had given him as a coming-of-age gift. Hands shaking, he loaded two chambers just to be safe and ready to frighten away whoever might be trespassing on the McKey property. But ready as his pistol was, John Henry himself was still so hung-over that he could barely stand without swaying, and the swaying made him so sick he thought he might wretch.

He staggered to the door of the cabin and out into the hot summer sun, looking around for the source of the sound, and didn't see at first where it was coming from. The clearing around the cabin was still undisturbed, the barn and the buggy house closed up as Tom had left them. Then the sound came again, more distinct this time, and his eyes followed it across the bend of the river to the far side of the swimming hole. There in the green shade of the overhanging trees, a gang of colored boys was stepping into the water. They were stripped naked, skinny-dipping like young men did, and laughing as they splashed in the shallows. Behind them, their homespun clothes hung on bushes along the sandy riverbank.

It should have been a pleasant picture, those careless colored boys sneaking out for a Sunday afternoon's frolic. But to John Henry, it seemed like a sacrilege. This was his swimming hole – his and Mattie's. He had brought her here that long-ago summer when her family had stayed with his at Cat Creek. He had watched her walk down into the river, the sun glinting off her auburn hair and the water making her cotton dress cling to the curves of her body. He had laid beside her here, in the grass along the riverbank, feeling an urge to touch her in a way he did not then understand. And then, his passion for her and his pain at losing her swelled up inside of him, spun together with the frustration at his useless life, and came flooding out in an anger he could barely control. He raised his pistol and without bothering to shout a warning, fired one shot across the river.

Unsteady as he was, the shot went over the heads of the boys swimming there, but they heard it whistle past, and ran yelling for the riverbank.

"Y'all get out of here!" John Henry screamed hoarsely, "damn you, get away from our land!" His whole body shook with the words, so hard he didn't think he could fire a second shot if he had to. But as long as the boys cleared out the way they were told, he wouldn't need to find out.

But one of the boys seemed not to understand, or care, that he had been justly ordered out of the water, and he stopped where he was and looked back across the river to where the shot had come from. Then, standing there naked in the water, white teeth gleaming in his dark face, he started to laugh.

It was the laughter, coming like a challenge, that made John Henry's liquored blood rise, reminding him of the laughter of the guard at the Courthouse the day the carpetbagger had come to town, the day the Yankees had taken his friends away to prison, the day his father had slapped him hard across the face and called him a shame. And then the pistol in his hand seemed to take on a life of its own, rising to the challenge and firing a shot square into the colored boy's laughing face.

The other boys heard the shot, saw their companion spin around, watched his blood flood into the river as he fell, faceless, into the water. For a moment, neither the boys nor John Henry moved, as the smoke of the gunpowder rose up into the air and wafted across the river, lazy as a summer's cloud. Then one of the boys screamed, ran toward the water, put out a hand as if to raise his fallen friend, then turned and raced into the woods, naked still. His companions, grabbing for what clothing they could reach from the bushes, ran after him into the trees.

In the still shadows of the swimming hole, the blood of the dead boy was turning the green water to crimson red.

The pistol dropped from John Henry's hand as he fell to his knees in the dirt.

"Oh my God!" he whispered, more a desperate prayer than a curse. "Oh my God, what have I done?"

"Looks like you've killed a man," Tom McKey said heavily, stepping up behind

334

him. In the yelling and the commotion of the last few moments, John Henry hadn't heard his uncle drive up in his new buggy, fresh back from church in Valdosta. "So I reckon we've got some plans to make."

"Plans?" John Henry said, bewildered. "What kind of plans?"

"How to get you gone before the sheriff hears of this. Lucky for you, it's Sunday, and the law won't want to be bothered with a colored boy's killin' just yet. That gives us a little time, anyhow."

And when John Henry didn't move, frozen like a dreamer in an awful nightmare, Tom grabbed hold of his shoulder and yanked him to his feet.

"One man's dead, John Henry," he said. "We've got to make sure another one lives. Now go on inside and brew some coffee to sober you up while I get that poor boy's body out of the river. His parents shouldn't have to find him like that."

~~~~~~~~~~

But Tom McKey already realized what John Henry was too stunned and scared to know: that whether the boy was found floating in the river or buried in a shallow grave, once word got around that a killing had taken place on the Withlacoochee, law men and curious folk from all over the county would be coming to the McKey land, looking for the killer.

"It ain't slavery days anymore," Tom tried to explain to him. "Back then, you killed a colored, you only had to deal with his master, or pay the price of him. We've been reconstructed now. A black man's life is equal to a white man's, in the law."

"But they were trespassin' on our land..." John Henry said in weak defense, still not believing what had happened. Surely, it was just some bad liquor dream he was having and he'd wake from it soon enough. It wasn't real. It couldn't be real.

But Tom went on talking as though it were all too real.

"The river ain't ours, John Henry, and you know it, only this stretch of land alongside of it. But there's land the law around here can't catch you on, and that's where we're headed, fast as I can get us out of here."

"What are you talkin' about?"

"I'm talkin' about Banner Plantation. Georgia law won't follow you down into Florida, not for a colored boy. Equal law don't mean equal justice, lucky for you. Now finish up that coffee and pack up your gear. Too bad your first ride in the buggy has to be for such a cause."

"The buggy? You're comin' too?"

Tom looked at him somberly. "I doubt you'd make it there on your own, the way you're lookin' now. Besides, you took to a dangerous road once to help get me safely home. I reckon it's my turn to do you the same favor. I just wish you and your Pa were on speakin' terms. Was a time, once, when Henry got you out of a fix like this without hardly anyone noticin'."

But John Henry shook his head and looked up at Tom with terrified eyes. "No Tom, I never was in a fix like this before."

Tom didn't even bother answering.

~~~~~~~~~~

Alone on horseback, John Henry could have made the ride to the McKey plantation in just a few hours. But in a buggy with a horse already winded from the trip back from Valdosta, the drive took until well past dark. But at least there was only a crescent moon that night and no bright moonlight to show off Tom's new buggy. With its shiny black paint and that bright gold stripe down the side, anyone seeing it racing across the Georgia state line would surely have remembered it.

John Henry knew that Tom was taking an awful chance, driving him down to Florida. Tom had nothing to do with the shooting, and could have just walked away from the whole thing. Helping his nephew escape from the law would make Tom an accessory to a killing, if the courts ever got wind of it. And the fact that Tom had taken the Hell-Bitch along for the ride, out of its scabbard and slid down between the leather seat cushions and the wood frame of the buggy, showed he knew what kind of danger he was in. For even after he'd delivered John Henry to Banner Plantation, Tom would have to find cause why he himself shouldn't be suspected of murder. It had happened in the river alongside his own property, after all, and within clear sight of his cabin.

"At least I went to church, Sunday mornin'," Tom said to his older brother Will that night, as he explained what had caused their unexpected visit. "The whole Methodist congregation can vouch for that, and Sadie'll say I spent the rest of the afternoon havin' supper with her family. Lucky for us all, I didn't make any big show of leavin' Valdosta when I headed back out to the river. Hopefully, nobody noticed me go."

"I reckon we'll find out soon enough about that, once the law starts lookin' into things," Uncle Will replied. Though he'd been fast asleep when Tom and John Henry arrived, he was wide-awake now, and considering the situation. John Henry was sorry to have caused him the trouble. Uncle Will was still not entirely healed of the wound he'd taken at the Battle of Malvern Hill during the War, though Uncle James McKey had done his best to repair the damage, and Will had a continuing kidney ailment that left him weak much of the time. And now, sitting in the oil lamp shadows of his parlor, he looked far older than his thirty-six years, with his pale face drawn and his sandy hair turning to gray.

"Let's not tell the sisters about this," he said quietly, nodding toward the bedroom where Aunt Ella and Aunt Eunice were sleeping. "You know how women can talk, and this needs to stay as quiet as we can make it. So who was this boy who took the bullet? Is his family well known around town?"

Tom shook his head, "I didn't see him before John Henry fired. The other boys were gone before I got a good look at 'em. And after, there wasn't much left to identify."

"John Henry?" Will asked, turning toward his nephew, "did you know the boy?"

John Henry thought back to that awful moment when the liquor and the anger overcame him and his pistol seemed to fire itself, but couldn't remember anything but sound and smoke and the boy falling faceless into the water. "I don't know, Uncle Will. I don't think so..."

Will sighed and sat back in his chair, considering. "Not knowin' him makes it more difficult, I reckon. Can't quiet his family with money, if we don't know who they are. Don't know who to watch out for around town, either. What about Henry?" he asked, turning back to Uncle Tom. "Does he know about this yet?"

"I doubt it," Tom said. "I didn't dare take the time to stop by and visit with him."

"Well, we'll have to get word to him first thing in the mornin', have him do what he can there to put an end to this. Henry's a powerful man in Valdosta. Surely he's got some influence with the law..."

"Pa won't help me," John Henry said. "He told me he wouldn't ever come to my rescue again like he did over the Courthouse trouble. He said I'd be on my own, next time I got in a fix with the law..."

He'd expected his uncle to have some sympathy for him in the face of his father's neglect, but Uncle Will's words put a whole new frightening light on things.

"This isn't just your fix, John Henry," Uncle Will said somberly. "It's all of ours, seein' as you chose to kill that boy on our part of the river. My name's on that land deed, too, along with Tom's. Supposin' somebody decides it was me who happened to be there today, takin' a look over things? Supposin' somebody decides I'm the one who did the shootin'?"

"But you weren't there!" John Henry exclaimed. "You've been in Florida the whole time, the sisters can prove that..."

Even in the shadows, John Henry could see the weariness in Uncle Will's eyes.

"What a man can prove and what he gets accused of are two different things. Oft times, an accusation's all it takes to ruin a man's good name. So, first thing in the mornin', I'll ride over to Belleville and send a wire to Henry, ask for his help. Though I'd rather take a hangin' myself then beg anything of him..."

For the first time since the shooting, John Henry looked beyond himself to what he had done to his family. As Tom had said, Henry's marriage to Rachel had left bad feelings all around. Now his uncles would have to throw themselves on Henry Holliday's mercy to keep the McKey name clean.

"I'm sorry, Uncle Will," John Henry said truthfully, "I am so sorry for troublin' you..."

"Seems like it's killin' that boy you ought to be sorry for, John Henry, not the trouble that's come after it. If you'd have kept your head this mornin', none of this would have happened. I fear Alice Jane was right in what she used to say about you."

"My mother? What did she used to say?"

Will paused a moment before answering, then sighed. "She feared there's too much tares in you, John Henry, and not enough wheat. I reckon maybe she was right."

~~~~~~~~~~

Tom drove back to Georgia that same night, taking advantage of the darkness and borrowing one of his brother's horses to make for a speedy ride. He left his own winded horse with Will, but he left the Hell-Bitch with John Henry in case any trouble should come down that way. And while Tom raced north before the sun, John Henry's mind raced as well. Though there'd been no talk of what he was to do with himself while his uncles settled things in Valdosta, it was clear to him that he couldn't stay long at Banner Plantation. Soon his Aunt Ella and Aunt Eunice, his mother's unmarried younger sisters, would awaken and wonder what had brought their favorite nephew for a visit. He could lie, of course, and tell them he had just wanted to come and see them all. But that wouldn't explain why he couldn't go back to Georgia for a while. And if the worst came, and Tom and Will couldn't get things settled after all, he might never be able to go back to Georgia again...

He sat down heavily on one of the straight-backed chairs in the parlor and stared at the family pictures lining the walls: silver frames around unsmiling faces, his McKey relatives all looking back at him somberly – Uncle Will, Uncle James, Uncle Jonathan who'd gone west to Texas...

Then he remembered the last time he'd been to visit Banner Plantation, when Tom had told him about his inheritance. There'd been something wild in him that night, when all he could think about was getting out of Valdosta, away from his restlessness, and heading west to Texas like his Uncle Jonathan McKey had done. Texas –

The thought of it settled down on his mind like an endless summer day. Wide, wild Texas, where a man could get lost and not have to think, let his sorrows burn away under that hot western sky.

"Texas," he whispered. "Texas."

Chapter Twenty

He didn't wait around to see if the law was coming after him or not. At first light, when his Uncle Will rode off to town to send the telegram, John Henry took Tom's quarter horse and headed south to Live Oak, the closest station on the Pensacola and Georgia Railroad. Among the things he'd learned while working for the Atlantic and Gulf Line before dental school were the names and stops of all the connecting railroads – and he knew that the fastest way to Texas from north Florida was by train to the Gulf and then by ship out of Pensacola to Galveston. Beyond that, he had only a vague plan in mind for what he'd do once he got to Texas, hoping to somehow find his Uncle Jonathan McKey whom no one had heard from since before the War, and whom John Henry hardly remembered knowing. But Jonathan shouldn't be too hard to locate, living on that big cotton plantation of his somewhere along the Brazos River...

But it was thoughts of the past, not the future, that occupied his mind as he rode into Live Oak, arranged for Tom's horse to be sent back to Banner Plantation, and bought a ticket west. His thoughts were on Mattie to whom he hadn't even been able to say a proper goodbye. He'd been in such a state the last time he'd seen her, holding her in the stained glass light of the Church of the Immaculate Conception and knowing that she could never be his, that he hadn't been able to bring himself to say farewell. And now here he was, gone from Georgia without a chance to tell her how he still felt about her – that he loved her and always would, no matter where he went.

It was a long train ride from Live Oak to Pensacola, two-hundred-fifty miles through scrub pine and small towns, and hellish hot with the windows of the rail cars closed up to keep out the sooty smoke and cinders of the steam engine. And even when the windows were opened up at each stop to let in the air, the steamy Florida heat was almost worse than the engine smoke. But the heat seemed appropriate to

John Henry, who deserved to be in hell for what he'd done. For though it was just a colored's life he had taken, it was a life nonetheless, and God would surely call him to judgment for it, he had no doubt of that. If there was one thing his mother had taught him, it was to fear God even when he didn't honor Him, and he was feeling plenty fearful now.

His fears didn't settle any as the train finally came to a stop on the far side of Escambia Bay from Pensacola.

"End of the line!" the porter called out. "Everybody out!"

"End of the line?" John Henry asked, glancing up from the newspaper he'd bought in Tallahassee, and which he'd been nervously reading for any mention of a shooting on the Withlacoochee River in south Georgia. "I thought this was the Pensacola line. How am I supposed to get over there from here?"

The porter raised the window shade and pointed. "You take the ferry across," he said, "cost you two-bits."

John Henry followed the man's gaze out the window, looking for the ferry dock, but what he saw instead nearly took his breath away. For though he'd been to the ocean before, sailing from Savannah to Philadelphia, he'd never seen anything like the Gulf of Mexico. The water was like liquid jewels: emeralds and sapphires shimmering in the summer sun, the sandy shore as white as oyster pearls. And littering the bay, the sails of a hundred tall-masted ships looked like so many white clouds against the brilliant blue of sky and sea.

"Looks like paradise," he said aloud, "like heaven almost."

"Wouldn't call it paradise this time of year," the porter replied. "It's quarantine season, June 'til November. Glad this train don't run that far, or I'd be in the middle of it."

"Quarantine?" John Henry asked. "For what?"

"Yellow Fever, and worse than usual this year. They say there's sixty-three dead in the city already, and plenty more close to it. Bad way to die, if you ask me. Fever and chills together, headache and gut-ache, then your skin turns yellow and the black vomit starts. Don't take long after that till you're dead. Real trouble comes in the buryin'. Can't wait long to get to it, in this heat, and some folks is too poor to buy a cemetery plot. So they bury 'em down on the sand-beach at night when nobody's lookin'. Problem is, high tide washes their dearly departed right back up again. It's bad, all right. That's why trains aren't allowed in this time of year, and ships can't get near the wharf until they've done a month in quarantine over at the Navy Cove. Makes the sailors plenty restless, havin' to cool their heels across the water like that when there's streetwalkers and such waitin' for 'em over in Pensacola. No sir, it's not much like paradise this time of year, if you ask me. Hell's more like it."

John Henry almost laughed at the awful irony of it. After running from one state and clean across another trying to escape from the evil he'd done, he'd ended up where he deserved to be after all, proving that his mother was right: you couldn't run from the wrath of God. But he was done running for a while, having spent the last of his money on traveling expenses, with only enough left over for a few days' room and board. He'd need to raise some cash before he could buy passage on a tall-ship sailing to Texas. But if Pensacola were anywhere near as wicked as the porter had described, raising some money there shouldn't be all that hard. Surely, with all those sailors and streetwalkers around, there'd be a saloon somewhere too, and a card game with an open chair.

~~~~~~~~~~

The city didn't surprise him any, in that respect. There were plenty of saloons along Main Street, across from the wharves on Pensacola Bay, and plenty more on the higher ground of the town proper. What did surprise him was how foreign the place felt, as he walked along the wood-plank sidewalks of streets named Alcañiz and Tarragona and Zaragoza. For though Pensacola had once been the capitol of the British colony of West Florida, it had spent more time under Spanish rule than English, and the warm breeze off the Gulf of Mexico was still lazy as a siesta.

It was the ocean breeze that folks blamed for the Yellow Fever. They said it blew noxious fumes from the southeast, so they kept their windows closed up at night against the cooling air. Though the shuttered windows of John Henry's rented room at the Tivoli High House made the nights close and stuffy, they also kept away the bothersome mosquitoes, so at least he wasn't scratching at insect bites all the time. He was lucky to have a room at all with his funds as depleted as they were. If the Tivoli House hadn't been seventy-years old and much declined from its days as Pensacola's first dance hall, even that would have been too expensive for his purse. So he didn't complain about the stuffiness of the room or the noise from the gaming tables downstairs, and he gratefully accepted the landlady's offer of writing paper and ink pen so that he could send a letter home. He had left Georgia rather hurriedly, he explained, and hadn't been able to pack all the niceties along with him.

He wrote first to Tom, telling him where he was and asking for him to send along his traveling trunk when he was finally settled somewhere. He was sorry, he said, for having caused the family so much trouble, and hoped that all was well with Tom and the rest of his McKey kin. Then, out of a sense of obligation, he wrote another letter and put it in the same envelope: a short note to his father, saying he was on his way to Texas. Henry would probably just toss the note into the parlor fire, once he read it, but John Henry knew he owed his father that much at least.

His letter to Mattie took longer to compose as he tried to find the right words to tell her that he was leaving, and why. But how could he tell her that it was his love for her that had made him go? How could he explain that it was his love that had made him angry enough to shoot that boy on the Withlacoochee River? She would never understand such passion, though she knew he had a passionate streak in him. She had called him prideful, arrogant, hotheaded, and had predicted that it would all get him into trouble one day. But she couldn't have foreseen just how bad that trouble would have turned out to be. Her gentle and virtuous heart could never have imagined him taking another man's life, and doing it so easily. Besides, it had all been an accident, just an awful, unintentioned, drunken mistake. Why burden her with something he hadn't meant to do, anyhow? So in the end, he decided not to tell her much at all, only that he was off to Texas to visit with his Uncle Jonathan McKey.

But he had more to do than write letters if he planned to be out of Pensacola before the Yellow Fever took him, too. There had already been one notable death since his arrival: a local politician who'd accused the Board of Health of giving the town a bad name with their strict quarantine. The man called the physicians on the board damned fools for warning him against visiting a quarantined ship. The doctors had little comment when the politician took ill and died ten days later. No, John Henry did not care to be long around Pensacola, so as soon as his letter writing was done, he began making the rounds of the saloons along the waterfront, trying his hand against those eager sailors fresh off the boat.

The porter had been right about the tempers of the sailing men. After their weeks at sea and a month of quarantine with their ships at Navy Cove on Santa Rosa Island, they came across the bay as ready to fight as they were to play, and ready to take offense at the smallest slight. So, just to be safe, John Henry took along his Uncle John's walnut-handled pistol, loaded up all around and ready to fire, and carried his Uncle Tom's big knife as well. The pistol slid easily into his trousers' pocket, but the knife was awkward without the leather scabbard Tom had left behind at the cabin.

He found himself being wary all the time, worrying that the heavy-handled thing would slide from its hiding place in his inside coat pocket. And maybe it was the distraction of worrying about the knife, or maybe it was just plain carelessness, but being so heavily armed turned out to be more dangerous than not being heeled at all, one hot summer night at the Grand Prize Saloon.

He'd chosen the Grand Prize because of its location on the ground floor of a grocery and ship supply store, which meant that it was likely to be filled with sailors with ready cash to wager, and by the looks of the women who went into the place, the sailors were ready to spend some money. The streetwalkers were easy to spot: their faces painted up and their dresses cut revealingly low, looking almost as hardened as the suntanned seamen they draped themselves around. But every now and then there was one who seemed too soft for that hard life, too young under the rouge and powder to be offering what those sailors wanted. And though John Henry tried not to pay any attention, keeping his eyes on the cards and his mind clear, that hot night he couldn't help but notice the girl that one of his card-playing companions had brought along to the game.

She was a little thing, tiny as Mattie around the waist but with a womanly endowment above and wearing a dress that showed off her figure. The sailor, a bad-smelling man with black hairy arms, seemed particularly pleased with the girl's looks, letting his free hand wander from around her little waist to the open bodice of her dress, fondling her right there in public. The first time he did it, John Henry caught a breath and tried not to let his surprise show. He was in a seaman's saloon, after all, and the girl was just a sailor's streetwalker — though she too seemed surprised by the touch of the man's hand on her breast. Although she didn't move away from him, her eyes fell away, as if she could remove herself from being there by pretending that she wasn't.

John Henry averted his own eyes, trying to concentrate on the cards. The girl was no business of his, nor was the sailor's crude behavior any real hindrance to the game. As long as the man kept putting down his money and letting John Henry pick it up, what difference did it make what else he was doing at the same time? And when he saw the sailor reach into the girl's dress a second time, he had to suppress his own unexpected reaction, wondering just what the sailor was feeling. But when the sailor reached for her a third time, John Henry's long years of training as a gentleman finally took hold of him, and he put down his cards deliberately and looked up with cool blue eyes.

"That's enough, Sir," he said, though the sailor hardly deserved the title. "Why don't you let the girl go while we finish this hand?"

" 'Cause my hand ain't through with her yet, that's why!" the man answered with a laugh, and to prove his point he grabbed her so hard that she winced and started to cry.

"Doesn't look to me like she's enjoyin' your company overly much," John Henry said, as the girl looked up at him with tear-filled eyes. "Looks like she's kind of young for you, besides."

"Hell right, she's young," the man said with a snarled smile, "just the way I like 'em. This one's thirteen come next month. I checked with her Ma, just to make sure. Said I'd pay her double if I was the girl's first. Can tell I am, the way she wriggles whenever I touch her." Then he pulled his hand from her breast and slid it down toward the full gathers of her skirt. "Bet she's gonna wriggle some more, once I get myself under here..."

It was all John Henry could take, and without thinking twice, he reached for his Uncle John's pistol, pulling it on the man so fast the sailor didn't have time to finish his thought.

"I said let her go," he commanded. "Right now."

The sailor caught a breath and his hand loosed just long enough for the girl to squirm away from him. Then he laughed, and his rancid whiskey breath poured over the table like an evil cloud.

"What do you think about that, boys?" he said to the other players in the game, sailors like himself. "Do we let this pretty boy tell us what to do with our shore leave?"

John Henry realized too late that he was a lone man in a brawl. The sailor's friends jumped him like it was their fight, too, wrestling the pistol out of his hand and yanking his arm up behind him so hard he thought it would break. And as his arm came up, the Hell-Bitch slid from his jacket pocket, clattering to the wood plank floor.

There was silence for a moment as the sailors all stared down at the giant knife. Then the big man started to laugh.

"Well, hell, if he ain't a sword-fighter! Come on, boys, let's show him how real fightin's done."

And all at once they were on top of him and he was face down on the barroom floor, smelling whiskey and vomit and hoping the blood he was tasting was his own. But there was nothing he could do to get away from the assault, only gasp for breath between blows and try to keep his face away from the sailors' fists. If they meant to kill him, it wouldn't take them long, the way he was pinned down and helpless to defend himself. Even the Hell-Bitch couldn't do him any good, on the floor beneath him with its swamp oak handle pressing up painfully against his aching ribs.

Then he heard a scream from somewhere up above, and after that a commotion of angry voices. And suddenly he was free again and being yanked to his feet by rough hands on his neck.

"What do you mean, startin' a brawl in my place?" said the man who held him. "Can't you read the sign? No firearms. No fightin'. You tryin' to get me closed down by the port police? Now get out of here before I take a few punches at you myself. And give him his pistol back, boys. I don't want him bringin' no theft charges against my place."

The man let John Henry go, and he fell to the floor again as his legs folded under him.

"I said get out of here," the man repeated, "and take your weapons with you." Then he turned away, cursing loudly.

John Henry pushed himself to his feet amid the jeers and laughs of the sailors who had assaulted him. The room around him swayed and he moaned as he bent over to pick up his uncle's knife. But it wasn't just the pain of the beating that he was suffering from. He had tried to be a gentleman, saving a lady from the sailor's lewd advances, but he'd made a fool of himself instead. And worse than that, the girl he'd hoped to save was sitting on the sailor's lap again, more scared now than she'd been before – and with cause. For as John Henry stumbled from the saloon, pushing open the doors into the noxious night air, he heard the sailor's ugly laugh echoing behind him: "You see what happens to them's that mess with me? You be a good little girl now, and won't no harm come to you like what come to him."

He knew without glancing back that the girl's eyes were looking somewhere far away.

~~~~~~~~~~

The landlady at the Tivoli House gave him rags and a bowl of clear water to wash off the blood. But there was nothing she could give him to wash away the shame he felt. Because of his impetuous actions, the sailor's girl would likely suffer more now than she would have suffered before. And what had his bravado won him, anyhow? Just a split and bloodied lip, a shooting arm strained and aching, and a back already turning black and blue from bruises.

A fine sporting man he'd turned out to be, unable to handle himself in a saloon full of gamblers! And what good was it to be fast on the draw if he couldn't keep ahold of his pistol long enough to pull off a shot? Worse than that, what good did it to do to carry a knife the size of a meat cleaver if it only made people laugh? It was the laughter that was the worst of it, the memory of it making him feel small and ridiculous. His father had said once that pride was about all they had left in life; now even his pride was gone.

But there was something more than shame that was burdening him. For try as he might, he couldn't forget the face of the boy he'd killed on the river, or the way his dead-aim pistol shot had blown that face away. Accident or not, he was still as guilty as the hell he'd found himself in and deserving of every bad thing that might come to him. His blood and bruises were nothing compared to what God would lay upon him for his sin: scourges and flogging and an eternity in fire and brimstone.

And as his shame turned to contrition, he fell to his knees beside the narrow bed. His mother had taught him how to pray those many nights at her own bedside, having evening prayers before she passed on. She had taught him to believe in the goodness of God, in Jesus' forgiving grace. And surely, sinner that he was, only Jesus could save him now.

His prayer was more a plea of desperation than the praises his mother had offered, but the words were the same: "Have mercy upon me, O God..."

And as he poured out his heart to heaven, the penitent tears welled up in his eyes and overflowed, wetting the bedcovers. It would take all night, at least, to confess all that he'd done wrong in his life, and beg forgiveness for it. But his mother had taught him that the angels heard every honest prayer, and wrote the words in God's holy book against the Judgment Day. He only hoped his angel mother wasn't having to hear him now.

~~~~~~~~~~

He prayed himself to sleep that night, and slept well for the first time in weeks. And when he woke the next day, the only pain he had left was the spreading bruising on his back and an aching in his shooting arm. But his heart was lighter than it had been since he left Mattie, and even his breathing seemed to be coming easier. And though he didn't know whether or not he was forgiven, he knew at least that he was repentant.

~~~~~~~~~~~~

The tall ship *Golden Dream* set sail from Commendencia Wharf, bound for New Orleans and Galveston, on a day so clear it seemed that sea and sky were one boundless wash of blue. Alongside the ship, windward, dolphins danced and laughed, daring the schooner to a race. And standing at the rail, watching them leap and dive, John Henry felt like laughing too.

He was leaving the past behind and sailing off into the future on a fine summer day. And though he'd used up nearly all of his gambling winnings buying his passage west, he didn't care. At the end of the voyage Texas was waiting, wide and wild and full of opportunity for a bright young man like himself. But there was one part of the past that he would never forget: Mattie, eyes full of affection, heart full of love. The Irish heirloom ring she had given him shone gold on his little finger, like a promise. Someday he'd come sailing back, take her in his arms again, and hear her speak the words that meant everything to him: *"I love you. I always have, and I always will..."*

But for now he was looking westward, across the Gulf of Mexico toward the bright blue of the rest of his life. He took a breath of fresh sea air, smiled, and faced into the wind.

The Southern Son Saga

continues in

Gone West

Author's Note

When I first set out to retell the story of Doc Holliday, I thought it would be so simple: just dramatize the known history, add in a bit of legend, and tie it all together with some old-fashioned Southern romance. And how else could one tell a tale that sweeps from the Old South to the Wild West and stars a man whose supposed sweetheart was the model for Melanie in *Gone With the Wind?* That was the story I had uncovered in my work with a Georgia museum: an amazing melding of Western legend and Southern literature.

But when I tried to make a timeline of the historical events, I found that the lines didn't connect properly and the accepted facts about Doc Holliday didn't add up. Of course, I wasn't the first writer to see inconsistencies in the accepted facts; others had run into them, too, and tried to explain them away by saying that Doc Holliday was, well, crazy. But crazy doesn't account for dates that don't add up and timelines that don't connect. Maybe, just maybe, the "facts" weren't facts at all. It soon became apparent that if I wanted to write about the real Doc Holliday, I'd have to find him first.

Thus began eighteen years of original research, discovering previously unknown court documents and deeds, reading old newspaper accounts and memoirs and letters, interviewing living family members and visiting all the places Doc Holliday had been in his adventurous life: from Georgia to Philadelphia to St. Louis, from Texas to Colorado, from New Mexico to Arizona, even down to New Orleans and up the Mississippi River. And somewhere along the way, I found that in trying to dramatize his life I'd discovered his life. Or a lot of it, anyway, enough to fill three volumes of novelized reality as I relived his life from childhood to his last days.

Southern Son: The Saga of Doc Holliday is not a history book, nor is it a simple work of fiction. It is a true historical fiction, combining the best history I could find in those eighteen years of research with the best story I could weave in almost as many years of writing. The Doc Holliday you meet here may not be the man you have seen in movies or other novels, but he is likely closer to the real person of John Henry Holliday – a Southern boy who had no idea that he was destined to become a Western legend. And the same could be said of his cousin Mattie, who didn't know that years later her name and character would be recast in the South's greatest novel by a younger cousin, Margaret Mitchell. Neither of them knew that one day they'd be famous; they likely would have been uncomfortable with the thought. But I think they'd like the portrayal I have given them here.

While you may not always admire the Doc Holliday you meet in these pages, a man whose legendary life was filled with very real human failings, I hope that you will come to understand him, as I have. Mattie Holliday, who knew him better than we ever will, loved him.

~~~~~~~~~~

I am indebted to many people for their help in this work, from Doc's early biographers to the archivists who aided in my original research to friends and family who gave encouragement along the way. The following is but a short list of those with whom I have worked personally:

Authors: Susan McKey Thomas ("In Search of the Hollidays"), Doc's cousin whose family history work started my own research and who became my dear friend over the years; Dr. Gary Roberts ("Doc Holliday: The Life and Legend"), Doc's most eminent biographer whom I met through Susie and who also became a friend as well as an advisor and collaborator as we were both writing our books; Casey Tefertiller ("Wyatt Earp: The Life Behind the Legend") whose late night thoughts on the streets of Tombstone helped me to get my work done; David O'Connell ("The Irish Roots of Margaret Mitchell's *Gone With the Wind*") for his unique insights into the story behind the story.

Holliday and McKey family members: Susan McKey Thomas, Jack McKey, Morgan De Lancey McGee, A. J. Young, Regina Rapier, Carolyn Holliday Manley, Constance Knowles McKeller, Robert Lee Holliday, and John P. Holliday who all contributed family history and the kind of family stories that bring the past to life.

Historians, archivists, and researchers: the late Franklin D. Garrett and the staff of the Atlanta History Center; Noelle King of the Margaret Mitchell House Museum in Atlanta; Anthony R. Dees, Catholic Archdiocese of Atlanta; Mary Ellen Brooks, Margaret Mitchell Archives at the University of Georgia Library; John Lynch & Bobby Kerlin of the Fayette County Historical Society; Joseph Henry Hightower Moore of the Clayton County Historical Society; J.P. Jennings of the Griffin Historical Society; Shirl Tisdale, Dental Medicine Library Archives at the University of Pennsylvania; Joan Farmer of the Old Jail Art Center, Albany, Texas; Harold F. Thatcher, City of Las Vegas Museum and Rough Rider Memorial Collection, New

Mexico; Robert Fisher, Arizona Historical Society; Christine McNab Rhodes, Cochise County Recorder, Arizona; Gary McClelland, Tombstone, Arizona; John Denious, Silverton, Colorado; Nancy Manley at the Mountain History Collection of the Lake County Public Library and Mary Billings-McVicar, Leadville, Colorado; Lois Ann McCollum of the Frontier Historical Society in Glenwood Springs, Colorado; and Dr. Arthur W. Bork, Prescott, Arizona, who knew and interviewed Kate Elder and shared his recollections with me.

Literary Agents and Editors: Catherine Drayton of Inkwell Management, Peter Rubie of FinePrint Literary, and Lila Karpf of Lila Karpf Literary Management. And especially to Dana Celeste Robinson, managing director of Knox Robinson Publishing, for her visionary guidance and dedication to quality historical fiction.

Members of the Holliday House Association, founding organization of the Holliday-Dorsey-Fife House Museum: Jeanne Brewer, Karlan Coleman, Michele Cox, Eleanor Ebbert, VelDean Fincher, Elizabeth McCombs Kissel, Nancy Meyer, Joan Neal, Dr. Kate Robinson, and LaVanda Shellnutt, along with advisor Dr. Tommy H. Jones of the Georgia State University Heritage Preservation Program.

Family & Friends who were my early readers, first critics, and stalwart supporters: Patricia Petersen, Samuel Shannon, Sterling Felsted, Jennifer Felsted, Heather Shannon, Ashley Wilcox, Ross Wilcox, Mack Peirson, Daniel Mikat, Michael Spain, Melinda Talley, VelDean Fincher, and Dr. Dorothy Mikat. Special thanks to Laura Pilcher, copyeditor extraordinaire, and to Dan and Sally Mikat for giving me long quiet weeks to write at their home on Mackinac Island, Michigan.

Finally, but never done, thanks to my husband, Dr. Ronald C. Wilcox, the real Doc in my life, who didn't mind sharing me with a much, much older man, and to my parents, Malcolm and Beth Peirson, for a house filled with books and a love of all things literary. John Henry and I thank you all!

Victoria Wilcox
Peachtree City, Georgia

For more information about the writing of Southern Son and the world of Doc Holliday, please visit www.victoriawilcoxbooks.com